GW00778095

CONFLICT ON THE YANGTZE

by

GREG KATER

CONFLICT ON THE YANGTZE
Copyright © GREG KATER 2019

First published by Zeus Publications 2019
http://www.zeus-publications.com
P.O. Box 2554
Burleigh M.D.C.
QLD 4220
Australia.

A catalogue record for this
book is available from the
National Library of Australia

All Rights Reserved

No part of this book may be reproduced in any form, by photocopying or by any
electronic or mechanical means, including information storage or retrieval
systems, without permission in writing from both the copyright owner and the
publisher of this book.

This book is a work of fiction.

The author asserts his moral rights.

ISBN: 978-1-921240-77-5

Image, used under license from Shutterstock.com
Michael Rosskothen/Shutterstock.com

© Cover Design—Zeus Publications 2019

Author Biography

Greg Kater is an Australian-based author. He lives in Sanctuary Cove, Gold Coast, Queensland and has recently retired from a 55-year international career in the resources industry. During 2018 he had three books published. *The Warramunga's War, The Warramunga's Aftermath of War* and *Skills of the Warramunga* are a trilogy of historical fiction.

Greg Kater's fourth book, *Conflict on the Yangtze*, follows on from the trilogy and is set in post-war China. After the Japanese defeat in the Second World War, fighting continued throughout China between the Kuomintang government, the Communists, Warlords and various gangs trying to establish their areas of influence. In the creation of his fourth book, Greg has been assisted by his experiences in China which he visited many times during his career.

Previous Works by Greg Kater

The Warramunga's War
The Warramunga's Aftermath of War
Skills of the Warramunga

Dedication

This book is dedicated to my business partner (Dolly) Fu Yuan
who still oscillates between Australia and China.
Also to all my Chinese friends.

Acknowledgements

I would like to thank Marilyn Higgins, Clive Dalkins and all the people at Zeus Publications for their friendly, helpful and competent work resulting in the publication of this book. I would also like to thank my editor Gail for her excellent structural editing and Julie Winzar for her fine editing and formatting. I am also grateful to my family for their support.

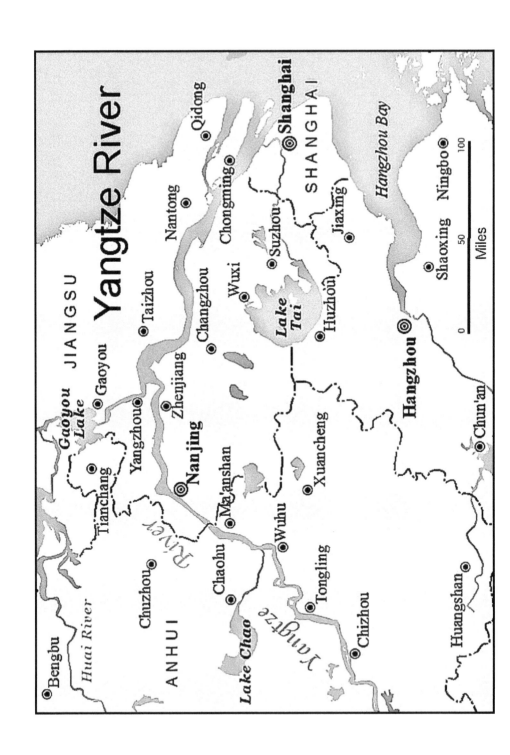

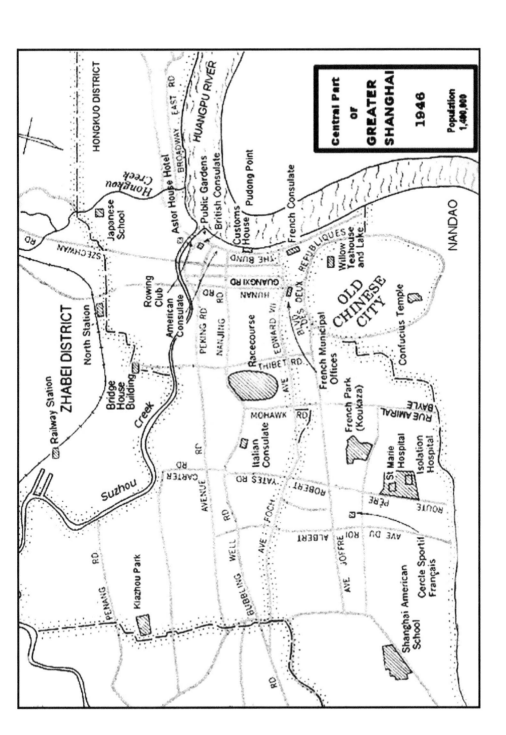

Central Part of GREATER SHANGHAI 1946

Population 1,400,000

HONGKUO DISTRICT

ZHABEI DISTRICT

HONGKUO DISTRICT

EAST RD

BROADWAY

HUANGPU RIVER

Hongkou Creek

Astor House Hotel

Public Gardens

British Consulate

Customs House

Pudong Point

French Consulate

Japanese School

SZECHWAN

RD

Rowing Club

American Consulate

THE BUND

QUANGXI RD

HUNAN

RD

REPUBLIQUES

BLVD DEUX

Willow Teahouse and Lake

OLD CHINESE CITY

Confucius Temple

NANDAO

North Station

Railway Station

Bridge House Building

Creek

Suzhou

NANJING RD

PEKING RD

Racecourse

EDWARD VII

THIBET RD

AVE

MOHAWK RD

Italian Consulate

French Municipal Offices

French Park (Koukaza)

RUE AMIRAL BAYLE

CARTER RD

RD

AVENUE

YATES RD

RD

FOCH

ROBERT

PÈRE

St Marie Hospital

Isolation Hospital

ROUTE

PENANG RD

Kiazhou Park

BUBBLING WELL

AVE

ALBERT

AVE DU ROI

AVE JOFFRE

Shanghai American School

Cercle Sportif Français

RD

The Bund
Shanghai 1946

The large building this side of the Customs House Clock Tower is the Hong Kong and Shanghai Bank Building. The nearest building (left foreground) is the Mercantile Bank of India.

The building with the pointed roof is the Cathay Hotel on the corner of East Nanjing Road. Left of that is the Palace Hotel.

The distant building, just left of the World War I Memorial, is the Astor House Hotel. Left of that is the tall Broadway Mansions building.

CHAPTER 1

The pervasive stench of human excrement, used as fertiliser in nearby rice paddies, assailed the nostrils of the two men creeping through the wooded area of broad-leafed trees and wind-tossed willows and scrub, towards the distant settlement backed by low hills. By now, they were about three miles west of the Yangtze River, in Zongyang County. Through the trees they glimpsed the waters of Lake Zhusi to the south. Large high-stepping cranes and smaller water birds ambled around the edges of the lake. The mountains cradling the town of Tongling loomed large and hazy behind them.

Commander Daniel Stafford looked back at his companion, Lee Drake. He nodded at him and continued edging forward, both men crouching below the level of the scrubby undergrowth. On the plains to their left were rice paddies and ahead was a large open field. They could make out the large bulbs of the poppy seed pods in rows extending to the dun-coloured houses and sheds on the far side of the field. No Chinese red-tiled roofs. Just very plain buildings bathed in sunshine.

It was late morning on this early June day in 1946, and the temperature was rising sharply as midday approached. Sweat was running down Stafford's back inside his shirt. He realised it would be like a cauldron exposed to the sun when they crawled through the poppy field, but he could see no other way of getting closer to the settlement. He noticed people moving around near the sheds. As he studied them through his binoculars, Stafford discerned that not all of them were Chinese. Three were obviously white men. English, American or both? he wondered, unable to distinguish their features at this distance. Putting down his binoculars, he looked around. Except for the buzzing of insects, it was extremely quiet here, unlike the previous night.

They had sailed up the Yangtze River from Nanjing through the night on a converted motorised junk, miraculously avoiding the occasional sandbanks in the river. Their progress was accompanied by the crackle of rifle fire on both sides of the river. Bandits,

1

Kuomintang government troops and Communist forces all shooting at one another in the dark. Except for sporadic bursts, the shooting had died away at daybreak when they disembarked from the vessel on the western bank of the river. The vessel was owned and skippered by an American experienced in navigating the river, who had somehow survived the Japanese occupation.

Stafford had an athletic build, was of medium height and his bright blue eyes and tanned face were topped by straight, light brown hair. He was an operative of MI6, which had sent him into Shanghai after the surrender of the Japanese to attempt to track down a suspected conspiracy smuggling opium out of China into the USA, Australia and the Philippines.

His colleague, Lee Drake, was also with MI6. While his father had been British, his mother was Chinese, and so during the Japanese occupation, he had been able to pass as a local, living in the old Chinese city west of the Bund in Shanghai. Through various channels, he had transmitted information on the situation in China through to London during the war without being detected by the enemy, although he had had a number of narrow escapes. He was thin and wiry, possessing more strength than his appearance suggested.

'I need to get a closer look,' Stafford muttered, looking at Drake. 'There's no other alternative. I'll have to crawl through that damned poppy field. You feel like following me?'

Drake nodded. 'You'll need someone to watch your back, boss.'

'Okay. So be it then. Let's go, Lee.' The two of them set off on all fours into the poppy field. The sun beat down on their backs from a cloudless sky, the foliage of the poppy plants providing little shade. Halfway across the field, Stafford realised that if anyone was alert in the settlement ahead, they might detect their presence via the small clouds of insects rising out of the crops ahead of them, continually signalling their progress. Expecting to hear a shout of alarm at any moment, Stafford was painfully aware that he and Drake had decided to travel light and were only armed with pistols for this reconnaissance.

A hundred yards from the small settlement and with the sun still slightly behind them, Stafford figured there was no chance of a light reflection from the binoculars, so he slowly brought them up to his eyes and peered cautiously over the top of some poppy bushes. Probably, on account of the heat, there were fewer people than previously moving around outside the buildings. He focused on one individual, a tall, heavily built man with a ginger beard and wearing a broad-brimmed hat, stressing something to a shorter Chinese man who was nodding vigorously. The ginger-haired man could be heard faintly, speaking in a sort of pidgin English, but with a marked cockney accent. Aha, thought Stafford, I know where you're from.

He looked back and shrugged at Drake, who was just behind him. He wasn't sure how he was going to get a look into these buildings without being detected. If they stayed where they were, they would be cooked by the blazing sun. Making up his mind that he would have to return to take a look at the sheds in the dark, he signalled to Drake to crawl back the way they had come. Drake nodded and set off back in the lead, crawling towards the trees at the eastern end of the poppy field.

If anything, the crawl back was worse. The sun was hotter, the insects seemed more numerous, sweat stung Stafford's eyes, and his knees were bleeding as he tried to keep as silent as possible.

Suddenly, he heard a shout behind them and the sound of heavy boots running towards them. Looking back, he saw several men running about 200 yards behind him. He yelled at Drake and they both leapt to their feet and ran as fast as they could away from the pursuers.

Three shots rang out and he sensed a bullet passing close to his head. Within 50 yards of the tree line, a bullet struck him in the shoulder, making him stagger. Drake looked back, but Stafford shouted at him, 'Don't wait for me! Get away, for God's sake.'

Drake took off and disappeared into the woods. However, just before Stafford reached the tree line, another bullet crashed into his back. He fell headlong onto his face, blood flowing out of his nose. 'Bloody hell!' he cried just before blacking out.

* * * *

It was a balmy June afternoon in Darwin with cloudless skies and fresh onshore breezes when the Avro Lancastrian from Dili touched

3

down at the airport northeast of the city. Two jeeps drove up close to the aircraft as soon as it arrived at the terminal and two men and two women got out. There was a cheer from the small group standing next to the vehicles as newlyweds, Jack 'Jacko' and Monique O'Brien, emerged from the aircraft.

Sarah, Jacko's half-sister, and their friends, Jamie and Carna Munro, hugged them enthusiastically, while their radio operator and general factotum, Garry 'Sparky' Speck, climbed into the aircraft in search of the baggage.

'You back. You back bikpela brother!' cried Sarah excitedly.

'Great to see you, Sar. How are your school lessons?' asked Jacko.

'Aye yu, lessons good. Spik proper Ingliss now,' she said, then carefully asked, 'How are you, Jacko?'

'I'm very well, thank you,' he replied. 'How are you, Sarah?'

'I'm very well, thank you,' she said with careful concentration, followed by a shriek of laughter.

'How was the honeymoon?' asked Jamie.

'You shouldn't ask such personal questions,' scolded Carna, winking at Monique and adding, 'You both look well. Is Dili a nice place to have a holiday?'

'Yes, beautiful, but like everywhere else, still with ruins from the war,' replied Monique. 'Even the lovely beaches had shipwrecks everywhere. But we didn't really care.'

'I didn't notice,' said Jacko, winking at Jamie. 'I only had eyes for my lovely wife.'

Monique blushed. 'We stayed in a lovely old Portuguese hotel close to the beach. It was like nowhere I've seen before.'

'I hope you were able to keep all the criminals under control while I was out of town, Cap,' Jacko said to Jamie.

'It was hard, Jacko, but we managed,' Jamie laughed.

Jamie and Jacko had met on the battlefield during the Syrian campaign in the early part of the Second World War. When Jamie was wounded, Jacko had carried him to a field hospital and later, they had worked together in intelligence with Colonel John Cook of MI6, based in Cairo, exposing and capturing German spies as well as successfully using false radio signals designed to confuse Rommel's Afrika Corps during the North Africa desert campaign. Jacko, a well-

4

educated half-Aboriginal of the Warramunga tribe in the central Northern Territory, had been a non-commissioned officer during the war and had a habit of referring to all officers as 'Cap'. At the end of the desert war, Jamie and Jacko had worked in intelligence together in the Pacific theatre. Following the defeat of the Japanese, they had, with the cooperation of MI6, set up in Darwin the northern Australia operations of the CIS, the Commonwealth Investigations Service. Since then, they had been involved in eliminating the operations of a number of gangs involved in criminal activities in the aftermath of war. These operations had necessitated travel to the Philippines and Malaya as well as to different parts of northern Australia. Jacko's half-sister, Sarah, a young Warramunga Aboriginal from Tennant Creek, had proved vital to some of the operations because of her remarkable tracking and bushcraft skills. She and Jacko were particularly close.

Jacko had originally met Monique, whose mother was Syriac and her father French, in Cairo during the war in 1941. It was love at first sight, but the two had not been able to start a real courtship until her parents, the Rousseaus, had migrated from Egypt to Australia in early 1946.

After recovering all the baggage from the aeroplane, Sparky drove one of the jeeps, with the three women happily chatting together. Jamie and Jacko went in the other jeep with the bags.

'I guess the girls will be pulling us to pieces in the other jeep,' said Jamie with a grin as he followed them towards the Darwin waterfront.

Jacko nodded, chuckling. 'As long as they put the pieces back together again.'

'I've had a message from Johnny Cook in London,' Jamie told him. 'It seems that MI6 has lost one of their operatives in China. He wants us to go there.'

'China!' exclaimed Jacko. 'Wow! Where in China?'

'Johnny said it was somewhere west of Shanghai,' said Jamie. 'A few hundred miles from Shanghai along the Yangtze River.'

'Sounds mysterious,' said Jacko. 'Why would he want to involve us?'

5

'I'm not sure, but I'll be talking to him on the radio this evening,' said Jamie. 'We have a sched at 6 o'clock. I'm sure I'll get more details then.'

'Okey dokey,' said Jacko. 'However, if we have to go to China, it might not go over too well with Monique. She's got visions of us spending the next few weeks looking for a house.'

'Yes, well, I'll know more this evening,' said Jamie. 'Carna might not be too keen on me going to China either. Although the war has ended, there are reports of full-scale battles between the Kuomintang government, the communists and the many bandit gangs all over China. I don't know how true they are.'

'Where there's smoke, there's fire, Cap.'

'You're probably right, Jacko.'

After Jacko and Monique had freshened up in their room at the Hotel Darwin, they all met on the verandah of the hotel overlooking the Esplanade and Darwin Harbour. The sun was setting in a blaze of colour reflected off the calm waters of Darwin Harbour, stirred by a gentle breeze. By the time Jacko had finished entertaining the others with amusing embellished anecdotes of interesting moments in the Portuguese colony, Sparky announced that it was 5.45 and he would warm up the radio for the schedule with Johnny Cook in London.

'What is the time in London?' asked Monique.

'It'll be 10 in the morning when it's 6 o'clock here,' said Sparky, heading off to the room where the CIS radio was set up.

'We'll follow in a couple of minutes,' Jamie said to Jacko.

'Monique, Sarah and I would love to come with you to hear what Johnny Cook has to say and what is so interesting in China,' said Carna, giving Jamie a beguiling smile.

'Okay, okay. But you'll have to be quiet,' said Jamie.

'You won't even know we are there,' replied Carna.

Sarah beamed at her.

When they had all gathered in the radio room, Sparky twisted several dials on the large Hallicrafter radio before picking up the microphone and starting to talk.

'MI6 London. MI6 London. This is CIS Darwin. Come in. Over.'

After some static, a voice came through from the other end. 'CIS Darwin. This is MI6 London. Johnny Cook here. How are things Down Under? Over.'

Sparky handed the microphone over to Jamie, who replied, 'Jamie Munro here, Johnny. Things are fine Down Under. You should come here one day and learn to walk upside down for a while. Jacko, Monique, Carna and Sarah are all here. What's the news of China? Over.'

'Hello all. Yes, China. As I mentioned before to you, we have lost one of our operatives. His name is Daniel Stafford. We don't know whether he is alive or dead. We do know he was shot west of Tongling, a village on the Yangtze River a few hundred miles from Shanghai. He was investigating a large field of opium poppies three miles west of the river, and a small settlement which we suspect is processing opium from the southern provinces, Guangxi and Yunnan, as well as locally grown stuff. This is being smuggled by boats along the Yangtze to some point near Shanghai and then shipped to the USA, the Philippines and Australia. Over.'

'How do you know where Stafford was shot?' asked Jamie.

'He was with another MI6 agent, Lee Drake. He was also shot at but managed to escape back to Shanghai. Drake's a good man. He saw Stafford fall. Over.'

'Can't the Chinese government do anything about it?' asked Jamie.

'We suspect the Kuomintang government, under Chiang Kai-shek, is probably complicit in the smuggling operation,' replied Johnny. 'Chiang needs money for his constant battles against the CCP, the Chinese Communist Party, and he probably gets a big kick-back from the opium sales. Nobody can accuse the Chinese Nationalist government of being incorrupt. Over.'

'Gonna be a bit difficult if the government's behind it,' observed Jamie. 'Over.'

'I think it's more like parts of the government turning a blind eye,' said Johnny. 'We know the government has links with bandit groups in the region. There are a number of foreigners involved in the opium operation as well. Drake told us that one of them is English, Cockney.

7

We're going to have to find out who else is involved and terminate it if we can. Over.'

'Yeah. It looks like you'd have to destroy the processing plant at that place on the Yangtze,' said Jamie. 'What's the name of the town again? Over.'

'Tongling. Over.'

'Yes. Tongling,' Jamie said. 'Then I guess if you can round up the people who are operating the boats on the Yangtze River, you'll have it nailed. Over.'

'Easier said than done,' said Johnny. 'But essentially, you are correct. I'm going to need your help though. My MI6 agents in this part of the world have their hands full with the desperate problems in Europe as a result of the aftermath of war. Especially in eastern Europe. You chaps are by far the best intelligence agents in the eastern hemisphere. Over.'

'I thought the Royal Navy had gunboats on the Yangtze River,' said Jamie. 'They could take care of the boats, couldn't they? Over.'

'That was before the war, Jamie,' said Johnny. 'We do have some ships at the mouth of the Yangtze and in the Huang River, but they're only there to protect any British people and possessions. The US Navy has a few ships in the Yangtze with Chinese government approval. It's all a bit tense and sensitive at the present time. China is now an independent country, although it's not always easy to know who's in charge in the regions. Over.'

'What would you like us to do?' asked Jamie. 'Over.'

'I'd like to meet up with you and Jacko in Shanghai in the next week. I haven't worked out how to get you there yet,' said Johnny. 'The best way might be for you to fly to Manila first. Then, with the help of our American friends, we can fly you to the Itazuke Air Base in southern Japan. We could then have a small navy ship take you from there to Shanghai. I'll have to check it out and let you know. Over.'

'What should we take to wear?' asked Jamie. 'Over.'

'It's summer and hot. Just summer gear and some long trousers for wearing in the Shanghai hotel,' replied Johnny. 'Anything else? Over.'

'The name of the Shanghai hotel? Over,' said Jamie.

'We'll probably book you at the Astor House Hotel north of the Bund. I'll confirm later,' said Johnny. 'I'll be calling your old friend, Harry Williams of American intelligence, soon to arrange a flight for you from Manila to Itazuke. That's all for now. We'll speak same time tomorrow. Over and out.'

'Over and out,' repeated Jamie.

'Astor House Hotel!' exclaimed Jacko. 'That sounds very grand.'

'Many of those buildings were built before the First World War,' said Jamie. 'Having been involved in a recent war zone it might not be too grand. But no matter.'

'It sounds to me as if you'll be leaving us girls behind, no?' commented Carna.

'Reluctantly, yes,' agreed Jamie. 'The situation in China is quite dangerous now, with government troops, communists and bandits in a state of civil war.'

'But not too dangerous for you?' exclaimed Carna.

'We... er... we'll be careful,' said Jamie.

'We'll move around like ghosts,' said Jacko with a broad smile. 'The Chinese baddies won't see us.'

'Me come! Me come!' cried Sarah.

'You'd better stay here, Sar,' said Jacko. 'We'll call you if we need you.'

'You need me, bikpela brother,' said Sarah with tears forming in her large eyes. 'All way need me.'

'I'll find out, Sar,' said Jacko with his arm around her shoulder. 'If we need you, we'll call you. In the meantime, you should continue with your schooling here in Darwin.'

With an angry look in her eyes, Sarah mumbled something under her breath and glared at Jacko, her lower lip quivering.

'If you are flying to Manila first, you can take Carna and me and leave us there,' said Monique. 'My parents are there. Papa is setting up a furniture factory in Cebu and a sales office in Manila. That's if Carna wants to join us, n'est-ce pas?'

'Of course, I'd be very happy to join you,' said Carna happily. 'You might need my Filipina skills and I'll be closer to my Jamie there while he chases after his baddies in China, no? But I don't want

9

to leave Sarah here on her own. Is it ok if she comes with us to the Philippines and I'll take over her English lessons?'

'Tank you, tank you, Car nah!' cried Sarah. 'You real prend.'

'Okay. If that's not a problem for you, Carna,' said Jacko.

'No problem at all if you don't mind, Jacko,' said Carna. 'We're all happy for Sarah to keep us company.'

'She'll be happy to be with you, Carna,' said Jacko, winking at Sarah.

'Should be plenty of room on the aeroplane if MI6 is organising it,' said Jamie. 'I hope you girls don't take any risks in the Philippines.'

'I know my former country better than that, you silly man,' Carna replied.

Jamie looked at the others and said, 'I think we all need a cup of tea.'

CHAPTER 2

It was just before 5.00 in the afternoon, Philippines time, when the telephone rang in the office of Harry Williams Jr, chief of the US intelligence agency, Office of Strategic Services, or OSS, in Manila. Harry had been gazing out the window of his office in the US High Commission Building on Dewey Avenue, watching sailboats on the glittering blue waters of Manila Bay.

He lifted the phone receiver and immediately came alert when he realised he was talking to Colonel John Cook of MI6 in London.

'Why, hello there, Johnny,' he said. 'I believe you managed to round up all the bad guys in Malaya after I left a month or so ago.'

'Yes, Harry. We certainly did with the help of our friends from Australia.'

'So, to what do I owe the pleasure of this call, Johnny?' Harry enquired.

'I'm going to ask for your help again, Harry. We're trying to track down the people behind a major opium-smuggling operation in China.'

'Ah, China!' exclaimed Harry. 'We've also been monitoring the situation from here. I believe some of that opium has found its way into the Philippines. Part of it, we believe, is bound for the USA. We're not sure where they're landing it. The Philippine Islands have thousands of miles of coastline. We haven't been able to nail it down yet.'

'Yes. We also haven't worked out who's behind it,' said Johnny. 'Last week, I lost one of my men in China. I've asked for the help of our Australian friends who will shortly be flying to Manila. Then I'll need your help to get them from Manila to the Itazuke Air Base, which I believe is now under USAAF control. From there, I'll be organising a Royal Navy boat to take them to Shanghai.'

'Not a big problem. I can help you there,' said Harry. 'Anything for my Aussie friends. I'd like to come along into China with them. This smuggling operation concerns us as much as you guys.'

'I'm sure Jamie and Jacko would be happy to have you along,' said Johnny. 'I know you worked well together on breaking up that kidnapping cartel in the Philippines early this year.'

'Yep, sure did. Jacko's parents-in-law, Henri and Bella Rousseau, are in the Philippines as we speak,' said Harry. 'They're in Cebu, but they'll be back in Manila the day after tomorrow. When I met her mother, I realised where Monique got her good looks from. When do you expect Jamie and Jacko to arrive there?'

'I'm still organising that,' said Johnny. 'I expect it'll be in two or three days. I'll let you know. I'll be there to meet you all in Shanghai.'

'What about the civil war that we keep hearing about?' asked Harry.

'I think the Kuomintang government and the communists are too busy fighting each other to worry too much about us. But we'll have to keep our heads down. The situation is tense, but I think we can handle it. We'll know more when we get there.'

'Gotcha, Johnny. Just call me again when you know about Jamie's and Jacko's arrival and I'll have an aircraft ready for sure.'

'Thanks, Harry. I knew I could count on you. I'll be in touch.'

'Okay, ciao!' said Harry, hanging up the telephone. Screwing up his eyes against the glare, he looked out the window where the sun was edging westwards, beginning its evening fall towards Bataan. It cast a coppery tinge on the surface of the bay. He scratched his chin thoughtfully as he watched a flock of gulls wheeling around outside. We'll have to keep our heads down. How do we do that? he wondered.

It was comforting to know that Johnny Cook, one of the most senior officers of MI6, was prepared to risk his own personal safety. Johnny was likely to know the true situation in China better than anyone. It would be nice to work with Jamie and that rascal Jacko again, whatever the risks. He decided he was looking forward to it.

* * * *

Lee Drake contemplated the familiar Ching and Ming Dynasty buildings characteristic of this part of the old Chinese City in

Shanghai from the old tea house in Fangbang Middle Road. Throughout the Japanese occupation, he had acted the part of a humble dealer in rare green teas and he lived in a small apartment above the tea house, where he was now waiting for his American colleague.

During the war, the occupying enemy had never suspected that he had a powerful radio setup in his apartment with which he had stayed in touch with London, as he still did. Last night he had been informed that Colonel John Cook himself would be arriving in Shanghai within the next week along with three other operatives, two Australian and one American. So, MI6 was serious about investigating the drug-smuggling operation. That's good, he thought. Since Dan Stafford had been captured, possibly killed, he hadn't been at all sure what to do.

He couldn't achieve much on his own. If he tried, he would risk his cover which enabled him to remain invisible to the nationalists, the communists, and the various warlord bandits such as the Eight Stars, the Green Phoenix Rising, the Flying Leaves, and the other gangs all trying to cement their areas of power in Shanghai, Jiangsu, Hunan and the neighbouring provinces. The Green Phoenix Rising gang was the most ruthless and dangerous in Shanghai, but the other gangs had influence in many other parts of the Yangtze basin. And what of the Kuomintang and the communists? Atrocities had been committed by all these groups since the war had ended. Not nearly as bad as the Japanese massacre in Nanjing, but just as ruthless. Since the war, it had become increasingly difficult to operate in China. Full-scale civil war had recently erupted between the Nationalist government and the communists in various parts of China, starting in the north. At least Western foreigners remained relatively unmolested as they went about their business in Shanghai, but for how long?

Most of the Japanese troops were being repatriated in a week or two. After the surrender, Chiang Kai-shek had asked the defeated Japanese to act as policemen in Shanghai until his Nationalist forces were able to take control of the city. Almost unbelievable! Drake shook his head. The strange thing was that it had actually worked. The Japanese had complied and conducted police work with their

13

usual efficiency and without upsetting the ordinary law-abiding citizens.

Now, with the Japanese leaving, the Green Phoenix Rising thugs were more evident throughout the city, in particular the worst thug of them all, Chen Xiao Lu, the local gang chief, a beefy moon-faced scoundrel with a long scar on his left cheek. The Nationalist government tolerated the criminal activities of such bandits because they were allied with them in the fight against the communists. The bandits were feared and hated, so this alliance only served to alienate the populace and diminish support for the government. Where would it all end?

Drake's thoughts were interrupted by the arrival of Peter Jackson, his American friend, who sat down at his table, ordered tea, and looked quizzically at him.

'What's up, Lee, old buddy?' he asked.

'Oh, hi Pete, or should I say Pierre?' said Drake with a chuckle.

After the Japanese attack on Pearl Harbour, Peter Jackson, who had run a pre-war shipping business in Shanghai, had moved from the American Concession north of Suzhou Creek to the French Concession south of it. As it had come under the control of the Vichy French, an ally of the Axis, it remained largely undisturbed by the Japanese. During the war, Peter had morphed into Pierre Leconte, a Frenchman, shipping goods up and down the Yangtze in a shallow-draft motorised junk, the Blue Dolphin. His true identity had never been uncovered by the occupation forces.

Jackson took a sip of his tea, smiled, and said, 'You can call me what you like here, Lee. On the river I'm still a frog.'

'We're going to have a further need for your expertise on the river, Peter old chap,' said Drake. 'I've heard that MI6 are sending in a team of four to follow up on our last debacle.'

'You guys are beggars for punishment,' said Jackson with a lopsided grin. 'I thought you would probably walk away from all that when you lost Dan Stafford.'

'Yes, well, we love a bit of punishment,' agreed Drake. 'One of the chaps who's coming is an American with the OSS, I believe.'

'Well, at least you'll have someone sane in the team,' said Jackson, laughing. 'I assume you'll want me to take you to the same place, opposite Tongling?'

'Probably. I'll have to let you know,' said Drake. 'Are you going to be around Shanghai for the next few days?'

'For the next few days, my only plans are for a lovely bit of fluff in Avenue Joffre,' Jackson smirked. 'After that, I'll be off back to Nanjing to get the Blue Dolphin ready. Let me know when your team will be arriving, Lee. You know how to contact me.'

'Yes. Have fun. I'll contact you as soon as I know more.'

'Oh, don't worry. I'll have fun, ol' buddy,' said Jackson, getting up and heading out the door into the busy, noisy street.

* * * *

Later that same day, as night was falling in Darwin, Jamie, Carna, Jacko, Monique and Sarah were seated around one of the larger tables at the Knickerbocker Steakhouse in Mitchell Street, discussing the latest radio communication from London between Johnny Cook and Jamie earlier in the afternoon. Johnny had informed him that he and Jacko, their wives and Sarah would be travelling on a USAAF aircraft for Manila leaving Darwin the following day. They would be staying overnight at the Manila Hotel. Carna, Monique and Sarah would stay behind in Manila while the men flew the following morning to the Itazuke Air Base at Fukuoka. Johnny informed Jamie that they would take on an additional passenger in Manila, their old friend Harry Williams of US Intelligence. As soon as they arrived at the Fukuoka port, a Royal Navy gunboat was scheduled to pick them up to take them to Shanghai.

'It'll be great to meet up with our old Texan friend again,' said Jacko.

'Yes, we'll have quite a team. Johnny seemed to think it's going to be difficult and probably dangerous, but the powers that be are desperate to put a stop to the opium smuggling,' said Jamie.

'Merde! I do not like this word dangereux, or how you say – "dangerous",' said Monique. 'Je suis désolé. You'd better come back to me, Jacko, or I'll... I'll...'

15

'You'll kill me, right?' he said, laughing.

'Oui. I kill you.'

'Why can't you men be just engineers or bankers?' asked Carna. 'I shall always have to fear for you when you go away to fight bad men.'

'If I was an engineer or a banker, you might not have fallen in love with me,' said Jamie with a grin.

'Si. Está bien! As you say, I might consider you very stuffy then. Aburrido!' Carna laughed. 'No! I think I love you, even if you are garbage man.'

'Nothing is worth doing without a little risk,' said Jacko, winking at Monique.

'D'accord. I like that word "little",' she said. 'I'll keep thinking on it.'

'Letim me know if you need me in China, bikpela brother,' said Sarah, who had been silently eating her steak, listening to the others.

'No probs, Sar,' said Jacko. 'If we need you I'll leave a message at the Manila Hotel. In the meantime, you make sure you keep up your studies with Carna. Your progress is terrific.'

'Aye you! You always full of it, bikpela brother Jacko,' she said as a tear trickled down her right cheek. Jacko gave her shoulders a slight squeeze.

'So, we'll be meeting Johnny Cook at the Bund on the Huang River and the other fellow when we get to the Astor House Hotel?' Jacko asked Jamie.

'Yeah, that's right, Jacko. His name is Lee Drake,' said Jamie. 'He's the only witness to the shooting of the other MI6 agent, Dan Stafford. Johnny reckons he's very reliable. Lived in Shanghai throughout the war.'

'Why didn't the Japanese put him in prison?' asked Carna.

'He's half-British and half-Chinese so he blends in with the locals in Shanghai,' Jamie replied. 'The few times he was questioned, he told the Japanese his father was French. The French Concession was under the control of the Vichy French, Japan's allies.'

'Ah, détestable Vichy!' cried Monique. 'So, French people were always safe in China during the war?'

'Yes, to a degree,' agreed Jamie. 'The Japanese generally left the French Concession alone, even though they were always nervous about all those white men walking around.'

'Weren't there Germans there as well?' asked Monique.

'Yes, there were. Some in Shanghai but largely in the north in Qingdao,' remarked Jamie. 'The Germans made the Japanese nervous as well, I believe. Not a great deal of trust between allies in China.'

'You can say that again, Cap,' said Jacko. 'The Nationalist government and the Chinese Communists were allied against the Japanese, but they hated each other more.'

'Merde! I'm not sorry that I'm not going,' said Monique. 'You boys can have China all to yourselves.'

'Well, I'm sure we won't be getting such delicious steaks when we're in China,' said Jamie.

'At least we'll have Chinese food, Cap,' said Jacko. 'I like those dumplings. I don't know if they'll be better than the ones in Darwin's Chinatown.'

'I guess we'll find out,' said Jamie. 'If everyone's finished here, I suggest we reconvene tomorrow morning over breakfast at the Darwin Hotel and work out what we should take with us.'

An hour later, Jamie and Carna were sitting on the verandah of their house at Doctors Gully sipping on mugs of hot chocolate. Contented, they looked over Darwin Harbour, its shimmering waters reflecting a silvery sheen from the near-full moon.

'It's always hard to leave you behind,' said Jamie, breaking the comfortable silence.

'It's hard for me too, but I wouldn't have it any other way, whatever I may say,' said Carna. 'I married you because you will always be my Jamie. I don't want you to change. I know it is too dangerous in China to have me around to worry about.'

'Yes. I have to admit that I'll feel more at ease knowing you're in your Philippines with the Rousseaus.'

'You are quite the loveliest of men,' she said, snuggling up to him and spilling both their drinks. 'I will be very angry though, if you let anything happen to you in China. Muy enojada!'

'In that case, I wouldn't dare let anything happen to me.'

'Especially as you will eventually be known as "Papá".'

17

'Papá? What are you talking about? Don't tell me...'

'Bueno. I won't tell you. But our bebé will come along anyway.'

'How… er... how? I mean...'

'The usual way, Jamie querido. The usual way.'

'Oh wow! When did you find out? I'm talking a lot of rubbish, aren't I?'

'Si, my darling Jamie. We have another thirty-two weeks to go, so you'll work out what to say by then, no?' she exclaimed, laughing.

'I know what to say now. Come here and let me hug you.'

'You can hug me harder than that. I'm not going to break.'

Jamie looked at her with admiration and said, 'You are going to make the most beautiful and wonderful mother.'

'And by Christmas this year when I'm fat, waddling like a duck, will you still think I'm beautiful then?'

'I will love you more than ever, waddle and all,' said Jamie, laughing. 'You will still be beautiful and the best mamá that ever was.'

'Por supuesto! Of course. And you will be a great papá, my handsome hero.'

* * * *

It was a cloudless blue sky when the USAAF Douglas C54 Skymaster took off from Darwin Airport with Jamie, Carna, Jacko, Monique and Sarah aboard. The only other passengers in the spacious cabin were fourteen American servicemen bound for the Philippines. After half an hour, the aircraft levelled out and was cruising smoothly when the captain of the flight sat down beside them and told them the flight would be non-stop to Manila.

'My name is Chuck Barton,' he told them.

Jamie asked how long the flight would take.

'We're cruising at 165 knots at a level of 20,000 feet,' he said. 'Flight time, ten and a half hours. We'll be landing at Nielsen Field airport at approximately 15:00 depending on the wind. That's three o'clock in the afternoon. I've been told that you guys are on a special mission which involves the USA and that I have to make sure you are well looked after. So, if there's anything you need, just ask. We have

18

a crew of four and one of them is a steward who will get you whatever you want.'

'That's very kind of you, Captain,' said Carna. 'Perhaps you could introduce us to your other passengers.'

'I could surely do that, young lady,' he said.

After being introduced to the American servicemen, most of whom were ground staff and aeronautical engineers with the US Army Airforce, the Australians settled down to nap, while the Americans played cards amongst themselves.

Except for lunch, they were left largely undisturbed until the captain announced they would be descending soon and were expected to land at Nielsen Field on time at 15:00.

As the aircraft taxied towards the terminal, they noted a large dark-blue car parked on the tarmac with the familiar figure of Harry Williams Jr standing beside it. Harry was wearing khaki shirt and slacks and his signature Texan hat. Although he wouldn't have been able to distinguish anyone inside, he gave a welcoming wave as the aircraft drew up close to where his car was parked.

His waving was more enthusiastic when Jamie and the others emerged from the side door of the aeroplane.

'Welcome back to sunny Manila!' he yelled over the aircraft noise as he walked up to greet them. 'Mah favourite Australians, their lovely wives and, of course, Sarah.'

'That's a great-looking car, Harry,' said Jacko. 'What is it?'

'It's the latest Plymouth P15S De Luxe,' said Harry. 'Very roomy and comfortable. I must confess the car isn't mine. It belongs to Paul McNutt, the US High Commissioner. He insisted I use it when he heard you guys were coming. He is still grateful for your intervention in that child-kidnapping operation a few months ago.'

'Will we have the chance to pay our respects to him?' asked Jamie.

'Not this time. He's snowed under with diplomatic stuff right now,' replied Harry. 'Perhaps when we return from China. He has instructed me to invite you to dinner. I'd like to hear more about this trip to China. Where would you like to go for dinner? You guys know the district pretty well.'

'Maybe we could go to that Spanish restaurant in Mabini Street where they play guitars,' suggested Jacko. 'We might be able to get Jamie to play with them.'

'Aha, you mean the Casa de la Cocina,' said Harry. 'Good choice.'

'So, Jamie will be playing the guitar for us there?' said Carna, grinning.

'Yes, yes, yes!' cried Sarah, clapping.

'No, no, no. Those people really know how to play guitar,' said Jamie quickly. 'I'm very second rate compared to those fellows.'

'I'm sure you're not so bad,' Carna said, winking at Harry. 'We'll see.'

'I think we should eat somewhere else,' Jamie protested.

The others, however, all agreed that the Casa de la Cocina was the best choice and after collecting their bags, they headed off to the Manila Hotel.

'Do you know if my parents have arrived yet?' asked Monique.

'Yeah, sure, Monique,' said Harry, smiling. 'They checked in this morning. They'll be wanting to hear Jamie on guitar also.'

'Bloody hell,' Jamie murmured.

'Don't swear, naughty boy!' said Carna.

CHAPTER 3

After checking into the Manila Hotel and freshening up in their rooms, the happily married couples and Sarah joined Henri and Bella Rousseau and Harry for high tea in the tea room at the Manila Hotel, an elegant affair with silver teapot, fine china cups and English scones. Harry asked Henri Rousseau about his plans for the Philippines.

'Over the next few days, with the kind help of Carna whose local knowledge is invaluable, I'll be investigating the best site for a Manila base somewhere near the port area,' explained Henri. 'After that we shall spend a week in the Visayan Islands. Manny Alvarez has informed me that there are wonderful stands of the finest narra wood in Samar, which he will arrange for us to inspect. Finer quality than any cedar or mahogany. There is also another timber we shall look at for unusual furniture items. In Manny's house, he has some chairs and tables carved from an ebony ironwood timber known as kamagong. He said he will show us where this grows on Leyte Island. There are so many amazing timbers in the Philippines, I am really excited about setting up a furniture manufacturing establishment in Cebu.'

'It sounds fascinating, Henri,' said Harry. 'Would you plan to live in Cebu?'

'Non, non. I would plan to visit often, but it is my intention to hire a top-notch manager of the operations once all the machinery is in place,' Henri explained further. 'I also plan to appoint our good Cebuano friends, Manny Alvarez and Oscar Choy, as directors of the enterprise to watch over it for me. They are noted successful businessmen themselves and have become trusted friends, n'est-ce pas?'

'It sounds as though you are well advanced in your planning, Henri,' said Harry. 'When will you be in operation?'

'I hope before 1946 is finished,' said Henri. 'But there is much to do. I have to talk to many hotels, restaurants, society leaders and others, both here and in other countries. Those who are likely to

21

require top-quality fine furniture. I shall also be concentrating on setting up the manufacturing project.'

'You are going to be very busy, sir,' said Harry.

'Oui. Très occupé. As you say, very busy,' agreed Henri. 'I like to be busy. But enough of me. I would like to hear more of this venture into China where, we are told, there is civil war in progress. Is it as bad as reported?'

'Well, it's not quite as bad as all that,' said Jamie. 'We believe that British and American citizens have remained untouched so far. We have to be careful, but we should be able to move around freely if we stay under the radar, so to speak.'

'I would hate for my daughter to lose her husband so soon after marriage,' said Henri seriously, looking at Monique.

'Papa, Jacko is very good at moving around without anybody noticing,' said Monique. 'I hate for him to go too, but that is his life, n'est-ce pas?'

'We shall have a lot of help from the Americans,' said Jamie, gesturing to Harry. 'Also, the British MI6. There is a very bad drug-smuggling operation which needs to be stopped.'

'Je comprends. Oui. I understand,' said Henri. 'Just take care of yourselves, s'il vous plaît.'

'We intend to do that, Henri,' said Jacko, smiling. 'You are also taking some risks. Don't get lost in that Samar jungle.'

'Ah, pas de problème. I'll have Manny and his men to help me,' said Henri. 'The girls can come with me or stay in Cebu with Bella.'

'I'll go with you, Henri,' said Carna. 'That's what I'm here for. I'm sure Sarah would like to come too.'

'D'accord! Thank you,' said Henri. 'Perhaps Monique and Bella can look around for suitable large sheds for the manufacturing in Cebu. Mr Choy said he had some to show us. Again, I am talking more about myself than your trip to China.'

'Don't worry about us in China, Henri,' said Jacko. 'We'll be back before you know it. I'm more worried about whether we can get Jamie to play guitar for us tonight at the Casa de la Cocina in Mabini Street.'

'Yes. Yes. Yes!' Carna and Sarah cried in unison, clapping their hands.

'I thought you fellas were my friends,' said Jamie with an exaggerated frown.

Harry stood up to go and said, 'I've organised another car besides mine so that we can all fit in this evening. The driver of the other car is José, who was your driver when you were here earlier this year. I'll be back at 7.30 and we'll leave from here?'

'That's great, Harry. Thanks for everything,' said Jamie. 'We'll be happy to see José again.'

* * * *

With night falling over Manila, they all stood outside the Casa de la Cocina and looked up and down Mabini Street.

'Oh là!' exclaimed Monique. 'I have never seen so many soldiers and sailors. Are they all American?'

'Pretty much,' replied Harry. 'There are plenty of our boys still here after the war.'

'Most of them have pretty young Filipina girls on their arms,' she said with a playful look at Jacko. 'I'm never going to allow my Jacko to come here without me.'

'My darling lovely wife, you know I only have eyes for you,' Jacko protested.

'I hope so. Otherwise you're in trouble,' she said mischievously.

'Let's go inside,' said Harry. 'I have a table booked for eight.'

As they entered the restaurant, the guitarists who were wandering around the tables started playing and singing a melancholy rendition of 'La Adelita', which had Carna clapping her hands. They sat down at a table with a distinctive yellow-and-red-checked tablecloth. Harry informed them he had already ordered the local delicacy, lechón, as well as several Spanish dishes including tapas, gambas al ajillo and paella, along with a bottle of Rioja tempranillo red wine.

The dinner passed in comfortable merriment to the strains of popular Spanish and Mexican music. Not a mention of China, Cebu, or exotic timbers. Jamie felt particularly relaxed until Carna got up from her seat, whispered something to one of the guitarists, and then returned to the table with a wicked glint in her eye.

Next moment, the guitar music quartet was standing behind Jamie and a guitar was thrust into his hands.

'What you like?' asked the band leader.

'I can only play chords. I'm not much good,' protested Jamie, blushing.

'Well then, we'll play "Cielito Lindo",' the guitarist replied. 'You follow with the chords and your companions have to join in "Aye, yi yi yi", no?'

With that, the combo broke into a rousing rendition of 'Cielito Lindo' and Jamie found, to his astonishment, that he was able to follow them just strumming chords. After the first stanza, most of the other diners joined in, clapping and singing the refrain with much hilarity. At the end of the song, there was loud applause from the other tables. Jamie handed back the guitar and, with the urging of the combo, stood and bowed to the room to further applause.

'Bravo! Such talent,' exclaimed Henri.

'It was only basic chords,' Jamie protested in a low voice.

Carna leant across and whispered in his ear, 'You are a wonderful entertainer, mi amor.'

'It's all right, Cap,' said Jacko, laughing. 'I don't think they have any guitars in China.'

'Thank goodness for that,' said Jamie. 'Now I think it's your turn to perform, Jacko. After dinner we should go to the Nipa Hut.'

'What is this Nipa Hut?' asked Henri.

'It's a nightclub just across the road from here,' said Jamie. 'They have a type of dancing where they continuously bang two bamboo poles together. The dancers have to keep skipping in between the poles before they crash together. It's a Visayan folk dance called Tinikling. We tried it when we were here earlier in the year. Jacko is our Tinikling champion.'

'Splendide!' cried Henri, clapping his hands. 'We must see this dance.'

'Well, I'm not a champion at all,' said Jacko. 'But I'll give it a go again.'

When they walked into the Nipa Hut bar, the Tinikling dancing was well in progress. Many American servicemen almost filled the place watching while two local dancers holding hands and facing

24

each other performed. Folk music on guitars and bamboo instruments created the beat to which two long bamboo poles were tapped on the ground about a foot apart and then against each other, repeatedly. The local dancers, both men and women, wearing straw hats and brightly coloured clothes, were stepping inside and out of the poles with bare feet, nimbly avoiding their ankles being crushed when the horizontal poles were bashed together. At the completion of each dance, the crowd gave the dancers appreciative applause. After a while, the dancers invited anybody in the audience to participate. One of the American servicemen stepped forward. Holding the hands of one of the local dancers, he performed well until the tempo became too fast for him and he limped away with an embarrassed laugh.

'The trick is not to look down,' said Jacko, taking off his boots and socks.

'We watch you with much anticipation,' said Monique, shaking her head.

When it was his turn, Jacko did indeed prove to be very adept at Tinikling. As the tempo increased, the bamboo poles crashed faster and louder, adding to the excitement of the action. Jacko's feet seemed to move in a blur and he kept his head up, looking straight at the local girl dancing with him. When it seemed the action could only get too fast to follow, the music suddenly stopped, and the onlookers broke into enthusiastic applause.

Puffing heavily, Jacko went over to Jamie and said, 'Your turn, Cap.'

'No. I think I'll give it a miss, Jacko. Your dancing would be a hard act to follow. Anyway, I've already done my performance.'

'I go now!' exclaimed Sarah, taking off her shoes and running over to the bamboo poles. She took Jacko's advice and looked only at the Filipina girl opposite her. She effortlessly kept time with the music, nimbly stepping in and out of the poles as the music became faster and faster. When the music stopped, she also received warm applause.

'Brother and sister! Excepcional!' said Carna, clapping her hands.

'My kid sister puts me to shame,' said Jacko, shaking his head.

'I think I like to try,' said Monique. 'Do you think they keep the music a bit slower for me?'

'I'll ask them, my love,' said Jacko, speaking to some of the dancers who nodded.

'They'll slow it down for the girls but not the boys,' Jacko reported.

By the time they set off home, Monique, Carna and Bella had each tried Tinikling. Arriving at the Manila Hotel before midnight, the girls discussed the lack of daring of the men, excepting Jacko, of course.

Harry wished them all good night and told them he would pick up Jamie and Jacko at eight o'clock the next morning to drive them to Nielsen Field airport for the flight to Fukuoka.

A short time later, Jamie and Carna were looking out the window of their hotel room over Manila Bay. There were many stars twinkling in the clear dark sky and they could make out the occasional flash from the Sangley Point lighthouse across the bay.

'Such a beautiful night,' sighed Carna.

'I think you have danced the Tinikling before,' said Jamie.

'I admit this. I'm Filipina, aren't I?'

'The most beautiful one in existence.'

'Oh phoo! Let's go to bed before I bang you on the head, mi amor. I'm not going to see you again for a week or more after tonight.'

'Yes, I'll miss you, but there's no reason for you to worry about my going to China.'

'As long as you come back to me, querido.'

* * * *

The USAAF Douglas C54 Skymaster took off from Nielsen Field airport in the morning into a cloudless blue sky, performed a long sweep to starboard over Parañaque, Manila Bay and Mariveles, before heading north-northeast towards Japan. Although there was seating for about forty, Jamie, Jacko and Harry were the only passengers.

After attaining cruising height, the captain, Chuck Barton, informed them that the flight time to Itazuke Air Base in Fukuoka would be seven hours.

'We should arrive at about 14:30, 2.30 in the afternoon Japanese time,' he said. 'We'll be cruising at 20,000 feet. Make yourselves comfortable, gentlemen, and don't hesitate to put your hands up if you need anything.'

'Thanks, Chuck,' said Harry. 'Empty plane. Put on just for us?'

'Not quite, Harry,' said Chuck with a grin. 'I should have said "yes", but I will be ferrying a group of USAAF personnel back from Itazuke to Clark Air Base after I drop you. Have a pleasant flight, guys.'

He waved and disappeared back into the cockpit, whereupon Harry produced a leather cup and five dice and challenged the others to a game of Balut, a game popular throughout the Philippines.

'Ah'm sure you remember this game from the last time you stayed in the Philippines,' he said. 'You know the rules. I suggest a cent a point. Okay?'

'No problem, Harry. I'm happy to skin you any time,' Jacko laughed.

The long flight over the East China Sea was interspersed with the occasional triumphant cry of 'Balut!' interrupted by a delicious lunch of hot roast chicken. The three Balut players were so engrossed in their game, they didn't realise the aircraft had begun its descent until they were almost over the Itazuke Air Base. A voice over the intercom telling them to fasten their seat belts finally ended the game.

By the time they touched down on the tarmac, Harry had calculated that Jamie had won $2.24, Jacko $1.04, and he himself was the big loser to the tune of $3.28.

'I don't think I'll take up gambling as a career, guys,' said Harry.

'Don't worry, Harry,' said Jamie, patting him on the back. 'The first drinks are on me when we reach Shanghai.'

'I'll hold you to that, Jamie ol' buddy.'

The Skymaster taxied over to a hangar where an old black passenger car was waiting with a young American serviceman standing beside it. After they disembarked from the side door of the aircraft, Jamie and Jacko followed Harry who walked over to the serviceman and introduced himself.

'I'm Corporal Hill, sir,' was the reply. 'I've been instructed to take you straight to the port area. There's a British ship waiting there for you.'

'Thanks, Corporal. What sort of car is this?' asked Harry. 'I haven't seen one of these before.'

It's a 1936 Toyoda Sedan, sir. It's a Japanese car. It goes okay and there's plenty of room for you all.'

'Excellent,' said Harry, kicking a tyre. 'We'll get our bags and be off.'

As they approached the port, the most prominent vessel to be seen was a grey ship, more than 100 yards long. The car drove up to the ship's gangway and the three men stood looking at it with bags in hand. A smart young officer came running down the gangway and introduced himself as Lieutenant Hamilton.

'Hello, Lieutenant,' said Jamie. 'I think your ship is the one taking us to China?'

'It is indeed, sir,' said Hamilton. 'This is HMS East Cape. If you come aboard right away, we'll be ready to leave in a short while.'

As soon as they were aboard, the gangway was taken in and the throbbing of the engine increased. Lieutenant Hamilton suggested they leave their bags on the deck while he took them to the bridge to meet the captain. By the time they reached the bridge, the ship was already moving away from the pier and in a short while was heading out to sea.

An officer with a tanned face and grey hair introduced himself as Captain Kenneth Wilson, skipper of HMS East Cape. After all the introductions, Jamie asked what sort of ship she was.

'This is a British frigate, Mr Munro,' said Captain Wilson. 'It's over 350 feet long and can cruise at over thirty knots. The East China Sea is pretty smooth at this time, so I estimate we'll take sixteen hours or so. I should be landing you at the Bund in Shanghai at 0700 hours.'

'A very impressive ship, Captain,' said Jamie.

'Yes, it is,' agreed Captain Wilson. 'The powers-that-be must believe you people are on a very important mission. So, welcome aboard the good ship East Cape, sir.'

'We're no longer in the armed services, so can we dispense with the formalities?' asked Jamie. 'I'm Jamie and these fellows are Jacko and Harry.'

'Okay! I concur,' agreed Captain Wilson. 'You chaps can call me Ken. From your accent, I assume you are Australians.'

'Jacko and I are Australian,' said Jamie. 'Harry's American.'

'Aha, a Yank!' said Wilson, smiling.

'Ah ain't no yankee, Captain. Ah'm from Texas!'

'Oh, yes. Quite! Sorry,' said Wilson. 'I've assigned Lieutenant Hamilton to look after you and show you where you can bunk down. You'll be joining us in the officers' mess for dinner and breakfast. So, I'll leave you in the hands of the lieutenant for now. You can call him Hugh if you like.'

Back on deck, they watched as the frigate headed out through a narrow passage between the mainland and a small island. Genkai Island, Hugh told them. After that, the ship picked up speed and headed southwest into the East China Sea. Hugh then showed them to three small cabins towards the stern of the ship, close to heads and shower rooms.

They stowed their gear and returned to the deck, mesmerised by the frigate cutting through the smooth water at speed, throwing up a bow wave high and wide. After a while they were joined by Captain Wilson who had to shout above the noise of the engines. He pointed out a large island in the misty distance on the starboard bow.

'That's Cheju-do. It's a Korean volcanic island. That's the cone of the volcano you see in the distance. It's over 6,000 feet high,' he said. 'We'll be abeam of the island in about three hours and after that, it'll be open sea to the mouth of the Yangtze River on the China coast. The sea is not always so smooth, so you've brought us luck this time. It'll still be dark when we enter the Yangtze delta, but we have excellent radar. The sun should be well and truly up by the time we drop you chaps at the Shanghai Bund.'

'We are certainly motoring along,' said Jamie. 'What's our speed, Ken?'

'Currently cruising at thirty-one knots. We should be able to keep that up all the way.'

'That's amazing, Ken,' said Jamie. 'Thanks.'

By the time they were abeam of Cheju-do, with its towering volcano reaching for the sky, the sun was dipping and the East China Sea had turned from blue-green to a deep coppery colour extending as far as the eye could see. Jamie, Jacko and Harry stared at the island until a loud bell sounded for dinner.

The following morning, as the sun rose, Jamie, Jacko and Harry were on the main deck again as the East Cape, at reduced speed and surrounded by shrieking seagulls, weaved its way up a river about 400 yards wide. The main river traffic comprised motorised and sailing junks and small sampans. Hugh Hamilton joined them, and Harry asked if it was the Yangtze River.

'No, no. This is the Huangpu or, in other words, the Huang River,' explained Hamilton. 'It flows into the Yangtze near its delta. We're about halfway between its mouth and the Bund. We're only doing about eight knots at the moment, so we'll be there in twenty minutes or so.'

A short time later, they sailed around a sharp left-hand bend in the river and beheld, on the starboard shore, a long row of impressive stone buildings, some with columns and gothic windows. A large clock tower dominated the central part of the row.

'Welcome to the famous Shanghai Bund,' said Hamilton, grandly gesturing to the buildings, as the frigate edged towards the piers in front of them.

CHAPTER 4

The three men were still up on the main deck staring in wonderment at the beautiful stone buildings, when the HMS East Cape was finally moored against one of the piers in front of the Bund. It was surrounded by varied boats and sailboats, some with one mast, some with two, all with Chinese crew yelling and chattering in a loud discordant chorus.

Jamie looked down at the crowded pier and spotted Johnny standing next to a slightly shorter man. He waved to him. The movement caught Johnny's eye and he waved back. Captain Wilson appeared on the deck and informed them that the gangway was being lowered and they could leave the ship in the next few minutes.

'That was an impressive and speedy voyage, Ken,' said Jamie, shaking his hand. 'Jacko and I have sailed on a Royal Navy ship before, but nothing as fast as this ship.'

'Yes, this frigate can go places in a hurry,' said Captain Wilson. 'Glad you enjoyed it. I wish you luck with whatever your mission is, chaps.'

They made their farewells, picked up their bags and were soon clambering down the gangway to the pier where they could see Johnny pushing through the crowd towards them.

'G'day, Johnny,' said Jamie as they shook hands. 'So, this is Shanghai. We never expected to see so many fine buildings.'

'Jamie, Jacko, Harry, great to see you again. Yes, all built during the early part of this century, mostly British architects,' said Johnny, looking around. 'Before the Japanese occupation, the building with the clock tower functioned as the Customs House and the one with 100 yards of frontage next to it was the Hong Kong and Shanghai Bank. Most of the other buildings were banks, shipping lines, or hotels. We can give you a tour later on, but now we'll go and check you in at your hotel. First of all, I want you to meet Lee Drake who is our local agent here.'

Lee Drake, who had been quietly standing back watching, stepped forward and shook everyone's hands as Johnny introduced him.

'Lee lived here in what they call the old Chinese City throughout the Japanese occupation,' said Johnny. 'He knows his way around.'

'There must be quite a story there,' said Harry. 'I'd sure like you to tell us about it when we've got time.'

'What are all these people on the pier doing, Lee?' asked Jacko.

'They're just here for a sticky-beak,' said Lee. 'A Royal Navy ship in the Huang River is a spectacle for them. There are a few US Navy ships about. Cruisers, destroyers, survey ships and a few old gunboats, but since last year they haven't ventured much up the Huangpu, mainly operating on the Yangtze River.'

As soon as they left the pier, the crowds thinned and they were able to walk freely, heading north along the waterfront. After walking 200 yards or so they noticed, on their left, an ornate red and white building with distinctive turrets on the top. Jacko commented that it was a beautiful and unusual building.

'That's the old Palace Hotel,' explained Lee. 'It's nearly forty years old and was one of the major hotels in China in its time, comparing favourably with the best hotels in Europe. Bit run-down now, though. The next much bigger building with the pointed green roof is the Cathay Hotel. It's owned by the Sassoons, one of the richest families in China. In between them is Nanjing Dong Lu – that is, Nanjing East Road, the main road through to the French Concession. I'll explain all this to you later.'

A further 300 yards found them at the southern end of a bridge crossing a narrow stream, which Lee told them was known as Suzhou Creek. After crossing the bridge, they turned right into Huangpu Road and arrived at a magnificent neo-classical Baroque stone building, the Astor House Hotel, with its many imposing arched windows. Walking up the front steps and through the entrance, they were impressed by the ornate ceilings and walls, noting that the wooden floors, stairs, bannisters and reception desk were of the finest teak.

Lee spoke to the girl at reception in rapid Chinese, and finally handed room keys to the three new arrivals.

'We're all on the first floor,' said Johnny. 'I'm in room 102 and your rooms are nearby. I suggest you throw your bags in your room and we'll meet here on the ground floor. They serve a nice morning tea in the dining room.'

Walking up the stairs to the first floor, the trio couldn't help but be impressed by the opulent décor of the hotel. The plush red carpet in the centre of the stairway continued through the hallway on the first floor, with gleaming teak floorboards on both sides. The hallway was lighted by chandeliers and furnished with elegant tables and chairs. In addition, large pots with indoor plants were spaced at intervals along the hall outside the rooms, which were large with high ceilings and filled with dark glossy teak furniture.

'This place seems to have survived the war pretty well,' observed Jacko when they met up again with Johnny and Lee in the ground floor restaurant. Tea, scones and jam were being served.

'Not all of it,' said Lee. 'Most of the other floors deteriorated during the war despite the Japanese using it extensively themselves. You'd be interested to know that Charlie Chaplin once stayed on the floor where you are now in the 1930s, and Albert Einstein stayed during the 1920s, on the third floor. In fact, many celebrities from all around the world stayed here during the Roaring Twenties. The Astor House Hotel was the centre of amusement, parties and dancing during that time. Big bands, big balls, expensive receptions. You name it, it all happened here.'

'The knobs hobnobbed, and the celebrities sparkled,' said Jamie, grinning.

'Exactly!' agreed Lee. 'But Harry would be more interested to know that General Ulysses S Grant once stayed in this hotel, way back in 1878.'

'Well, I'll be damned! Ulysses S Grant!' exclaimed Harry, shaking his head. 'What's the large building with the red roof on the other side of the road from this hotel?'

'That's the old Russian Consulate,' explained Lee. 'The Chinese government has forbidden the Russians from occupying it again since the war. They fear it would only encourage the Chinese Communists.'

'A lot of intrigue going on around China right now, no?' said Harry.

'You'd never believe the half of it,' said Lee. 'There are, in fact, many Russians living in Shanghai. Most of them are White Russians

33

who escaped into China after the revolution. They fear the communists more than anyone.'

'I can well imagine,' muttered Jamie, shaking his head. 'Are the communists likely to win the civil war between them and the nationalists?'

'Certainly that is a possibility, but it's hard to know who'll eventually win,' Lee conceded. 'The defeat of the nationalists in Jilin a couple of months ago, in the northern Manchurian region, is an example of what can happen. The Kuomintang government tried to take control of Siping City but lacked troops. So, Chiang Kai-shek recruited the local bandit gangs to help him secure the city. This angered the local population, as the gang members used their newfound power to rape and pillage. Lacking any popular support, the government was defeated by the communists. This is happening in a number of places in China. The Kuomintang are rapidly losing the hearts and minds of the people.'

'Would these same bandit gangs be involved in the opium-smuggling trade we've been sent here to investigate?' asked Jamie.

'Different gangs, but same scenario,' said Lee. 'The government is essentially corrupt. You can be sure that a number of Kuomintang Nationalist leaders are in it up to their necks.'

'As well as a few foreigners?' added Jacko.

'As well as a few foreigners,' agreed Lee. 'Their main base of operations is on the western side of the Yangtze River opposite Tongling. We believe that's where they refine the opium, some of which is grown there. Most, though, is barged in from distant provinces such as Guangxi. I observed a couple of Englishmen there before Dan was shot. One of them was a big fellow with a red beard. We didn't get close enough to find out much. Colonel Cook knows most of this.'

'From now on, we'll be working together closely, so just call me Johnny, Lee. The other chaps do.'

'To get to this place where the opium is refined, will we sail in a boat from here?' asked Harry.

'No. We'll take the train from here to Nanjing. It's about 190 miles upriver from here,' said Lee, smiling. 'That'll be another interesting experience for you. The trains are something else. The railway station is not far from here, on this side of Suzhou Creek.'

'So, I guess we'll have a boat waiting for us at Nanjing?' Harry surmised.

'Yes, Harry. A compatriot of yours. An American, Peter Jackson, will take us up the river from Nanjing to Tongling,' explained Lee. 'He has a rough-looking motorised junk which is more operational than it looks. He and his crew know the river backwards.'

'Was he here throughout the war?' asked Jamie incredulously.

'Yes. After Pearl Harbour he became Pierre Leconte of the French Concession in Shanghai,' Lee chuckled. 'Presented himself as an ardent supporter of the Vichy French! He didn't discriminate, chartering his boat to the Japanese conquerors and the Chinese resistance equally, while at the same time, feeding me information to send to the Allies.'

'Can't wait to meet this guy!' said Harry.

'The last time you and Dan Stafford sailed with him down the river was during the night, wasn't it?' asked Jamie.

'Yes, that's right,' agreed Lee. 'We arrived at the opium centre in the morning and Dan wanted to get a closer look during daylight. In hindsight, a huge mistake. The bandits sighted us in the poppy field.'

'We'd like to have a look at the opium setup during the night,' said Jacko. 'That means your friend, Peter Jackson, sailing up the river during the day. Is that feasible?'

'Sure. He often travels up and down the river in daylight,' said Lee. 'It's best you stay out of sight though. Some trigger-happy characters might take a pot shot at you.'

'What about Jackson? Don't they shoot at him?' asked Jamie.

Lee nodded. 'They do, regularly. He's built a bullet-proof shelter around the wheelhouse which is big enough for three men, so he hasn't been worried so far.'

'So, it looks like we'll have to leave Nanjing in the morning to get there by dark?' said Jamie. 'Will the train get there in the morning?'

'That's doubtful,' said Lee. 'The arrival time of the train is uncertain at the best of times. It often has to stop to avoid fighting or to repair the rails. We'll most likely have to stay a night in Nanjing or somewhere further up the Yangtze. Peter Jackson will advise us on that.'

'What's the situation in Nanjing?' asked Johnny.

'It's quiet at the present time,' replied Lee. 'The government is in firm control there, but that doesn't mean there aren't incidents once in a while when some of the criminal gangs cause a bit of havoc.'

'I guess the government has firm control here in Shanghai?' mused Johnny.

'Oh yes. The government and the Four Families are pretty much in control of everything,' said Lee wistfully.

'The Four Families? Who are they?' asked Jamie.

'Well, the family of Chiang Kai-shek, of course. Then the Soong, Kung and Chen families,' said Lee. 'They own just about all the commerce. When we've finished our tea, we'll go for a walk around the city and I'll show you.'

'Okay. Fantastic. I'm ready to go when you are,' said Jacko eagerly.

After crossing back over the bridge, they walked along the waterfront known as the Bund while Lee related a brief history of each of the large stone buildings as they passed them. Many American servicemen were amongst the crowds of local Chinese on both sides of the main street. Pedlars moved amongst them shouting in shrill voices. Distinctive two-wheeled horse-drawn carriages, rickshaws and a few 1930s-model cars plied their way up and down the street. Most of the rickshaws conveyed American GIs.

'The first building was the Banque de L'Indo-Chine, the second Glen Line shipping. The US Consulate has set up office there since the war,' Lee said, pointing to various buildings. 'The third building is Jardine Matheson & Co. Then Yangtze Insurance followed by Yokohama Bank, which handled most of the Japan–China trade. The next tall building is the Bank of China, followed by the Cathay Hotel, owned by Victor Sassoon, a very wealthy businessman. The Cathay, when it opened in 1929, took over from the Astor House Hotel as the centre for big dances, big bands, celebrities, you name it. After the beautiful Palace Hotel, which I've already told you about, is that building with the elegant columns. It was the Chartered Bank of India, Australia and China. Next is the North China Daily News

36

building. That newspaper used to be the leading English language newspaper since 1850, but it exists no more. Then the Bank of Taiwan, which was a Japanese Bank. Next, that large building was the Russo–Chinese Bank, the first building in Shanghai equipped with a lift. The tall light-coloured building, now empty, used to be the Bank of Communications, which handled all the revenues from the railways, post, telegrams and shipping. Then we come to the famous Customs House with its tall clock tower. The chimes of the extremely accurate clock are exactly the same as those in Big Ben in London. After that is the largest building with the dome on top, the Hongkong & Shanghai Bank. Between this building and the next one, the China Merchants Steam Navigation Company building, is Fuzhou Road. I'll take you up there now and show you the old Chinese part of town. For your information, if we had continued down the Bund, seven buildings further on from here is the old Shanghai Club, the meeting place of all the gentry in the nineteen-thirties. It's most famous for its bar – a hundred and ten feet long. It's vacant these days. I'm sure you won't miss seeing it.'

'That's very instructive, thanks, Lee,' said Jamie. 'You certainly know the area well.'

'Yes, I've lived here a while,' said Lee with a wry smile. 'Shortly, you'll be looking at some much older buildings, quite different to those on the Bund, most of them from the Ming and Qing Dynasties.'

They walked to the west up Fuzhou Road away from the river, Lee Drake pointing out areas of interest, all around them the loud multi-language chatter, the rumble and clatter of cart wheels, and the honking of car horns. They finally arrived in a square dominated by ornate old Chinese buildings, largely dark brown with light inlays and red and green curved roofs, all in various stages of disrepair.

'We are now well into the old Chinese City of Shanghai where I've lived for the past six years as a modest tea merchant. Some of these buildings are as old as the Ming Dynasty. The Japanese left this area largely untouched. Up ahead is the marketplace. You can buy almost anything there. Many of the goods for sale are black-market items. I'll show you.'

The marketplace was crowded, mainly with American GIs looking for souvenirs and handing out chocolates to children following them around. Lee led them to a few of the stalls where food, clothing and medicines were displayed.

'Take a close look at the medicines over here,' said Lee, indicating a prominent stall.

'I think I see what you mean,' said Jamie, looking closely at an array of medicines, bandages and surgical instruments. 'Most of these have Red Cross and United Nations Relief and Rehabilitation Administration wrappings.'

'Exactly. Most of these stalls are outlets for the Four Families,' said Lee. 'The USA, in particular, has sent considerable aid to China since the war. Chiang, Soong and their cronies have stipulated that all relief goods and money be delivered to a government relief authority. From there, the goods are stored in warehouses owned by the Four Families to be sold at high prices. The money, of course, is siphoned off into selected bank accounts designated by the government, and some of it probably finishes up in banks in the Bahamas or similar.'

'That's bloody dreadful,' said Jacko.

'Goddamn it! So that's where our American aid disappears to,' exclaimed Harry, shaking his head. 'Goddamn!'

'I'm telling you this so you know what you're up against here,' said Lee. 'You'll have to regard almost everybody as a potential enemy. The government is not necessarily your friend.'

'You've certainly made that clear,' said Johnny. He added, 'There are a lot of young white girls amongst the crowd. Quite a few pretty ones. Where do they come from?'

'Russians. White Russians,' said Lee. 'They're all hoping to catch the eye of young GIs to take them away from here. There are thousands of them. Further up the road, into the French Concession, are all the nightclubs and brothels, where most of the girls are Russians. Very sad. Now you've seen all this, I'll take you to one of the better Chinese eateries around here for lunch.'

'What a great idea,' said Jacko. 'I'm hungry.'

Seated at a round table in a restaurant cooled by overhead fans, Lee suggested that he order all the dishes for the five of them to share. After speaking at length to a waiter in rapid Chinese, Lee told them he was sure they would find the food delicious and said they would have to use chopsticks.

'No problem,' said Jacko, 'I think we're all not too bad with chopsticks. Although I'm not sure about Harry.'

'Don't worry about me,' said Harry. 'I'll manage. So, what will we be eating, Lee?'

Lee laughed and said, 'The first rule about good Chinese cooking is never to ask what you're eating. It might put you off. If it tastes good, then it's good.'

'You certainly speak Chinese fluently,' observed Jamie.

'Well, I should do. My late mother was Chinese. She was from Nanjing. Like her, I can speak several dialects. Mandarin, Cantonese, and even the local Shanghai dialect.'

'Your English is also perfect,' said Johnny.

'My father was English,' explained Lee. 'I went to the British School here in Shanghai.'

'Is your father still alive?' asked Jamie.

'No. Killed in the war,' said Lee, as the dishes started arriving at the table. 'We'll be drinking tea, which is safe here. I suggest you don't drink water unless it's been boiled.'

'What about beer?' asked Jacko.

'The beer is good,' said Lee. 'Outside Shanghai, you'll be lucky to find cold beer, though.'

'Well, I'd better have some cold beer while we're here,' suggested Jacko, waving at the waiter.

'Tell him bīng píjiu!' said Lee.

Jacko said, 'Bing... er... I'll leave it up to you, Lee.'

Lee ordered beer for everyone in another burst of rapid Chinese, and the waiter returned with five cold fifteen-ounce bottles of local beer.

'Hmm. Not bad,' said Jacko after tasting his beer.

'That's high praise from a Territorian,' Jamie chuckled.

'Yeah, I think I'm gonna like Shanghai,' agreed Jacko.

'Even with all the corruption we've seen and heard about, Jacko?' asked Jamie, winking at the others.

'I'd rather not think about that while I'm eating,' Jacko smiled.

'I agree with you there, Jacko,' said Lee.

'A country with good beer can't be all that bad.' Jacko grinned.

Lee looked carefully at Jacko and said, 'I think you have some other heritage in your background besides British, Jacko. Indian, maybe?'

'Nah! I'm true-blue Australian, mate,' said Jacko with a smile. 'Half Aborigine. Something like you, Lee. A bit of this and a bit of that. Do you think I could pass for Chinese?'

'With a bit of make-up, you could,' said Lee.

'Don't think I could ever learn the language, though. Sounds a bit quick for me.'

CHAPTER 5

Throughout the afternoon, Lee Drake led his willing sightseers through many of the back streets of Shanghai, pointing out places and buildings of interest, even including some of the more popular nightclubs which, he said, became very lively after ten at night.

'By that time, the streets around here will be full of cheerful innocent young servicemen from the States cavorting in the streets,' said Lee with a chuckle. 'Every beautiful young girl, whether Chinese, Russian or whatever, will be advising them how to spend their dollars.'

'Are dollars legal currency around here?' asked Harry.

'Dollars, pounds, rupees, pesos, anything but Chinese money,' said Lee. 'To pay for the army, the government is printing new money so fast, inflation is out of hand. By next month you'll need a wheelbarrow-full of Chinese notes to buy a loaf of bread. Everyone is happy with US dollars, Harry.'

A couple more hours found them beside the Suzhou Creek, not far from the bridge to the Astor House Hotel.

'I'll leave you chaps now,' said Lee. 'You can see the hotel. I have a few things to do. I'll radio London that you're all here. You can have dinner in the hotel tonight, if you like. They probably even serve a roast there.'

'Fine. Where shall we meet you tomorrow morning?' asked Johnny.

'I'll have breakfast with you at 0700 in the hotel dining room where we had tea this morning,' replied Lee. 'It's only a short walk from there to the railway station on the north side of the creek. The train leaves around nine.'

'Wait! Wait! Weapons,' exclaimed Jamie. 'We'll need some weapons. Jacko and I brought our handguns, but we'll need some rifles. Can you organise them for us?'

'No problem, Jamie,' said Lee. 'Peter has an assortment of rifles on his boat. American three-O carbines, .303s and the odd STEN gun. You can have your pick.'

'That'll do us,' said Jacko, chuckling.

'Are you sure you don't want to stay at the Astor House tonight?' asked Jamie. 'It might be more convenient for you.'

'No. I'll be fine,' said Lee. 'I'll come to the hotel in the morning.'

'I guess you're pretty used to being on your own after all this time,' said Johnny.

Lee winked at them. 'Who said I'll be on my own?'

With that, and a wave of his hand, he quickly disappeared into the narrow streets south of Suzhou Creek.

Johnny smiled and said, 'An amazing chap. He certainly has his finger on the pulse.'

'It's almost too much to take in,' said Jamie, as they started walking towards the bridge. 'I guess this is what's called a melting pot.'

'A melting pot indeed,' said Johnny. 'But which way will it flow when it melts?'

'Don't know, Johnny, but I'm just about ready for another cold beer,' said Jacko. 'That bing whatever!'

I think it's bīng píjiu,' said Johnny. 'That's what Lee said.'

'Yeah, that'll do,' said Jacko. 'You can be the one to order the drinks, Johnny.'

'Okay, no problem,' Johnny laughed. 'I think they all speak English at the hotel anyway.'

They crossed the bridge and walked past the old Russian Consulate building to the front door of the hotel. Looking out towards the Huang River, they saw several docks in front of the hotel that were a hive of activity, with many Chinese workers, toiling like ants, frenetically loading goods in boxes, chests, barrels, packages and sacks into boats large and small. As they watched, two of the boats set sail down the river towards the Yangtze delta, while eight or nine others, still with coolies swarming all over them, looked as though they were preparing to sail.

'I'll have to ask Lee what that's all about,' muttered Johnny as they walked into the hotel.

Dinner was a sombre affair that evening in the elegant hotel dining room, with each of the men lost in his own thoughts, pondering what was ahead of them a long way west of Shanghai up the Yangtze

42

River. They were the only guests in the dining room. The roast of the day was beef served with a poor excuse for a Yorkshire pudding, boiled vegetables, and thin light-brown gravy. They had nearly finished the main course when Johnny finally broke the silence.

'Talk about the great unknown,' he said. 'We know quite a lot now about the general situation in China, thanks to Lee, but we know almost nothing about the opium smugglers we're trying to track down. We do know where they're operating from. But except for a big Englishman with a red beard and a cockney accent, we know nothing about the people along the supply chain which reaches as far as the USA. Not the best start to the investigation, what?'

'Hell's bells!' exclaimed Harry. 'Blind men in a fog at night time.'

'Apart from having a close look at the opium centre which we know about, we may be able to gather some information by asking questions along the river,' said Jamie. 'The opium has to be transported by boats on the Yangtze. Someone must know something. What type of boats? Who's in charge of the boats? There must be someone running things from Shanghai. We'll have to take careful note of all the boats using the river.'

'Yes, yes. Lee, with his knowledge of the region and the language, will be the key man,' said Johnny. 'I don't know if we'll be able to recruit any other locals to help us out.'

'Doubtful,' said Jamie thoughtfully. 'As Lee says, we can't really trust anyone.'

'I dunno,' said Jacko. 'As we go along, things could get clearer and we might find all sorts of people who don't like the government, the communists or the bandits. Some local fellas might be happy to help us. You just never know.'

'You're right, Jacko,' said Johnny. 'You never know till you try. Things will probably look a lot clearer once we've been on the job for a few days.' He paused and then said, 'I wonder if the dessert is better than the main course.'

'I might have another cold beer instead of dessert,' said Jacko.

'I think I'll join you,' agreed Jamie.

'Make it three,' said Harry.

Johnny nodded, waved at the waiter, and ordered four cold beers.

* * * *

Breakfast at the Astor House Hotel was typically English with poached eggs, bacon, toast, marmalade and tea. Lee had arrived on the dot at 7.00 am and they all ate with an air of anticipation.

'Do you reckon the train'll be on time, Lee?' asked Jacko.

'Oh yes. The train will leave on time,' replied Lee. 'Whether it reaches Nanjing on time or at all is the question.'

'That bad, huh?' said Harry.

'The main thing will be to get on it,' said Lee with a sardonic smile. 'There'll be crowds waiting to board. Too many for the train.'

'Oh? How can we be sure we'll get on then?' asked Johnny.

'Leave it to me,' said Lee.

They looked at one another while Lee tucked into his eggs. Then Johnny cleared his throat and said, 'You might satisfy my curiosity, Lee. Yesterday afternoon there were boats of all sizes being loaded at the docks in front of this hotel. There were hundreds of coolies loading large boxes, chests, crates, sacks and barrels. Do you know where all that would be going?'

Lee laughed. 'Yes. I suspect I know where all that would be going. The wealthy families often use the Hongkew docks down there to ship out portions of their wealth. The Soongs, Chiangs, Kungs and Chens would have had a large ship waiting outside the Yangtze River mouth to collect all the goods you saw being loaded. They'd include priceless artefacts as well as gold.'

'Goddamn it! Couldn't somebody stop these people, these Four Families?' asked Harry.

'Those Four Families are the power behind the government,' said Lee cynically. 'They also have the support of the British and American governments.'

'We can't get involved in this political stuff,' said Jamie. 'We should just focus on the smuggling operation and try to stay out of the way of the political leaders and warring parties.'

'That's all you can do,' agreed Lee. 'When you've finished breakfast, we'll take off. First of all, I need to know if you chaps have any silver coins like florins.'

44

'I have quite a few florins here,' said Johnny, pulling them out of his pocket.

'I have two silver dollars, if that's any use,' proffered Harry.

'Silver dollars! Why, Harry, that's better than ever,' exclaimed Lee. 'I need to cross the palms of a couple of railway officials, and nobody around here trusts paper money much. Silver dollars are perfect!'

'Do you need these florins?' asked Johnny.

'I'll take those too. In case,' said Lee.

'I've got some Australian silver florins,' said Jamie.

'Yes, I'll take them,' said Lee, slipping all the coins into his pocket.

The streets on the north side of Suzhou Creek were relatively deserted as they wended their way to the railway station. After a short distance, they passed a light-grey, eight-storey Art Deco building just north of the Shanghai Post Office. Lee informed them that it was the Bridge House Building, a former hotel. The Japanese Kempeitai, Japan's equivalent of the German Gestapo, had occupied the building during the war.

'On most nights, you could hear the tortured screams across the other side of Suzhou Creek,' he said grimly.

As they drew near the Shanghai Railway Station, they found a vast crowd of Chinese people in front of them, all calling and shouting at a harassed railway guard who was checking tickets. The crowd, pushing and shoving, slowly filed through a narrow gate leading onto the platform. Lee told the others to stay where they were and then he disappeared through the crowd towards the station. The crowd waiting to get through the gate seemed to grow larger as they watched.

It was a half-hour before Lee reappeared accompanied by a uniformed railway guard who beckoned them to follow him up a narrow lane away from the crowd. Following a circuitous route, they found themselves next to the rear guard's van. On that side of the van, they were concealed from the crowds on the platform. The guard climbed up through a sliding door, followed by Lee and the others. Lee later told them he was the chief guard.

Another uniformed railway official and a government soldier sat in the front end of the van watching them. Lee handed the chief guard one of Harry's silver dollars and four of the florins. The dollar quickly disappeared into the guard's pocket, and he then distributed the florins to the other two men. The four new arrivals were treated to wide smiles all round, then the chief guard said something in Chinese and ushered them to the rear of the van where a large number of mail sacks were stacked.

'He suggests we make ourselves comfortable amongst these sacks during the journey,' explained Lee. 'That's good advice. There'll be a bit of rocking around and stopping and starting. We'll be underway soon. The carriages behind the engine are already full to the brim.'

The locomotive ahead was puffing, snorting and spouting steam above the clamouring of those of the angry crowd who had been unable to get through the gate. Suddenly, the train lurched forward with much screeching of iron wheels and Jamie, who had not yet sat down, was nearly thrown off his feet.

'Now I know why the guard said to sit!' said Jamie, sitting down heavily as the train stopped and started a few times before finally moving forward at a more even pace.

'I've still got your other silver dollar, Harry,' said Lee loudly above the noise.

'Keep it. Keep it. I'm glad I brought them,' said Harry. 'I might even have more in my backpack here.'

'Good, we might need them later,' said Lee.

'What about the crowd who missed this train?' asked Jacko. 'Will they have to wait until tomorrow?'

'No. There should be a second train leaving from another platform sometime later,' said Lee. 'Heaven knows when. This is the only daily train that leaves roughly on time.'

'So, how do you chaps like the Chinese rail system?' asked Johnny, smiling.

'I'll let you know after we get to Nanjing,' replied Jacko.

The train picked up speed and they all settled down in silence, looking towards the soldier and the guards seated up the front of the van preparing to play cards. They plainly heard the choof-choof-

choof of the locomotive, and the clackety-clack of the railway tracks became almost mesmerising.

'Well, it's a darn sight better than walking,' said Harry with a straight face.

'Yeah, it's better than a poke in the eye with a sharp stick,' said Jacko, nodding.

Harry chuckled, 'Yeah, that too.'

Jamie stared out of the open guard's door on the left side of the van. Small square fields, paddies, clusters of houses, carts, solitary people, an occasional carabao or water buffalo, creeks, hills, all flashed past as the train sped along the tracks. Occasionally, a gust of wind blew black smoke from the locomotive into the van, but for the most part the breeze through the open door was pleasant. Probably doing fifty miles an hour, Jamie estimated. As Harry had suggested, better than walking. At long intervals the train sped past railway stations without slowing down.

Just as they were all being lulled into drowsy sleep, the train slowed with sudden jerks and a loud squealing of brakes. They looked at Lee, who shook his head and shrugged. From there, the train crawled along for another half-hour and then slowly sped up again, only to brake again after a short while.

After another extended period of crawling, the train accelerated and for an hour or so maintained a relatively even speed. The guards and the soldier at the front of the van became engrossed in their card game and Jamie and the others lay back watching the scenery flashing past.

Suddenly, the brakes were again applied, accompanied by the familiar squealing and screeching of metal on metal, and then the train came to a complete stop. In the silence that followed, they heard shooting ahead. The soldier in the van picked up his rifle and aimed it down the track, looking for a target. They all looked at Lee who shrugged and appeared unconcerned.

'A daily occurrence around here,' he explained. 'Kuomintang shooting at communists, bandits shooting at bandits, peasants taking pot shots at each other. Who knows? The soldiers on the locomotive have mounted machine guns. If the train is attacked directly, the soldiers will open fire. The delay shouldn't last long.'

With that, the chatter of a machine gun opening fire was followed by silence. Two minutes later, with a sudden lurch, the train moved slowly forward again. Sporadic rifle fire could be heard but it was now further away. The train maintained its frustrating snail-like progress for another half-hour and then picked up speed again. There was further sporadic rifle fire on both sides as they sped along and at one time, they were startled by the sound of a ricochet off the side of the van. Lee's face remained impassive so the others relaxed, while the chief guard and his friends went back to their card game.

It was well after midday when, after a few more slow-downs and speed-ups, Jamie noticed that they were passing more slowly through a large town backed by misty hills. Red- and green-tiled roofs, people moving around the streets, tall pagodas. The tallest and most picturesque pagoda sat atop a high wooded hill behind the town.

Jamie looked at Lee who said, 'We're passing through Zhenjiang, the provincial capital of Jiangsu. Only fifty miles to go. If you look through the eye slots on the right-hand side of the van, you'll be able to see the Yangtze River.'

The chief guard stood up and, laughing to himself, opened the sliding door so that they could all easily see the river. Many junks, sampans, barges, and other craft dotted the immense brown waterway like ants crawling over a vast claypan. The surface of the river glimmered with reflections from the afternoon sun.

'My first view of the mighty Yangtze,' said Jacko. 'We learned about it in school. I never thought I'd see it. It's so wide!'

'Yes. About a mile or so wide here,' said Lee. 'We shouldn't have to pass through any more gun battles between here and Nanjing. That doesn't mean we'll travel at a sensible speed all the way. We'll probably arrive after three in the afternoon, which isn't bad for this trip. I've had much longer.'

The chief guard went back to the card game with his colleagues.

Several Chinese appeared close to the railway track, looking up at the white men standing at the door of the van. Jacko realised they had jumped off the train, taking advantage of the relatively slow speed. They passed through a large railway station and the train did not stop, but several hundred more of its passengers leapt out of their carriages onto the platform.

'That's the way it works in post-war China,' said Lee. 'You wouldn't have seen them, but a few people would have jumped onto the train as well.'

As Zhenjiang disappeared into the misty distance behind them, the train picked up speed with loud chuffs of steam from the locomotive and soon it was travelling again at an even speed. Clackety-clack! Clackety-clack! They caught glimpses of the huge river through the pine trees between the rolling hills until the chief guard stood up and closed the right-hand door.

'Should be there in less than hour,' said Lee. 'Bandits permitting!'

Over the next forty minutes, the train pushed on through low rolling hills with only a few areas of flat lands. Then Lee pointed out a large mountain, purple in the heat haze of the afternoon, through the open door on the left side of the train.

'We're almost there,' he said. 'At the foot of that purple mountain is the tomb of the Hongwu Emperor, the founder of the Ming Dynasty more than 550 years ago. It was a favourite tourist destination in Nanjing before the war. It's just this side of the city. Won't be long now.'

'I wouldn't mind having a look at that,' said Jacko.

'Won't have time,' said Lee.

Through the trees they glimpsed numerous tiled roofs. With the usual squealing and screeching of brakes, the train lurched to a much slower speed and they realised they were coming into a major railway terminal.

As soon as a platform appeared level with the left-hand door of the van, Lee said, 'Be ready to leave as soon as the train stops. Our friend the chief guard doesn't want to get into trouble, so he wants us out of here as quickly as possible.'

As soon as the train staggered to a stop with much hissing of steam and screeching of brakes, the five men grabbed their packs and stepped onto the platform. They were soon surrounded by the milling crowds of disembarking passengers, including several who had climbed down from the roofs of the carriages.

'Goddamn! Did those guys travel all the way on the roof?' exclaimed Harry.

'They're the third-class passengers,' said Lee with a sardonic grin. 'Welcome to China's capital city. Stick close to me, chaps. We're heading down to the river docks.'

'Right behind you, Lee,' said Jamie, and they set off briskly to the west of the railway station.

CHAPTER 6

As Johnny, Jamie, Jacko and Harry followed Lee away from the railway station, they noticed a large expanse of water to their left.

'Is that the Yangtze River right there?' asked Harry.

'No, no. That's the Xuanwu Lake. Black Tortoise Lake,' said Lee. 'The legend is that a black dragon which looks like a tortoise lives there. We've still got about two hours' walk ahead of us before we get to the river where Peter Jackson keeps his boat. He usually hangs out in a bar, the Honglong, close to the river, so I'm sure we'll find him there. We can eat there.'

'That's good,' said Jacko. 'I'll be hungry by the time we get there. Do they have cold beer?'

Lee laughed. 'They'll have beer, Jacko. Not sure if it'll be cold.'

Passing through the streets of the city, they saw that many of the buildings were ancient and ornate, mostly single storey. A few tall towers dotted the landscape. They crossed various small bridges over canals, which pervaded the city. Rickshaw pullers yelled at them as they passed, while pedestrians often stopped to stare at them.

Jacko, at one stage, cocked his ear and asked Lee, 'Some of those rickshaw fellas were yelling out, "Buy mog... something". What's that?'

Lee laughed and replied, 'They are just commenting that there are white devils around.'

'I wonder if they include me,' said Jacko.

'Don't worry, Jacko. They even include me,' said Lee.

Rounding the corner of a street, Lee held up his hand and they all stopped. He was staring down the next street with a look of intense concern. Turning to the others, he said, 'I've just sighted Chen Xiao Lu about 200 yards ahead of us. Luckily, he's looking the other way. We've got to take a detour.'

He led them on a circuitous route through narrow streets and lanes and Jamie asked him who Chen Xiao Lu was.

'He's the bandit chief of the Green Phoenix Rising Gang,' explained Lee. 'Nasty piece of work. If he'd seen a group of white devils approaching, he would most probably have assaulted us. Just robbed us if we were lucky.'

By late afternoon, they could see the mighty river ahead, and Lee stopped and gestured for them to enter a colourful doorway on the side of the road. It was dark after the glare outside. A man waved at them. His bright-blue eyes were set in a tanned weather-beaten face above a droopy light-brown moustache and his face was shaded by a floppy hat. He was seated at a large round table in the corner of the room, his gaze fixed on them as they entered. Lee waved back at him with enthusiasm and they advanced on the table.

He introduced his good friend, Peter Jackson.

'You've brought the whole cavalry with you this time, Lee,' said Jackson. When he stood up they could see he was slim and over six feet tall.

'A mixture,' responded Lee. 'Colonel Johnny Cook here is my boss from MI6. Harry Williams is one of your compatriots. He's with the OSS. Jamie Munro and Jacko O'Brien are the Australians I was telling you about on the blower.'

'Mighty pleased to meet you folks,' said Jackson with a southern drawl. 'I'm particularly pleased to meet the colonel who pays some of my bills. How was your train trip?'

'Uneventful,' replied Lee. 'But we only just avoided running into our old friend, Chen Xiao Lu, between the railway station and here.'

Jackson whistled and remarked, 'That ol' bastard! So, he's in Nanjing. Up to no good, I expect. Lucky you missed him. Anyway, you made good time getting here.'

'You must have a radio here, Peter?' said Jamie.

'That's right, Mr Munro sir,' said Jackson. 'On the boat. I talk to Lee regular-like. That's how I knew y'all were coming.'

'Can a man get a cold beer here?' asked Jacko.

'I'll see what we can do,' said Jackson, who then shouted to someone in a back room. 'Hey Wu! Wu! Wan fan he bīng píjiu! Kuàisù!'

'Sounds good,' said Jacko. 'All that for a cold beer?'

'Naw! Not only for the beer. That's just my rough Mandarin. I asked for something to eat as well, Mr O'Brien,' said Jackson. 'I'm not as fluent as Lee, but they seem to understand me here.'

52

'Please call me Jacko, Peter. Nobody ever calls me Mr O'Brien unless they're angry with me.'

'Yes, good idea,' added Johnny. 'All first names here, Peter. I'm Johnny.'

'Suits me,' said Peter. 'You guys can even call me Pete if you like. I answer to all sorts of names. Don't blame me if the beer's not cold enough, Jacko.'

'I'll have to blame someone, Pete,' said Jacko.

'Yeah. Sure. Everyone blames me,' said Peter, looking carefully at Jacko. 'I think you've got some Indian or Asian background in your heritage, huh?'

'No. Pure Australian, mate,' said Jacko with a mischievous grin. 'Half white devil and half Aborigine.'

'Aha, a bitsa. Just like my good friend Lee here,' said Peter, laughing.

'Yeah. A bitsa. That's me. Dunno how you would say that in Chinese,' said Jacko. 'Where's the beer?'

'Just coming, mate. Here's Wu now,' said Peter, as a short plump Chinese man tottered in carrying a tray full of beer bottles and a variety of steaming dumplings. Peter spoke again in Chinese to Wu, who nodded and left with an empty tray.

'These dumplings are made in heaven,' said Peter. 'If you dip them in this hot chili sauce here, it puts lead in your pencil. Wu will bring us some more dishes in a while. So, guys, what are your plans?'

'We want to get to the place on the river where Daniel Stafford was shot just before dark,' said Jamie, 'to get a look at that opium setup under cover of night.'

'Yeah, thought you might. I told Dan at the time, he'd never get close to the treatment centre without being seen,' said Peter, scratching his chin. 'It's about 140 miles upriver, so we'd never make it tonight. Let's see – if we take off as soon as we've finished this excellent food, we could get about forty-five miles upriver, tie up next to the village of Ma'anshan, and stay on the boat overnight. From there, it's about ten hours to Tongling so we'd easily get you there by nightfall tomorrow. How does that sound?'

'Sounds good to me,' said Jamie, looking at the others who all nodded.

At that moment, Wu arrived with extra dishes of duck, lamb, crab, and vegetables. Peter said, 'Eat up, guys, this is the only dinner you'll get today. They serve a good breakfast, though, at a place I know in Ma'anshan.'

'They seem to be a bit trigger-happy around here,' said Harry. 'Are we likely to get shot at between here and this next place you're talking about, Pete?'

'Naw, not likely, Harry,' said Peter. 'The government's pretty much in control of things between here and Ma'anshan. But there might be a few bandits, commies, or peasants taking pot shots at us tomorrow. You'll be all right if you keep your heads down.'

Changing the subject, Jacko said, 'This Chinese food's the best, Pete. Especially the duck. Makes up for the not-very-cold beer.'

'Yeah. Old Wu knows how to cook up a spread,' agreed Peter.

In the late afternoon, with the sun dipping towards the hazy western hills, they arrived at the docks. Moored to one of the piers was an immense wooden Chinese junk with a tall mast in the centre and a high quarterdeck gleaming in the late afternoon sunlight. A short mast was set near the stern.

'Wow. You've got some ship here, Pete ol' buddy,' said Harry, wide-eyed at the sight. 'Is that a standard type of Chinese junk?'

'Not really, Harry. It was originally a motor torpedo boat or MTB. Seventy-seven feet long,' explained Peter. 'I bought the hull as surplus from the US Navy for almost nothing, but without all the armaments. Just the hull and the twin engines. The superstructure and fittings were all built here to my specification. If pushed, it could get up to twenty knots, but I never go much more than ten knots along the Yangtze. It pays to remain below the radar, if you know what I mean. That wheelhouse up there on the quarterdeck doesn't look it, but it's built from bullet-proof steel with cladding painted to look like timber.'

'Well, you've taken my breath away, Pete,' said Jamie.

'Yeah, I had visions of sailing up the Yangtze River with one of those brown sails pushing us along,' said Jacko.

'We have one of those sails, great big gaff rig thing, but it's only for show,' said Peter. 'Step aboard, guys, and meet the crew of the good ship Jin Shayu. They already know Lee, of course.'

They all clambered up a short gangway to the deck of the junk. Four men and a young girl were busy in different parts of the boat. They all stopped what they were doing and stared at Peter and the five new arrivals.

Peter gestured to the nearest man, a tall elderly Chinese with white hair, a straggly beard, and a face as weather-beaten as Peter's. 'This is Fu Qian, my sailing master. He and I have been close friends since before the war.'

Pointing to a short stocky man up on the quarterdeck he said, 'That fellow is Wing Huan, helmsman of this fine vessel. That chap with oil on his clothes, hiding behind the mast, is Mr Chou. Chou Shan Li. Answers to the name of Stanley. He's my engine man. Top marine mechanic.'

Then gesturing to the other two who had been busy near the bow of the boat, he said, 'Those two young kids make up the rest of the crew. On the right is Li Yuan. She speaks a little English and answers to the name of Lily. She is bow crew and spare helmsman. The young guy to the left, who also speaks a little English, is Jin On. We call him Goldie. In Chinese, Jin means gold. Goldie is deck crew, general factotum, and sometime cook.'

He ended with a bow saying, 'I, of course, am your skipper.'

Peter then spoke to his crew in Chinese. The new arrivals heard their names mentioned and nodded in turn. The crew members then all came forward and shook their hands.

'You all come from England?' enquired Li Yuan in a soft voice. She was petite and attractive and her long straight hair was halfway down her back.

'Not all,' replied Jamie, deliberately speaking slowly. 'Johnny comes from England, Harry from the USA and the Philippines. Jacko and I are from Australia.'

'Ah. Aust-lalia. Have heard, long way from here,' she said, smiling.

'Yes, Lily, a long way from here,' said Jamie, not sure what else to say.

'Kangaroo, yes?'

'Yes, Lily. Kangaroos.'

'Enough chitchat!' interrupted Peter, pointing to Chou. 'Stanley. Engine. Go, go, go!'

Stanley laughed as he went down a ladderway, repeating, 'Go, go, go. Ha ha!'

The rest of the crew sprang into action. Lily and Goldie released the hawsers and Fu and Wing disappeared into the wheelhouse. Soon, the engine started with a throaty roar and the junk was backing away from the pier into the huge river behind.

Peter shouted something in Chinese to the wheelhouse and then turned to Johnny and the others. 'While they get the boat going upriver, I'll show you guys around. We'll go down that ladder before the quarterdeck. Lee knows his way around the boat already.'

Peter showed them around the cabin with tables, seats, bunks and teak cupboards. A door led into a toilet towards the bow. He opened one of the larger cupboards, which was stacked with rifles, and told them they could choose their weapons when they went ashore.

'The hull is obviously steel rather than wood, so if any shooting starts tomorrow, you'll be quite safe down here below decks,' he said. 'There's not likely to be any excitement before we get to Ma'anshan, so you'll probably prefer to be on deck. If there is some shooting, you know what to do now.'

'That's excellent. You've got a great boat,' said Jamie.

'I've got one question,' said Jacko. 'When I was at school we learnt about a place called Nanking. Is that different from Nanjing?'

'Same place, Jacko,' replied Peter. 'Just a matter of dialect. During the time of the treaty ports, the British had their own pronunciation for certain cities. I use the same dialect as the locals. Simple as that.'

'Thanks, Pete. I'm learning all the time,' said Jacko. 'One last thing. When you mentioned the name of your boat, I noticed that it had a "Jin" in it. Does the name mean gold something?'

'Good observation, Jacko,' said Peter. 'Jin Shayu means Golden Shark.'

'Golden Shark,' said Harry. 'Great name, Pete.'

'Well, guys, let's go back on deck and see how our helmsman is going, eh?' said Peter.

By this time, the Jin Shayu was well out in the middle of the mighty river, leaving a white frothy wake astern on the brown surface of the water. Peter informed them that the current was not strong at this time of the year and they would be making about ten knots relative to the land.

'It'll be four hours or so to Ma'anshan,' he said. 'Both Fu and Wing have very keen eyesight, and they know this river like the backs of their hands. We should have no problem avoiding sandbanks and other river craft.'

Once the sun had set in a blaze of orange glory, there was no moon to lighten the world around the boat as it carved through the waters of the Yangtze, throwing out a white bow wave shimmering with phosphorescence. Jacko leant on the port-side rail watching lights flickering on the distant shore. Lights from other boats passed them regularly and occasionally, Jacko could make out the dark shapes of unlit junks and barges as the Jin Shayu surged past them. The sky was clear, and the stars seemed brighter than usual. The continuous throbbing of the powerful engines, the twang of a halyard beating against the mast, and the creaking of stays and shrouds set up a rhythm like the percussion section of an orchestra. Jacko marvelled at the faith Peter Jackson had in his sailing master and helmsman as the Jin Shayu pressed ahead into the darkness; however, it seemed that his faith was certainly justified.

Occasionally, they heard the distant crackle of gunfire, although not close enough to the river to be of concern. It's a pity, thought Jacko, that after all these years of war the Chinese still can't find peace. Staring at the stars, his mind wandered to thoughts of Monique. Two bright-green stars gleaming out from the Milky Way gave him a feeling she was watching over him.

He remembered when he had first looked into those sparkling green eyes five years before, during the war. It was near the Great Pyramid of Giza to the west of Cairo. Monique had been spending her spare time acting as a guide, a dragoman, for foreign soldiers visiting the Giza pyramids. He had been spellbound by her charm and beauty but had thought, after that day, he might never see her again. But now she was his wife. Jacko thought he must be the luckiest man in the world.

Further astern, on the starboard side of the boat, Harry was in deep discussion with Johnny. They had been chatting to Lee Drake, who had just left them to look in on the wheelhouse. Their conversation had reverted to the subject of Peter.

'So, you mean to tell me that Peter Jackson is not an MI6 operative?' exclaimed Harry.

'No. We charter him and his boat when we need him,' explained Johnny. 'The rest of the time, he does charter work for the government and other units of the political spectrum. We get to learn a few useful pieces of information from that.'

'How did you find him?' asked Harry.

'He's a close friend of our man, Lee,' said Johnny. 'They were friends before the war and watched each other's backs during the Japanese occupation. Peter wanted to remain independent after the war.'

'The OSS could use a man like Jackson full time,' mused Harry. 'Would it upset your plans if I asked him to become a full-time operative for us?'

'It wouldn't worry me a bit as long as we could use him once in a while,' said Johnny. 'As an American, he's more likely to accept working for the OSS.'

'Yeah. That's good. I'll ask him,' said Harry. 'He would still be able to charter for you as well as the government and all that, but we'd get all the information. Peter would make more money that way. The OSS is, in many ways, similar to MI6. Intelligence is our lifeblood.'

'I'm sure London would agree,' said Johnny, chuckling. 'I don't expect we'll be at war with the USA anytime soon.'

'Sure as hell hope not,' said Harry, laughing.

Peter and Jamie were up near the bow of the boat, the bow wave sparkling with phosphorescence. Pete was pointing out to Jamie where different villages were located when they heard Harry's laugh astern of them.

'Happy fellow, that OSS guy Harry,' remarked Peter.

'Yeah. Harry's been a big help to us on several occasions,' said Jamie. 'We worked with him earlier this year to break up a ring of child kidnappers in the Philippines. We couldn't have done it without Harry. Good man.'

The boat had recently slowed to navigate between several islands in the middle of the river. As they passed the southern headland of a large island on their port beam, Peter pointed out some lights in the distance on their port bow.

'That's Ma'anshan ahead,' he said. 'Won't be too long now.'

'Is it a big place?' asked Jamie.

'Not so big,' said Peter. 'Used to be just a mining town. The Japanese set up a steelworks there during the war, although I think that was bombed out. They still mine coal and other minerals around the immediate area.'

'You know a lot about all these places, eh Pete?' observed Jamie.

'I've been up and down this river many a time, ol' buddy,' said Peter. 'Yeah, many a time.'

'How far upriver have you gone with the Jin Shayu?' asked Jamie.

'I've taken her a few times to Yichang, but no further,' said Peter. 'Yichang's about another thousand miles further on from here. It's a large port just before you get to the Three Gorges.'

'The Three Gorges?'

'The Three Gorges are where the Yangtze becomes narrow for about 120 miles, confined by steep cliffs on both sides,' explained Peter. 'There are swift currents and rapids and you need a lot of power to get up the narrowest parts of the river.'

'So, the slower boats can't get up there, I presume?'

'The slower boats are hauled up through the narrows by many people walking along the riverside with lots of ropes,' said Peter, grinning. 'It's a sight to behold.'

'Wow. The boats are hauled against the current by people pulling ropes?' said Jamie, astonished.

'Yeah, that's right. Hundreds of people,' said Peter. 'It's pretty risky too. The paths on the side of the river are narrow and men fall in every day and drown.'

'Would the Jin Shayu have to be hauled up if you wanted to go through the Three Gorges?' asked Jamie.

'No, no. This little lady could motor up easily,' said Peter. 'Particularly at this time of year. I've just had no call to go up there.'

'Fascinating!' said Jamie. 'It's a hell of a long river.'

'It goes well beyond the Three Gorges,' said Peter. 'Past Chongqing in Sichuan province and eventually up into Tibet.'

'Thanks for the geography lesson.'

'You're most welcome. As you can see, the lights of Ma'anshan are getting closer. I'll leave you now. I have to go to the wheelhouse and have a word with Fu.'

Fifteen minutes later, with practised ease, Fu slipped the Jin Shayu alongside a pier and the junk stopped with a churning of reversed rudders. Wing and Goldie had the boat firmly moored to the pier within seconds.

CHAPTER 7

Jacko awoke from a deep sleep and briefly wondered where he was. It was still dark, but he could hear someone moving around on the deck above him. In the cabin of the large boat, someone snoring softly in another bunk competed with the sounds of water lapping against the hull. Rising quietly, he climbed up the ladderway to the deck and in the half-light of early dawn made out Peter, Fu Qian, Lily and Goldie engaged in various activities around the boat.

'Good morning, young fellow,' Peter greeted him as he approached. 'Looks like it's gonna be a fine day. We'll be heading up the hill shortly to have some vittles. You can wake the rest of your team now if you like.'

Jacko rubbed his eyes, looked up the hill where the village was taking shape in the early dawn, waved back at Peter, and went back below.

'Wakey, wakey, fellas,' he said, walking around the cabin. 'The skipper says it's time for breakfast.'

This was greeted by everything from groans to gratitude and in a short while, everyone was climbing onto the pier and following Peter up to the village.

The owners of the little restaurant greeted Peter and his crew like a long-lost friends, 'Ni hao, ni hao, ni hao!' and much bowing with clasped hands.

The guests were placed at the largest round table in the centre of the room. The owners then hovered around with bowls of rice, numerous small dishes and pots of green tea. There were few other customers at that time of the morning.

'What do you think of the Chinese food in China, sir?' Lee asked Johnny.

'Always different and always delicious, Lee,' he replied. 'But I'll get indigestion if you keep calling me sir. Just call me Johnny.'

'Yessir... er... Johnny. Sorry.'

'I have a question, Lee,' said Jacko. 'The locals here keep saying ni hao. Is that good morning or hello or something like that in Chinese?'

'You've got a good ear, Jacko,' said Lee. 'It means hello.'

'Ah! My first Chinese words,' said Jacko, nodding. 'Ni hao.'

Everyone had his own thoughts about what the day ahead might bring, so there was little further conversation over breakfast. In less than half an hour, with the sun already rising over the hills behind Ma'anshan, they were all back aboard the Jin Shayu and underway up the river again.

Everyone was on deck when Peter climbed down from the wheelhouse and said, 'In the next couple of hours we'll be passing Wuhu on our port side. Before the war, Wuhu was one of the major British treaty ports for trading on the river. Rice and timber mainly. The Japanese had a lot of trouble with resistance fighters during the occupation but now, unfortunately, it's a hotbed of warlords and bandits. Although we'll be half a mile from either bank, I'm sure we'll come under fire. They won't do much harm to the boat, but everyone, including the crew, must be either below decks or in the wheelhouse after the next hour.'

'You're the skipper,' said Jamie.

'When you're down there in the cabin you can select which firearms you want to take ashore from our store,' said Peter. 'I'd suggest the three-O carbines, but it's up to you guys.'

'Yeah, thanks, Pete,' said Jamie. 'Is it okay if we stay on deck for the next hour?'

'Sure, Jamie, but if you hear any gunfire, keep your heads down,' he said with his sardonic grin.

He climbed back up to the wheelhouse and the others sat around the deck idly watching the traffic on the river. Several smaller junks sported their familiar brown sails with long, near-horizontal wooden battens. Others motored without sails. Other traffic included barges, sampans and the occasional Bermuda-rigged sailboat.

After half an hour, they were all astonished to see on their starboard bow a grey warship heading downriver close to the western bank. Although it was still several miles away, Jacko, with his keen

62

eyesight, was able to make out white letters on the bow of the ship, 'CS-10'.

As he watched it rapidly closing the gap, Peter appeared beside him and said, 'That's the old USS John Blish. It's conducting hydrographic surveys along the Yangtze River. All its big guns were removed after the war. Part of the aid to China by the good ol' US of A.'

The USS John Blish drew abeam of the Jin Shayu and Peter took off his hat and waved it. Some of the crew on the US ship waved back.

'Does the US Navy have any other ships on the Yangtze, Pete?' asked Jacko.

'Hell yeah! A couple. The USS Eaton is somewhere along the river at this time. Not sure where. It's a destroyer with plenty of firepower.'

'A destroyer?' exclaimed Jacko. 'In support of the Chinese government, I suppose?'

'No. I'm told it's mainly to protect American interests, Jacko,' said Peter with a rueful expression. 'I don't think they'll support my interests if it comes to the crunch.'

'No. Probably not,' Jacko agreed, grinning.

'Anyway, after all that excitement, it's time for everyone to get out of sight,' said Peter in a louder voice. 'We'll be getting close to "pot-shot corner" soon.'

After half an hour, Lee was in the middle of explaining some of the features of the Yangtze River when Peter, Lily, Stanley and Goldie rushed down into the cabin.

'Trouble!' said Pete. 'Goddamn pirates ahead of us. Grab yourselves a gun. We need everyone on deck to repel boarders.'

'Good opportunity to try out the three-Os,' said Jamie as they went to the gun cupboard. 'What's happening, Pete?'

'There are five motorboats in the centre of the river a mile ahead, waiting for us,' said Peter, handing out carbines and picking up two hand grenades. 'If they try to board us, don't argue. Shoot to kill.'

'Okay, Skipper,' said Jacko. 'Does this happen often?'

'One of the dangers of travelling by day,' said Peter as he led the way up to the deck. 'They'll aim to kill us all and take the boat. Try to stay out of sight.'

As they quickly crept to the bow, Jamie and Jacko noted the five motorboats ahead slowly cruising in a line, side by side, towards them. They were open boats with large outboard engines on the sterns. Each carried armed men, all watching the junk intently. Jacko sensed someone else crouched beside him and saw it was Lily holding a Winchester rifle. He looked back to see the others amidships. Johnny, Harry and Stanley were crouching down on the starboard side; Peter, Lee and Goldie on the port side, all armed with carbines. That should do it, he thought.

Sneaking a look over the woodwork at the bow, Jacko estimated there were at least eight men on each of the bandits' boats, all armed with rifles or machetes. Within 100 yards, some of the bandits opened fire. Peter gave a yell and the Jin Shayu surged forward, heading straight for the centre boat.

The other four boats changed direction, closing in at speed on the large junk. Peter yelled, 'Open fire!' as the Jin Shayu hit the centre boat with a loud crunch, sinking it, while grappling hooks came flying through the air from the other boats. The sudden surge of speed created a bow wave which swamped one of the closest pirate boats, causing it to capsize, although some of the bandits had leapt off it and were hanging onto the sides of the Jin Shayu.

Jacko saw that three of the bandits from the smashed centre boat had managed to hold onto the bow in front of him and were trying to climb up. Pulling out his knife, he slashed the hands of two of them who disappeared under the junk. When the third man's face appeared above the hawse, Lily shot him between the eyes.

Jacko and Jamie looked astern where several bandits were trying to board on both sides. The other three boats were being towed behind the junk by their grappling hook lines. From the stern, Peter threw a grenade into one of the towed boats, which was smashed to pieces in a satisfying explosion. Bodies were thrown into the river by the blast. From their position in the bow, Jamie, Jacko and Lily were able to pick off some of the bandits who were trying to climb the sides into the junk. Stanley was swinging an axe, cutting two of the lines attached to the grappling hooks and cleaving an attacker's head.

As they charged back from the bow to help the others, Jacko noticed Johnny grappling on the deck with a ferocious-looking bandit who was trying to stab him. Peter and Lee were also wrestling with two bandits who had managed to get aboard. Jacko moved like lightning, stabbing Johnny's attacker in the neck, shooting Lee's with his pistol, and stabbing the other bandit in the kidneys. The fight was finally ended when Stanley was able to cut the remaining lines. Three bandits, who were still clinging desperately to the side of the junk, were quickly dispatched with shots from Lily and Goldie. The remaining dead bandits were tossed over the side.

'Well done, shipmates,' said Peter. 'Damn good job!'

'Bloody hell!' exclaimed Jacko. 'Determined little bastards, weren't they? That surge in speed certainly caught them by surprise!'

'Yer pretty handy with that knife, young fellow,' said Peter. 'You can join my crew any time you like.'

'My wife would never forgive me,' said Jacko, laughing.

'Those bandits in the five boats seemed to know we were coming, Pete,' said Johnny. 'Do you think they'll be waiting for us at Tongling?'

'No. I wouldn't worry about that,' said Peter. 'They sure knew we were coming, but the Jin Shayu was what they were after. Someone probably saw us when we arrived at Ma'anshan and sent word to the baddies.'

'Do you think they had anything to do with that Green Phoenix Rising mob we heard about in Shanghai?' asked Jamie.

'Naw. That gang doesn't operate this far up the river,' replied Pete.

'Nothing like a bit of excitement to start the day,' Jacko laughed.

'Look at this damned deck,' said Peter with feigned indignation. 'It's like an abattoir here. We're gonna need the high-pressure pump. Goldie! Get that pump going pronto.'

'Does it happen often?' asked Johnny, looking down at his bloodstained shirt.

'I usually avoid passing through this region during the day,' said Peter. Pointing ahead, he added, 'You see that sharp right bend in the river ahead? The river narrows just before the bend, so I would ask you all to go back down below, 'cause we're gonna get fired on there for sure. Lily and Goldie can go below too, after Goldie finishes washing down the deck.'

'You're the skipper, Pete,' said Jacko, as he headed to the ladderway.

'Sure am, ol' buddy.'

Time seemed interminable to Jamie down in the long cabin where they were unable to see what was going on. The six portholes, three on either side, were just slits and allowed only restricted vision. He started to pace up and down while the others, seated on the bunks, watched him. The faces of Lee, Lily and Goldie were inscrutable. Harry was helping Johnny with antiseptic on the minor stab wounds he had sustained, and Jacko was sitting back looking totally relaxed. Jamie admired his friend's ability to stay calm through any situation. The only sounds in the cabin were the bow waves slapping against the hull and the creaking and clanging of rigging.

'Luckily, most of the blood on my shirt was from the bandit,' said Johnny, slipping on a clean shirt. 'Those pirates certainly knew we were coming. Do you think it's likely the men at the opium plant know we're on the way?'

'Yeah, maybe, although Pete doesn't seem to think it's likely,' said Harry. 'We'll ask him again later. He knows this river backwards.'

A short time later, they felt the tilt of the boat as it steered to starboard around the long bend in the river. Through the narrow portholes, Jamie saw that the land was closer than before on both sides of the boat. They were still sailing around the bend when the first rifle fire started. Bullets hit the deck and ricocheted off the hull and the wheelhouse above, but the Jin Shayu motored on at an even speed regardless.

After completing its turn, the junk sped up and the sounds of shooting receded. Jamie, who had continued pacing, finally decided that worrying about what he couldn't see would not achieve anything, so he sat down on one of the bunks with a sigh.

Eventually, the boat slowed right down and seemed to be turning to port.

Peter suddenly appeared at the top of the ladderway and called out, 'Goldie and Lily! I need you both to help replace one of the shrouds cut by a slug. Grab some cordage from the locker and we'll fix it now. The rest of you can come back up on deck.'

'Just one thing, Pete,' said Johnny. 'I'm still wondering about those pirates. Are you sure this has nothing to do with the criminals at Tongling?'

'Different thing,' replied Peter. 'As I told you before, someone in Ma'anshan must have noticed our arrival and rode through the night to Wuhu to warn the bandits. The Jin Shayu was what they were after. With this boat they could control that part of the river. Nothing to do with the opium. Come on deck and I'll show you something.'

From the deck they could see they were in a small inlet off the river next to a small village. Approaching a jetty, the boat glided to a stop and Peter and Stanley jumped ashore and secured it with hawsers looped over some cleats.

'Where are we, Pete?' asked Jamie, looking around at the scene.

'It's a little fishing village south of the river. Xiaozhou. You'll be quite safe here,' said Peter. 'Not much of a town but they do have a great little eatery here. We might as well have an early lunch as we won't stop after this. You can try some fresh Yangtze seafood.'

'Sounds good to me,' said Jacko. He looked at Johnny who was limping a bit. 'How are you feeling now, Johnny?'

I'll survive thanks to you,' replied Johnny. 'Just a few scrapes and bruises, but nothing that a good meal of fresh fish won't cure.'

'That's the spirit,' said Peter, laughing. He looked up at the top of the mast where Goldie was threading some cord through a block to replace the broken shroud and called out, 'You and Lily join us, Goldie, when you've finished!'

Disembarking onto the jetty, Fu and Wing joined them. Peter said something to them in Chinese and they both laughed as the group set off up a small rise into the village.

The restaurant comprised several round tables sheltered by a tiled roof with no walls. Peter was as well known here as he had been in Ma'anshan. There were even more smiles when Jacko replied, 'Ni hao.' Soon, several hot and cold dishes and cups of green tea were spread around their table. Cooking was done on an open fire under

67

the same roof, and occasional billows of smoke wafted over to them. Goldie and Lily, having completed their work on the mast, arrived and eagerly tucked into the food.

'Well, what do y'all think of our river cruise so far?' mumbled Peter with a mouth full of fish.

'Quite exciting,' replied Jacko. 'Is it always like this?'

'Naw. Not always. Sometimes worse.'

'Worse! Bloody hell.'

'Just razzin' ya, guys,' Peter laughed. 'This is fairly normal for a day trip. Usually better at night. How's the fish?'

'The food's delicious. D'you reckon we'll have much more trouble between here and Tongling?' asked Jamie.

'Not much,' said Peter. 'Maybe the odd pot shot. If you keep your heads down, you should be all right up on deck.'

They were interrupted by waitresses bringing more steaming dishes to the table. Then they sat in silence, each deep in thought about what might be awaiting them once they reached their destination.

Back on the boat, the crew rushed around getting the vessel ready for departure and in a short while they were cruising upriver again. The usual junks, sampans, barges and other sailing boats dotted the river around them. Apart from the ever-present seagulls, different types of birds flew around the boat, some diving for fish in the wake. A flock of elegant black-necked cranes flew past them, while crested ibis and brightly coloured birds flew around the banks of the river. There were parts of the Yangtze River where peace and tranquillity prevailed, Jamie thought. Not at all typical of reality.

They sat under a tarpaulin spread over the sail boom to protect them from the heat of the sun. The breeze generated by the speed of the boat made conditions markedly more pleasant despite the risk of gunfire from the riverbanks. The river narrowed in parts to less than half a mile wide. They frequently heard the chatter of gunfire in the distance but nothing near the river. The junk circumvented several sandbanks and islands in the river which itself, curved through hilly to mountainous terrain.

Peter, who spent most of his time in the wheelhouse, occasionally joined them on deck to point out small villages, tall pagodas,

68

mountains and other places of interest which he knew well. After rounding a long left-hand bend in the river, Peter informed them that it was only about fifteen miles to the point where he had taken Dan Stafford and Lee previously.

'I don't want to land you much before nightfall, so we'll slow the boat a little,' he said. 'That way we shouldn't alert your quarry. Who's going ashore?'

'Just Lee, Jamie, Jacko and Harry,' said Johnny. 'Our plan is for Lee and Jacko to get a closer look at the opium plant setup under cover of darkness. Jamie and Harry will stay back in the trees this side of the opium field to provide backup if necessary. I'll stay aboard. I'd appreciate if I could use your radio, Pete. Were you planning to go ashore?'

'No. No. My sole commitment and responsibility is to my boat,' responded Peter. 'I'll do everything I can for you on the river. Away from the river, that's your lookout.'

'Gotcha!' said Harry. 'We couldn't have even got to first base without you, ol' buddy.'

'Yer welcome, Harry,' said Peter, chuckling.

The boat cruised steadily south at five to six knots. For the next hour or so, they could see the river was about half a mile wide and relatively straight for miles ahead. At one stage a shot rang out from the bank and they all ducked.

'Just a peasant taking a pot shot,' said Peter, a broad smile showing below his droopy moustache. 'Most of 'em couldn't hit the side of a barn from ten paces.'

The river ahead was divided into two separate channels by a large island group. Reducing speed to about three knots, the boat steered to starboard towards the western channel.

'This is the Buckminster Island group,' Lee explained. 'Our landing point is not far ahead. On this side of the islands, we can't be seen from Tongling which is over on the south-east bank. Although the town is safe and under the control of the Kuomintang, there's a probability that some of the government officials, if not the leadership, are involved in some way with the opium smugglers. So, it's better not to be seen from the town.'

69

As the sun began setting towards the misty western hills, the boat drifted to a wooded section of the bank until the hull touched with a gentle scrape. The crew quickly threw out a gangway onto the shore and Peter stepped down from the wheelhouse.

Jacko asked him, 'Have you got any more grenades, Pete? Fishing line?'

'Yeah, Dan Stafford left a bagful of grenades. Stacks of fishing line,' replied Peter. 'Goldie, go and get that bag. It's in the for'ard locker. And some fishing line.'

'Thanks, Pete. I'll take five or six grenades and some line,' said Jacko.

'This is where we leave you,' Peter said. 'When you return, Lee knows what to do. The Jin Shayu will be anchored near the north-west end of the island over there. Good luck, guys. Make sure you've got all your gear and your guns. There's no moon tonight, so don't get lost and don't get shot! I'm not that good at extracting slugs from bodies.'

'Yeah, thanks a lot, Pete. I hope we'll be back tomorrow morning sometime,' said Jamie.

'Unshot!' added Jacko, laughing.

CHAPTER 8

With Lee and Jacko in the lead and Jamie following, they walked westward through the woods. There were few sounds except for the twittering of small birds and a background buzzing of insects. In the brightness of the sunset shining through the trees, their progress was rapid, with Lee taking over the lead. Jacko, just behind him, asked what the strong smell was.

'Here, they use human faeces as fertiliser,' Lee replied. 'As we get closer to the rice paddies, it'll get stronger. You'll get used to it. It's a common thing in China.'

'I don't think I'll get used to that,' said Jacko. 'Where's the poppy field?'

'Still more than a mile ahead,' replied Lee. 'We'd better be silent when we get close. There might be workers in the field.'

Jacko nodded, and they continued at a brisk pace with the light slowly fading. After twenty minutes, it was obvious they were near the end of the wooded area and Lee pointed ahead. Arriving at the fringe of the woods, they saw the opium poppy field ahead covering a flat treeless plain. A mile or so away, on the other side of the field, were the beige buildings Lee had previously described to them, with green hills behind, hazy in the evening light. To their left they could see Lake Zhusi glimmering in the sunset. Beyond the lake to the left of the poppy field were extensive rice paddies, the source of the strong ever-present stench. To the north of the poppy field and to their left were more hills and isolated woods as well as various small farmhouses in the distance.

'Don't look much like poppies to me,' observed Jacko.

'No. Those large green bulbs are the unripe poppy seed pods from which they extract the opium,' explained Lee. 'They cut an incision in the pod and a milky viscous fluid oozes out. That's the raw opium.'

'Lots of bulbs,' said Jamie. 'Must produce a lot of opium.'

'Not only from here. We believe even more comes down the river from other provinces west of here,' said Lee. 'Guanxi, Hunan, Sichuan.'

'Big operation!' exclaimed Jamie.

'Well, the poppy field's deserted,' said Jacko. 'Not much cover there. I can see why Stafford was spotted.'

'Yes. It was never a clever idea to go in the daytime,' said Lee. 'Dan insisted, with unfortunate consequences.'

'You did well to escape yourself,' said Jacko.

'Yes. I was lucky,' said Lee.

Jacko was intently studying the buildings in the half-light of dusk. 'There are two trucks on the left side of the large central shed,' he said. 'They're being loaded with sacks of some sort.'

'I see them too,' said Lee, screwing up his eyes. 'They're getting ready to ship some of the opium out. We'll settle down here until it's dark and then Jacko and I can take off.'

'Suits me,' said Jacko.

'I've got some cork here which I can burn to blacken our faces,' said Lee.

'That's good. Now I'll get to look like my grandfather,' said Jacko, chuckling.

* * * *

'That damned boat had better be on time in the morning,' said Ned Brandon, spraying scraps of food from his mouth.

'It will. It will,' said Eddie Wang, looking at Brandon malevolently. 'Why you worry so much?'

'That bloody spy we shot has me feeling edgy,' said Brandon. 'I'm sure that's not the end of it.'

Eddie Wang addressed a dapper little man across the other side of the table. 'Will you be going back to Shanghai on tomorrow's boat, Sir William?'

'Yes, Eddie. It'll drop me off at Baoshan before heading out into the China Sea,' he replied. 'I'll find out what I can about your spy when I get to the city.'

Sir William Founding, attached to the British Consulate in Shanghai, was short and grey-haired with a groomed moustache. He had an air of elegance, even in casual clothes. Studying his six companions at the round dinner table, he was struck by the atmosphere of general discontent.

Next to him, on his left, sat Roddy Braithwaite, a thickset individual with unruly black hair, a bedraggled moustache, a prominent scar on the side of his left cheek, and a marked northern England accent. In charge of security. On the other side of him sat Wei Lijun, the chief chemist, one of their key men in the preparation of the opium. He was a tall thin Chinese from Anhui with neatly combed thick black hair, his mouth drooped on one side giving him a permanent frown. Next to him was Motoi Tanaka, formerly wartime Kempeitai chief in Shanghai, a humourless trained assassin wanted by the government for war crimes. Sir William was always somewhat unnerved by the flat hardness of his eyes.

Seated next to Tanaka, Eddie Wang was a short balding Chinese with an eye patch which made him look like some sort of river pirate. His mixture of a New York and Chinese accent sounded strange in comparison to his pale yellowish face. Originally from Hong Kong, he had spent a good part of his adult life in New York and had close contacts with influential families involved in organised crime. This gave him a level of respect amongst the others. Eddie Wang had organised much of the financing for the opium operation. Next to him was Ned Brandon, a large Londoner with red hair and beard and a distinct cockney accent. Brandon, often known as 'Red Ned', was an untidy eater and Sir William didn't enjoy watching him stuffing his mouth, leaving some of the food behind in his beard. He was nominal manager of the local operation. When angry, his face competed with the colour of his hair. Between Brandon and Sir William was a chubby Chinese with long disorderly black hair covering his shoulders, who ate as though he hadn't eaten in days. Feng Gang Li was a mechanic in charge of transportation.

Some of the group's general irritation was due to a sudden shower of rain the previous day. It had damaged part of the opium which had been set out for sun-drying before bagging. There had also been problems with the supply of hessian bags and the motor of one of the trucks. Short fuses amongst a disparate group.

Sir William relied on Eddie Wang to maintain calm amongst the group. A glare from his single eye was often enough to mitigate dissension.

The mood at the table was not softened by the tasty dishes spread over it. If anything, the atmosphere was becoming tenser as more small glasses of fifty-four per cent baijiu, the locally produced liquor, was consumed with regular toasts of gan bei! Bottoms up!

Feng Gang Li finally stood up and said, 'I go and check on the trucks.'

'Wait! Before you go, Feng. What is the exact tonnage on those trucks now?' Brandon asked, spraying crumbs on the table and floor as he stood up.

'Eighteen tons, seven hundredweight, fifty-four pounds, boss,' replied Feng.

'All right. Make sure it all gets on the boat tomorrow. One more toast before you go!' Brandon said loudly, holding up a full glass. 'Gan bei!'

'Gan bei, boss,' responded Feng, downing the contents of his glass.

Feng half-staggered as he left. Sir William had managed to avoid most of the toasts as, he noted, had Eddie Wang. The others were well on the way to being half-plastered. Even the usually taciturn Motoi Tanaka. His hard eyes were looking glassy. Sir William shrugged his shoulders. One of the many hazards of doing this type of business in post-war China, he thought.

After the last bottle of baijiu had been consumed, the diners all headed, some staggering, towards their sleeping quarters in the huts south of the central treatment shed. In contrast to the previous loud cries of 'gan bei', almost complete silence finally settled on the base under a starlit sky.

It was three o'clock in the morning when the large Kunming wolfdog chained up on the north side of the large central shed started barking. Ned Brandon woke with a start, sending a sharp pain through his head. Clasping his forehead, he mumbled, 'Bloody dog!'

Stumbling around his room, he managed to pull on his pants and boots and make his way to the door. Once outside, he realised he had forgotten his torch. He grabbed the torch and a handgun and rushed back outside, where he collided with Roddy Braithwaite in the dark. He switched on his torch and observed the other man who looked as hungover as he felt.

'Something's disturbed Zhiming,' Braithwaite muttered. 'We'd better have a look.'

'Of course, yer bloody fool,' said Brandon. 'D'ya think I'm up 'cause I like to go prancing around in the dark?'

Before they had gone far, the barking stopped abruptly. The men looked at each other and started walking quickly towards the other side of the shed.

Halfway there, Braithwaite yelled, 'Zhiming! Zhiming!'

This was greeted by a snort and a snuffle from the direction of the dog. As they turned the corner of the shed, Brandon's torchlight revealed the bulky shape of the dog sleeping in his kennel to which he was attached by a chain. He was snoring softly.

'Sometimes Zhiming has a bad dream,' explained Braithwaite as they walked back. 'He'd bark louder than that if there was any danger.'

'You should train your bloody dog better,' said Brandon, feeling sick. His head was throbbing so much he wasn't sure he would make it back to his bunkhouse.

Within the next quarter of an hour, silence again descended on the buildings at the base.

* * * *

Earlier in the night, with the boat anchored across the river just west of the northern tip of Buckminster Island, Peter, Johnny and Harry were in deep in conversation.

'Harry would like to engage you full time with US intelligence, the OSS,' Johnny was saying. 'It would be more reliable than MI6 chartering you part time.'

'OSS? I dunno,' muttered Peter.

'You'd still be free to do the odd charter for MI6,' Harry cut in. 'But the OSS would pay you and your crew and pick up all the expenses for your boat.'

'I'd have to be free to be able to charter to others,' said Peter firmly. 'The government authorities never cause me any grief as long as I can deliver for them when they need me. The money's good. I do the odd charter for the communists as well, so they leave me alone the rest of the time. I've even done a charter for some of the warlords. Keeps the bandits off my back most of the time. Not all though, as you know.'

'Ain't no problem there, Pete ol' buddy,' said Harry. 'The OSS would be happy for you to keep doing exactly what you're doing now. Chartering to everyone, even to my friends in MI6. We'll just pay you on top of all that.'

'You mean I could keep all the money other people pay me?' asked Peter incredulously. 'What do you guys get out of it?'

'We just want you to keep us up to date with everything you're doing as well as anything you see going on,' said Harry. 'Y'see, intelligence is our business. The OSS needs to know as much as it can. Everything you tell us helps towards the security of the old US of A.'

'Yeah, and if I get into trouble, will the old US of A come to my rescue?' Peter asked with a cynical expression.

'As much as we can, we'll do that,' said Harry. 'I can't guarantee anything, but you'll be no worse off than you are now. While there are US Navy ships in the Yangtze, we'll be able to do something. That mightn't always be the case.'

'An honest answer,' said Peter, nodding. Then pointing at Johnny, he said, 'What about him? Do I tell you everything that MI6 is doing?'

'I have no problem with that,' said Johnny, smiling. 'I don't expect Britain will be at war with the USA anytime soon. We share a lot of information with the OSS anyway.'

'Hmm. It sounds good,' said Peter. 'I'll just have to think about it.'

'Yeah, sleep on it,' said Harry. 'No hurry. We'll chat about it tomorrow.'

'The river is hardly stirring,' observed Johnny. 'It should be easy to sleep tonight.'

'Good time of year. It isn't always like this,' said Peter with a chuckle. 'In the early spring when the snow is melting on the slopes

76

in Hunan, Sichuan and Tibet, there are strong variable currents, sandbanks suddenly build up, and parts of the Yangtze can be treacherous. We always have to be on our toes then. Goodnight, guys.'

The river indeed was hardly stirring, the only sound caused by ripples lightly slapping the hull. All those aboard the Jin Shayu slept soundly until the distant honk of a wild goose woke Goldie, who had been sleeping on the deck. He leapt up and peered through the darkness towards the western bank. After a few minutes, a torchlight flashed out twice to the southwest.

Goldie rushed down to the main cabin and shook Peter awake.

'Lee is back,' he said. 'Southwest.'

Peter jumped up and called softly to the others. 'Stanley, get that engine started. Fu and Wing to the wheelhouse. Lily on deck. Let's get underway.'

In a short time, the large junk's engine was throbbing, the anchor was weighed, and they were steadily heading upriver to the opposite bank. Two more flashes from a torch and they were drifting alongside the bank in almost total darkness.

Harry watched anxiously as a plank was thrown onto the bank and three figures holding torches ran up it onto the boat. The third figure had a large shadow at his heels.

'What the hell is that thing, Jacko?' called Peter, shining his own torch on to him. 'Goddamn it, it's a bloody dog. It's one of them big Chinese wolfdogs!'

'Meet my new best friend, Zhiming,' said Jacko, smiling. The dog looked around at everyone without fear, his tongue hanging out and his tail wagging, but stayed close to Jacko.

'Where the hell did you pick him up from?' demanded Peter.

'He was the guard dog at the sheds,' replied Jacko. 'I gave him some beef jerky. At the same time, I gave him a good talking to. He agreed to join the good guys if I took him off the chain. He's on our side.'

Jamie burst into laughter. 'I couldn't believe it when I first saw Jacko with the dog! He's done some amazing things since I've known him but this takes the cake. The baddies didn't even notice he was gone!'

'No, Lee attached the chain to a hessian bag inside his kennel and made some amazing dog noises when they looked into it,' said Jacko, laughing and pointing to a smiling Lee. 'I couldn't leave Zhiming there. That's what they called him. What does Zhiming mean anyway?'

'Deadly,' replied Lee, still laughing. 'He's deadly! Zhiming.'

'That's not a good name for such a friendly dog,' said Jacko. 'Maybe I'll call him just Ming. Does that mean anything in Chinese?'

'Good name for a dog,' said Lee. 'That's what it means. Ming means "Name".'

'Well, Ming'll do. Eh, Ming?' said Jacko, as the wolfdog looked at him and wagged its tail. 'See! He likes it.'

Peter Jackson, who was also laughing, looked at the dog, then at Jacko and said, 'I don't normally allow animals on my boat, but in your case, I guess I'll have to make an exception.' He laughed again and shook his head. 'So, you took their guard dog? Never seen anything like it.'

Jamie patted the dog on the head and said to Jacko, 'I haven't had a chance to ask you. What did you and Lee find out?'

'There are quite a lot of people there,' said Jacko. 'Most of them are coolies. We didn't get much of a look at the others, although one of the men who came to check on the dog was a big, burly, bearded fellow with a cockney accent. Same as the fellow Lee saw when Stafford was shot. The main thing we noticed was that they've loaded up two 10-ton trucks with sacks ready to take somewhere. My guess is to a boat for shipping.'

'Probably tomorrow morning,' agreed Lee.

'I created a little surprise for them,' said Jacko. 'Using the fishing line and five grenades, I set up a booby trap in the large central shed. I learned that from a mob of commandoes in Malaya. There's a lot of gear in there.'

'What do you think is the next move, Jacko?' asked Jamie.

'I think Lee and I, and of course Ming here, should go ashore again just before dawn, Cap,' replied Jacko. 'We'll stay in the bushes this side of the poppy field to see where those trucks go. You don't need to come this time, Cap.'

'It's another two hours until first light, so we might as well keep the boat here till then,' said Peter. 'Goldie, Lily, get some hawsers ashore to attach us to those trees.'

As the two young crew members scurried ashore, Jacko asked, 'Have you got something to eat? We're all hungry and Ming needs some more jerky.'

Peter looked at him, shook his head again chuckling, and said, 'Yeah, I'll get the three of you, and the dog, something. Then we can all get some shut-eye for the next little while.'

By the time the sun was showing above the mountains to the east, Jacko and Lee, together with Ming, were well on their way to the intended position at the edge of the woods. Once there, they noticed there was a deal of activity around the left side of the central shed and soon after, the two heavy trucks began driving towards them along the southern side of the poppy field. Near the end of the field they veered off, skirting the edge of Zhusi Lake towards a point on the river well south of where the Jin Shayu was moored.

They decided to return to search the river further south from the junk. As they turned to leave, they heard in the distance behind them a series of explosions. Looking back across the poppy field, they saw smoke emitting from the large central shed and people rushing around in panic.

'I think you've managed to surprise them, Jacko,' said Lee.

'Yeah, I'd reckon, Lee,' agreed Jacko, patting the wolfdog beside him. 'They'll have the heebie jeebies about that lot. Let's get back to the boat. C'mon, Ming.'

An hour later, they were back on board the vessel which set off upriver, staying close to the shoreline of Buckminster Island and cruising at about five knots. The junk was halfway along the length of the island when they sighted two large white boats moored to a pier on the western bank. As they drew closer, they could see that hessian sacks were being loaded onto one of the boats from the two trucks they had seen earlier.

'We'll continue down to the end of the island about four miles further and then turn around,' said Peter. He turned to Harry. 'Do you want me to follow that loaded white boat all the way down the river, Harry?'

79

'Yeah, sure do, Pete,' agreed Harry. 'We should follow it at a distance to see what they do. Would you be able to contact one of those US Navy ships in the Yangtze on your radio?'

'Sure can, ol' buddy. The USS Eaton and the USS St Louis are on the river or just outside the mouth. Which one do you want?'

'Either one, Pete,' said Harry. 'If the white boat starts to head out into the China Sea, we'll want one of them to pick it up. The boat might be armed, so the navy ship has to be ready for a fight.'

'No problem there, Harry,' Peter laughed. 'The USS Eaton's a destroyer and the St Louis is a light cruiser. Before we get close to the Yangtze delta, I'll find out which one is in the best position to stop that boat.'

'That'll do it, Pete. I didn't realise the States still had so much firepower around here now,' said Harry.

'You sure you're in intelligence, Harry?'

'And up yours too, Pete,' said Harry, laughing.

CHAPTER 9

Pandemonium reigned throughout the opium base. The heebie jeebies indeed! People were rushing aimlessly in all directions trying to find the perpetrators of the explosions, unable to understand how such a thing could happen. Was it an inside job? Was there a traitor? What was the extent of the damage? Some local Chinese workers ran away, and stories of spirits and ghosts circulated around the base.

'Red' Ned Brandon, redder than ever, walked up and down roaring at everyone; the more he roared, the more his headache intensified and the more his words became unintelligible.

Roddy Braithwaite stared incredulously down at the hessian bag stuffed with straw attached by the chain to the kennel. Could that be what he had thought was the dog last night? But hadn't he heard Zhiming making dog noises and snoring? Where the hell was Zhiming? He was trained to attack any strangers. Braithwaite pulled at his moustache, making it even more bedraggled. His head ached. Bloody Chinese fire-water! He could still taste the liquor in his dry mouth.

Eddie Wang told everyone he encountered to calm down. His expression was grimmer, more piratical, than usual as he entered the ruins of the central treatment and packing shed to assess the damage. A few of the workers who had been lucky to escape with their lives gave him the news that the chief chemist, Wei Lijun, and two others had been killed. Three more were wounded but still alive. Wang shook his head slowly. Who to talk to? Ned Brandon seemed to be off his rocker. Motoi Tanaka was out in the poppy field looking for tracks, mumbling to himself and occasionally slashing at the plants with his sword. Wang thought he was probably too hungover to be of any use anyway. Sir William and Feng Gang Li had left with the trucks. He asked one of the chemical assistants to assess the damage and report to him as soon as he was finished.

Back in his office, he asked his secretary to find someone to drive him to the pier where the trucks would be loading the ship. He needed to talk to Sir William. There was something odd about the whole affair.

His state of mind was not improved when his secretary returned to inform him that the jeep was up on the hoist in the mechanics' shed and they would have to wait until Mr Feng returned with the trucks. She also told him that most of the workers had run off, scared by the rumours of spirits and ghosts. Bad feng shui!

Eddie Wang threw his hands in the air and cried, 'La shi!' He then exploded with some far worse Chinese swear words, apologised to his secretary, and went outside to find Brandon or Braithwaite and tell them to pull themselves together and get ready to take the other boat into Shanghai to warn Sir William about what had happened.

He found Braithwaite first. 'You're a total idiot, Roddy, believing you could leave security to one damned wolfdog. When Feng Gang Li returns, tell him to get that bloody jeep off the hoist right away. He can drive you and Red to the pier to take the other boat into Shanghai and tell Sir William what's happened. Urgently! Take Tanaka with you. No baijiu or any other alcohol! You must try to find out who did this and kill them if they're still in China. Understand?'

'Yes, Eddie. I understand,' said Braithwaite. 'When do you want us to leave?'

'Yesterday, you idiot.'

* * * *

'The loaded white boat is just pulling out into the channel now, Pete,' said Lee.

'Roger that,' said Peter. 'I'll get Fu to keep us at about 500 yards behind her. He'll be able to see her easily from up there in the wheelhouse.'

'Do you think we'll be attacked by river pirates again on the way back down the river?' asked Jamie.

'I doubt it,' replied Peter thoughtfully, pulling one side of his moustache. 'My guess is that the government has probably warned most of the gangs off from disturbing that opium boat. After the mauling we gave those bandits near Wuhu earlier, I don't think they'll try it again.'

82

'Nah! I don't reckon,' declared Jacko.

'How's your dog?' asked Peter.

'Happy as Larry,' said Jacko, chuckling. 'I reckon he didn't like those bad fellas much.'

'Having the dog with us is propitious, Jacko,' said Lee. 'It's his year. This year in China is the Year of the Dog.'

'Hey! It's your year, Ming,' said Jacko, rubbing the dog behind the ears.

'Well, I hope he's house-trained,' said Peter, shaking his head.

'I'll have a talk to him about that,' said Jacko with a broad smile.

'That white boat's picking up speed,' said Peter. 'I'll go and talk to Fu while you talk to your dog. Ciao!'

After the motorboat ahead had settled down to a cruising speed of six knots, the Jin Shayu matched their speed, maintaining a distance of 500 yards behind. The sky was cloudless, a bright blue contrasting with the brown surface of the Yangtze. Other boats sailing up and down the river paid them no attention.

Peter decided to raise the sails on the main mast and the small mast at the stern. He explained that this would probably make them less conspicuous, as they would conform to the appearance of the other junks on the river. Goldie, Lily and Stanley all rushed around hoisting halyards and securing sheets until the bright brown-red sails shone in the sunlight above the junk. The only flaws in the sails were a few patches and bullet holes from previous expeditions.

'Very pretty, Pete,' said Jamie. 'Will they increase the speed?'

'No, no. We'll maintain the same speed,' replied Peter. 'There's a nice warm breeze from the south, so the sails will help a bit, although the winds can be fluky on the river. We'll use less fuel and from a distance it will look as though we're only under sail.'

After a little more than an hour, the two boats entered the large bends in the river. During the first bend to the right, Lee pointed out the village of Liuduzhen on the northern bank. He said there had been recent fighting there, but things had calmed down now. Several fishing boats accompanied by wheeling and screeching gulls were moored in front of the village.

Over the next two hours, they followed the white opium-laden boat around the next large bend to the left, hazy multi-coloured hills

83

and mountains dominating the landscape on both sides. Jamie and some of the others became mesmerised by the slow progress and the regular pulse of the diesel engines. Not so Ming! The wolfdog acted as though the river was his natural domain, alert to everything going on around him and wagging his tail. He was happy for any of his newfound friends to pat him, but he always stayed close to Jacko.

Nearly past the great bend in the river, Lee pointed out a village on the starboard side.

'That's the town of Digangzhen,' he said. 'It's not large, but it has some of the most beautiful Buddhist shrines along the Yangtze. It also has a small harbour off the river where they construct junks and other boats.'

'You're a regular tourist guide, Lee,' said Jacko. 'That's interesting.'

Just then, a shot from the other side of the river made yet another bullet hole in the mainsail. Everyone ducked close to the deck.

'I don't think that fella's a Buddhist,' observed Jacko.

'No, definitely not,' agreed Lee. 'Luckily, he's not much of a shot either.'

'Just stay alert all the same!' shouted Peter from further astern. 'Keep your heads down through the narrow parts.'

Lee chuckled. 'You're the boss, Pete!'

'Glad you realise that!'

Still at six knots, the boats continued along the twenty-five-mile north-east stretch of the river towards the sharp left-hand bend at Wuhu. With the wind almost astern, at times the sails were able to sustain the boat speed without assistance from the engines. At other times, as mountains on the southern side of the river occasionally created a wind shadow, the engines came into play again. The day was warm with a cloudless sky and, with the boat running before the wind, there was little breeze across the deck to temper the heat of the sun, so the passengers stayed in the shade of the mainsail. In a state of drowsy reverie, they sat staring at the changing scenery. Small villages, hills, mountains, people, animals, and infrequent pagodas rising in their magnificence above coloured roofs, wheeling gulls and other birds always in attendance.

For the next three hours, they could hear the sporadic crackle of gunfire in the distance, but no one shot at the boat. It was already late in the afternoon and Jamie was beginning to wonder whether the white boat ahead would continue downriver during the night. It was another half-hour before they saw the hill above the sharp left-hand bend through a light mist which had settled on the river.

Peter came down from the wheelhouse to the deck and said, 'In a little while, I suggest y'all go down below decks. The sharpshooters on that hill might want to test their marksmanship on us again.'

'Do you think the opium boat is likely to stop in Wuhu for the night?' asked Jamie.

'No. That's potentially hostile territory for those smugglers,' responded Peter. 'The Kuomintang has no control there. I think they'll anchor behind one of the river islands this side of Ma'anshan. If they do, we'll go on to Ma'anshan and wait for them in the morning.'

'That makes sense,' said Jamie. 'You don't reckon they'll keep sailing through the night, Pete?'

'Naw! Their cargo's too valuable, Jamie. They might hit something in the dark. Or something might hit them,' Peter replied with a rueful smile. 'Get below, you lot.'

Later from the cabin, they could feel the junk steering around to port and as predicted, hear occasional bullets hitting the deck and ricocheting off the wheelhouse or the hull, but not with the same intensity as before.

After passing Wuhu, everyone was back on deck. There were plenty of other craft on this part of the river; however, the Jin Shayu was easily able to keep the white boat in sight. An hour later, Peter's prediction proved correct when the boat ahead steered to port towards a branch of the river leading to the western side of a large island. The junk didn't follow but steered towards the eastern branch, the main part of the river.

'My guess is they'll anchor for the night near a village on the west bank,' said Peter. 'The village has the splendid name of Xiliangshan. Lee might know what it means.'

Lee shook his head. 'Your guess is as good as mine. Large mountain, I think. I could be wrong.'

85

'Whatever. They'll be able to get food supplies there if they need them,' continued Peter. 'We'll carry on to Ma'anshan and stay there for the night. They may even have some cold beer for my ol' buddy Jacko.'

'Bloody beauty!' exclaimed Jacko. 'I'm with you, Skip. Lead on.'

'Now that we're not keeping pace with that slowcoach, we'll stir this baby up to ten knots and have the first beer in your hand in two hours,' said Peter, laughing and climbing up into the wheelhouse.

As they approached the small inlet near the town of Ma'anshan, night fell in a brief crimson blaze. In the glow of the boat's running lights, the pier loomed ahead and in a short time the boat was moored to it. The lights of the town appeared welcoming and soon they were walking up the hill towards the small restaurant where they had previously dined. Ming irrigated every tree and post as they walked. They were greeted with the same enthusiasm as previously. 'Ni hao! Ni hao! Ni hao!' along with beaming smiles and much kowtowing.

Jacko, who had been practising his few Chinese words, cried, 'Bīng píjiu! Bīng píjiu! Xiè xiè.'

He was immediately rewarded when a dozen green bottles of beer were carried to the table, but slightly disappointed when the 'bing' part of the order did not eventuate. The beer was not very cold but gratefully accepted. In a cloud of fragrance, the table was soon filled with tasty dishes, bowls of rice, and assorted dumplings. They even served a lamb shank for Ming whose tail wagged in a blur.

Peter looked at Jacko who was deftly filling his plate with his chopsticks. 'I think you're beginning to take a shine to China, Jacko.'

'Yeah, Pete. Great tucker, but it's got one big drawback.'

'Yeah? What's that, Jacko?'

'No Monique. My wife's not here.'

Peter laughed. 'Yeah. Well, every place has its defects. China's got more than a few of those right now, unfortunately.'

'Have you thought of moving somewhere else, Pete?' asked Jamie.

'Naw. I've been here so long, I'm part of the furniture now,' replied Peter. 'I might have to think about it sometime in the future though. Probably depends on which side wins the civil war, but I'll be around here for a few more years yet, I reckon.'

'Well, since we're all here, I think we need another plate of dumplings,' said Jacko with a grin. 'I know gluttony's a sin, but I can't resist them. Anyway, without sin there wouldn't be any forgiveness.'

Jamie laughed. 'Don't worry, Jacko, I'll order some more dumplings and forgive you for your sins.'

Everyone put aside their thoughts about the opium smugglers for the next hour or so. After dinner, they returned to the Jin Shayu and after a brief discussion about when the opium boat was likely to pass their position the next day, they all settled down for the night.

As dawn broke, they were all awake and alert, but Peter seemed unconcerned and relaxed. The morning sky was cloudy and there was a light mist on the river and in the hills. Humidity was much higher than the previous days. Peter jumped onto the pier and looked out at the river.

'They'll be a while yet. Even if they set off right now, they'll still be another three hours if they maintain their speed at six knots,' he said. 'We've got plenty of time for breakfast. After that, we can have a look at the ancient temple close to here.'

'Ancient temple?' exclaimed Harry. 'Yeah. That'd be good if we've got time.'

'If you look over there to the south, you can see its pretty black-tiled roof,' said Peter. 'It's an old Buddhist temple. It's known as the Xiaojiuhua Temple.'

'You've taken over from Lee as the chief tourist guide, Pete,' said Jacko.

'Always at your service, ol' buddy,' said Peter with a bow. 'Let's go eat.'

Back at the restaurant, Jacko remembered to say, 'Ni hao!' and was greeted by, 'Ni hao! Ni hao! Ni hao! Zao shang hao!'

'Never known a mob to be so happy to see me,' Jacko commented as they all sat down at the round table. 'Must be my handsome dial.'

'Yeah. Can't think what else it could be, Jacko,' said Jamie. 'Maybe your great command of the language.'

'Yeah, that must be it,' agreed Jacko as dishes were laid on the table before them. Ming was again presented with a lamb shank, to his tail-wagging enthusiasm.

An hour later, they stood before the Xiaojiuhua Temple. It was built largely of dark woods and tiles, had three levels of ornate Chinese roofs, and stood serenely in a garden shaded by large trees.

'You sure that white boat won't slip past us, Pete?' asked Harry.

'You'll never survive in China if you worry too much, Harry,' said Peter with a twinkle in his eye. 'Anyway, Lily and Goldie are watching the river closely. C'mon, I'll show you around as chief tourist guide.'

In the cool, dark interior, with intricate carvings and exquisite pearl and gold inlays in the dark wood, they could make out a large golden Buddha. Local people were lighting incense sticks and standing them up in tubs set out for the purpose. Jacko stepped up to a monk and bought an incense stick. Jamie immediately followed.

'You can never be too careful, Cap,' said Jacko, chuckling.

Back on the pier, Lily informed them there was still no sign of the opium boat. Peter instructed Stanley to start up the engines and the crew to prepare the boat for a quick getaway upon sighting their quarry.

It was another half-hour before Lily cried out that the white boat had emerged from the mist and was cruising north in the centre of the river.

Peter yelled a few orders in Chinese and in less than two minutes, the Jin Shayu was unmoored and motoring out of the Ma'anshan inlet into the river.

Because of the mist, the junk closed to within 300 yards of the opium boat. The traffic on the Yangtze River was relatively heavy at that time of day and both vessels had to occasionally weave around other boats, but the white boat was distinctive and easy to follow. The hills and mountains on both sides of the river were dark shapes against the grey sky and it was impossible to distinguish the shoreline. There was little breeze and Peter decided to only hoist the stern mizzen sail and not the mainsail as they motored down the river, now in a north-easterly direction. As before, noisy gulls flew around the boat, regularly diving into its wake to catch fish.

'We should be at Nanjing by about two in the afternoon, guys,' Peter told them. 'I don't think the opium boat will stop there or anywhere. The river is wider from here, so they may decide to keep going now, even in the dark, until they're out into the China Sea, but we'll see.'

'Hours before we get to Shanghai, I'll have to radio the USS Eaton to wait for them outside the Yangtze delta,' said Harry. 'What'ya reckon, Pete?'

'I agree, Harry,' said Peter. 'But at this pace it's still a helluva long time before we get to Shanghai. It'll be after dawn tomorrow at the earliest if they do decide to sail through the night. So, you can relax for a while.'

'I'm getting stiff and bored from too much relaxing,' complained Harry.

'Me too,' said Jacko. 'But old Ming here doesn't seem to mind.'

'He your dog now,' said Lily, patting Ming on the head. 'Velly nice dog.'

'You want him?' asked Jacko.

'Yes, want him but Peter not like me to keep on boat,' she said sadly, shaking her head while Ming licked her hand. 'He fliendly.'

'Yeah, he likes you,' said Jacko. 'I'll take him to Shanghai and try to find him a good home.'

'My aunt. She live in old city. She like this dog,' said Lily.

'Give the address to Lee and we'll see if we can find her,' said Jacko. He winked at her and said, 'If we find her, I'll explain to Ming to be good friends with your aunt.'

'My aunt, she be velly happy,' she said, clapping her hands. 'You good man. You talk to dog.'

'Lily!' yelled Peter from the quarterdeck. 'If you're finished chitchatting, the mizzen sail is flapping. Secure the sheet. Hěn kuài!'

'Shì. Yes, boss,' said Lily, scampering to the stern.

As Peter had guessed, the city of Nanjing was off their starboard beam by early afternoon and the white boat in front showed no sign of stopping or changing speed. The Yangtze River trended easterly from this point, the mist had lifted, and the Jin Shayu had dropped back to 500 yards behind. Peter walked up to the bow and stared at the opium boat ahead, silently contemplating it for a while, then turned back to address the others.

'At this pace it'll already be nightfall before we reach Zhenjiang,' he explained. 'They might stop there but I doubt it. I think they'll push on. Fu has eyes like a cat, but I'll need a couple of guys with good eyesight to watch their boat after dark. We don't want them giving us the slip. Jacko and Lee claim to be able to see in the dark, so I nominate you guys to take turns to stand at watch through the night from the bow. Okay?'

'Not a problem, Pete,' said Lee.

'You're the skipper,' said Jacko.

'Yes I am,' Peter laughed, his teeth glistening below his droopy moustache.

'Anyway, we'll have our eagle-eyed wolfdog Ming to help us, Pete,' said Jacko, grinning. 'He hates those baddies.'

'Yeah, yeah, yeah,' said Peter. 'If that damned dog of yours wants to pee, make sure he doesn't do it on the windward side of the boat.'

'I'll explain it to him,' said Jacko.

CHAPTER 10

'Magnifique! Magnifique!' exclaimed Henri Rousseau as he gazed upwards at the stand of narra trees, his face glistening with raindrops. Many of the trees soared up to 100 feet, with the trunks five to eight feet in diameter. The wet ground at his feet was strewn with the elliptical leaves and yellow blossoms from the trees.

One of the local men, Jacob, stepped up to Henri and showed him a sample of the timber sawn into a small plank. The wood was a yellow-rose colour and it was scented like sandalwood or cedar. Henri took it and after inspecting it closely and weighing it in his hand, exclaimed again, 'Magnifique!'

He turned around to Sarah and Carna, who were watching him, and smiled. 'This is the finest timber I have seen for the making of fine furniture,' he said. 'Heavy, hard and beautiful. Such quality. Mahogany is second rate to this. Even better than teak. Magnifique!'

The day before, Manny Alvarez had transported Henri, his wife Bella, Monique, Carna and Sarah on his large double-outrigged bangka, the Pulo Draco (Red Dragon), from Cebu City across the Camotes Sea to the small village of Giporlos on the southern coast of Samar Island, the most eastern of the large islands in the Visayas. The bangka was moored to a long pier beside the village. After staying overnight on the boat, Manny had organised a wartime Willys jeep with driver for them. He told them that Jacinto the driver could speak some English and was familiar with the stand of narra trees Henri wanted to inspect. However, apart from the driver, the jeep was only suitable for three passengers, so Bella and Monique elected to stay behind.

After a bone-jarring drive of over twenty miles on the roughest road Henri had ever experienced, they arrived at the small village of Hernani on the east coast of Samar. To add to their discomfort, it rained all the way causing the jeep to slip and slide from one pothole to the next. As Manny had informed them before they left, Samar had only two seasons. Wet and wetter.

They arrived in Hernani in the early afternoon, and a friend of Jacinto invited them out of the rain into his nipa hut and offered them rice, fish and fruit, which they gratefully accepted. Henri noticed that Carna was often hesitant when she translated for them.

As they sat on the floor of the nipa hut eating, Henri quietly asked Carna whether she was having any trouble with the local dialect.

'Yes. They have a very different language, Waray Waray,' replied Carna. 'It's difficult for me, but some of them also speak some Tagalog and Cebuano, as well as a little Spanish, so we can understand each other. It's an interesting exercise.'

'Oui. I can imagine,' said Henri, nodding. 'Do you understand any of this, Sarah?'

Sarah shook her head, but Carna said, 'Sarah is good at reading body language, so she mostly understands what's going on even if she doesn't know the words.'

This brought a beaming smile from Sarah and she gazed devotedly at Carna with her large eyes. By this time, many others from the village had entered the hut and were standing around staring at the newcomers, including several children.

Carna spent some time in deep discussion with their host, often chuckling as they both strove to understand each other.

She then turned to Henri and said, 'This man, whose hospitality we are currently enjoying, knows all about the narra trees. His name is Angelo Reyes. He can guide us to the best trees, but he says it will take a few hours to walk there. It's too late to go today as we wouldn't make it back before dark. He says we can sleep in his hut overnight and set out early in the morning.'

'That's very kind of him,' responded Henri. 'How do I say thank you to him?'

'Just say, salamat,' she replied.

'How about many thanks?' he asked further.

Carna thought for a moment and replied, 'In Waray that is damu nga salamat.'

Henri touched Angelo on the shoulder and said, 'Damu nga salamat.'

Angelo looked at him, smiled broadly, and touched Henri on the shoulder saying, 'Diri, diri!'

This exchange created a degree of gaiety amongst the onlookers who laughed and chattered amongst themselves.

'I think you have won some new friends,' said Carna, laughing.

'Thanks to you, my dear,' acknowledged Henri, waving to the crowd.

It rained heavily overnight but eased off in the morning. Henri said to Carna that he was amazed at how dry they were in a nipa hut constructed mainly from bamboo and the leaves of tropical plants. She told him that, for centuries, the Filipinos had been skilled in such construction.

The trek to the stand of narra trees, led by Angelo, was only five or six miles; however, it took a large part of the morning as they had to wade through several streams and there was nothing that could be described as dry land. At times, Henri had to be assisted in climbing up or down slippery banks, but there were plenty of willing hands to help him, as five other locals as well as Jacinto had accompanied the group. After arriving at the narra wooded area, Henri decided that the discomfort of walking while wringing wet was well worthwhile. He still found it hard to believe the extent of the beautiful narra forest. Magnifique! Sarah, who had walked the entire distance in bare feet, was slightly puzzled by his enthusiasm, but realised he was happy with what he saw. She saw that Carna was also pleased and this made her happy.

The return trek to Hernani was just as wet and slippery, and they arrived back at the road by early afternoon, drenched to the skin. Angelo insisted that they stay for lunch in his hut. Having forgotten part of the phrase he had used before, Henri thanked Angelo with, 'Salamat. Salamat.' Angelo laughed and bowed.

They all tucked into their lunch largely in silence, using sign language to indicate how delicious the food was while Angelo maintained a broad smile. Henri handed him an envelope with some pesos and he nodded, smiling even more broadly.

After lunch, Angelo spoke to Carna at length, pointing up the road. Other locals joined in the conversation, pointing in the same direction. Eventually Henri, who was ready to return to the boat at Giporlos, asked Carna what it was all about.

'Angelo said that there are some foreigners, white men, living up the road near Llorente,' she explained. 'They have taken over some sheds and huts constructed by the Americans after the Leyte landing in 1944. They don't think the foreigners are Americans. According to Angelo, they unload sacks from small boats, store them in a shed, then load them onto larger boats. Nobody here knows what they're doing. The local people of Llorente are paid to do the loading, but when there is no boat around, armed guards keep them away.'

'Intéressant!' exclaimed Henri, standing up and bowing to Angelo. 'But it is time for us to get back to Monsieur Alvarez and his boat.'

Carna spoke again to Angelo who talked quickly, pointing to the north. It was obvious he was concerned about something.

Carna then said to Henri, 'He is requesting that since we are also foreigners here, we take a short drive to Llorente to find out what they're doing. He says it is more likely that the foreigners will explain it to us. It is only six miles.'

'Six miles on these roads is like sixty miles on proper roads,' said Henri irritably. Then he sighed resignedly and added, 'We owe Angelo much. The timber he has shown us is worth a king's ransom. He is truly an angel. Perhaps we could just add an extra hour to our journey to investigate these mysterious strangers who have the local people so worked up, n'est-ce pas?'

Carna spoke to Angelo who smiled, shook her by the hand, shook Henri by the hand, and much to her astonishment, grabbed Sarah's hand and shook it. Sarah had been silently watching the exchanges and sensed that the locals were frightened by the white men up the road. If Henri was going to confront them, she must be alert.

Angelo accompanied them out to the jeep where Jacinto was waiting with the engine already idling. Henri didn't quite know what to say, so trying to mimic Carna's accent, he looked at Angelo and said, 'Amigo.'

Angelo laughed and responded, 'O-o, amigo yes.'

Heading north along the coast, they found the road rough but not as bad as before, and within twenty minutes they could see a large shed and several army demountables above a beach of black sand. A few small fishing bangkas were pulled up onto the beach. A long pier jutted out from the headland to the south of the beach. About three-quarters of a mile beyond the shed, they could see the small village of Llorente, some concrete block houses, nipa huts, and the skyline dominated by a church spire.

Jacinto followed the road past the beach inland from the large shed and drove into the village. Leaving the jeep, he walked over to a group of locals who had been watching them. He spoke to them briefly and then they all started talking at once, pointing agitatedly south towards the shed and the pier. Henri, Carna and Sarah sat silently observing this performance while several curious children surrounded the jeep.

After a while, Jacinto, followed by some of the local men, returned to the jeep and said, 'They tell me that whenever a ship comes in, they are paid to load or unload it and then told to stay away until the next ship. There are three white men and two Chinese. They are scared of them. One of them tried to look around the sheds and they beat him up.'

'Merde! They beat him? What sort of people are these?' exclaimed Henri.

'We'll ask them,' said Carna. 'They can only tell us to go away.'

'Oui. Yes. I suppose so,' agreed Henri. 'Jacinto, let's go back down the road and stop at that big shed.'

'Yessir.'

On arrival at the shed, they saw two men standing at the front staring at them. One was a tall burly Chinese with a belligerent expression and a STEN gun, the other a white man with curly black hair and an untidy full beard. Carna whispered to Henri to let her do all the talking. She said they might be politer to a woman.

The bearded man walked up to the car and said in a strong Glasgow accent, 'I think you must be the ones we've been expecting. Did Sir William send you?'

Carna was taken aback by the question. As she descended from the jeep, she said, 'Sir William? Er... yes. Sir William.'

The Scotsman nodded to the Chinese, then said, 'Good, good. Both of you come along and I'll show you around. My name's Hamish McIntyre. You can call me Mac.'

Carna looked back at the jeep as Henri was getting out. Sarah wasn't there. Where is she? she wondered. Henri caught up with her and they followed the bearded Scotsman.

They walked through a doorway into the large shed and Carna, composing herself, said, 'I am Carna, and may I introduce you to Henry?'

'Carna? You are Filipina?' asked McIntyre without curiosity.

'Yes, I'm Filipina,' was all she could think of replying. Who are these people and who is Sir William? she wondered. They found themselves inside a small office. A window into the main part of the shed gave them a view of thousands of sacks stacked up in neat piles throughout the space.

'So, Henry, I presume you are interested in the last lading inventory?' asked McIntyre, sitting behind a desk and gesturing to two chairs on the other side.

Henry nodded and mumbled, 'Yes, of course.'

'Did Sir William give you an ETA for the next boat from China?' McIntyre asked, stroking his beard and watching them closely.

Henri and Carna looked at each other with astonishment then as Carna cleared her throat to reply, McIntyre interrupted.

'You don't even know who Sir William is, do you?' he shouted. 'Who the hell are you?'

Henri stood up indignantly and said, 'Monsieur Mac, or whatever your name is, I would suggest you don't speak like that in front of a lady.'

'Och! So, a Frenchie, eh? Whoever you are, your efforts to spy on us have come to naught,' challenged McIntyre with a malicious grin. The armed brawny Chinese whom they had seen outside came rushing in, having heard the shouting. McIntyre said to him, 'These people are spies, Joe. What should we do with them, eh?'

'We are not spies, Monsieur,' objected Henri, his face flushed. 'We are private citizens from Australia only interested in the local timbers. Our interest in your enterprise was purely idle curiosity as we passed by. We are sorry to have troubled you and we shall depart now.'

'Depart now?' repeated McIntyre. 'I don't think so, Frenchie.'

'You can't detain us here,' Henri insisted.

McIntyre, who remained seated, thoughtfully stroked his beard again. Looking up at Henri, he said, 'You think not? I can assure you that you shall be my honoured guests for the next few days or until the man I was expecting arrives. He can decide what to do with you.'

Carna spoke up in a soft voice. 'We know nothing of your enterprise. You have nothing to fear from us if you let us leave now.'

'Och aye, Filipina. And pigs may fly,' said McIntyre. 'Joe, take these two to the east cabin and lock them in. Then find Nick and Huang and we'll all meet here. Oh aye! Take the key to their jeep and tell the driver to git.'

'How dare you treat us like this!' Henri protested.

'Do what you're told and go with Mr Gao here,' said McIntyre grimly. 'I warn you that Gao Jiang is from Shaolin in Henan, China, and is an expert in kung fu. So I suggest you go along quietly.'

Further protestations were silenced as the ferocious-looking Gao Jiang threatened them with his STEN gun. He led them past the pier to a demountable hut on the headland east of the main shed.

After they heard the key turn in the lock, Henri asked Carna where Sarah was.

'She just disappeared when we arrived at the shed,' said Carna. 'I'm sure she sensed something was wrong. Particularly when she saw that armed thug.'

'They are all thugs,' said Henri. 'We shouldn't have come here. We should be on our way back to the boat by now. Merde!'

Carna began exploring the hut they were locked in. It had metal walls and two rooms. The room where they had entered had two single beds, some chairs, and a small kitchenette. The other, smaller room had a shower, basin and toilet. The windows were far too small for any chance of escape. She sat down on one of the chairs and was soon lost in thought about the situation.

Her thoughts were interrupted when Henri asked, 'So Sarah just vanished? Elle a disparu.'

'Don't worry, Henri,' said Carna. 'She is out there somewhere. She will not abandon us.'

'Merde! But what can she do?' protested Henri. 'Such a little girl. Alone.'

'She'll think of something, Henri,' said Carna soothingly. 'I've seen her do some remarkable things. She'll at least find someone to help us.'

Shrugging his shoulders in resignation and shaking his head, Henri sat down on one of the beds sighing as a squall swept over the hut, the clamour of the wind and heavy rain on the corrugated iron drowning out all other sounds.

* * * *

Night had fallen on the Yangtze River and they had all just finished eating a dinner of noodles and a meat dish that Lily and Goldie had cooked before they saw the lights of Zhenjiang on the starboard bow. Jacko and Lee were at the bow discussing in subdued voices the geography of the Yangtze River with Ming beside them, alert.

The opium boat was easy to see. As soon as it was dark, that boat had turned on a large spotlight on its bow, lighting up the river in front of it. It was showing no sign of leaving its position in the centre of the river. The Jin Shayu carried only its running lights and amongst all the other green and red running lights of other craft on the river, it was virtually invisible to anyone looking aft from the boat ahead.

Peter joined them on the bow for a while and commented that it was unlikely there would be any stops and they would be going through the night. He reiterated that it would be best from now to stand three-hour watches each and keep a weather eye on the opium boat. They were to report to him if the boat changed speed or veered to the side of the river. Lee asked Peter if he wanted to be alerted to any likely collision with other craft on the river. Peter replied that Fu and Wing were experienced at sailing in the dark and departed, muttering a comment about teaching his grandmother to suck eggs.

After midnight, the river took a long right-hand turn to the south and was noticeably wider. Jacko reported back to Peter in the wheelhouse that their quarry had increased its speed.

'Indeed it has,' he agreed. 'To maintain our distance, we're already up to eight knots. The river widens further on, so they might decide to go faster. We'll have to keep an eye on 'em. At this pace we'll pass Kaisha Island in about six hours. It'll be light by then.'

98

'How far to the mouth of the river from that island?' asked Jacko.

'Aw. About another eighty-five miles,' said Peter, scratching his moustache. 'Probably get there by about 1600.'

'We'll have to tell Harry,' said Jacko. 'He'll want to contact a US Navy ship before then.'

'Okay. I'll do that, Jacko,' said Peter, grinning. 'Just keep your eye peeled on that boat and let us know if it does anything different.'

'Okey dokey. No problem, Pete,' Jacko responded. 'She's easy to see.'

Returning to the bow, Jacko settled down to watch the opium boat silhouetted by its own forward spotlight. Lee and Ming were asleep, both lightly snoring beside him, adding to the sounds of the night dominated by the pulse of the junk's twin engines. The crackle of sporadic gunfire could occasionally be heard in the far distance as well as the infrequent screech of gulls diving into the boat's phosphorescent wake. Jacko sensed a presence beside him and glanced at Jamie who was standing behind him.

'G'day, Cap. Can't you sleep?'

'Yeah, but something woke me,' Jamie answered, sounding puzzled. 'I had a weird feeling that something was wrong.'

'No, Cap. She's all okay here,' said Jacko breezily. 'I've got the opium boat in sight and it's still in the centre of the river.'

'No, it's not that,' said Jamie, sitting down. 'I had a dream. I dreamt that Carna was in trouble.'

'Couldn't be, Cap,' said Jacko. 'She's with Monique's family and our Cebuano friends, Manny and Co. They're probably all having a great time of it.'

'Yeah. Of course, you're right, Jacko,' said Jamie. 'They'll all be safely tucked up in bed at this time of night, but I can't seem to shake the feeling there's something wrong.'

'Dreams can often seem real when they're not, Cap,' said Jacko, studying his friend's face in the dim glow of the running lights. 'I'm sure nothing's wrong. Carna knows her way around the Philippines and she wouldn't take any risks.'

'It's certainly a beautiful night, Jacko,' said Jamie, looking up at the stars. 'I think I'll go back to my bunk and try to dream of happier things.'

'That's the spirit, Cap. Goodnight.'

Jamie went back down to his bunk with the sense of helpless fatalism he often felt when he knew there was nothing he could do even if his foreboding was correct.

CHAPTER 11

It had been raining all day. From a distance, Sarah had observed Henri and Carna being hurried along by an armed guard to a hut, the furthest from the road. She had watched them enter the hut and seen him turn a key in the lock, put the key in his pocket, and quickly return in the rain to the large shed. The guard was a big man with thinning hair, a flat nose, and an angry expression. He didn't look like the local people. More like some of the Chinese men she and Jacko had encountered in Malaya a few months previously.

Sarah stayed where she was, hidden amongst thick foliage, until night fell. She had been soaked through to the skin for a long while and hardly noticed the rain as she pondered what she should do. The jeep was still there but the man with the gun had removed the ignition key and sent Jacinto away. The driver had walked north along the road and, as far as Sarah could speculate, was probably staying with friends in the nearby village.

She figured that if she ran all night down the road towards Giporlos, where Manny Alvarez's boat was, she could get there by morning. Bella and Monique were there. But what could they do? In any case, the bad people might hurt Carna and Henri or take them somewhere else while she was away, as it would take her a long while to return. She dismissed that idea and decided she must try to free Henri and Carna herself.

What would Jacko do? She decided to hold onto that thought. She knew he wouldn't abandon his friends, even for a day. What he would do, she decided, was to get closer and study the whole situation. Like a shadow, she crossed the road and worked her way through an area of coconut trees and thick tropical growth until she was level with the hut and only a short distance away from it. As she settled down to study the scene, there was movement to her left and she watched a man she hadn't seen before walking from the shed towards her, carrying a large bag. He also looked Chinese, although thinner, and he had long wet hair and a straggly beard. Reaching the hut, he leant a rifle up against it and proceeded to set up a sort of tent from the bag he had been carrying. Satisfied that the tent was properly erected, he sat on a folding chair inside it with his rifle.

Sarah scrutinised the hut but couldn't work out how she would be able to get her friends out of there. The walls looked solid and the windows were tiny. Even if she broke one of the windows, she doubted that even she with her tiny frame would be able to squeeze through. What would Jacko do? Occasional squalls came in from the sea, the heavy rain almost blotting out her view of the hut.

She was starting to weep with frustration when she noticed, after a heavy squall, some of the corrugated iron on the roof rattling in the brief high wind. The roof! That could be the way in. If she could lift one of those sheets of corrugated iron, she might be able to create a big enough hole for Henri and Carna to escape through.

Jacko had told her that some hours after midnight was when guards were not so alert. She had no concept of hours; however, she knew it was best to wait a while to catch the guard unawares. She sat down with her back up against a tree, oblivious to the rain running down her face, mentally reckoning what a while would be, and went to sleep.

After that while, about two hours, her eyes popped open and she stood up to appraise the area. The rain had eased, and she could see the guard's feet at the mouth of the tent. There was no movement from the direction of the shed or the road. Searching around, she found a thick branch about two feet long, heavy enough to be used as a waddy club. Grasping this in her right hand, she moved silently towards the tent. Standing next to the opening, she yapped like a small dog. The guard groggily shook his head, stood up, and peered out of the opening. Sarah brought her waddy down hard on his head. The guard teetered on his feet for a second and then slumped back into his folding chair.

Sarah reached inside and picked up his rifle then gave the guard another thump with the butt on the side of his head. That's what Jacko would do! Looking around, she made sure that her actions had not attracted any attention. Not likely with the rain dampening any sounds. She went around the back of the hut where she found a vertical metal water pipe running up the side nearly to the roof.

102

Within seconds, she was on the roof pulling at the ends of some of the corrugated iron sheets that had worked loose in the winds.

Pulling with all her strength at the loosest sheet, she finally managed to dislodge it and threw it onto the ground. Below where the sheet had been, some wooden beams held white insulation material which she easily pushed through with her feet. Looking down, she saw a washbasin below her. Holding onto a beam, she clambered down to the washbasin and from there leapt to the floor.

Carna had not slept well, filled with anxiety and disturbed by the sporadic heavy rains beating down on the metal roof. She was half asleep with her mind drifting when she heard a whisper in her ear, 'Ka Na, Sarah. Ka Na, Sarah.'

Suddenly alert, she sat up and exclaimed incredulously, 'Sarah?'

'Aye yu, Carna. It is me.'

'I knew you'd come!' said Carna, standing up. 'Can you get us out of here?'

'Aye yu, Carna. Where Hon Ree?'

'I'll wake him,' said Carna, going to the other bed and shaking the occupant. 'Henri, Sarah is here. We must go quickly.'

'Quelle? Wha...? Comment? Sarah? Yes. Yes. I'm awake,' said Henri, sitting up on the bed. 'I'll follow you.'

Entering the bathroom, in the dim light they saw the hole in the ceiling above the basin that Sarah had made. Sarah helped Carna climb onto the basin so that she could easily reach the beams above her. Sarah gave her a push from below and Carna climbed onto the roof. She lay down and dangled her arms down to help Henri, whom Sarah was already helping climb onto the basin. With Carna pulling and Sarah pushing, Henri was finally able to pull himself out onto the roof.

'I'm getting too old for this,' he mumbled.

Carna was about to position herself to help Sarah up when she realised the small black girl had already joined them and was pointing out the water pipe on the side of the hut. Sarah went down first and helped Carna and Henri to climb down the pipe in turn. Sarah picked up the guard's rifle, handed it to Henri, and led them towards the palm trees and scrub to the south of the hut. Once hidden in the foliage, they stopped to get their breath and Carna gave Sarah a warm hug. Sarah smiled and thought, that's the way Jacko would have done it!

'Where shall we go now?' Henri asked in a hoarse whisper.

'Place of Angelo,' said Sarah. Holding hands with Carna, she led them inland to the road. Pointing south she said, 'Go now,' and set off at a brisk pace.

The rain had eased to a misty drizzle, just enough to soak them to the skin. After marching for two hours, the sounds of dogs barking and pigs snorting indicated they were near Hernani. It was still dark, but they could see a faint glow on the eastern horizon.

As they approached Angelo's nipa hut, a male voice asked, 'Hin-o? Hin-o? Who's there?'

'It's Carna, Henri and Sarah,' replied Carna.

Angelo, wiping the sleep from his eyes and giving them a broad smile, spoke, with Carna translating. 'Come in, come in. We were worried about you. Where's your jeep? Has something happened to you?'

As the sun rose, Carna and Henri explained the details of their earlier frightening experiences and eventual rescue by Sarah, while his family served up hot rice, fish and eggs for breakfast. Angelo kept apologising for having caused them so much trouble. Henri told him not to worry and that it was not his fault. He presented him with the carbine rifle he had carried with him. He said that they were very tired and needed somewhere to sleep where the bad men would be unable to find them.

'Angelo says he has just the place,' Carna said, looking at Angelo who seemed relieved to be able to help. 'They have a nipa hut in the rainforest just behind the village. No one will find us there.'

'That is very kind of you,' said Henri.

'But he asks where Jacinto is,' Carna said. Angelo looked puzzled.

Sarah, who had sat quietly throughout the discussion, stepped forward and touched Angelo on the arm. 'Jacinto in village near bad men.'

'In Llorente?'

'Aye yu. Llorente,' she said. 'I go gettim. Bad men have key to jeep.'

Angelo said he would send his eldest son, Almado, to accompany them. 'He can help you find Jacinto in Llorente and he knows how to hot-wire a jeep,' Carna translated.

'Hot-wire? What is hot-wire?' asked Henri.

'It's a way of starting a car without a key, Henri,' said Carna. 'Sarah, you can't go back. You are much too tired.'

'Not tired, Ka Na,' said Sarah, beaming. 'I sleep on Manny boat.'

'Don't let those horrible bastardos catch you, Sarah,' Carna said, giving her a hug.

'Bastards not see me, Ka Na,' she responded, laughing.

Carna couldn't help herself from bursting into laughter. 'Ay! Guau! Your English is really something now, Sarah.'

* * * *

The rising sun sent myriad glimmering reflections off the surface of the Yangtze River. As Peter had predicted, the junk was now abeam and to port of Kaisha Island, a large flat landmass enshrouded in the morning mist. The Jin Shayu maintained its distance behind the white boat, which hadn't deviated all night from its course in the centre of the river. The speed of the two boats remained at eight to nine knots. Cranes, swans, geese, ducks, herons, storks and the inevitable noisy seagulls flew in flocks over the numerous river craft.

Off watch, Jacko was sleeping, with Ming's head resting on his stomach. He awoke, rubbed his eyes, and sighted Jamie who was standing several yards astern of him looking intently ahead. Ming sat up and wagged his tail.

'G'day, Cap,' he said. 'How'd you sleep?'

'Like a log after I last saw you, Jacko,' replied Jamie. 'You were right. It must just have been a bad dream. I'm sure Carna wouldn't be in any trouble in the Philippines. I'm pretty relaxed about it now. Has that boat ahead stayed in the middle of the river all night?'

'Sure has, Cap,' agreed Jacko.

'I think they've taken the speed up a notch,' said Lee. 'I'll go and wake Peter below.'

Peter was soon on deck. He had a word with Fu in the wheelhouse and then joined the others at the bow.

'The river's about three miles wide just ahead, so our friends have cranked her up to eleven knots,' he said, unconsciously stroking some shape into his droopy moustache. 'Even at that speed it'll be another eight or nine hours before they get out of the river into the China Sea. So relax, guys. I've already asked Goldie and Lily to rustle up some breakfast.'

'Do you want Jacko and me to keep watch here?' asked Lee.

'Naw. After we've eaten, Harry and Johnny can take over,' said Peter. 'You guys have a nap. I'll take over the wheel to give Fu and Wing a break.'

'Now you've mentioned breakfast, I'm bloody hungry, Pete,' said Jacko, standing up stiffly and stretching.

'Should be plenty, even for you, Jacko,' Peter laughed. 'And your dog!'

'Dunno. You fellas better get in first or there mightn't be any food left,' said Jacko.

'How is it going?' asked Johnny as the others arrived down in the large cabin.

'Really burning along now, Johnny,' said Jacko. 'Pete reckons we're doing eleven knots.'

'When do we get to the mouth of the river?' asked Harry.

'About mid-afternoon,' responded Peter. 'You've still got time before you have to alert the US Navy, Harry. I'm fairly sure the USS Eaton will be the one near the delta. We'll give them a call after breakfast.'

'Perfect, Pete,' said Harry.

'Is anyone going to shoot at us in this part of the river, Pete?' asked Johnny.

'Unlikely. Anyway, we're too far from the banks.'

* * * *

'Cor Blimey!' exclaimed Nick Bradford, a short, bald, thickset man from the English Midlands.

He, Hamish McIntyre, Luke Atkins, and 'Joe' Gao Jiang stared in shock and astonishment at the unconscious Huang Lei flopped in the folding chair outside the hut.

106

'How the hell did they get out, Joe?' yelled McIntyre.

'There's a hole in the roof in the bathroom,' replied Gao. 'They got out there.'

'So! Are you telling me the old man and the young girl climbed out through the roof and overpowered Huang?' McIntyre demanded. 'Incredible!'

'Must have had help, boss,' said Gao. 'His carbine has disappeared too.'

'Can't see any of the locals helping them,' said McIntyre, who then looked at Atkins and remarked, 'They said they were from Australia, Luke. Maybe they were part of an investigation. Do you think they'd know about our setup?'

'Can't see how, Mac,' replied Luke. 'Anyway, you said one was a Frenchman and the other a Filipina. Hardly investigators from Australia.'

Luke Atkins was a tall baby-faced Australian, clean-shaven and with fair hair. He was in Samar coordinating the shipments of opium destined for Australia. He looked at the body in the tent and asked, 'Is he dead?'

'No, but he's in a bad way,' said Bradford. 'We'll have to get him inside on one of the beds.'

'When you've done that, I want you and Joe to search that bloody village. See if they're there. Be as rough as you like,' instructed McIntyre. 'Luke, come to the office with me.'

Sarah and Almado were walking through the scrub on the western side of the road and had just sighted the shed and huts ahead, when they saw two men leave the shed and walk over to the jeep parked outside on the side of the road. One of them was a short, stout, bald white man, the other Sarah recognised as the big Chinese who had locked Carna and Henri in the hut the day before.

They watched as the men drove the jeep towards Llorente and decided to continue walking to the village to see what happened. Sarah was confused about what to do when they got there. The bad men were driving Jacinto's jeep, which they had been hoping to take. Were the bad men looking for Jacinto? Did they think Carna and Henri were hiding there? What would Jacko do? She decided that Jacko would go to the village, stay concealed and have a look.

Confident now that this was the right decision, she strode along, with Almado following close behind.

They were within 100 yards of the first house in the village when Sarah stopped and stared at the dense scrub to her left. She heard someone whisper, 'Missie!' and realised it was Jacinto hiding in the bushes.

Jacinto gingerly looked out from his hiding place to confirm it was Sarah and Almado. He smiled broadly and asked, 'Where your friends, Missie?'

Almado answered for her. 'Safe at Hernani. We come to get the jeep.'

'No chance,' said Jacinto. 'Bad men are driving it.'

'Maybe we can steal it from under their noses,' suggested Almado.

'Aye yu. We steal it,' agreed Sarah.

'It will be dangerous,' said Jacinto.

Almado laughed and said, 'We know that. We'll go to the village and have a look-look.'

'Aye yu. Look-look,' repeated Sarah, smiling, then touching Jacinto on the shoulder she said carefully, 'You stay here.'

As they continued through the scrub to the village, Almado told Sarah that he was used to danger. He and his father, Angelo, had been part of the local resistance against the Japanese during the war. They had become expert in bushcraft during their time harassing the enemy. Sarah didn't quite understand it all but got the message that Almado didn't fear a bit of action. She smiled to herself.

Close to Llorente, they heard screaming coming from one of the houses and after a short while, the two armed men in the jeep emerged looking angry and strode into another house.

Almado pointed at the jeep parked in the centre of the road and whispered, 'Maybe they leave the keys in the jeep.'

Sarah nodded and said she would have a look. Almado protested, 'No, no. You are too different, Sarah. If they see me, I am just another stupid local. I'll go. If I have a chance to drive it, get ready to jump aboard when I come past.'

Sarah smiled and nodded and Almado worked his way into the village. After a while, Sarah could see him wandering nonchalantly out into the open. He slowly approached the jeep and looked at the dashboard from the side, but quickly walked away when an angry shout came from the bald man who ran out of a house waving his gun. 'Get away from there!'

In a short while, the big Chinese joined him. They spoke to each other, looked around, and walked towards the church. After they had entered, Sarah heard angry voices echoing from the building then out of the corner of her eye, she saw Almado swiftly climb into the driver's seat of the jeep and start it up. After a fast U-turn, the jeep roared down the road towards her. She stepped onto the side of the road and leapt into the passenger seat when the jeep reached her. Arriving near the place where they had left Jacinto, Almado skidded the jeep to a stop and called his name. Jacinto emerged from the bushes and leapt into the back of the jeep.

In spite of the noise of the engine at full throttle, they could hear yelling behind them and a rifle bullet whining overhead. Speeding past the bad men's huts, they were soon out of sight of the village. Almado burst into laughter and slowed down a little to a more reasonable pace for the rough road.

'This is the most exciting day I've had since the war!' he exclaimed. 'I feel like going back and beating up those bad men.'

'Hindi. No, no, no!' cried Jacinto. 'We must get out of here.'

'Walang problema! Don't worry, Jacinto,' said Almado, laughing. 'We're not going back.'

Sarah started laughing also. She wasn't quite sure why. Part of it was relief and part was being caught up in Almado's merriment. They had successfully stolen the jeep back. Jacko would approve!

CHAPTER 12

It was early afternoon when the white boat began heading for the starboard shore, well short of the delta and just before Changxing Island which divided the Yangtze River in two. Harry raced down to the cabin and woke Peter who was having an after-lunch nap.

Peter watched the white boat from the bow and said, 'They're heading for Baoshan. Looks like they plan to drop someone or something off there.

'What's at Baoshan?' asked Harry.

'It's a short drive from there into Shanghai,' said Peter. 'My guess is they'll drop someone off and then continue to the mouth of the river. I'd better radio the USS Eaton again and tell them what's happening.'

'Yeah, good idea, Pete,' said Harry as Peter climbed into the wheelhouse.

The opium boat steered straight towards a pier on the south side of the river and moored within minutes. The Jin Shayu slowed to a drifting speed with its bow pointed towards the right-hand channel while Lee and Jacko studied it carefully through binoculars.

'Someone's getting off the boat,' said Jacko. 'Dapper little fellow. I think he's the only one. He's climbed into a car and the boat has just left the pier.'

'It's on its way again, that's for sure,' said Lee.

'The destroyer should see them in two hours or so,' said Peter, 'I'll confirm that with the USS Eaton now. We'll stay on their tail to make sure.'

'Are you going to drop us off at Baoshan also?' asked Johnny.

'Nah. As soon as we reach Baoshan, I'm going up the Huang River, better known as the Huangpu, and drop you guys in style at the Bund,' said Peter with a wide grin. 'Now, I'll just make that radio call.'

They were not aware that an identical white boat, empty of cargo, was at that time passing Kaisha Island and had just picked up speed. It was motoring down the river towards Shanghai at eleven knots.

'Red' Ned Brandon, whose face was now almost the colour of his hair and beard from exposure to the sun, was up at the bow angrily muttering to himself while he studied all the other boats on the river.

Near the stern, Roddy Braithwaite sat dejected, idly gazing at the boat's wake. He was still wondering what could happened to his wolfdog, Zhiming. The dog was too smart and too well trained to accept food from strangers, but the intruders must have found a way to poison or dope him. Bloody mystery! Occasionally, he glanced at Motoi Tanaka who sat unmoving across from him, his face like a statue. I wouldn't want to get on the wrong side of him, thought Braithwaite. Assassin written all over him. We'll be in Shanghai by this evening and if the intruders are there, we'll find them and kill them. Slowly! Very slowly!

* * * *

It was raining heavily again when Henri, Carna and Sarah were saying their farewells to Angelo and his family at Hernani.

'It is a good thing if we leave now, n'est-ce pas?' said Henri to Angelo. 'I can't thank you enough for your kindness. It is my intention to set up a sawmill here when there are fewer bad men around. I will employ many local people.'

Carna translated Henri's words and then Angelo's response. 'No, no. It is me to thank you, sir,' responded Angelo. 'Again, I am sorry for being responsible for putting you and Miss Carna in such danger.'

'Non, non. Think nothing of it,' protested Henri.

Carna explained to Angelo that they should leave before danger came down the road looking for them. She said that if anyone asked him or Almado, to say they had never met them.

'Diri! No, never met you,' repeated Angelo, winking.

With a last wave, Jacinto, Henri, Carna and Sarah ran out through the rain into the vehicle and were soon slipping, sliding, and bumping down the road to Giporlos where they were sure that Manny Alvarez and his boat, with Monique and Bella aboard, would be waiting.

And waiting they were. Monique was so worried that she had left the boat and was pacing up and down in the rain. They were supposed to have returned long before now. She wanted to walk up the road to

111

look for them, but realised it was much too far. She pictured her father and the others lying injured beside the crashed jeep with no one to help them. Or worse, they had been captured by Japanese soldiers who didn't know the war was over. She had heard stories that many such units remained in the forests of the Philippines. Oh Jacko, you are so far away when we need you. She tried to stop thinking about all the other dreadful things that might have overtaken her father and friends.

Bella was sitting under cover in the boat silently sobbing, while Manny was plying her with cups of coffee and telling her that Samar was a safe place now the war had ended.

The only sounds were the rain falling, the chirping of birds in the trees and unidentifiable noises of wildlife, until everyone was alerted by the distant groans from the north of a labouring motor drawing closer. Monique started to run up the flooded road but then, realising there was no sense in that, she stopped to listen.

She jumped up and down when Jacinto's jeep suddenly appeared from around a curve in the road, swaying from side to side and throwing waves of water as it drove towards her. Next moment, Manny was beside her, waving at the jeep and advising Monique to go back to the boat and tell her mother.

As the jeep pulled up beside the pier, Henri emerged stiffly from the passenger seat while Manny assisted Carna from the back seat. He looked around to find Sarah standing beside him, staring at him with a broad smile.

'Son of a gun!' he said, 'Welcome back. We all thought you'd had an accident.'

'It's a long story,' said Carna. 'I feel like a drowned rat. We are all drowned rats.'

'Samar is drowned rat country. We'll get you some dry clothes on the boat,' said Manny. 'You can tell us your long story when we are underway. We'll be back in Cebu just after dark.'

After a quick word with Jacinto before he drove off, Manny leapt aboard the Pulo Draco, issuing orders to the crew, and in a short while the double outrigger was heading south towards the Surigao Strait.

After dressing in dry clothes and eating hot food, Henri and Carna related the story of their incarceration and rescue to a rapt audience. Their descriptions were occasionally punctuated by Manny's expression of amazement, 'Son of a gun!' Sarah was looked on with admiration by everyone present when Henri related how she had come to their rescue. She sat silently smiling, embarrassed by the attention.

* * * *

Navigating up the relatively narrow Huangpu, the Jin Shayu was almost in sight of the Bund when Harry descended from the wheelhouse to inform Johnny and the others that the USS Eaton had managed to intercept the white boat and had the crew under lock and key for interrogation. They had confirmed that the cargo comprised many tons of a substance suspected to be opium. The captain had directed US Navy personnel to crew the white boat to the Subic Bay Naval Base in the Philippines.

Within twenty minutes, the junk was secured to the pier in front of the Customs House, whose landmark clock tower was just chiming six o'clock.

'My crew'll take care of the boat. Why don't you guys buy me a cold beer at the Palace Hotel just up the road?' suggested Peter, tugging on his moustache. 'They won't worry about your dog there, Jacko.'

'Bloody good idea,' agreed Jacko. 'I'll be in that. Ming won't drink much.'

Just as Jacko was about to step ashore, he saw Lily beside him and asked her, 'How do you say goodbye in Chinese, Lily?'

'Zàijiàn,' she replied and then, grinning playfully, she said, 'Zàijiàn, kangaroo man.'

'Zàijiàn, Lily.'

'I think we might owe you lots and lots of beers, Pete,' said Jamie.

'Don't worry about that,' said Peter, laughing as they set off towards the Palace Hotel on the Bund. 'Johnny's MI6 has been paying me well and I've decided to take up Harry's offer and become a permanent part of the OSS which, I hope, will pay me equally well or even better.'

'Good for you, Pete,' said Harry. 'The drinks are on me.'

Sitting up at the bar of the Palace Hotel with cold beer in their hands, the talk was humorous and light-hearted until Johnny asked Lee, 'Are there many British army platoons still around in Shanghai?'

'Yes. Four or five that I know of,' replied Lee. 'They're stationed here to help keep order until the government can take over control.'

'What about commandoes?'

'Yes. At least one of them is a commando unit, Sir,' Lee responded. 'They're stationed in and around the old rowing club this side of the Suzhou Creek, maybe 100 yards west of the bridge to the Astor House Hotel.'

'Do you know any of them, Lee?'

'No. I usually stay away from the army,' Lee chuckled. 'I'm supposed to be a local, remember?'

'Yes, yes. Of course,' said Johnny. 'I might go and see their commanding officer tomorrow and ask if they're prepared to help with the complete destruction of that opium treatment facility up the Yangtze.'

'Don't see why they wouldn't be, sir.'

'Enough of talking shop, you guys,' interrupted Peter loudly. 'It's time for another beer, and you're wasting good drinking time.'

* * * *

It was a gala affair, entertaining most of the influential dignitaries in Shanghai at the palatial house of Soong Tse-ven, better known as T.V. Soong. He was a commanding figure, a handsome man in his early fifties, with horn-rimmed glasses and a ready smile. A Harvard and Columbia alumnus, he spoke English with a cultured American accent.

He was deep in conversation with the US Consul General, along with his elder sister, Soong Ai-Ling, who was married to the wealthy H.H. Kung, Finance Minister of China, when he heard his doorman announce the arrival of the acting British Consul General.

Excusing himself, he walked over to personally welcome Sir William Founding. 'Greetings, Sir William,' he enthused, shaking him by the hand. 'I trust you had a pleasant trip. Now let's find a quiet corner.' He handed Sir William a glass of French champagne and led him out to the dark terrace overlooking the garden.

'Fine party, T.V.,' said Sir William, gazing out into the garden lit by multi-coloured electric lights hidden in the shrubbery.

'Yes, yes. Thank you, Sir William,' said Soong to the dapper but diminutive man beside him. 'How is our little Yangtze venture going?'

'Going well, T.V.,' said Sir William. 'I came in on the boat earlier today. It had more than eighteen tons of merchandise aboard and should be well on the way to our base in the Philippines to be hidden amongst the copra ready for final shipment.'

'Good. Good. That's excellent,' said Soong, nodding. 'So, no problems, eh?'

'Things have been a bit tense since the shooting of that British agent,' said Sir William. 'There have been no more incidents, so I expect things to settle down.'

Another man appeared on the terrace, smoking a cigar. He was a chubby Chinese with a round face and a shadow of a moustache.

'I thought I saw you disappear out here,' he said behind a puff of cigar smoke. 'Is there anything I should know?'

'I don't know if you've met my brother-in-law, Sir William,' said Soong. 'H.H. Kung, originally from Guangxi. Married to my elder sister. This is Sir William Founding, attached to the British Consulate in Shanghai.'

The two men bowed to each other and Soong continued, 'Sir William has just returned from our little venture up the Yangtze. Everything is going well there.'

'Ah! Good. Good. Wonderful way to expatriate hard currency,' said Kung. 'Spend the money here, make the profits overseas.'

'H.H. is always thinking only of money, Sir William,' said Soong, laughing. 'We should return to my guests.'

After the banquet, when more food had been left on the tables than eaten, the old grandfather clock in the hallway was chiming midnight. One of the servants approached Sir William and whispered in his ear.

115

A look of astonishment crossed his face and he hurried to the front door where he was confronted by the slightly bedraggled figure of Ned Brandon.

After a brief urgent discussion, Sir William rushed back inside looking for his host. Finding him in one of the drawing rooms, he pulled him aside and asked to meet him on the terrace.

'Are you telling me that someone attacked our facility again?' demanded Soong. 'This time they got away?'

'Yes. It must have happened soon after I left on the boat,' replied Sir William. 'Some of my men have just arrived in Shanghai to inform me.'

'What about the boat you arrived in, Sir William?' asked Soong.

'That is safely away in the China Sea and should be in Samar in a few days,' said Sir William.

'Well, that's a blessing. Can you find out who the saboteurs were?'

'If they're British, I might be able to find out through my office, T.V.'

'How much damage, Sir William?'

'I'm meeting with the men in the morning. I'll let you know after that. I should leave now and bid you goodnight.'

'When you find out who the saboteurs are, crush them,' said Soong angrily. 'I'll let H.H. Kung know. Ciao!'

* * * *

The following morning, Jacko awoke and briefly wondered where he was. There was a soft sound of snoring beside him and when he turned, the snoring stopped and he found himself looking into the eyes of Ming, whose tongue was hanging out of the side of his mouth in expectation. He remembered that since the Astor House Hotel had a strict ban on dogs, Lee had suggested Jacko camp at his pad in the old city. Ming would not leave Jacko's side.

After he had washed, he found Lee boiling up some tea in the kitchenette. 'I'd better take my friend for a walk, before he feels the need to irrigate your flat,' said Jacko.

'Have a quick cup of green tea, then we'll all go for a walk,' said Lee. 'There are many trees which need irrigation between here and a little restaurant where I usually have my breakfast.'

'Sounds perfect to me,' said Jacko. 'Nice little hideaway you have here.'

'Yeah, "hideaway" is right,' said Lee, chuckling. 'I was here during the whole Japanese occupation sending messages to MI6.'

'How did you send messages?' asked Jacko.

'There's a small radio hidden in that bench seat you were sleeping beside,' said Lee. 'Anyway, let's go. I'm hungry.'

'Me too,' agreed Jacko. 'Ming also. He could eat a whole bandit right now.'

When they reached the restaurant, they were engulfed by a torrent of greetings, 'Ni hao! Ni hao! Ni hao! Zao shang hao! Ni hao!' and many smiles while a waiter raced off to find a goat's shank for Ming.

Meanwhile, after an early breakfast at the hotel, Johnny and Jamie were wandering down the south side of Suzhou Creek west from the bridge looking for the old rowing club. Inside the old building, they found a young officer, slim, clean-shaven with curly brown hair, poring over some maps with three other soldiers.

He noticed the two men standing at the door and asked, 'Hello. Is there anything I can do for you gentlemen?'

Followed by Jamie, Johnny walked in and said, 'My name is Colonel John Cook. I was hoping to find the commandoes' headquarters. Is this it?'

'Indeed it is,' agreed the officer. 'I am Captain Jeremy Cowper. Which unit are you from, Colonel?'

'I'm no longer with the military. I'm with MI6,' said Johnny, showing Cowper an identification badge and shaking him by the hand. 'This is my colleague, James Munro from Australia.'

'Ah, yes. Anything I can do for you, sir?'

'Well, yes, there could be,' said Johnny. 'What are you chaps involved in at the present time?'

'Ours is just a peace-keeping role at the moment, sir,' said Cowper. 'We're here to hold the fort until the Chinese government can take over full control. We've also been assisting ex-pat British citizens who've run into trouble or need help to leave China. I can't tell you how boring it's been.'

'So basically cooling your heels, eh Jeremy?' said Johnny. 'I've got a proposition I'd like to put to you. It has the sanction of the governments of Britain and the United States.'

'I'm all ears, Colonel,' said Cowper. Indicating his companions, he said, 'I should introduce some of my NCOs. This is my right-hand man, Sergeant Bill Smythe. These other two fellows are Corporal Tony Bray and Corporal Tod Burnside. We call them the two TBs.'

'Nice to meet all you chaps,' said Johnny. 'Let's sit down, and I'll give you the full story.'

'Sounds interesting,' said Cowper, indicating some chairs. 'How about rustling up some tea, Tod?'

'Coming up in a few minutes, Captain.'

When they were all seated, Johnny explained about the opium field and treatment plant up the Yangtze River opposite Tongling. He described the earlier loss of one of the MI6 operatives, their recent trip upriver, and the sabotage to the opium plant. He also detailed the cruise down the river in pursuit of a boat laden with tons of opium, subsequently taken into custody by the US Navy.

'Their confederates in Shanghai would probably know about the sabotage by now,' added Johnny. 'I doubt they would know their shipment's been hijacked by the US Navy yet though. The navy boys are going to keep it quiet.'

'Looks like you chaps have been busy, what?' said Cowper. 'Is there some action in it for us?'

'That's what I was going to propose,' replied Johnny.

'We'd welcome it,' said Cowper, smiling. 'Our only excitement in recent weeks has been conducting mock battles in the swamps and paddies of Pudong, the other side of the Huangpu.'

'We believe the sabotage to the opium plant near Tongling is only a temporary setback for the criminals,' explained Johnny. 'If your men could go in there and make a proper job of it, there'd be a lot of happy people amongst our allies. I'll give you a map of the area.'

'Perfect job for us,' said Cowper. 'I will have to mention it to our Consul General in Shanghai, as the powers that be are a bit sensitive about the situation at the moment.'

'So, you have to get it approved by the powers that be?' asked Johnny.

'Well, I'll mention it, but I didn't say I won't do it if they don't like it,' said Cowper, winking and laughing. 'Where can I reach you, Colonel?'

'We're at the Astor House, the other side of the creek,' Johnny replied. 'I'd prefer it if the powers that be didn't know where we're staying. I'll come back here later on anyway to see how you've got on.'

'Good-oh! I'll set off for the consulate now,' said Cowper. 'I should be back by late morning, though you never know with these political types. In the meantime, Sergeant Smythe can organise our equipment.'

'It's a fairly long trip up the Yangtze,' said Jamie. 'You'll need a good fast boat.'

'No problem there. We've got such a boat at our disposal,' Cowper responded. 'See you later in the morning.'

As they all walked out of the old rowing club, he waved and said, 'Ciao!'

CHAPTER 13

Sir William Founding pushed a stray lock of hair back from his forehead and held the telephone receiver to his ear. He stared at the view of the immaculate garden through the window of the Consul General's office without seeing it, his anger almost overwhelming him.

'For God's sake! There must be someone who knows something, Ned,' he said with exasperation. 'These people are not ghosts. They must have a base in Shanghai. Check the hotels, restaurants, clubs, brothels. Ask around, for God's sake! Call me again as soon as you've got something.'

Simmering, he slammed the phone down, then idly watched barges navigating the Huangpu in the distance.

There was a knock on the door and a young English secretary poked her head into the room. 'Sir?'

'What?' he yelled, making her jump.

'Someone to see you, sir.'

'Er... yes. Sorry,' he apologised. 'Who is it?'

'It's Captain Cowper, sir,' she said in a quavering voice. 'He says he's with the 4th commando assault group.'

'Ask him to wait,' said Sir William curtly.

Commando assault group? What the hell is that? he asked himself. With Sir Alwyne away, there are too many things to deal with I don't know anything about. Too many things! He glanced once more out the window and then pressed the button on his desk. When she opened the door, he asked the secretary to show Captain Cowper in.

The officer who entered had an erect military bearing but to Sir William, his boyish face made him seem far too young to be an officer in an assault group.

'Yes. What is it, Captain?' he asked briskly.

'I was looking for Sir Alwyne Ogden, sir,' replied Cowper.

'Sir Alwyne is temporarily overseas, Captain,' said Sir William. 'I'm the acting Consul General while he's away. I'm Sir William Founding. What can I do for you?'

'Ah... er... we've had a request from MI6,' said Cowper, who did not know the man behind the desk.

'MI6? What does MI6 want?' asked Sir William.

'We've been asked to destroy the base of a smuggling enterprise,' said Cowper. 'It's a two- or three-day operation. I thought I should let you know.'

'A smuggling operation? Where?' asked Sir William, suddenly alert.

'I believe it's about 300 miles up the Yangtze River, Sir. Near Tongling,' said Cowper. 'MI6 and the US authorities are involved.'

Sir William coughed and glared at him. 'We can't take these matters into our own hands, Captain. The politics are sensitive. We have to let the Chinese government handle this type of thing. Who have you spoken to?'

'Colonel Cook, sir. He's from MI6 London,' said Cowper. 'He says the British and US governments are keen for us to go ahead with the demolition.'

'Hmm. Leave it to me, Captain,' said Sir William tersely. 'I'll contact the local Chinese government authorities and get them to handle it. Where is this Colonel Cook staying?'

'I don't know, sir,' Cowper said, saluting and marching to the door.

As soon as the door closed behind him, Sir William smiled, humming a happy tune under his breath, and picked up the telephone.

* * * *

Hamish McIntyre studied the new arrival who had just arrived from Tacloban in a 4x4 Dodge truck. He was a large man, a good fifteen stone, with small, close-set, glaucous eyes under a straight incongruous eyebrow extending over both eyes. The absence of good looks in his plump amorphous face was offset by a strong authoritative manner. In a refined London accent, he introduced himself as Trevor Clark, an associate of the Chinese Soong family.

'We were expecting you earlier,' said McIntyre cautiously. 'We had a visit from a middle-aged Frenchman whom we thought, at first, was you.'

121

'A Frenchman?' queried Clark, raising one side of his single eyebrow. 'You thought he was me? What did you do with him?'

'We locked him up together with his Filipina interpreter for you to interrogate, but they escaped,' explained McIntyre. 'They seemed to have no idea about our operations.'

'Yes, well, I hope not,' said Clark. 'Where did you lock them up?'

'In one of the demountables,' replied McIntyre. 'Huang Lei was on guard but somehow they knocked him out. They escaped through the roof of the hut.'

'My God! Where did they go?' asked Clark, a look of astonishment crossing his large face.

'We don't know,' said McIntyre, nervously tugging at his beard. 'We've questioned the people in the local villages up and down the coast. No one admits to any knowledge of them.'

'No, they wouldn't, would they,' said Clark gravely. 'To business! I came to tell you that you can expect the next boat from the Yangtze River in a day or so. Have you enough merchandise ready for the shipment to Australia?'

'Ten tons of copra with four tons of opium secreted inside the bundles,' replied McIntyre. 'We expect the freighter later in the week. Luke Atkins will accompany that cargo to our Australian depot.'

'Jolly good,' said Clark. 'At least you've got that properly organised, even if you can't contain stray Frenchmen. The Yangtze riverboat will have eighteen to twenty tonnes of opium aboard, more than enough for the next shipment to the United States. You'll need about forty-eight tons of copra to bundle up with that lot.'

'We've got about twenty tons of copra here already, Mr Clark,' said McIntyre. 'Nick Bradford is confident we can buy another forty tons from the local farmers in the next week or so.'

'Good. I must say, the smell of all that copra is putrid,' said Clark, squeezing his pudgy nose. 'Don't know how you stand it.'

'You get used to it after a while,' said McIntyre. 'The stink deters customs from looking too closely at the shipments.'

'Yes. That's so.'

'Will you be going back to China on the Yangtze riverboat when it arrives, Mr Clark?'

'No. I've got an aeroplane waiting for me in Tacloban,' explained Clark. 'I'll be flying back to Shanghai. So, can I report that everything is going well here?'

'Yes, we don't foresee any problems,' said McIntyre. 'Other than a strange Frenchman.'

Clark laughed. 'I wouldn't worry too much about that, old man. I can't see British or American intelligence using a middle-aged Frenchman to check into the remote areas of the eastern Philippines. Does it rain like this all the time?'

'Yes. Most of the time.'

* * * *

In the late morning, Jamie and Johnny were standing at the southern approach to the Suzhou Creek bridge discussing the possibility of the commando involvement in the demolition of the opium treatment centre. Many locals were crossing back and forth across the bridge.

'Jeremy Cowper should be back from the consulate soon, Jamie,' Johnny was saying. 'If you go and wait for him, I'll join you in about half an hour. There are a couple of things I need to get from my room in the hotel.'

'Do you know where Harry is?' asked Jamie.

'He and Peter would be with the American Consul General by now, in the Glen Line Building about fifty yards from where we're standing,' said Johnny. 'Jacko and Lee will be dropping by the hotel around midday.'

'Okay, I'll see you shortly,' said Jamie, waving as he headed towards the old rowing club.

When he arrived, Jeremy Cowper had not yet returned but Corporal Tony Bray suggested he wait in the planning room while he brewed up a pot of tea. Jamie and Tony were poring over some maps of the Yangtze River when Jeremy appeared twenty minutes later.

'Hi, Jamie,' he greeted him. Glancing at the maps spread out on the table, he asked, 'Where's our MI6 man?'

'Johnny should be here any moment,' Jamie replied. 'How'd you get on with the Consul General?'

'Unfortunately, Sir Alwyne Ogden, whom I know well, wasn't there,' replied Jeremy. 'The acting CG is Sir William Founding who I haven't met before. He was insistent that the Chinese government could handle the situation and we should have nothing to do with your baddies at all.'

'That's disappointing,' said Jamie. 'I would have thought the government was too busy fighting a civil war with the communists to worry about an opium operation.'

'I would think so too,' agreed Jeremy. 'When I was talking to Sir William, I was reminded of a Shakespearian quotation: "That man doth protest too much, methinks." I felt a bit uncomfortable. I did mention Colonel Cook but I didn't tell Sir William where he was staying.'

'Speaking of whom, Johnny should have been here by now,' said Jamie. 'I have an uneasy feeling about this too. I think I'd better go and check on him.'

'I'll come with you,' said Jeremy. 'I hope I haven't dropped a clanger. If Sir William told anyone else in the consulate about Johnny Cook, it wouldn't be hard to track down his hotel.'

On arrival at the Astor House Hotel, Jeremy and Jamie spoke to a nervous receptionist who informed him they had missed Colonel Cook by about ten minutes. On further questioning, between sobs, she told them that Colonel Cook had been accompanied by two rough-looking foreigners and a scary man who looked like a Japanese. Colonel Cook was bleeding from the nose and mouth and the men had to drag him from the hotel.

'Did you call the police?' asked Jamie.

'It's no good calling the police,' said Jeremy. 'Most of them are Japanese police contracted by the government until it can take full control of Shanghai. They'll soon be going back to Japan and they're not interested.'

'Can we have the key to his room?' asked Jamie.

'Sir, he has his key,' she said tearfully. 'I have a master key. I shall open the door for you.'

The master key wasn't necessary as the door had been smashed in and the lock broken. There were signs of a struggle; furniture overturned and broken glass. Jamie and Jeremy looked at each other, baffled.

Jamie asked the receptionist, 'Did you tell them what room he was in?'

'Yes, sir,' she replied in a small voice. 'They threatened me.'

Jeremy scratched his cheek. 'I wonder how they knew what hotel he was in.'

The receptionist, through a flood of tears, blurted out, 'A gentleman called earlier and asked if the colonel was staying here. I couldn't deny it.'

'Don't worry. It's not your fault,' said Jamie.

'Sir William must have told someone else,' he said thoughtfully. 'Unless he's involved.'

When they returned to the ground floor, Jacko and Lee were standing at the reception desk. They could see the dog, Ming, sitting obediently outside the front door.

Jacko took one look at them and said, 'You look like you've seen a ghost. What's happened?'

'Johnny's been beaten up and abducted,' explained Jamie. 'Couple of white men and a Japanese. I'll get the receptionist to describe them for me. You fellows haven't met Jeremy Cowper. He's in charge of a commando unit. These fellows are Jacko O'Brien and Lee Drake.'

'Good to meet you, Jeremy,' said Jacko, as he and Lee shook hands with the commando. 'I've got a lot of respect for commandoes.'

'Glad to meet you chaps,' said Jeremy. 'I might have been the one to let the cat out of the bag. I mentioned Colonel Cook's name at the consulate this morning.'

'While you're getting those descriptions, Cap, I'll just slip up to Johnny's room and see if I can find some laundry,' said Jacko. 'It's 102, right?'

'Laundry?'

When Jacko joined them again on the ground floor, he had a bundle of clothes under his arm.

Jeremy laughed and said, 'Funny time to be running a laundry service.'

'I want to test the nose of a close friend of mine,' said Jacko, pointing to the dog on the front step. 'I'm totally lost in a big city, but Ming might be able to find his way around. There's some rather choice underwear here. If he has a good sniff of it, it might give him a decent trail to follow.'

'He'll have to have a good nose,' said Jeremy. 'There's a million smells in this city.'

'Yeah, it'll be a good test for him,' said Jacko, going outside to sit on the steps next to the large wolfdog. Lee went outside and joined him.

Shortly, Jacko returned with the bundle of clothes and dumped them on the desk, asking the receptionist if it was possible to have them washed.

Behind him, Jeremy laughed and said, 'Are you asking her if there are any Chinese laundries in China?'

'Er... yeah. I see what you mean,' said Jacko, as the smiling receptionist gathered up the clothes. Before returning to Ming and Lee outside, he told them he still had a pair of Johnny's underpants in his back pocket.

'Your friend seems to have a lot of confidence in that dog,' Jeremy said to Jamie, who was writing down the descriptions of the abductors given by the receptionist.

Jamie picked up his notebook and said, 'If Jacko's confident, he's probably right.'

'Do you fellas want to gabble all day, or do want to come with us?' Jacko yelled from the front door.

'We're coming! We're coming,' responded Jamie, heading to the door with Jeremy.

The Bund was alive with civilians of all nationalities, American GIs, horses, motor cars and rickshaws, none of which seemed to distract Ming who trotted ahead of the men, occasionally looking back to make sure they were still there. Passing the Cathay Hotel, he sniffed around, with curious passers-by watching him, and then ducked up Nanjing Road to the right. After trotting for two blocks, Ming started to run, weaving through the crowds until the men, who were running as hard as possible, were unable to keep up and the dog disappeared into the distance, where Nanjing Road ran past the Shanghai Race Club course.

They stopped, and a panting Jeremy said, 'I hope your dog knows what he's doing, Jacko. I know what I'm going to do. I'm going to get the troops together and take a cruise up the Yangtze River. The information about Colonel Cook was relayed to your kidnappers by someone in the consulate. We'll blow up that opium establishment for you, and damn the consulate!'

'Good one, Jeremy,' said Jamie. 'Anything else you need from us?'

'No. I've got the map, Jamie. Good hunting. Hope you find your dog.'

'You're a man after my own heart, Jeremy,' said Jacko.

After Jeremy Cowper had disappeared up one of the side streets towards Suzhou Creek, Lee looked at Jacko and asked, 'What about your dog?'

'He'll be back,' replied Jacko confidently, 'I'm sure he'll find us if we stay on this road. We'll just keep wandering in the same direction.'

'Nothing much else we can do,' agreed Lee. 'There's about a million places Johnny could have been taken. I know Shanghai pretty well, but it's a big city.'

'Perhaps if we come across a small restaurant, we could have a cup of tea,' said Jamie, smiling. 'The British always reckon a cup of tea solves everything.'

'Good thinking, Cap,' Jacko chuckled. 'If they've got a lamb shank, Ming would be able to smell it from miles away.'

'There's a nice little place a bit further up the road on the corner of Fujian Road,' offered Lee. 'Good tea. Can't promise the lamb shank.'

'Ming's not fussy, Lee,' said Jacko. 'Any meaty bone will do.'

'Don't forget to say "ni hao", Jacko,' said Lee.

'No worries. I've got that down pat.'

* * * *

Peter Jackson and Harry Williams were seated across a desk from the chief of the consulate, General Walter McConaughy, who had just received a message from his attaché.

'Just had a wire from the USS Eaton which will interest you, gentlemen,' he said. 'One of the crew of the opium boat told them it had been bound for the east coast of Samar.'

'Samar?' responded Peter, puzzled.

'Samar is the most eastern of the Philippines Visayan Islands,' explained Harry. 'Just east of Leyte where the first landings took place.'

'Do you know it well, Harry?' asked General McConaughy.

'Never been there,' admitted Harry. 'I've been close to there in Surigao. I believe Samar is a large producer of copra for export.'

'Well, you know more than I do,' said General McConaughy. 'But then the Philippines is your jurisdiction. Are there any big towns on the east coast of Samar?'

'Not that I know of, General,' said Harry.

'Why Samar?' asked Peter.

'I'll have to do some research,' said Harry. 'Must be a reason.'

'Well, whoever's expecting that boat has a long wait ahead,' observed General McConaughy. 'I'm sure we can leave it to you and your OSS to find out why, Harry.'

'Yes, thanks, General.'

'Glad you could drop in, gentlemen,' he said. 'Call my attaché if you need any more help while you're in Shanghai.'

'Thank you, sir. You've been a great help already,' said Harry as he and Peter shook hands with him and headed for the door.

Outside the Glen Line Building, the Bund was as crowded and noisy as ever, pedestrians, rickshaws, horses, and the occasional motor car rushing up and down the waterfront.

'I'm not going to take you all the way to Samar in the Jin Shayu, Harry,' said Peter with a humorous glint in his eye.

'Never going to ask you, Pete,' Harry laughed. 'I wonder what's happened to our Brits and Australians?'

'If they're not back at your hotel, I must tell you it's a big city, Harry,' said Peter. 'While you decide which direction to walk in, how about some Chinese food?'

'You've got a great idea there, Pete. Lead the way.'

More than a mile to the west, Jamie, Jacko, and Lee were on their third pot of green tea and had just started to eat from a large dish of dumplings when they heard a yelp and Ming emerged from the crowded pavement and sat beside Jacko with his tongue hanging out.

'Good boy! You found us,' said Jacko admiringly and then holding his nose added, 'God, you smell awful, Ming. Where have you been?'

'I think I know where he's been,' said Lee. 'Between here and Avenue Joffre in the French Concession, there's a swampy area. It's about half a mile south of us. When the sewerage overflows, which it often does, it flows into that swamp. It smells just like that.'

'Do you think they've taken Johnny to a swamp?' asked Jamie.

'No, but there are a lot of old buildings around it. He could be in any one of those or somewhere beyond that area,' explained Lee. 'The swamp wouldn't have done Ming's nose any good.'

'Doesn't matter. We'll order a shank for Ming now. He looks hungry,' said Jacko. 'After that, I'll give him a good sniff of Johnny's underpants and we'll all get underway.'

'Okay. I just hope Ming's as good as you think he is,' said Lee.

'You know where Johnny is, don't you Ming?' said Jacko. The dog looked at him and wagged his tail. 'See? I told you. Ming's got the whole thing sorted. Let's get that shank bone before he jacks up on us.'

Lee and Jamie glanced at each other, shaking their heads. Twenty minutes later, Jacko gave the underpants to Ming to sniff and the trio set off south along Fujian Street following Ming, who had to weave through occasional crowds of pedestrians but maintained a steady walking pace.

CHAPTER 14

Johnny Cook slowly regained consciousness. He had no idea where he was, but he was well aware of the beating he had endured. He was lying on a hard floor unable to open his eyes because they were clotted with blood. He wondered grimly if there were any parts of his body that didn't hurt. They must have tired of beating him when he'd passed out. He gritted his teeth – even that hurt. If he could just stand up, but the mere effort of raising his head increased the ringing in his ears to a roaring and he lay back, panting. It was useless. He couldn't find the strength to sit up, let alone stand. He was sure they would kill him when they returned.

Who were they? Something to do with the opium shipments, for sure. They knew his name, but how could they have connected him with the sabotage of the opium treatment plant?

He tried to look around but could only see out of tiny slits between the clotted blood. The room looked like an empty hotel room. Some old curtains and furniture. He felt a carpet or mat underneath him. Unpleasant smell. His underpants were wet where he had urinated on himself. The pervasive smell was more than that. He tried to keep his brain working. If I give in to despair, I might as well be dead already, he thought.

By now, the others would know he had been abducted. There was no way they would ever be able to find him in such a large city. Millions of people. The locals not particularly sympathetic to foreigners. Any witnesses would not want to get involved. He thought of his father who always used the phrase 'fine kettle of fish' when things went wrong. I'm certainly in a fine kettle of fish now. This thought made him want to smile but only succeeded in reminding him how cut and chapped his lips were. Let's face it, Johnny old boy, you've had it.

* * * *

The crowds thinned along Fujian Road as they approached the open swamp area, and the smell grew stronger. Ming confidently led the way along the eastern perimeter of the swamp, with his tongue out and ears alert. There were a number of fine old buildings on the far side of the swamp in various stages of disrepair.

'Johnny could be held prisoner in any one of those buildings,' said Jamie.

'If he is, I reckon it's got to be one of those in the centre, Cap,' said Jacko, concentrating on the view ahead.

'Why do you say that, Jacko?' asked Jamie.

'Ming was carrying some of the swamp with him when he found us, Cap,' said Jacko. 'Stands to reason. After following Johnny's scent around the swamp and finding the right building, he took a direct line back across the swamp to try and find us.'

'Makes sense,' agreed Lee.

'Yeah, maybe,' said Jamie. 'We'll see where he leads us.'

'He seems to know where he's going,' said Lee.

'He knows all right,' said Jacko with more confidence than he felt.

After passing the swamp, Ming turned to the right and led them west along the pavement opposite a row of old buildings. He suddenly stopped and growled, then looked back at Jacko. A man had just walked out of one of the buildings in the centre of the row, a narrow four-storey mansion with a marble façade and columns on either side of the entrance. Jacko and the others hid quickly with Ming amongst some bushes, from where they could observe the man on the opposite side of the street.

'Ming knows him, for sure,' said Jacko.

The man was of medium height, plump, with curly black hair and a bushy, untidy moustache. He lit a cigarette and looked around while he smoked. Eventually, he threw away the butt, held his nose, and went back inside.

'Must have gone out for some fresh air,' said Jacko, chuckling.

'Yeah. Very fresh,' said Jamie, also holding his nose. 'Do you think Johnny's in there?'

'I'm sure of it, Cap.'

'What do you suggest, Jacko?' asked Jamie. 'I'm sure you've been hatching a plan.'

'Not fully hatched yet, Cap,' replied Jacko. 'Lee and I will cross the street and walk up to the front of the building. If nobody takes any notice of us, we'll duck inside and look for Johnny. You and Ming should stay here and watch for any suspicious characters entering the building. Ming will probably growl if he knows them. Give us a loud hoot to warn us.'

'Okay. Are you both armed?' asked Jamie.

'I am, Cap. Loaded pistol and my trusty knife,' said Jacko. 'Lee doesn't need to be armed.'

'I've got a good knife, Jacko,' said Lee.

'That'll do. Okay, let's go,' said Jacko. 'Stay here, Ming. Stay, boy!'

The dog gave a low groan as Jacko and Lee walked across the street and started along the pavement towards the front door of the building. Reaching the door, Jacko looked around, patted Lee on the shoulder, and both men disappeared into the doorway. The building was surprisingly cool after the outside heat and humidity. It was also very quiet. It seemed deserted. They carefully searched the ground floor and then crept up a marble stairway to the first floor. Rooms led off a wide, dimly-lit corridor over the length of the building. Moving quietly to the nearest door, Jacko opened it using downward pressure on the handle to minimise noise. The room was empty.

Opening the second door on the same side of the corridor, there was a screech as the rusted hinges protested. A voice from further up the corridor yelled, 'Is that you, Ned?'

Lee froze, uncertain about what to do. He then saw Jacko move like a speeding shadow in the semi-darkness towards the source of the voice and in an instant, heard a thump and a gurgle followed by silence.

'Jacko?' he called softly.

'Up here, mate,' said Jacko, emerging from one of the doors. 'I think he's the only one. Let's find Johnny.'

After throwing open several more doors, they found one locked. The doors were solid timber and it took three well-aimed kicks before the old door gave way, revealing the figure of a man lying in the middle of the floor.

Jacko knelt down beside him and felt his pulse, saying, 'Johnny. Can you hear me?'

A grimace of pain crossed Johnny's face, his eyes flickered, and he emitted a dull groan.

'He's been badly beaten, Lee,' said Jacko. 'We'll need something to carry him on. Let's see if we can find a light cot or something.'

'Yes, he's in a bad way,' said Lee, then grabbing Jacko by the arm he added, 'I hesitate to ask this, Jacko, but what did you do to that criminal in the other room?'

'Yeah, don't ask, Lee,' said Jacko. 'Let's see what we can find to get Johnny out of here.'

After searching some of the rooms on the same floor, the best they could find was a thin, stiff, single mattress. Holding the ends of a blanket spread beneath it, they decided they would be able to carry Johnny through the streets without causing him too much pain.

They put the mattress over the blanket next to Johnny's prone figure and carefully rolled him onto it with much groaning and moaning from Johnny.

'I think all his ribs are broken, Jacko,' observed Lee.

'If we don't get him out of here, those bastards will break more than that,' said Jacko grimly. 'Let me know when you're ready to lift your end.'

Lifting the whole bundle off the floor, they carefully stepped out into the corridor and walked towards the stairs.

On the other side of the street, Jamie became alert when he saw a large red-haired man with a red beard. He was walking towards the building. Jamie put his hands on either side of his mouth and let out a loud owl hoot, although to him it sounded more like a roar. The large man looked around, shook his head, and entered the doorway.

Lee, Jacko and their load were halfway down the stairs when they heard the hoot from Jamie and they were carefully laying Johnny down across one of the steps when they heard someone yell out from the bottom of the stairway, 'What the hell are you doing?'

They were facing a large red-bearded man with a revolver pointed straight up at them.

'We are just cleaners, sir,' said Lee in a humble Chinese accent.

'Yeah, and pigs may fly,' growled the man. 'Come down here where I can see you.'

In the next instant, a shadow moved swiftly through the doorway and in a flash, the man dropped his gun when Ming bit into his arm with a loud growl.

'Good boy, Ming,' said Jacko, leaping down the stairs, picking up the revolver, and whacking the big man over the head with it. As he fell in a heap, Ming was at his throat until Jacko called him off.

'That's okay, Ming. He won't be going anywhere for a while,' said Jacko. 'Come on, Lee. Let's get Johnny down the stairs before anything else happens.'

'I'll give you a hand,' said Jamie who had just entered. 'Did you hear my hoot?'

'We heard it all right, Cap,' said Jacko, laughing. 'Sounded like an eagle owl being strangled.'

'How's Johnny?'

'He's in a bad way, Cap,' replied Jacko. 'We'll have to carry him all the way to the old city where Lee reckons we can hide him.'

They had just emerged from the doorway when they were confronted by a Japanese policeman.

'Nani shiteru no? What you doing?' he demanded.

They all stared at him for a moment and then Jamie stepped forward and said, 'We have a very sick man here. Do you speak English?'

'Hai! Yes! Speak some Ingrish,' said the policeman. 'Ret me rook at him.'

Jacko and Lee laid their load down gently and pushed back the blankets. Jacko had his hand on the haft of his knife as the policeman peered at Johnny.

'This man has been tortured,' said the policeman. 'Looks like Kempeitai torture.'

'Kempeitai torture?' exclaimed Jamie.

'Hai! During war the Kempeitai tortured many people in Shanghai,' said the policeman. 'Very bad. I do not rike Kempeitai.'

'So, you won't object if we carry our friend here to safety?' asked Jamie.

134

'Carry dangerous,' said the policeman. 'Ribcage corrapse. I help you. I get car, take you to safe place. Wait here. Won't take rong.'

They looked at each other as the policeman trotted off.

Jamie nervously looked up and down the street then spoke to the others, 'Do you think the Kempeitai are involved with this?'

'I thought they'd been disbanded,' said Lee. 'Maybe they have a Kempeitai thug working for them.'

'Do you trust that policeman?' asked Jamie.

'Seemed all right to me,' said Jacko. 'I'm not sure we'd be able to carry Johnny all the way to the old city without killing him.'

'Yeah, well, let's hope none of the other gang members show up,' said Jamie. 'Particularly that Kempeitai bloke. Here comes the policeman now, I think.'

Two cars pulled up in front of the building, one an open Lincoln from which emerged the policeman, the other a 1930s Oldsmobile.

'I borrowed Rincoln from a friend,' said the policeman. 'Good back seat wounded man to rie down.'

'That's great,' said Jacko. 'You have probably saved his life. We don't even know your name.'

'Ah, so! Name Seiki Abe,' he said, bowing.

After introducing themselves to Seiki, they all carefully lifted Johnny with the mattress underneath onto the back seat of the Lincoln.

'That's good. One of you come with me. The rest in other car,' said Seiki. 'You all Ingrish?'

'Jacko and I are from Australia,' said Jamie.

'Ah. Too hard for Japanese to pronounce,' said Seiki, smiling. 'I say Straya.'

'That'll do, Seiki,' said Jacko. 'We'd better get going before any more thugs show up.'

'Hai, hai. You correct,' said Seiki, jumping into the driver's seat of the Lincoln. 'Ret's go.'

Jamie sat beside Seiki in the front seat while Jacko and Lee got into the Oldsmobile. It was quickly ascertained that their driver did not speak English. The two cars carefully weaved through the narrow streets towards the old Chinese City to the southeast.

After a long, slow journey, they stopped outside an old Ming Dynasty three-storey building with an ornate Chinese roof and elegant doorway flanked by bulbous red lanterns. Seiki Abe jumped out of the lead car and beckoned to the others.

'We carry your man inside,' he said, opening the back door of the Lincoln.

With infinite care, they carried Johnny up to the first floor where Seiki led them into a room with a bed on which they gently lowered their groaning colleague.

'I get help,' said Seiki, scampering to the door. 'Not rong. Wait.'

In a nearby washroom, Jamie found a clean towel. He wet it and carefully mopped Johnny's sweating forehead. After a while, his groaning subsided to a low moan and the men stood around, not sure what to do.

In a short while, Seiki returned with a short Japanese doctor and two young nurses, one Japanese, one Chinese.

'This Doctor Nakamura. He rook at patient,' he said.

As they all watched the doctor carry out his examination, Seiki introduced the two nurses as Yuko and Yuan. He said they would stay and look after Johnny until he was recovered. He told them not to worry. Neither the doctor nor the nurses would say anything about the patient to anyone.

The doctor finished his examination of Johnny and spoke to Seiki in Japanese. The others didn't know what they said but twice heard the word 'Kempeitai' from the doctor. The latter said a few words to the Japanese nurse, Yuko, bowed to the men, and left.

'He say your friend in bad way,' explained Seiki. 'Broken ribs, fracture in cheek, bad bruises. Need rots of rest.'

'He mentioned "Kempeitai",' said Jamie.

'Hai! Injury typical of Kempeitai torture,' said Seiki. 'Doctor seen it before. One of torturers was Kempeitai. Yuko give your friend injection now. Painkiller. Binding around ribs. Rots of rest, he be good in time. Take time.'

'We have a lot to thank you for, Seiki,' said Jamie. 'How can we repay you?'

'We all go back to Japan in three weeks. Government miritary porice take over then,' said Seiki. 'You tell your Ingrish leaders not all Japanese bad people.'

'I'll do that. Will Yuko be leaving too?' asked Jamie.

'Hai! All go. In three weeks your friend orright,' said Seiki, smiling. He then bowed and said, 'I come back rater.'

'Thank you and sayonara,' said Jacko.

Seiki laughed and waved as he left. 'Sayonara.'

'Don't tell me you speak Japanese, Jacko?' asked Jamie.

'Two words, Cap. Hello and goodbye,' said Jacko, grinning. 'Konnichiwa. Sayonara. Learnt that at school.'

This was greeted with a low tittering laugh from Yuko.

'My accent's probably not too good, Cap,' said Jacko. 'I think we should go and find Harry. Things could get dangerous when the criminals find their hostage gone.'

'I'll go,' said Lee. 'Nobody will give me a second glance. Your hotel will be the most dangerous place for a while. If Harry's there, I'll bring him back here. Then you can all hide out at my place. It's not far from here.'

* * * *

Harry was indeed back at the Astor House Hotel. After digesting the news about Samar as the destination of the opium boat, along with a large Chinese lunch, Harry had spent some time with General McConaughy's attaché at the US Consulate arranging a flight for himself to Manila. He had been informed that he could catch a USAAF flight the following morning to the Nielson airfield in Manila from the Kiangwan Air Base in the north part of Shanghai. Peter told him that he would be able to take him down the Huangpu in the Jin Shayu and drop him at the airport early in the morning. It was ten miles downstream from the Bund. He suggested Harry should collect his gear from the hotel and stay on the boat overnight.

Harry was just checking out when Lee arrived and told him about the attack on Johnny.

'They kidnapped him directly out of the hotel?' Harry enquired incredulously. 'Where are you all now?'

'Johnny and the others are in the old city,' said Lee. 'It was Jacko's dog that found him. We were lucky to get Johnny out of there, but he's in a bad way.'

'Ah'll be doggoned!' exclaimed Harry. 'I was just checking out. I'm gonna put my gear on Peter Jackson's boat.'

'I'll check Jamie and Jacko out too and take their bags with me,' said Lee.

'I'll give you a hand, Lee.'

* * * *

Sir William Founding walked out of the British Consulate and was surprised to find Ned Brandon and Motoi Tanaka waiting outside. Brandon had a bandage around his head, bruised cheeks, and a hangdog expression.

Looking anxiously around, Sir William told them angrily, 'I've told you we are not to be seen together. Follow me.'

He walked ahead of them away from the Bund, west along South Suzhou Road to a quiet park where they stood under a large shady tree beside Suzhou Creek.

'What the devil's happened to you, Red?' he demanded.

'I was attacked by a mob of men at the Ninghai residence,' Brandon explained. 'They killed Roddy, beat me up, and took Colonel Cook away with them.'

'They rescued Cook?' exclaimed Sir William incredulously. 'How many of them were there?'

'At least a dozen, Sir William,' replied Brandon in a low voice. 'Motoi wasn't there and I was overwhelmed.'

'This is bad,' said Sir William. 'Cook will be able to describe both of you. Your attackers also know what you look like, Ned. You'd better lie low for a while.'

'Cook almost dead,' said Tanaka. 'Not describe anything.'

'Yes... yes... um. Be that as it may, I'll talk to Soong and get his men to comb the city for these dozen men,' said Sir William, glaring at Ned. 'I assume that they include Cook's companions at the Astor House Hotel, Munro, O'Brien and Williams?'

'Yes sir, they would,' agreed Ned.

138

'It's better if Tanaka goes to the Astor by himself and checks if they are there,' said Sir William. 'I'll talk to Soong. He can get hundreds of men combing the city for Colonel Cook and these men. They won't be able to hide for long.'

'Yes, I go to Astor House now,' said Tanaka.

After he had gone, Sir William looked critically at Ned Brandon and asked, 'Were there really a dozen attackers, Red?'

'Quite a lot, sir,' replied Brandon. 'Not sure how many. I was knocked out.'

'How the hell did they find you?'

'There was a dog,' said Brandon. He pulled up his sleeve and showed the savage teeth lacerations on his arm.

'A dog?' exclaimed Sir William with astonishment. 'What sort of dog?'

'A Chinese wolfdog,' replied Brandon. 'It looked like Roddy Braithwaite's dog, Zhiming.'

'Unbelievable!' shouted Sir William. 'Go to our house in the French Concession and don't show your face until I tell you to.'

'Yessir.'

'I'm off to talk to Soong.'

CHAPTER 15

Major Joe Stevenson of the Philippine Constabulary in Cebu studied the five people sitting staring expectantly at him from the other side of his desk.

'I've been in touch with the US High Commission in Manila and told them about your ordeal in Samar,' he explained. 'They said that the chief of the OSS, Harry Williams, will be arriving in Manila tomorrow and that we should wait for his arrival before taking action against the people who held you prisoner. He's flying in from China where he's been working with your husband, Mrs Munro, and your brother, Miss Nangala.'

'Then we should do away with formalities, Major,' said Henri Rousseau. 'My name is Henri, and the ladies are my wife, Bella, Carna, Sarah and my daughter, Monique.'

'Excellent. Please call me Joe. I know Jamie and Jacko well. I have heard of you all from Jacko and am most interested to meet Sarah Nangala, his sister.'

'Jacko is also my husband,' said Monique. 'Will he be coming with Harry Williams?'

'No, he and Jamie will be following later, I understand,' said Joe. 'I'm not sure when. I've been instructed that when Harry arrives I am to give him my full support. He should be in Cebu the day after tomorrow. He suspects the operation you saw on Samar may have something to do with the investigations they've been conducting in China. I believe you weren't able to work out what they were doing in Llorente.'

'Non, non. The local people told us they were buying up all their copra for export,' said Henri, 'and that they were conscripted once in a while to unload sacks of unknown material from boats into their shed. They also loaded bundles of copra into other boats. That's all we know.'

'Very mysterious! I'm sure Harry will be able to tell us more when he arrives,' said Joe. 'Where are you people staying?'

'At the Magellan Hotel, Joe,' said Carna.

Joe nodded with a smile. 'Ah, of course. That's where Jamie and Jacko stayed when they were here before. Do you have plans for lunch?'

'We thought maybe at the hotel,' said Henri.

'No. You must have lunch on me,' said Joe. 'I have a lot to thank Jamie and Jacko for. They solved a very difficult case for us early this year. Their favourite place to eat was the Sailor's Log Cabin in the port area. It's more American-style cooking. Not French or Filipino. But I'm sure you'll like it.'

'That is very hospitable of you, Monsieur... er... Joe,' said Henri. 'We would be delighted to join you for lunch.'

'Great. You can tell me more about your proposed manufacturing business in Samar and Cebu over lunch,' said Joe. 'I'll just go and organise the vehicles.'

* * * *

Jamie looked in on Johnny to find the two young nurses carefully washing him. He was fast asleep, and Jamie assumed the painkillers had done the trick. The nurses smiled at him and Yuko put her finger to her lips to indicate silence. Jamie nodded and left the room. As he closed the door, he heard someone climbing the stairs.

'Is that you, Jacko?' he said.

'No, it's your old buddy from Texas,' replied Harry. 'Lee and I have got all your gear from the hotel, and something else. Pete Jackson knew the quartermaster at the US army barracks. We've been given two GI uniforms for you guys to wear. Complete with garrison caps and all. One's a sergeant and one's a corporal. There are so many GIs around, if the baddies are looking for you, your best disguise is to be dressed as US soldiers. I'll leave it to you to work out who should have the higher rank.'

Jacko appeared, Ming at his heels, from a room further down the corridor and Jamie called out to him, 'Hey, Jacko! Guess what? You've been promoted to corporal in the US army. Harry's brought us some uniforms.'

'That'll suit me, Cap,' said Jacko cheerily. 'What are you? Four-star general?'

141

'I'm a lowly sergeant, Jacko,' said Jamie, laughing.

'Nothing lowly about being a sergeant, Cap.'

'The baddies have got your names from the hotel,' said Lee. 'They'll all be out looking for you, but they won't notice a couple of GIs amongst the many American soldiers in Shanghai.'

'We'll need some chocolate to hand out to the kids,' said Jacko. 'We'd better practise our American accents, Cap.'

'How's Johnny?' asked Harry.

'He's alive and he's got two charming young ladies giving him a body wash,' said Jamie. 'Trouble is, he doesn't know about it. They've knocked him out with painkillers.'

'I have further news for you,' said Harry. 'When Pete and I were at the US Consulate, General McConaughy told us he had received a wire from the USS Eaton. The opium boat they captured was bound for Samar in the Philippine Islands.'

'Samar!' exclaimed Jacko, suddenly tense. 'That's where Henri Rousseau and the girls were going to look at timbers. Bloody hell!'

'Don't worry, Jacko,' said Harry. 'Samar is lightly populated but it's a big island. Very unlikely for them to have run into any smugglers. I've arranged to fly back to the Philippines tomorrow morning to find out more.'

'You haven't got a spare seat, have you?' Jacko asked.

'Not on this flight, but there'll be lots of aircraft taking troops to Manila over the next few weeks,' said Harry.

'I don't think we can leave Johnny,' said Jamie. 'We certainly can't ask the British Consulate to take care of him, can we?'

'I guess not, Cap,' said Jacko morosely.

'If we could discover who in the consulate gave out the information about Johnny, we could neutralise him,' said Lee. 'Although you're not Brits, I'm going to need your help.'

'How could we help with that?' Jamie asked.

'Our number one suspect has got to be the acting consul, Sir William Founding,' said Lee. 'I will establish his identity through a friend of mine. After that, we can take turns to follow him around and see where he goes and whom he sees. We'll be inconspicuous. He won't look twice at a Chinese or a GI.'

'How will we know if it was him?' asked Jamie.

142

'We know the four big families are involved, otherwise the government would have stepped in long ago,' Lee explained. 'If we see Sir William hobnobbing with the Soongs or the Kungs, then we'll know.'

'Then we eliminate him, right?' said Jacko.

'Yes. We must,' Lee agreed. 'You chaps can then take off and I'll make sure Johnny is looked after. After all, he is my boss.'

'That sounds great,' said Jacko. 'I don't feel at all easy in a gigantic city like this. I never get lost in the bush, but I'm lost all the time in Shanghai. When I was young, I used to think that Darwin was the big smoke. Compared to this, Darwin's just a small village.'

'I'll ask the US Consulate to put you on an aircraft to Manila whenever you're ready,' said Harry.

'They'll have to,' Jacko retorted. 'They must look after their GI corporals.'

'Speaking of which, I suggest you chaps put on those GI clothes now and wc'll pay a visit to thc British Consulate. As I said before, I've got a good friend there.'

After Jamie and Jacko had changed into their American uniforms, they left the building with Harry and Lee. Ming stayed close to Jacko. They had not gone far when they saw Seiki walking towards them.

He bowed to them and said, 'Ah so! You become Amelican now. That is good. Many Chinese men rooking for you. Easy to see. They have velly dark-brown shirts, ormost brack. Where you go now? Don't go Astor.'

'No. We won't go there,' said Jamie. 'We're going to the northern end of the Bund, but we'll stay well away from the Astor. Thank you for everything, Seiki.'

'It's good. I am going to see how your fliend is now,' said Seiki. 'Doctor Nakamura come again soon.'

'We have a lot to thank you for,' exclaimed Jamie.

Seiki laughed. 'You see. Not orr Japanese bad man.'

'I agree with you there.'

They noticed, dotted amongst the crowds, quite a number of Chinese with dark shirts looking carefully at foreigners but ignoring American soldiers. Jacko smiled to himself. Hiding in plain sight! Perfect. Almost perfect, because it was possible someone might recognise Ming. There were other dogs around although none as big as Ming. However, the dark shirts paid the dog no attention.

Arriving outside the fence bordering the garden in front of the British Consulate building, they walked along it towards the entrance. The imposing two-storey building at the northern end of the Bund stood some distance back from South Suzhou Road. It had immaculate clipped lawns bordered by flower gardens and large shady trees. Next to the entrance were trees and shrubs, and Jamie suggested they wait there amongst the bushes later in the afternoon to see who came and went.

'We don't know Sir William Founding from a bar of soap,' said Jacko.

'I can solve that,' said Lee. 'I'll go in now and find my friend. I'll ask him what Sir William looks like. Simple!'

'Good idea, Lee,' said Jamie. 'We'll wait here.'

Waiting near the gates of the British Consulate, they noted pedestrian traffic was much thinner along South Suzhou Road than in other parts of the city; however, even here a number of Chinese with the distinctive dark-brown shirts were patrolling the area. Some of them glanced at the two men wearing GI uniforms but paid them little attention.

'Good disguise, Cap,' remarked Jacko.

'Sure is, Jacko,' agreed Jamie.

'What state you from, Cap?' asked Jacko, chuckling. 'I'm from Saskatchewan.'

'That's Canada, Jacko.'

'Damn, and it took me a while to practise pronouncing it,' said Jacko. 'Okay, I'm from Tennessee.'

'I'm from the blue grasses of Kentucky, Jacko,' said Jamie. 'Next door to your state.'

'Neighbours, eh Cap?'

'You're darn tootin', buddy!'

Lee ran out of the building through the garden and told them that the acting consul had an afternoon meeting and would shortly be leaving the consulate. He said his friend had described him as a short, trim man always impeccably dressed, and that he was wearing a grey suit and dark-blue tie. He would probably also be wearing a light-grey fedora hat.

'That's him right now,' said Jamie as a man of that description emerged from the building.

'That looks like the fellow who got off the opium boat at Baoshan,' said Jacko.

'I think we've pegged him, Jacko,' agreed Jamie. 'Let's see where he goes.'

Sir William walked through the gate and turned left along the pavement outside, setting off at a brisk pace. After following the south side of Suzhou Creek for about half a mile, he turned left into Fujian Road, with the three men and Ming trailing 100 yards behind. Another quarter of a mile brought him to Nanjing Road where he hailed a rickshaw, which continued south along Fujian Road, the rickshaw puller running through the scattered pedestrians. There only being one other available rickshaw at the Nanjing Road corner, Jamie and Lee climbed aboard, Lee telling the puller to follow the other rickshaw. Jacko, running behind, found he could keep up without too much trouble. Ming trotted along beside him.

Half a mile further on, after passing through areas of entertainment with crowds of Chinese, Russian women, GIs, and other foreigners, they turned to the right into Avenue Joffre with its wide boulevard and imposing commercial buildings, finally turning into a quiet leafy street with giant plane trees on both sides. Sir William's rickshaw stopped outside a mansard-roofed mansion with stone terraces and large French windows and dormers, set back from a high railed fence.

They paid off their rickshaw puller further down the street and then Lee quietly told the others that this was the main house of T.V. Soong, prominent industrialist, businessman and financier. They watched from a distance as Sir William pressed a button and a servant ran to the gate to admit him.

'Soong is very close to President Chiang,' explained Lee, 'but he may not have much faith in the longevity of the Kuomintang government as it's rumoured he's shipping most of his wealth out of the country. Some of the other members of the four big families are reputed to be doing the same.'

'If he's so wealthy, why would Soong be involved with Sir William in the opium venture?' asked Jamie.

'It would be small fry for him but a useful way of making money overseas,' Lee explained. 'Nobody ever accused the four big families of being incorrupt.'

'You're well informed, Lee,' said Jacko, who had got his breath back after running.

'I've lived in Shanghai for a long while, Jacko.'

'Well, I suppose there's nothing to do but wait,' said Jamie. 'At least we know that Sir William is up to his neck in this opium-smuggling operation.'

'You fellas can go back to the house to see how Johnny's progressing,' offered Jacko. 'Ming and I'll be able to take care of the eminent Sir William.'

'You sure, Jacko?'

'Never a problem, Cap.'

'Yeah, I suppose Sir William is the key man in the opium operation,' Jamie said uncertainly.

'Of course! He's the head of the whole thing,' said Lee. 'Once we cut off the head, Soong will probably wash his hands of the operation. Hopefully, he'll call off his army of dark shirts who are looking for us.'

'Off you go,' said Jacko. 'Ming and I'll do the head-cutting.'

'Okay, Jacko. You might have a long wait though,' said Jamie, as he and Lee began walking back towards Avenue Joffre.

'No worries, Cap. As you know, I come from the wait-awhile part of the Territory.'

Jacko settled down with his back against the trunk of a plane tree, Ming lying beside him, concealed by a flowering bush fifty yards down from the gate to the Soong mansion. There were almost no pedestrians or traffic in the street. It was as though people avoided it. He ignored the bees buzzing around his head and fell into a trance, dreaming about Monique far away in a distant land.

The metallic sounds of a gate opening alerted him and through the bushes, he could see the dapper Sir William and an imposing well-dressed Chinese accompanied by uniformed bodyguards standing together chatting on the pavement outside the fence.

Soong's articulate voice carried over the distance. '... then Lo-yi told me she only buys all those shoes to look beautiful for me. I couldn't really care if she wore frogman flippers, but I can't tell her that.' Laughter. Then Sir William mumbled something. Soong's voice again. 'Don't worry, William. We'll catch your adversaries. Relax. Ciao!'

The gate clanged after Soong and his minders, and Jacko watched the short natty figure of Sir William hurrying towards his position. Jacko signalled to Ming to stay quiet and as Sir William passed, Jacko emerged from his concealment and brought the butt of his revolver down heavily on his fedora hat. The small man fell to the ground unconscious, breathing fitfully. Jacko dragged him down the pavement close to a low stone wall and felt his neck for the pulsing carotid artery, cut it with his knife, and stood back from the spurt of blood. As life seeped from the body, he lifted it and threw it over the stone wall.

'That's for Johnny,' he muttered. Ming watched him with his head cocked to one side and then followed him back to Avenue Joffre, where Jacko turned left towards the old city. He had been walking for twenty minutes with Ming at his heels when the dog emitted a growling bark, and he felt a movement behind him. He moved swiftly to the side, twisting around with his right hand held rigid. A heavy object glanced off his shoulder as the side of his swinging hand connected with the neck of his assailant, a muscular Asian man, whose eyes rolled up showing only the whites. Life faded from his face as he crumpled to the ground.

Ming started barking again and Jacko heard shouting behind him up the avenue. He saw a red-bearded man with a bandage around his head accompanied by five men wearing dark shirts, yelling and pointing at him as they ran towards him. Jacko whipped around and raced down Avenue Joffre, Ming in pursuit. He and their pursuers were often hindered by crowds of strolling people, outraged faces turned towards them. Jacko had a clear start and reaching an intersection he turned left into a narrower street, looking right and left for some means of escape. He was spurred on by the shouts and heavy footfalls of his pursuers and felt he was putting distance between them as he turned and weaved through the many side streets.

147

Realising, as he ran, it was probably because of Ming that he had been identified, he yelled at the dog to go. Go he did. Within seconds Ming, racing ahead, was gone.

Jacko had lost his GI garrison hat and knew he had to find somewhere to hide fast before he ran into more of the dark shirts. Turning a corner into yet another side street, he saw a drainpipe leading up the side of a three-storey building and leapt up it. Hand over hand, he climbed up the thick metal drainpipe until he could heave himself onto the tiled roof. He managed to slip behind a brick chimney halfway up the pitched roof before he heard the hue and cry of his pursuers as they turned into the street and raced past him. Breathing heavily from the exertion, he thought about the man who had tried to knock him out in Avenue Joffre. He was Asian but didn't look Chinese and he hadn't been wearing a dark shirt. His face looked more Japanese. Jacko smiled and wondered if it was the Kempeitai who had tortured Johnny. He figured from the reaction to his karate chop on the assailant's neck, he had probably killed him.

His thoughts were interrupted by shouting back and forth below. His pursuers had lost him, and he could hear footsteps running all over the place. They were also knocking on doors. Angry voices. He nestled down in his position behind the chimney and told himself it was going to be another case of wait-awhile.

After a couple of hours, there was even more noise below. Banging on doors, loud voices, footfalls. Jacko peeped around the side of his chimney. Damn! There must be an army down there, he thought. They were searching all the houses, men's and women's voices were raised in protest, doors were being broken down in unoccupied dwellings. They're bloody determined, he thought. I'll be up here a while longer. I could do with a drink of water. A cold beer would be better.

It was almost nightfall before the noises subsided and quietness, except for the passing of occasional traffic and birds twittering in the nearby trees, fell upon the street below. From his perch, Jacko detected little movement below but decided to wait a while longer. He wondered whether they had discovered the body of Sir William Founding yet. Whether they had or not, the baddies were certainly after his blood. The red-bearded man was definitely the one he had knocked out when they rescued Johnny. Should have done for him then, he thought. That man won't rest until he finds me. It's a shame I lost my soldier's hat. Makes me stand out from the GI crowd. I'll have to find some other form of disguise... or another hat. Where the hell am I? He stood up and stretched. Bright lights from Avenue Joffre glowed through the trees to his right, giving him a rough idea of the direction to the Bund.

There was silence in the street as he made his way down the drainpipe. Halfway down, he heard footsteps and froze, hardly breathing. The footsteps moved on, however. Just a passing pedestrian. On the ground, he decided to stay in the network of narrow streets while making his way east. After passing Fujian Road, he recognised where he was. Turning right, he headed towards the old city, keeping to the narrow streets as much as he could.

CHAPTER 16

After a quick snack, Jamie and Lee had just returned to the old Ming Dynasty building when they heard Ming give a happy yap. Jacko appeared out of the darkness of the street and rubbed his head.

'Did you catch up with our friend?' asked Jamie.

'Our friend is no longer with us, but I had a bit of strife on the way home,' said Jacko. 'That big red-headed fella nailed me because I had Ming with me and he sent the army after me. One of them tried to cosh me over the head, but luckily, I got him with a karate chop. He looked Japanese to me. Managed to give them the slip.'

'Glad you got away, Jacko. Ming arrived here hours ago and refused to move from the door,' said Jamie. 'Not even for food.'

'Food! I'm starved. Bloody thirsty too,' said Jacko, still patting Ming. 'How's Johnny, Cap?'

'Much better, Jacko. The girls managed to get some beef soup into him and it's brought some colour back into his face. Doesn't look dead any more.'

'I'd like to ask him something, Cap,' said Jacko. 'Can he talk?'

'Yeah. With some difficulty but he's not bad,' said Jamie. 'He'd like to see you.'

They all went upstairs and entered the room. Yuan was sitting by Johnny's side. Jacko looked down at him and coughed.

Johnny opened his watery eyes, gave a ghost of a smile, and said, 'Hi Jacko.'

'Hi yourself, boss. The fellow who tortured you, was he a Japanese with high cheekbones and nearly bald on top?'

'Yes. Exactly like that, Jacko.'

'I think I killed him with a lucky karate chop this afternoon, Johnny.'

Johnny gave a twisted grin, wincing in pain, and said, 'I bless you, Jacko. God blesses you. You will join the angels.'

With that, Johnny fell asleep and they all tiptoed from the room.

'We'd better put some food into you, Jacko, before you become an angel,' said Jamie, chuckling.

'Have you fellas eaten already?' asked Jacko.

'Yes, but we'll join you and have a couple of cold beers,' replied Jamie.

'Ah, cold beer! The words have an angelic ring to them, Cap.'

'There's a great Chinese restaurant just down the road from here,' said Lee.

'Lead on, Macduff,' said Jacko. 'I could eat a horse. C'mon, Ming.'

'You'd better tell your dog to stay out of sight at the restaurant, Jacko,' said Lee. 'That's how you were identified before.'

'I'll tell him,' said Jacko, grinning. 'He can eat his shank under the table.'

'We'll have to get you another garrison cap as well.'

'Once the commandoes have blown up the opium plant, and with the termination of Sir William, there's no reason for us to stay in China,' said Jamie, as they walked down the street. 'Once we're sure that Johnny's on the mend, we could follow Harry to the Philippines in a day or so.'

'Those dark shirts will be watching all the ports and airports,' said Lee. 'It'll be risky for a while.'

* * * *

The following day was particularly warm and humid in Shanghai, and by the afternoon most people had deserted the streets to escape the sweltering heat. In the western part of the city, it was considerably cooler inside the Soong mansion where, in the mid-afternoon, T.V. Soong and his wife, Lo-yi, were entertaining the Kungs with a sumptuous high tea. They were cooled by a newly installed American air-conditioning system supplemented by slow-moving overhead electric fans.

H.H. Kung's wife, Ai-Ling, Soong's elder sister, was chatting to them about her recent visit to Chongqing where she had attended several functions with her youngest sister, Mei-Ling, in support of her husband the President, Chiang Kai-shek, and the Kuomintang government.

They were interrupted by a tentative knock on the door of the lounge room. The door opened and a servant stood there, coughed, and said, 'Sir, someone to see you.'

Soong looked at the servant's face and detected some agitation. Excusing himself, he left the room with the servant. His chief of security, Li Huan, was waiting for him in the hallway. Soong eyed him and asked, 'What is it?'

Li Huan answered, 'A gardener has found a dead body five houses away along the road, Zhu.'

'So?'

'We think it is the visitor who was here yesterday, Zhu.'

'Visitor? You think... Wait here.' Soong returned to the lounge room and told his brother-in-law and their wives he had to take care of something but would be back in a short while.

He followed Li Huan down the street where two of his security guards were waiting beside a low stone wall. He peered over the wall and found himself staring at the bloodied body of Sir William Founder. It was hard to comprehend. What could have happened?

Rattled, he stepped back from the wall, composed himself with an effort, and told Li Huan, 'It is a good thing if this body disappears somewhere no one can find it, Li. Can you take care of that?'

'I can take care, Zhu. It will be done.'

'Only you and your men should know. Not a word to anyone else, Li.'

'I understand, Zhu.'

Soong returned to his house, queasy, but he managed to smile as he entered the lounge room.

Lo-Yi looked at him with concern and said, 'Is something wrong?'

'No, no, my love. Just a small matter, nothing to worry about.' Soong sat down and addressed Ai-Ling, 'Tell me more about Chongqing, Meimei.'

After half an hour of listening to the ladies discussing the events of the times, Soong said to Kung, 'I have a matter of business to discuss with you, H.H. If the ladies will pardon us, we'll go to my study and I'll show you something.'

In his study, Soong stood with his hands behind his back staring out the window overlooking the garden.

'Sir William has been murdered,' he said without turning around.

'What? Where? Who could have done such a thing?' gasped Kung.

Soong turned around and looked at him. 'I'm not so concerned about the who, why, or wherefore, H.H. This opium project has been quite lucrative over the past six months, but I think it's about time to write it off. It's become too messy. What do you think?'

Kung nodded. 'I completely concur with that, brother. If it's too messy, we don't need it. We have plenty of other things going for us. Chiang won't want any scandals at this time either. Better to wash our hands of it.'

'Good. We won't have anything more to do with it. Whoever murdered Sir William will have little chance of involving us,' said Soong.

'What about your militia who are all over Shanghai looking for those English?' asked Kung.

'I'll get Li Huan to send them back to their barracks,' replied Soong. 'Let's go and rejoin the ladies.'

* * * *

Harry Williams Jr gazed out the left side window of the aircraft at the western coast of Luzon through haze and scattered clouds. As promised, Peter Jackson had motored down the Huang River in the early morning and dropped him near the Kiangwan Air Base where he was met by a USAAF lieutenant who escorted him to the C-54 Skymaster waiting on the tarmac. A group of US navy personnel was standing around chatting and he was informed they would accompany him to the Subic Bay Naval Base in Zambales, northwest of Manila Bay.

'Subic Bay? Are we going to Subic?' he asked.

'Yes, sir,' replied the lieutenant. 'Your flight has been redirected to Subic Bay at the request of the navy. They are holding the crew of the opium boat there and have critical information for you before you go on to Samar.'

'Critical information? That's good.'

'That's all I know, sir, except I was told to tell you that the Skymaster will fly you down to Cebu straightaway after you've met the naval interrogator in Subic.'

After refuelling at Taihoku on the island of Taiwan, the C-54 was off the coast of Northern Luzon by early afternoon. Through a light haze, Harry could make out the old coastal town of Vigan, with its ancient Spanish churches and the strip of black-sand beaches stretching from Ilocos Sur south to La Union. He turned to answer a question from the young marine sitting beside him, when the captain of the flight announced they would be landing at Subic in forty minutes.

'Your first time in the Philippines, sir?' asked the marine.

'No, I've lived in Manila since the war,' replied Harry. 'I haven't been to Subic Bay yet, though.'

'It's still a bit of a mess, sir,' the marine explained. 'The Japs destroyed many of the facilities before they left, but there's a lot of construction going on now.'

The construction was very much in evidence as they landed on a new concrete airstrip. After taxiing over to a metal hangar, Harry disembarked to be greeted by a group of naval officers who escorted him to an office in a single-storey building behind the hangar.

Harry was introduced to Captain Tyler Barnes who handed him a file. 'Our guys have spent some time sorting out the separate stories of the crew of the boat picked up by the USS Eaton, Mr Williams. I've had all our notes typed here so that you can read them in detail.'

'That's just what I need, Captain,' said Harry. 'Can you give me the facts in a nutshell?'

'Sure can, Mr Williams,' said Captain Barnes. 'As far as we know, they've been shipping the opium to a small village on the east coast of Samar. Llorente. There, they hide packages of opium in tight bundles of copra and ship it off to the US of A or elsewhere where it's declared as copra. Copra has an unpleasant smell so, I guess, the customs are discouraged from looking too closely. They wouldn't expect opium from the Philippines in this day and age.'

'Hey, that's just great, Captain. I'll study your notes carefully,' said Harry enthusiastically, 'I owe you one, and next time, please call me Harry.'

154

'Glad to be of assistance Mr... er... Harry,' said Captain Barnes. 'I'm known as Tyle. Next time you can buy me a bourbon. Your aircraft to Cebu will leave as soon as it's finished refuelling. Good luck and take care.'

On boarding the Skymaster again, the co-pilot told Harry that once they were off the ground, they could radio ahead for a hotel reservation if he wanted one.

'Ah yes, friend. The Magellan, thanks,' said Harry. 'I think some people I know will probably be there.'

* * * *

Night had just fallen and the view over the poppy field had faded into darkness. Eddie Wang was restless and irritable. Brandon, Braithwaite and Tanaka should have returned by now. What the devil was going on? Although he was hungry, he was reluctant to go to dinner and listen to Feng Gang Li cndlcssly explaining to him in excruciating detail the problems with the vehicles and the lack of spare parts.

It had been a massive job exhorting the few remaining local workers who hadn't run away to clean up and fix the mess created by the saboteurs. He felt exhausted, wrung out, and alone. They must return soon. He sighed. I need to know what's happening. Have the saboteurs been found? Did the last boat reach the sea safely?

He thought he detected some movement in the poppy field but there was no moon and it was too dark to be sure. Having only one eye, he decided it was playing tricks on him. No! There it was again! Perhaps the men had finally returned. Not before time. There was a new shipment of raw opium from Guangxi due in the next day. They'd need all hands on deck.

Suddenly, he was shocked to find himself surrounded by a large group of men in military uniform. A British voice sharply demanded his name.

'Wha... who... who are you?' he stammered.

'More to the point, who are you, my good man?' countered Captain Jeremy Cowper.

155

'My... my name is Eddie Wang. I am farm manager,' said Wang in a low voice.

'We are here to blow up your farm, Mr Wang,' said Cowper. 'Who else is here?'

'Blow up farm?' exclaimed Wang incredulously.

'Yes. Big bang. You can be blown up with it or come with us. Your choice,' said Cowper. 'Who else is here?'

'Just mechanic, Feng, and some local peasants and cook.'

'Sergeant Smythe will go with you while you get your mechanic,' said Cowper, nodding to his sergeant. 'You can tell all the locals to run away.'

As Sergeant Bill Smythe accompanied Wang, tears of frustration running down his cheeks, to one of the sheds, Cowper directed his men to proceed with the planned demolition. Men carrying heavy backpacks ran into the different buildings, while Cowper looked around the outside of the sheds with his torch. Satisfied there were no other gang members hidden nearby, he returned and waited at the front of the largest shed.

The first to arrive back was his sergeant with the two Chinese: a grim, one-eyed Eddie Wang and a rough-looking man with long straggly hair. In less than fifteen minutes, they were joined by the rest of Cowper's commando company.

Cowper asked Corporal Tony Bray, 'Anyone missing, Corporal?'

After a pause, Bray replied, 'All present and correct, sir.'

'Very good. We'll take these two characters with us, unless they want to stay,' said Cowper. 'Back to the boats, men.'

The two characters referred to had no desire to stay, so they and the commandoes were soon swallowed up in the darkness to the east of the sheds. As they reached the bank of the Yangtze River where their two boats were moored, the stillness of the night was shattered by a mighty explosion, and the western sky lit up like a gigantic fireworks display. The commandoes stopped for a moment to look back at the flickering light, then all quietly embarked for the trip back to Shanghai.

* * * *

Earlier in the evening, Red Brandon had desperately continued his search for the hatless man in a GI uniform whom he had first sighted in company with Roddy's dog, Zhiming. He was accompanied by eight of the Chinese militia, only known to him as the Black Minbing, as they combed the streets. He was particularly angry that the fugitive had killed Tanaka right in front of him and then vanished. How the hell had he got away? Dusk had fallen by the time they left the former French Concession and entered the old Chinese City.

At that moment, another Chinese in a dark shirt ran up to them and said something to the leader of his group. There was a loud discussion in Mandarin and the leader turned to him, bowed, and without a word, they all departed. Bewildered, he stared after them and then wandered along the road, his mind filled with consternation.

Wondering what he should do, he suddenly came alert when, across the road, he saw three people entering a Chinese restaurant followed by a dog. Zhiming? He was convinced it was the dog when he noted that one of the trio was a hatless GI. He was accompanied by a Chinese and another GI. A sergeant. I've got you, he thought. His triumph was short-lived as he contemplated his lack of support. They couldn't have left him at a worse time. He decided the best thing would be to keep the trio in the restaurant under surveillance and find out where they went after their meal. Perhaps they might lead him to that British colonel who had escaped.

Staying in the shadows, he melted into a dark doorway where he could watch them. They were drinking beer and their laughter reached him and made him angrier. No sign of the dog. He must be under the table. He smiled grimly to himself. As soon as I find out where they're based, I'll search out the Black Minbing and we'll kill the bastards, once and for all. Zhiming too, the bloody traitor.

He had to wait for more than an hour and was stiff from standing for so long without moving. The road was busy, with revellers everywhere and rickshaw drivers running up and down, carting mainly foreigners. Finally, he saw the men stand up from the table and pay the bill. As they were leaving, Zhiming followed them, wagging his tail.

Suddenly, Zhiming stopped, the bristles rising on his back, and looked across the road where Red was standing. He shrank back further into the doorway and held his breath. The hatless man yelled, 'Ming!' at which the dog gave a yelp and then followed the trio up the road.

Staying on the other side of the road from them, he followed them at a distance, weaving through throngs of pedestrians. No dark shirts around anywhere. The men ahead walked for only two blocks before they turned into the doorway of an old Ming Dynasty building. Creeping along the pavement until he was opposite the building, he checked that they were inside out of sight. After writing down the address in his notebook, he chuckled to himself and went in search of dark shirts.

Although he walked for miles around the city, his search proved fruitless. He found himself in Avenue Joffre and remembered he had previously been directed to a house where he had met Sir William Founding in the western part of the old French Concession. It was a large mansion belonging to an influential Chinese, a close friend of Sir William. He wasn't sure where Sir William himself lived but thought he might be dining with his Chinese friends. If not, they would know where to get hold of him.

* * * *

T.V. Soong was, in fact, entertaining some close friends at his house as well as the American Consul, General Walter McConaughy, and his family. They were all seated at a long dining table and Soong was laughing at an amusing anecdote recounted by the general, when one of his security guards entered the dining room and caught his eye. Excusing himself, he stood up and followed the guard from the room.

'What is it?' he asked.

'There's an Englishman at the front door. He's been asking for Sir William Founding, Zhu,' the guard replied.

'An Englishman? What does he look like?' Soong enquired.

'Red hair and a beard, Zhu,' explained the guard. 'I would describe him as shabby. He smells bad.'

'I think you could show him into the small lounge near the front door,' said Soong thoughtfully. 'Give him something to drink and I'll see him in about ten minutes.'

Soong went out to the terrace, looked at the stars, and considered the situation. Why did this man want Sir William? What did he know? He remembered that a few days before, a man of a similar description had come to see Sir William to tell him about the saboteurs at the opium plant. That was probably it. He couldn't find Sir William and thought he might be here.

He let fifteen minutes go by before walking into the small lounge room, his eyebrows raised questioningly. The large red-headed man, holding a glass of Scotch whisky, stood up when Soong entered and looked at him nervously.

'My name is Soong. Sir William is not here this evening,' said Soong. 'Is there anything I can help you with?'

'I'm not sure, sir. I'm Ned Brandon. I've been working with Sir William on a project along the Yangtze River,' said Brandon. 'I thought you might know where he is.'

'No, I'm afraid not, old chap,' said Soong. 'I know Sir William, but I haven't seen him for a day or so. Is it important?'

'I've been on the trail of some fugitives. Saboteurs. I've been able to track down where they're staying,' said Brandon, feeling less nervous now. 'I had some men supporting me earlier in the day who Sir William said were organised by you. They seem to have deserted me. I need help to arrest these fugitives.'

'I see,' said Soong. 'Wait here and I'll see what I can do.'

'Thank you, sir.'

Soong left the room and asked the security guard to find Li Huan. When his chief of security arrived, Soong took him out onto the terrace and said, 'There's a fellow with a red beard in the small lounge room near the front door, Li Huan. Take him somewhere and make him disappear so that no one ever finds him.'

Li Haun bowed and walked to the lounge while Soong went back to the dining room to rejoin his guests.

CHAPTER 17

It was a bright sunny day in Cebu when Harry Williams went downstairs for breakfast at the Magellan Hotel.

'Why, I do declare!' he exclaimed, laughing and looking at the five astonished faces in the dining room. 'Howdy, folks!'

'Harry!' Carna yelled, jumping up and running over to him. 'Where did you spring from? We weren't expecting you until tomorrow. Are Jamie and Jacko with you?'

'Naw, they're still in Shanghai. Got in from China last night meself,' he replied, joining them at the table. 'It was late. Well after your bedtime. I'm mighty glad to find you here. We'd heard of some criminal activity on Samar. Jamie and Jacko were worried that you might have run into trouble when you went over there.'

'We did! We did!' exclaimed Carna. 'Henri and I were captured and locked up by some evil bandidos.'

'Well, I'll be doggoned!' exclaimed Harry.

'We were rescued by my guardian angel,' said Carna, pointing at Sarah who smiled shyly. 'Mi espíritu guardián!'

'Goddamn! I'll order some vittles and you'll have to tell me all about it,' said Harry. 'I've got some stories to tell you too. You first.'

It was already mid-morning by the time all their stories had been exchanged. When Carna, Henri and Monique related their adventures in Samar, with Sarah contributing only the occasional nod or giggle, Harry kept shaking his head in amazement. Harry followed this with his own detailed description of the trip up the Yangtze River, the sabotage of the opium treatment plant, and the pursuit of the boat bound for Samar. Sarah joined in the laughter when Harry embellished his story of Jacko's adoption of the Chinese wolfdog, Ming.

'Bikpela brother good dogman,' she exclaimed, giggling.

He also told his subdued audience about the kidnapping, torture and rescue of Johnny Cook.

'Merde! China must be a dangerous place,' speculated Henri.

'Yes and no,' said Harry. 'The Chinese are generally nice peaceful people. I can't say the same about some of their leaders though. The danger comes because of a major power struggle in China as well as greed and corruption in the aftermath of war. Our role in ending the opium-smuggling operation is only a small component in the scheme of things.'

'Who will win this civil war between the government and the communistes, Harry?' asked Henri.

'No one knows, Henri,' said Harry, shaking his head. 'No one knows.'

'So, will you be going to Samar, Harry?' asked Carna.

'Yes, for sure. You people have done much of my work for me already,' said Harry. 'You've confirmed that the base of the smuggling operation is in Llorente. I'll call my old friend, Major Joe Stevenson, of the Philippines Constabulary, and bring him up to date.'

'He is already up to date, Harry,' said Carna. 'He has been waiting for you.'

'Well, I'd better go see him,' said Harry, standing up and stretching. 'No time like the present.'

'You might need me to interpret on Samar,' said Carna.

'Joe will have plenty of Filipino speakers amongst his troops,' said Harry. 'However, they might need one of you to come and show us where everything is.'

'I will not allow my husband or daughter to go back,' exclaimed Bella firmly.

'I know where everyting is,' broke in Sarah, standing up.

Harry regarded the small black girl and said, 'I'll talk to Joe and let you know. I think it might be a good idea.'

'Aye yu. Good idea, Har Ri,' agreed Sarah. That's what Jacko would say, she thought.

'I'll be off now. Catch y'all later.'

* * * *

At daybreak on the eastern shores of Samar Island, the weather was not so clement. Patches of heavy rain fell in squalls with winds

161

gusting up to fifty miles an hour, creating white caps on the ocean swells. Loading of the cargo freighter bound for Australia had been temporarily suspended because of the weather. The freighter, Brown Dolphin, was a 70-foot ketch with a large hold in the centre of the boat between the main and mizzen masts.

The crew remained aboard to protect the boat in the foul weather. The rough sea, beneath dark threatening clouds, pounded up against the shore. The freighter, almost lost in spray, was jerking and tossing at its moorings against the pier, which shook and quivered under the onslaught of boat, wind and tide.

Inside the main shed, it was a gloomy group who watched the ominous figure of Trevor Clark pacing up and down, his close-set eyes flashing under his single straight eyebrow.

'The signal to the Brown Dolphin's radio was clear. It's all over, gentlemen,' he was saying.

Hamish McIntyre shook his head. 'It's a helluva thing. No explanations?'

'No. As soon as the boat is loaded, I shall return in the truck to Tacloban where my aeroplane is waiting,' said Clark. 'I suggest you chaps all go with the boat to Australia. No point in staying here. There won't be any more boats coming. It's all over.'

'What I do in Australia?' demanded Gao Jiang. 'I go back to China with you.'

'Me too,' piped up Huang Lei, his head still swathed in bandages.

'No one comes with me,' said Clark. 'No room in the aeroplane. The four big families don't want to see any of you again, anyway. It's all over. You can keep whatever money you get from selling the opium in Australia.'

'Luke's Australian, but the rest of us have never been there,' protested Bradford.

'Luke can show you the ropes then,' said Clark irritably.

'They can't all come. The boat has a full crew,' said Luke Atkins. 'Apart from me, there's only space for two more.'

'Well, I'm going for sure,' said McIntyre.

Nick Bradford looked at Gao and Huang, who eyed him with hostility. Bradford said, 'I should go to Australia too.'

162

'Coz you're a bloody white man?' exclaimed Gao belligerently.

'I'm more familiar with opium than you are,' said Bradford angrily.

Gao picked up a bolo, a large local machete, and said menacingly, 'When I hack your head off, there's room for me in the boat.'

Clark drew out a pistol, pointed it at him, and said, 'Nobody's hacking anyone. Drop it, Joe. You and Huang can come with me in the truck as far as Tacloban. After that, you're on your own. I can't take you any further. My aeroplane's not big enough. There's nothing for you back in Shanghai, anyway.'

'When the weather improves, we'll finish loading the boat, then we can all leave,' said McIntyre.

'All settled then,' said Clark.

'Not settled. Where our money?' protested Gao.

'I have some money with me,' said Clark. 'I'll give you your money when the boat is loaded. The ones who stay behind can get a bit more than the ones who go in the boat.'

Gao glowered at the men around him, muttering in Chinese, while Huang pulled at his wispy beard and burst into tears. Fine lot of co-workers these, thought Clark. And does it never stop raining around here?

* * * *

Jamie, Jacko, Lee and, of course, Ming were having breakfast at the small restaurant down the road from their new base in the Ming Dynasty building, when they were surprised to see Seiki walking across the road towards them. The Japanese policeman greeted them warmly with a broad smile.

'I have good news for you,' he said. 'The word around the streets of Shanghai is that the dark-brown shirt gunji are no ronger rooking for GI with no hat. Or gone. You have no more fear from dark shirts.'

Jacko jumped up and shook him by the hand, saying, 'You bring music to the ears of a hatless GI. My American accent wasn't much good anyway. Your blood's worth bottling, Seiki!'

Seiki stared at him, confused. 'Wha... my brad?'

163

'Don't worry about that, Seiki,' said Jamie, laughing. 'He means that you are a very good friend. Just a stupid Australian saying.'

'Ah so! I am happy for you,' he said, smiling. 'You good friend too.'

'Will you sit down and join us for breakfast, Seiki?' said Jacko.

'Just for short time,' replied Seiki. 'Just some rice and fish. How Mr Cook?'

'He's much better this morning, thanks to you,' said Jamie. 'He's happy to have two such beautiful nurses.'

'Ha ha! Hai! That orways good thing,' agreed Seiki. 'How rong you stay in Shanghai?'

'We'll be going to the US Consulate later on to see if they can arrange a flight to the Philippines for us,' said Jamie. 'Hopefully tomorrow.'

'Ah so! Phirippines. Yes,' said Seiki. 'Mr Ree can stay to rook after Mr Cook, hai?'

'Yes. He is definitely on the mend now,' said Lee. 'After this episode, I think Colonel Cook will probably want to direct operations solely from London in the future.'

'There's still that red-bearded mongrel out there somewhere,' said Jacko. 'If he appears again I'll get Ming to take a bite outta him. Don't think Ming likes him much.'

'What you pran to do with dog?' asked Seiki.

Jacko scratched his chin, shaking his head slowly. 'Yeah. Big problem. I don't think the US Air Force will let me take him with me. Anyway, Harry tells me, if I take him to the Philippines, they might eat him. Canine caldereta. Do you want to look after Ming, Lee?'

'No, but thanks, Jacko,' said Lee. 'I have enough trouble looking after myself.'

'Talk to our Chinese nurse, Yuan,' suggested Seiki. 'She rikes your Ming. She make good friend with him when he wait for you, night before rarst.'

'That's an excellent idea, Seiki,' said Jacko. 'I'll have a chat with Yuan. If she wants to look after Ming, I'm sure he'll want to look after her.'

'Well, sounds like we might have a solution there,' said Jamie. 'As soon as everyone's finished breakfast, we'll go down to the Glen Line Building on the Bund and talk to the US Consul.'

'I go and check with Yuko and Yuan and Cook San,' said Seiki when they stood up to leave. 'Doctor Nakamura come soon. See you rater.'

At the US Consulate, Jamie and Jacko were shown into an office and introduced to Major Don Blake, attaché to General McConaughy, the US Consul. Ming sat outside watching the building while passers-by gave him a wide berth.

'Yeah, Harry Williams told me all about you guys,' he said, gesturing for them to be seated. 'What can I do for you gentlemen?'

'Harry Williams suggested you might be able to help us with a flight to Manila,' explained Jamie.

'There's a flight scheduled for Clark Field in the Philippines leaving early tomorrow morning from the Kiangwan Air Base,' said Blake. 'We've got room on that flight for you two. Nothing going to Manila for a week, though. Clark's only fifty miles northwest of Manila so you should be able to get some road transport there.'

'Yeah, that'd be fine, thank you, Major,' said Jamie. Then he looked at Jacko and said, 'Shouldn't be too much trouble finding a flight to Cebu from Manila.'

'Cebu? You guys going to Cebu?' asked Blake, looking at a schedule on his desk.

'Yes, Cebu in the Visayan Islands,' replied Jamie.

'The US military has got quite a few personnel movements between Clark Field and the Mactan Airfield in Cebu over the next weeks,' said Blake. 'I'm sure they'll be able to accommodate you from Clark to Mactan. I'll just have my secretary type up a letter of request to show them when you get to Clark Field. I'll also let them know you're coming. You shouldn't have any trouble. Just wait here.'

After he returned with the letter, Jamie shook him by the hand and said, 'We're extremely grateful to you, Major. Many thanks.'

'You're welcome, Mr Munro,' said Blake, smiling. 'Mr Williams told me the operation you're working on involves smuggling drugs into the USA. He said it was of the highest priority. So, I wish you all

165

success. It's possible the air force could have you into Mactan Airfield by tomorrow evening.'

After leaving the consulate, Jamie and Jacko wandered along the Bund with Ming at their heels. They stopped for a while to watch the diverse shipping loading and unloading along the waterfront. The usual bustling crowds of pedestrians and rickshaws were noisily rushing in all directions.

'Plenty of activity, Cap,' said Jacko. 'Here and now, you'd hardly believe there'd been a war, eh?'

'No, I suppose it was always like this before the Japanese invasion,' said Jamie. 'It's a pity there's a civil war going on in the rest of the country now. We might as well get back to the house and tell Johnny about our departure and prepare our things for an early start tomorrow. It'll be good to catch up with our wives, eh Jacko?'

'Yeah, I reckon, Cap. Better than good! In the meantime, I've got to talk to a nurse about a dog. C'mon, Ming.'

* * * *

As earlier arranged by Harry, Major Joe Stevenson and Lieutenant Ricardo Gamboa of the Philippines Constabulary arrived at midday at the Sailor's Log Cabin near the waterfront in Cebu where Harry introduced them to Henri, Bella, Monique, Carna and Sarah. Over lunch, Joe laid out a map of Samar on the table and pointed to Llorente on the east coast.

'Si! That's the place where we were held prisoner,' cried Carna. 'We would still be there if not for mi mejor amiga, my best friend, Sarah here.'

Sarah averted her eyes, an embarrassed flush in her cheeks as they all looked at her with open admiration and nodded.

'What I propose is this,' continued Joe. 'We'll take two boats. We've got two fast boats, former MTBs, which could reach Giporlos, in southern Samar, from here in about ten hours. It will take a few hours this afternoon to get them ready. We'll be leaving before dawn tomorrow morning, probably around three am. I guess you'll be coming along, Harry?'

'Wouldn't miss it for the world, Joe.'

166

'Good.' Addressing Henri, Bella, Monique, Carna and Sarah who were all staring at him, he added, 'Because you are familiar with the region, I'd like one of you to come along too.'

'Non, non, non!' cried Bella. 'I told you before. I won't let my husband go. Or Monique.'

'Don't worry, Madame Rousseau,' said Joe. 'I was thinking only of Sarah who had the initiative to bring off that amazing rescue of your husband and Carna.'

'Aye yu. l come,' exclaimed Sarah.

'Très dangereux!' said Monique. 'You must stay here, Sarah.'

'I would also prefer you stayed here, Sarah,' said Carna, giving her a brief hug. 'But whatever I say, you'll go anyway, no?'

'Aye yu. Go anyway.'

'Well, I think we're all agreed. Glad to have you aboard, Sarah,' said Joe. 'You'll be going in the first boat with three of my best men, including Lieutenant Gamboa. You'll disembark at Giporlos and walk to Llorcntc to prcvcnt any of thc criminals cscaping that way by land. The second boat, with me aboard, will skirt around Calicoan Island and approach Llorente from the ocean. I'll have five of my constabulary unit with me, and Harry. We hope the essence of surprise will avoid any resistance.'

'Those bandidos are well armed, Major Stevenson,' said Carna. 'Be careful.'

'We shall, Carna,' he responded. 'Don't worry. My men are well trained to handle any resistance. They will also be instructed to keep Sarah as safe as possible. Please call me Joe.'

'Si! The locals speak the Waray Waray language in Samar, Joe,' she explained.

'A couple of my men are from that area, Carna,' said Joe. 'No problem.'

'No problem,' repeated Sarah with a beaming smile.

'That's right, Sarah,' said Joe. 'You'd better get to bed early tonight. I'll have you picked up at the Magellan at two-thirty tomorrow morning.'

'Aye yu, boss. No problem.'

As they were rising to leave, Manny Alvarez entered the Sailor's Log Cabin and exclaimed, 'Son of a gun! Here you all are. What's happening?'

'We're off to Samar tomorrow to round up the baddies, Manny,' said Joe.

'Son of a gun! You need my boat, no?'

'No, Manny. Not this time. I'm taking two MTBs to Samar. You can go fishing tomorrow,' said Joe, laughing.

'Well, if you need me, you know where I am,' said Manny. 'Are all of my friends from Australia going with you?'

'No, just Sarah,' said Joe.

'Ah! The heroína of Llorente!' said Manny, laughing. 'If you get into trouble, Joe, she will be there to save you.'

'You're right, Manny.'

'Aye yu! You right, Manny,' Sarah laughed.

* * * *

Overnight, the wind and rain eased off considerably along the east coast of Samar. The heavy waves that had washed into the shore, streaming over the pier and freighter, had reduced to moderate rollers hours before dawn. Trevor Clark awoke and instructed McIntyre to rouse his men and some locals to set up lights on the pier and resume loading the copra bundles.

'Gaisi de waiguo ren! Damned foreigners,' grumbled Gao to Huang, observing McIntyre, Bradford and Atkins rushing to comply. 'What will become of us? They all have way out. We are thrown on trash heap.'

For the next few hours there was considerable activity between the shed and the pier. As dawn broke, the freighter was reported to have a full load.

The Australian, Luke Atkins, informed McIntyre that as soon as the freighter had taken on more fuel it would be ready to leave.

'They had to use some fuel to pump out the water from the bilge,' he said. 'The captain, Colin Flinn, reckons it's best to top it up before we go.'

'Aye! O' course! Na kinch. We'll git tae it, then,' said McIntyre, his Scottish brogue pronounced as he became more excited at the thought of leaving.

'When will the damned boat be ready to leave!' yelled Trevor Clark, walking towards the pier from the main shed.

'Soon, soon, Mr Clark,' replied McIntyre, slightly out of breath from carrying two five-gallon jerry cans of diesel. 'Just have to top her up.'

'Well, get going as soon as you can,' said Clark tersely. 'The sooner we all get away from here the better.'

'How come a' th' hurry?' asked McIntyre combatively.

'Because, you Scottish twit, the project has been compromised. It's entirely likely that your Frenchman was not the innocent visitor he seemed,' Clark replied sarcastically. 'You don't want to be caught here with your pants down, do you?'

'No, no. I guess not,' said McIntyre. 'Anyway, we should be underway within an hour or so.'

He rushed along the pier with his jerry cans, muttering, 'Humourless boring old bastard.'

Looking back over his shoulder, he saw Clark's glaucous eyes, below a knitted forehead, glaring at him from the start of the pier. He couldn't have heard that, he thought to himself. He shrugged. Anyway, I won't have to worry about him any more once we get underway. Glad to see the last of him.

* * * *

As dawn was breaking, the two MTBs chartered by the Philippine Constabulary had already crossed the Camotes Sea and were heading southeast along the coast of southern Leyte. Through his binoculars, Joe Stevenson could see the southern tip of Panaon Island ahead on the port bow. The clouds in the east were clearing and although there was a slight mist, visibility was good.

'Looks like we're in for a nice day. In another hour we'll pass Panaon and from there head up north to Samar,' he said to Harry. 'We'll part company with the other boat in about another three hours.

169

When we're abeam of Homonhon Island, we'll take off east while the other boat will stay on course for Giporlos.'

'What time will we get to Llorente?' asked Harry.

'Ah, let's see,' replied Joe, looking at his watch. 'I guess around mid-afternoon. The other boat'll be into Giporlos well before that. Just after midday, I reckon.'

'Those smugglers will get a bit of a surprise when they see us charging in,' said Harry, grinning.

'They sure will. We may come under fire though. Are you up to that, Harry?'

'As we Texans say, Joe, this ain't my first rodeo!'

CHAPTER 18

The sun was rising into a cloudless blue sky when the C54 Skymaster took off from the Kiangwan Air Base in the north of Shanghai, heading out over the China Sea.

Jacko gazed thoughtfully out the window of the aircraft at the sea below. Foremost was his exhilaration at reuniting with Monique, perhaps later in the day. He was worried that Sarah might be overcome by being in such a strange place without him. She would be happy having Carna there, however. He felt strangely bereft at his earlier parting from Ming. He had been unusually emotional as he and Jamie had left the house in the old city. He had looked back at the smiling young Chinese nurse, Yuan, sitting on the front steps with her arms wrapped around the neck of the large Chinese wolfdog that had stared back at him with sorrowful eyes. He'd had an affinity with Ming he had not shared with other animals. I miss that dog, he thought.

The ever-friendly Seiki had driven the two of them out to the air base. He had seen them onto the Skymaster with much bowing, handshaking, and assurances that their colleague, Johnny Cook, was in good hands.

Breaking from his reverie, Jacko looked around at his fellow passengers, mainly GIs homeward bound as well as USAAF personnel reassigned to the military air base at Clark Field. Most of them were playing cards with loud exclamations and laughter. Jamie, beside him, was sitting back with his eyes closed. Perhaps dreaming of his Carna? Jacko glanced out the window again, decided that Jamie had the right idea, and sat back and shut his eyes also. I miss that dog.

He awoke when the captain announced they would be landing at Clark Field in half an hour and to fasten seat belts. He could make out the Philippines coastline on the left side of the aircraft as they flew over the Lingayan Gulf before starting their descent over rice paddies and farmland approaching Clark Field.

When they touched down, a few Americans cheered as though they hadn't expected a smooth landing. The GI next to Jamie

171

explained that Clark Field had been seriously damaged during the war and they hadn't been sure about the recent state of repair of the airstrips.

'It was a nice smooth landing,' commended Jamie.

'Yeah, it's cool man,' said the GI. 'They must've resurfaced the runway.'

After alighting from the Skymaster, Jamie and Jacko noticed construction in progress all over the base. They were met by Captain Bruce Meyer, a short brisk officer who asked them if they were the Australians they were expecting.

'That's us,' said Jacko. 'You got it in one! I'm Jack O'Brien and this is Jamie Munro.'

'Good. I've got instructions to put you on a flight to Mactan Airfield,' said Meyer. 'It will be taking off in about an hour. In the meantime, I can offer you gentlemen a questionable cup of coffee in our mess.'

'That sounds perfect,' responded Jamie.

'Okay. This way, gentlemen.'

'You wouldn't have a cold beer, would you?' ventured Jacko.

'Sorry, sir. The club doesn't open until six in the evening,' said Meyer. 'Hot coffee or cold lemonade is all we can offer you now.'

Seated in the mess hall, Jamie asked, 'How many aircraft do you have here at the moment?'

'I'm not sure I'm supposed to tell you that, but what the hell! You're the good guys,' Meyer chuckled. 'Most of the US aircraft have moved to other fields closer to Japan, but we've still got a number of B29 bombers of the 313th Bombardment wing. So-called super-fortresses. A couple of fighters and a bunch of derelict aircraft, mainly P-38s cannibalised for parts.'

'Lots of construction going on,' remarked Jamie.

'Oh yeah! Plenty. We're even building a super-duper golf course,' said Meyer. 'You guys can shoot a few holes when you're here next.'

'That sounds like the best type of shooting,' said Jamie. 'Never played, but I'll have a go.'

'We can lend you some sticks,' said Meyer. 'What do you think of the coffee?'

'Questionable,' replied Jacko.

'Yeah. We're hoping to get some good stuff in next week,' said Meyer. 'Your flight should be ready soon, so we'll go back to the airstrip now.'

'Are we taking a B29?' asked Jacko.

'In your dreams, buddy,' Meyer laughed. 'It's the same Skymaster you came in. You should be at Mactan by this evening. If you want to reserve a hotel room in Cebu, ask the captain.'

'Thanks a lot, Captain Meyer,' said Jamie.

'You're welcome, guys. Take care.'

They took off and passed over Manila Bay and soon after, Jamie was able to identify the large lake, Laguna de Bay, through the left-hand side window of the aircraft. He was about to point it out to Jacko when he saw that his colleague had already lapsed into sleep. I don't know how he does that, he thought. Lucky sod! His smile means he's probably dreaming of Monique. Don't blame him. I can't wait to see my Carna again. With that on his mind, he closed his eyes and lay back in his seat.

* * * *

By the time the first MTB, carrying Joe Stevenson, Joe's men and Harry Williams, had rounded Calicoan Island headed north along the Samar east coast to Llorente, the second MTB was already moored to the pier at Giporlos. Lieutenant Gamboa, Sarah and the other two men disembarked and set off on foot heading north along the road.

Harry and Joe's MTB pitched gently in the ocean in three-foot swells under a nearly cloudless sky. Looking to the east, all Harry could see was an empty ocean except for the sails of a distant yacht on the horizon. In the moderate conditions, the boat was able to increase speed to sixteen knots, creating a rougher ride and making its passengers hold on to avoid being tossed around.

'Should be there just after three o'clock at this rate,' Joe told Harry. 'The smugglers at Llorente are in for a big surprise.'

'Yeah, but it feels like I'm riding a wild bull right now,' said Harry.

Joe laughed. 'You told me before that this wasn't your first rodeo!'

'Yeah, but this ain't no ten-second buck-jumping.'

'You wouldn't want Sarah and the boys to arrive before us, would you?' asked Joe, shouting above the roar of the engines.

'Naw, keep it up, cowboy!' Harry shouted back. 'No time to mosey now.'

Within three hours, they were headed towards the coast near Llorente. A church spire with a large cross was prominent above the village off the starboard bow, while off the port bow they could see a pier extending out from the headland south of an extensive black-sand beach. Behind the pier they distinguished several sheds, but there was no sign of activity around them.

As the MTB approached the pier, Joe Stevenson and his men had their firearms ready for any opposition. They moored the boat to the pier and the men quickly spread out and ran towards the sheds, which they searched one after the other.

'The whole place is deserted,' said Joe to Harry. 'There's been recent activity here but no one's around. No boats! Curious!'

'Yeah. There's quite a bit of copra in the main shed and a few bags of powder, which I suspect is opium,' said Harry. 'Perhaps the villagers know what's happened.'

Joe spoke to two of his men, who trotted off to the village while the rest resumed their search of the sheds. One of the men emerged from the hut nearest to the pier and shouted to Joe who, with Harry, followed him inside.

Joe studied the hole through the roof in the wash room and said, 'Hmm. Looks like we've found the hut from which Henri and Carna escaped. We've sure come to the right place. But where is everybody?'

'Beats me, Joe,' replied Harry, puzzled.

Returning to the main shed, they waited for the others to arrive back from the village. When they did, they informed Joe that a boat had left earlier in the day, a sailing boat with two masts. Some of the bad men had departed with the boat, the villagers said, but three had headed south towards Hernani in a truck. All of them gone.

'Goddamn it! We'd best get around to Giporlos to back up the others in case they've encountered that truck,' said Joe.

One of his men, Sergeant Juan Benitez, saluted him and said, 'Sir. Better way. We can go down coast to Matarinao Bay. I know this area. There's a pier near a barrio behind Anahap Island. On the road ten miles south of Hernani. If you drop some of us there we can go along the road to Giporlos and meet you there. Much quicker.'

'Excellent plan, Sergeant Benitez,' said Joe, clapping him on the shoulder. 'Let's get underway. Everybody aboard!'

They sped away from the pier and Joe asked Sergeant Benitez, 'What's the name of the barrio?'

'The locals now refer to it as General MacArthur, sir.'

'I suppose they would,' said Joe, laughing.

* * * *

Earlier, Sarah, Lieutenant Gamboa and the other two constabulary officers, Matty and Tomas, were six miles north of Giporlos where the muddy road they had followed joined the coastline, when they heard loud voices ahead. They all quickly melted into the rainforest on the left side of the road and listened to the voices raised in argument.

'You follow me, okay?' Sarah whispered to Gamboa and the others, setting off through the trees. They had to walk briskly to keep up with the diminutive black girl ahead and Gamboa marvelled at how easily she moved through the thick bushland, almost as though she had lived in Samar all her life.

Although it was not raining, the foliage continually dripped and they were all wet by the time they had drawn close to the source of the altercation. Creeping towards the road, Gamboa and the others could see a truck bogged in the mud in the centre of the road. A large, ugly, angry white man, in front of the truck, was berating two men with Chinese features who were staring back at him. A Filipino driver was sitting at the wheel of the truck. The white man was swearing loudly at the others and pointing at the truck, his clenched fist trembling with rage, his eyes suffused with red. The Chinese were covered in mud and sludge. They had been trying to push the truck out of the bog and had finally given up.

Sarah noted that one of the Chinese men had a bandage around the top of his head. She smiled when she recognised him as the man she had knocked unconscious when she liberated Henri and Carna. Gamboa signalled to his men, indicating that all three of the fugitives were armed with pistols. He decided that the best plan was to wait to see what eventuated.

As he was watching the scene, Sarah tapped him on the arm, drew his knife out from its pouch behind his back, smiled, and then disappeared into the dense foliage before he could react. Wondering what she was up to, he returned his attention to the men at the front of the truck. By this time, the white man's voice had become hoarse. He was now menacing the two men with his pistol and instructing them to gather leaves and branches to put in front of the tyres. Nodding, they walked towards the tree line, behind which Gamboa and his men were hiding, and sulkily started to pick up sticks and leaves.

Gamboa, his men, and the two Chinese all stopped to stare at the truck when they heard loud hissing sounds and watched in startled silence as the rear tyres went flat.

'Bloody hell!' the white man yelled hoarsely, looking at the trees. 'There must be someone in the forest! Go and find him.'

The two men drew their pistols but hesitated as they assessed the wisdom of plunging into the thick jungle-like growth. Gamboa jumped when Sarah suddenly appeared beside him and handed back his knife. Neither he nor anyone else had seen her stab the rear tyres. He smiled at her and then waited to see what happened next. The two Chinese were only about ten yards from where he was standing. In spite of the white man's urging, they remained where they were.

Then the Chinese with the bandage around his head suddenly drew his pistol and started shooting into the trees. Gamboa, Sarah, Matty and Tomas all hit the ground and lay flat as bullets whined overhead. The second Chinese joined in, shooting indiscriminately into the rainforest. But soon, both men ran out of ammunition and for a while, the only sound was the metallic chorus of cicadas.

They heard the white man mutter, 'Damned fools!'

The Chinese returned and the three men stood frozen in front of the truck, staring at the forest. Finally the white man, whose anger had dispelled, ordered the other two to reload their pistols and start

176

walking. He told them they would try to pick up a fishing boat at Giporlos.

Sarah and the constabulary officers followed them, still concealed in the trees. They had only walked about 400 yards when they heard a shout from behind them. Turning around, they saw several armed and uniformed men passing the bogged truck and approaching the three men at a run.

With a howl of rage, the larger Chinese opened fire while the other two leapt into the rainforest. The white man plunged into the foliage only to find himself stopped short and looking into the barrel of a large revolver held by Lieutenant Gamboa. The other Chinese with the bandaged head blundered through bushes where he was hit over the head again by Sarah brandishing a heavy lump of wood.

The gunfire had ceased when Gamboa and his companions emerged from the forest to be greeted by the newly arrived members of the Philippine Constabulary.

He pushed the white man into the road with the barrel of his revolver and noted the large Chinese lying sprawled and bleeding on the ground. His other two men were carrying the unconscious bandaged Chinese, laying him down on the road.

Sarah beamed at Gamboa and the newcomers.

'Looks like you didn't need our help, sir,' said one of the men, a sergeant.

'You helped all right, sergeant,' said Gamboa. 'Until you arrived, we weren't sure what to do. Handcuff these two. How's the large fellow?'

'I think he's dead, sir.'

'You can't hold me like this!' yelled the white man. 'I'm a representative of the British government.'

'Yes? What's your name?' asked Gamboa.

'My name is Trevor Clark. I'm attached to the British Consulate in Shanghai.'

'You're a long way from there, sir,' said Gamboa with a smile. 'Show me your papers.'

'I... I don't have them with me,' said Clark. 'I demand you take me to Tacloban where I have an aeroplane. I demand diplomatic immunity.'

177

'You are very demanding, sSir,' said Gamboa. 'You'll come along with me and my men to Giporlos. I'll ask my commander what to do.'

'I have money. I'll pay you to take me to Tacloban,' Clark pleaded.

'Keep it. We'll work out what to do with you when we get to Cebu,' said Gamboa tersely, then turning to the sergeant he said, 'what about that other fellow? Will he be able to walk?'

'He's just coming around, sir,' replied the sergeant. 'The lady hit him a good one. I think he'll be okay in a moment.'

'What's his name?' Gamboa asked Clark.

'I only know him as Huang. Now look here, I demand...'

'Oh, shut up!' said Gamboa impatiently.

Three hours later, after half-supporting and half-dragging Huang along, they arrived at Giporlos and were all ensconced in the MTB which had earlier landed Ricky Gamboa, Sarah, Matty and Tomas in Samar. It was estimated that the other boat, with Joe and Harry aboard, would catch up with them from the east coast in another two to three hours. Most of the men fell asleep and the silence was only broken once in a while by protestations from Trevor Clark.

'It is often said that we Filipinos can sleep on a clothes line in a typhoon,' Gamboa confided to Sarah who was eating a sandwich.

'Aye yu! Me too. I sleep good,' she replied with a chuckle.

'You hit Mr Huang pretty hard.'

'Hit 'im twice now.'

'I didn't see you at all when you stabbed those rear tyres on the truck. You're like a shadow,' said Gamboa. Sarah smiled, winked at him, and then closed her eyes to sleep.

In the late afternoon, they were all awake when they heard the growl from the engine of the other MTB. When they had moored the boat, Gamboa explained to Joe and Harry how they had captured the prisoners on account of their truck being bogged, and the assistance of the men he had disembarked at the General MacArthur village. He also explained about the cantankerous Englishman. Harry laughed loudly when told of Sarah's role in the events while Joe went to question Clark, who was sitting on the deck of the boat glaring at him with his hate-filled close-set eyes.

'You've been a naughty boy, Mr Clark,' Joe said with a grim smile.

'You can't hold me, you scum!' yelled Clark, his ugly face turning a shade of purple. 'I'm a British citizen. I've got diplomatic immunity.'

'I see. Well, we have evidence that you've been engaged in criminal activities in the Philippines,' said Joe.

'Evidence? What evidence?' demanded Clark.

'We've brought with us the bags of opium you left behind in Llorente,' said Joe. 'Ring a bell?'

Clark stared at him, then trying a new tack, said, 'Sir, I am a very wealthy man. If you can just take me to Tacloban, I can make it worth your while. All of you.'

'Tacloban? What's in Tacloban?' asked Joe. 'Another smuggling operation?'

'I have an aeroplane there,' said Clark. 'It would be easy for you to take me there in this boat. I need to fly to Shanghai, today.'

'Don't think you'll be flying anywhere for a while,' said Joe, who then told his men to get both boats ready to leave.

'We'll be travelling through the night,' he explained. 'We'll take it easy and should be into Cebu by first light. Lieutenant Gamboa can take Mr Clark here in this boat and I'll take Huang with me in the other boat. He might be able to tell me something before we arrive in Cebu.'

'You can't... you can't...' stuttered Clark, almost frothing at the mouth.

'I can, and I will!' Joe snapped back. 'Okay, men. Whenever you're ready, let's vamoose.'

'Vamoose!' repeated Sarah with a peal of laughter.

Within ten minutes, the two MTBs were out in the Leyte Gulf headed south to pass through the Surigao Strait. A fiery sun was slowly sinking towards the mountains of Leyte on their starboard side.

For a while, Trevor Clark kept up a monologue in a loud but pleading voice. Realising that he was being ignored, he stopped and spent the next hour muttering and swearing to himself as the two boats sped along, side by side, into the darkness.

179

CHAPTER 19

It was already after last light when the C54 Skymaster touched down at the Mactan Airfield. Jacko and Jamie had been dozing but came instantly awake when they felt the aircraft touch the runway. Jacko looked around the cabin at the two GIs, rubbing his eyes.

'Can't wait to see Monique, Cap,' he exclaimed. 'Never been so impatient. I hope to hell the girls and Henri are all okay.'

'Me too, Jacko,' said Jamie. 'The old heart's jumping with anticipation.'

After the aircraft had pulled up next to the terminal, Jacko and Jamie were standing and stretching when the captain entered the cabin from the cockpit and asked them, 'Have you guys got transport to Cebu?'

'No. We'll see if we can get a taxi or something,' said Jamie.

'You can come with us,' said the captain. 'The landing barges across to mainland Cebu aren't working at this time of night. We've got a boat and we can drop you at the port area. I'm Charley Blunt, by the way.'

'We'll accept your offer with pleasure, Charley,' responded Jamie, shaking him by the hand. 'I'm Jamie Munro and this is Jack O'Brien.'

'Just get your baggage and we'll meet you at the gate,' said Charley, opening the outside door, setting the steps and exiting the aircraft.

A large brown military Chevrolet and driver were waiting by the gate. Six men, Charley, his co-pilot, the two GIs, Jamie and Jacko crammed themselves into the car. They drove down to a pier on the western coast of Mactan Island where a large blue motorboat waited. After a smooth crossing on the calm waters of the Mactan Strait, the boat pulled into a pier at the port area of Cebu.

Jamie and Jacko said their goodbyes and after hailing a kalesa, a one-horse cart, they set off up to the Magellan Hotel.

Partly mesmerised by the clip-clop of the horse's hooves as the kalesa climbed the hill towards the hotel, Jamie muttered, 'I reckon they'll all be asleep.'

'Doesn't matter, Cap. They won't mind waking up for us.'

'Reckon you're right, Jacko.'

At the empty reception desk of the hotel, they endured a frustrating few minutes ringing a bell. Finally, a security guard appeared.

'I get someone for you,' he said, disappearing through a door beside the desk. A few minutes later, a sleepy girl in a receptionist's uniform appeared. At first, she hesitated to believe they were the husbands of two of the guests but finally told them the room numbers of Mrs Munro and Mrs O'Brien and gave them spare keys.

'I'm gonna break the world sprint record, Cap,' said Jacko, darting up the hotel stairs with Jamie close behind.

Jacko was first to arrive and made such a noise opening the door, a startled Monique was sitting up in bed staring at him as he entered.

Recognising him, she leapt out of bed, crying, 'Mon Dieu! My God! Mon Jacko! Tu es là. When? How? I am talking too much, mon amour. I am so happy. Happy to see you.'

By comparison, Jamie crept into the room where Carna was sleeping soundly and, walking over to the bed, he looked at her face dimly lit by moonlight through the window. What a beautiful angel, he thought to himself. Almost a pity to wake her.

When he put his hand gently on her forehead, she opened her eyes and shrieked, 'Jamie! Mi amor! You frightened me half to death. Canalla encantador. I hate you and love you at the same time. I didn't know you were coming.'

'We had no chance to warn you,' said Jamie as she rose from the bed and hugged him tightly. 'Sorry to frighten you.'

'No importa! It doesn't matter. You're here. Gracias a Dios. Thank God. Just kiss me and hold me tight,' she cried, the words pouring out rapidly. 'I am so happy.'

It was after four o'clock in the morning when Jacko woke up. He crept out of the bed without waking Monique and sat down on a small couch which he moved to face the window. He gazed out at the eastern sky. There were dark clouds on the horizon, but the rest of the

181

sky was lit by stars and a crescent moon. He was thinking about his half-sister Sarah. She was out there somewhere. Monique had told him that she had insisted on going with the constabulary group to Samar and they hadn't been able to stop her.

Jacko smiled. Even he had never been able to stop her when she had made up her mind. He sensed, somehow, that she was safe, but anxiety lingered in his mind. He noticed movement and soon Monique was sitting beside him.

She laid her head on his shoulder and whispered, 'Worried about Sarah?'

He nodded. 'I'm sure she'll be safe, but she's such a little girl. One day she will try to do too much.'

They sat in companionable silence until the eastern horizon lightened, signalling a new day. Jacko stood up and stretched.

'Sitting here is not going to change anything,' he said. 'We might as well have a short nap and then go down to breakfast. I'm hungry.'

'Bonne idée, good idea, mon Jacko. I am hungry too. For food and for you.'

'I'm very happy about that, my darling.'

Henri and Bella had finished their breakfast by the time the others arrived in the hotel dining room.

'Mon Dieu!' Henri repeated several times. 'I am surprised and happy to see you both here. Safe and well. Bon. Bon. You came last night?'

'G'day Henri, Bella,' Jacko replied, giving them both a brief hug. 'We scared our wives to death last night. I hope they will forgive us one day.'

'Already forgiven but not forgotten,' said Carna, laughing.

'I'm so happy to see you,' said Henri, gesturing for them to sit down at the table. 'You know Sarah is in Samar?'

'Yeah,' agreed Jacko. 'She's pretty good at looking after herself.'

After breakfast, they all went out to the terrace overlooking the tops of palm trees to the distant Camotes Sea. Henri was expounding at length about their ordeal in Samar and their rescue by Sarah when they noticed a brown military car heading up the hill to the hotel.

'I think that's her!' said Jacko, running to the front door of the hotel in time to see Major Joe Stevenson, Harry, and Sarah emerge from the car.

'Brada Jacko!' Sarah shrieked, leaping up the steps and hugging him. 'Plenty worry 'bout you in China place.'

'I was more worried about you, Sar,' said Jacko, laughing. 'I hear you've been bashing baddies over the head with sticks.'

'Aye yu! Bigpela brata! Er ... brother,' she said, as Joe climbed the steps behind her, also laughing. 'Me bashim again.'

'Again, Sar?'

'She sure did,' said Joe, grabbing Jacko by the hand and shaking it. 'I don't know what we would have done without this little tiger.'

'Little tiger,' she repeated, grinning.

'Are you fellas hungry?' asked Jacko.

'C'd eat bigpela crocodile, Jacko,' said Sarah.

'I'll make sure the cook's still around,' said Jacko, running into the dining room.

While they ate a hearty breakfast, Jamie briefly explained that the smuggling operation in China had been effectively neutralised and opium shipments from China would be unlikely to start again.

Joe then narrated to a willing audience how he and Harry had planned to attack the opium shipping point in Samar, found it abandoned, and missed the last freighter. He described how they had captured two of the smugglers and brought them back to Cebu.

'One of them's an Englishman. Arrogant dude,' Joe explained. 'The other's a Chinaman named Huang. When we told him that it was this little girl who rescued Henri and Carna, he burst into tears. He couldn't believe us. He lost a lot of face for a Chinese. I didn't have the heart to tell him that she was the one who whacked him again.'

'Whacked him again!' repeated Sarah, squealing with laughter.

'Did they tell you where the last freighter was bound for?' asked Jamie.

Joe shook his head. 'Naw. Huang let slip it was a sailing boat. We did see a sail on the horizon when we headed up the coast to Llorente. Mighta been it. Anyways, we'll start interrogating them this morning. You guys might want to come along.'

'Yeah, Jacko and I'll be in that for sure,' said Jamie enthusiastically.

'Me too!' said Sarah.

'Are you sure you don't need to rest, Sarah?' asked Carna.

'No, Ka Na. Want to see Chineepela cry again,' she said, chuckling.

'Probably won't be able to stop him talking when he sees Sar again,' said Jacko. 'Bring along a big stick, sis.'

'Aye yu. Big stick.'

'I think I'll leave you younger guys to it,' said Harry. 'I've been dreaming about a soft mattress to lie on all night. Age is catching up.'

An hour later, Jamie, Jacko, Sarah and Joe sat across from a dejected Huang Lei in an interrogation room at the Philippines Constabulary headquarters. Huang was sweating as he stared back at them nervously, trying desperately not to look in Sarah's direction.

Joe finally broke the silence by introducing Jamie and Jacko to Huang, telling him that they were the ones who had destroyed the source of opium supply in China. Huang looked down at his feet and shook his head.

'You are guilty of criminal acts in this country,' he continued. 'If you answer our questions truthfully, it will have a big bearing on what happens to you.'

Huang remained silent, still with downcast eyes.

'We know a freighter, a motorised sailing boat with a cargo of copra and opium, left Llorente a few days ago,' said Joe in a calm voice. 'Where was it going?'

No reaction from the Chinese.

'There is no one to protect you now,' went on Joe. 'No one in China. No one here. Why don't you tell us where the boat went?'

'How about giving Sarah a big stick and leaving her alone with Huang?' said Jacko suddenly.

Startled, Huang looked up at Joe then at Sarah but remained silent.

'Who are you scared of?' asked Joe. 'Mr Clark will probably hang for his crimes and, unless you answer us, so will you.'

'I don't know where boat go,' said Huang. 'Somewhere in Australia.'

'Okay,' said Joe, handing Sarah his truncheon and telling Huang, 'we'll leave you now with Sarah. I know you lost a lot of face when Sarah got the better of you in Llorente. After she gets through with you now you won't have any face left.'

Huang looked at them incredulously when they stood up and headed towards the door, leaving a beaming Sarah holding Joe's large truncheon.

As they filed through the door, Huang yelled, 'Roper! Roper!'

They all came back into the room and sat down again, staring at Huang who winced when Sarah slapped the truncheon against her palm.

'Roper? Where's Roper?' asked Joe.

'Must be the Roper River,' said Jacko, glaring at Huang. 'Did they say it was the Roper River?'

'Yes, sir,' replied Huang, nodding vigorously. 'They say Roper River.'

'Do you know where that is?' Joe asked Jacko.

'Yeah. Big river. Flows into the Limmen Bight, Gulf of Carpentaria,' said Jacko. 'Makes sense. Big wide river. They could load the gear onto trucks below Roper Bar and cart it onto the bitumen near Mataranka.' Jacko was referring to the narrow strip of paved road extending over 1,000 miles from Alice Springs to Darwin.

'Roper Bar?' asked Jamie.

Jacko nodded. 'Yeah, Cap. Roper Bar. A natural rock weir about sixty miles from the coast. A small freighter could get all the way up there. They must have some trucking point east of the Bar. There's a police station there.'

'Need anything more from this prisoner?' asked Joe.

'No. Don't think so, Joe,' replied Jacko. 'Would you like us to leave Sarah with him for a while? Beat him up a bit?'

This brought a groan from Huang who put his face in his hands.

'No. I'll be asking him further questions to provide more evidence against our ugly Englishman. I also want to know where the freighters bound for the USA were headed. It needn't involve you guys any more. We'll keep Sarah in reserve,' said Joe, winking. 'You can use my car and driver for the rest of the day. Send the driver back

185

here by six and I'll meet you up at the Magellan. You can tell me all about China.'

Sarah was shrieking with laughter as she left with Jamie and Jacko.

'Well, I think we'd better get back to Darwin as soon as possible and have a look at the Roper River region, eh Jacko?' said Jamie.

'Yeah. It's a helluva long river, Cap. My guess is we'll find what we're looking for downstream from Roper Bar. They would more likely truck the opium south to Borroloola to avoid the police station.'

'Do you know that Roper River country at all, Jacko?'

'Nah. Learnt all about it in geography class, Cap.'

'Excellent, Jacko. Lucky you paid attention. Let's see if we can organise a flight to Darwin for seven in the next day or so,' said Jamie. 'I'll ask Harry when he wakes up.'

'Bloody good, I reckon, Cap.'

'Bloody good!' repeated Sarah.

A few hours later after Joe had arrived, they were all sitting on the verandah of the Magellan Hotel with cool drinks in hand, watching strata clouds in the east changing colours as the sun went down behind them.

'Baja California,' said Joe triumphantly.

'Baja California? Where's that?' asked Jamie.

'It's a large peninsula just south of California on the Mexican side,' replied Joe. 'The opium smugglers from Samar have been unloading their cargos on the Costa de Oro. Tijuana. It's not far south of San Diego. The border's quite porous around those parts. I've alerted the OSS to take care of it.'

'So, your Chinese friend spilled the beans,' observed Jacko.

'Yes. I put my truncheon on the table in front of him and mentioned Sarah,' said Joe with a mischievous grin. 'Couldn't shut him up after that.'

'Scary young bird, my sister,' said Jacko, provoking a loud giggle from Sarah.

'So, when are you guys leaving? Have you booked a flight?' asked Joe.

'Unfortunately, Harry couldn't organise something for us directly from Cebu to Darwin,' said Jamie. 'We'll all fly to Manila tomorrow

186

evening and then from Manila, Harry's arranged a USAAF flight to Darwin for us the following morning.'

'Nothin's too good for my Aussie friends,' said Harry.

'So you'll have a few more hours to enjoy the delights of Cebu,' said Joe. 'Speaking of delights, I've brought an extra car with me, as there's nine of us. I suggest we all mosey down to the Sailor's Log Cabin for a juicy steak. You can tell me all about your trip up the Yangtze River over dinner. What do you say, guys?'

'Best suggestion I've heard all day,' said Harry.

'That's just the ticket, Joe,' said Jacko.

'Yay! Just the ticket,' repeated Sarah.

* * * *

It was late afternoon when the weary group stepped off the Avro Lancastrian aircraft at the Darwin Airport two days later. Henri couldn't stop yawning and was relieved when Jacko pointed out Garry 'Sparky' Speck and their friend, the Darwin police chief, Superintendent Russell Fitzgibbon, waiting for them on the tarmac.

'G'day, Fitzy,' greeted Jamie as the superintendent approached. 'Glad to see your smiling face.'

'Yeah. Sparky gave me a cryptic message that you would be going after some smugglers down in the Roper, Jamie,' said Fitzy, shaking his hand. 'Anything I need to know?'

'Yeah, too right!' said Jamie. 'A mob have been shipping opium from China via the Philippines from there. We don't know anything about them, but we'll be going down to Roper Bar in the next couple of days to find out.'

'Opium, eh? Bloody hell!' exclaimed Fitzy. 'I'll come with you if you like. I can bring a few of my men.'

'That'd be good, Fitzy,' said Jamie. 'Jacko and I might go ahead first to work out the lay of the land. After that we'll almost certainly need some backup. Anyway, we'll discuss it this evening. Are you free for dinner?'

'For you fellas, I'm always available, mate,' said Fitzy. 'When we've got your luggage loaded, Sparky and I'll take you mob into town.'

187

'Could do with a cold beer, Cap,' said Jacko.

'Why am I not surprised, Jacko?'

Sparky dropped Jamie and Carna off at their house near Doctors Gully and then drove Sarah to the Darwin Hotel where the Rousseaus, Jacko, Monique and Fitzy were waiting for them.

'Why don't all you people freshen up in your rooms and I'll go and rustle up some maps of the Roper River,' said Fitzy. 'I'll be back in about half an hour. By that time Jamie and his beautiful bride should be here. Once I've shown Jamie and Jacko the maps, we can slip along to the Knickerbocker for a steak.'

'Always steak,' said Henri, chuckling. 'I should open a French restaurant in Australia one day to show you real food. Vraie cuisine.'

'I'll be in that,' said Jacko. 'Do they cook dumplings in France?'

'Stupide!' exclaimed Monique. 'Come on, Jacko. We'll go and have a wash in our room. Dumplings! Merde!'

Fitzy chortled as he drove to the police station to collect the maps. What a mob of characters, he told himself. Bloody effective, though!

As predicted, half an hour later Jamie and Carna, freshly washed and changed, arrived at the hotel. Fitzy spread out a map on one of the tables on the hotel verandah, pointing out the location of Roper Bar. Jamie and Jacko studied the map, with Sarah watching them closely. She didn't understand what the map showed them but was sure it must be important. Henri and the three wives sat at another table and chatted.

'There's a young policeman at Roper Bar,' Fitzy said. 'The nearest settlements are an Anglican mission, the Roper River Mission, just north of the Bar in southern Arnhem Land, and to the west is a cattle station, Roper Valley Downs. Most of the Aborigines in Arnhem Land live around the missions or work on the cattle stations. A smuggling operation downstream from Roper Bar would get little disturbance or interference, but my guess is most of the locals around Roper Bar must know about it, even if they don't know what it is. Few secrets in that part of the world.'

'Do you know the policeman at Roper Bar, Fitzy?' asked Jamie.

'Yeah. Chief Constable Jake Bradwood,' replied Fitzy. 'Good young fella. Has three black police on his staff. Does the rounds over a large area. Knows everyone by now.'

'Yeah, well it seems to me that the best plan of attack would be for Jacko and me to go on ahead. We'll confirm our plans tomorrow. We could leave the day after tomorrow and make some enquiries in the Roper region,' said Jamie. 'You and your men could follow a day later. Tell anyone who asks that you're only there to visit the police station at Roper Bar. By the time you get there, Jacko and I hope to have gathered enough information about the smuggling project to know where it is and to plan what we can do about it.'

'Whoa! Me come too, bikpela brother,' said Sarah.

'No, no, little sister. You have to take care of your studies here,' said Jacko, winking at Jamie. 'You have to learn to say things like "I will come too", for example.'

'I will come too,' said Sarah carefully.

'Hey, Sar. That's not bad,' said Jacko, smiling broadly. 'Okay! I reckon you can come too.'

'Yay!'

Jacko hugged Sarah.

Fitzy laughed then cleared his throat, asking, 'Did you find out anything about the Roper operations?'

'No. I don't think the fellow we questioned knew anything about that,' replied Jamie. 'We don't know how much opium they have on site, but we do know there's another boat on the way.'

'There won't be any more boats after that one,' said Jacko. 'We've managed to throw a spanner into their source of supply. But we think that the boat will be carrying a lot of the stuff.'

'Yeah, well. We'll have to throw a spanner into their venture too, won't we?' said Fitzy.

'We might borrow your map when we take off, Fitzy, if you don't mind,' said Jamie.

'It's all yours, Jamie,' said Fitzy. 'I'm looking forward to this venture. So, who's for a bloody big juicy rump steak?'

CHAPTER 20

The Brown Dolphin, a 70-foot ketch, was just off the west coast of the lush green island of Waiwo, Netherlands New Guinea, sailing at around twelve knots over calm azure seas, propelled by its powerful diesel engine and a steady north-easterly wind.

Hamish McIntyre climbed out of the cabin onto the deck, blinking in the sunlight. He looked seedy and pale after days of seasickness and engine noise, the clatter of halliards against the masts, and the constant smell of diesel fuel that didn't help a pounding headache.

'Where are we, Col?' he asked the captain, Colin Flinn, who was at the long tiller concentrating on the sails.

Bloody landlubbers, Flinn thought to himself as he answered, 'We're just off the coast of Waiwo Island. We'll be sailing down the coast of Dutch New Guinea for the next twenty-four hours or so before we duck in to pass the northern tip of Trangan.'

McIntyre nodded, causing pains to shoot through his skull. He didn't have a clue what the captain was talking about but was unwilling to question him further. He wished the deck would stop moving around even if only for a short while. He was hot and sweating as he looked at the land passing on the port side. Rocks, jungle and patches of white sand. He shuddered. Luke Atkins was sitting with his back against the main mast looking for'ard, chatting to and laughing with the other two members of the crew who were sunning themselves on the foredeck. Luke was obviously enjoying himself. Bloody Australians, he thought. Sea travel, they can shove it. The Englishman, Nick Bradford, had if anything suffered worse than him and was still lying below on a bunk, groaning. Damned Sassenach!

Flinn interrupted his thoughts. 'We're over halfway.'

McIntyre groaned. Halfway! Another four or five days of enduring this, he thought. God! But there was nothing he could do about it. Maybe he should try a bit of that opium they were carrying. The thought of his share of the valuable cargo calmed him a little until a welling in his throat made him rush to the side of the boat.

'Not to windward, you stupid bugger!' yelled Flinn. 'Bloody hell!'

Too late, McIntyre realised that it was up to him to clean up the side of the boat where he had vomited. He would have to wash his shirt too.

'You blighters never learn,' said Flinn. 'You always let fly to the lee side.'

'Yeah, yeah, yeah,' muttered McIntyre as he went below in search of a bucket and mop. I never want to see a boat again after this, he thought.

* * * *

Early the following morning, Jacko was woken by a knock on the door of his hotel room. Garry Speck was there to ask him to go and listen to something in the radio room.

'I've been cruising through the band signals on our radio for the past few days and I've discovered a frequency I'd like you to listen to,' he told Jacko. 'It transmits at seven.'

'Yeah, okay, Sparky. I'll be with you in a jiff,' said Jacko.

Jacko found Sparky sitting next to their large Hallicrafter radio, adjusting the dial. The radio was only transmitting static.

'Any time now, Jacko,' he said.

'I'm all ears, Sparky.'

Suddenly there was a brief explosion of sound followed by a clear voice, 'BD to RV. BD to RV. Over.'

'RV here. Go ahead BD. Over.'

'BD. S 2 point 92. E 131 point 87. Eleven K. Over.'

'RV. Got that BD. Anything else? Over.'

'BD. Negative. Over and out.'

'RV. Out.'

The sounds from the radio reverted to static and Jacko asked, 'What was that about, Sparky?'

'I've written it all down. I'm pretty sure it's a small ship giving its position, but it's not using the normal ship-to-shore channels,' explained Sparky.

'Ah. Can you work out the position, Sparky?'

'Yeah. I'm sure that the latitude is 2.92 degrees south and the longitude 131.87 degrees east. I'll just plot that on our map.'

After carefully plotting the latitude and longitude, Sparky turned to Jacko and said, 'That boat is just off a cape with the delightful name of Fak Fak, Jacko. The cape is part of Dutch Papua New Guinea. At the last transmission, the boat was northwest of there, so it's headed south. It might be your boat from Samar.'

'Yeah. Possible. What does Eleven K mean?'

'I'd say eleven knots, for sure. The speed of the vessel.'

Jacko scratched his chin thoughtfully. 'If it is our boat, Sparky, do you think you could estimate the time of arrival at the Roper River?'

'Yeah, I'll try, Jacko.' Sparky then made some measurements on the map and started some long-hand calculations. Ten minutes later, he said, 'They're still about 1,200 nautical miles from the Roper River, so if they maintain that speed, it would be another 110 hours, or about four and a half days. So they should be there just after dark, four days from now.'

'That's bloody amazing, Sparky. Your blood's worth bottling.'

'You've told me that before, Jacko.'

'Just to be sure, keep tuning into them every morning, Sparky. I believe we can contact you through the police radio at Roper Bar when we get there. I'd better go and see if Jamie's surfaced yet. He'll be very interested. See ya later.'

Jamie observed that they might have plenty of time to take care of the mob on the Roper River before the boat arrived.

They spent most of the day planning with Russell Fitzgibbon, organising supplies, and learning more about the Roper River country from friends in Darwin who knew the region. They also went out to the airport to see Henri and Bella on a flight to Brisbane. Fitzy had managed to book them on the flight, as Henri was keen to return to complete the setting up of his furniture sales centre there.

Monique was a little teary that evening as they sat on the verandah of the hotel eating an early dinner. It was not so much the departure of her parents. She was upset at the thought of Jacko chasing criminals again so soon after their return to Darwin.

'I know it is what you do, Jacko, but I can't help worrying every time you put yourself in danger,' she said.

192

'Don't worry about me. Danger has trouble catching up with me in the Australian bush,' he said, grinning. 'Anyway, I've got Sarah here to look after me.'

This was greeted by a giggle from Sarah as Monique added, 'Come back to me, Jacko, and take care of Sarah, too.'

'Si! You must take care of Sarah,' agreed Carna. 'I'll be angry with you if anything happens to her.'

'What about me?' said Jamie, putting on a pained expression.

'I am also angry with you if you don't come back,' she said, trying not to smile. 'And you must also look after Sarah.'

'Who's going to look after me?' complained Jacko.

'I'll look after you, Jacko,' said Jamie, laughing.

'Okay, that's settled,' said Jacko. 'Jamie looks after me, I look after Sarah, and she looks after Jamie.'

'You are impossible, Jacko,' Monique laughed.

'Whoever looks after who, we'd better get an early night,' said Jamie. 'We're off very early in the morning. Time for shut-eye.'

It was still dark when Jamie, Jacko and Sarah set off down the bitumen in their Willys jeep. They had already passed through Adelaide River by the time the sun rose. Two hours later, after passing through the old gold workings around Pine Creek, they drove through tropical savanna shrublands, and past rugged rock outcrops and the large red sandstone escarpments bordering the gorges along the Katherine River. After reaching Knott's Crossing, the low-level concrete river crossing that was well above the usual water level at that time of year, they entered the town of Katherine and pulled up at Knott's Store to refuel and buy sandwiches.

The owner of the grocery store, Fred Knott, greeted them from behind the counter. Then he raised his eyebrows and exclaimed, 'G'day! I know you fellas. Jamie and Jacko. Am I right?'

'Guilty as charged, Fred,' replied Jamie.

'Still chasing bad men?'

'Yeah, a whole new mob of baddies, Fred. Bad bastards. We need to buy some more petrol from you.'

'Not a problem. Is that your jeep next to the bowser, Jamie?'

'Sure is. That's the one. We might also get some fresh sandwiches to take with us,' said Jamie.

'Yeah. I'll just fill up your jeep first,' said Fred. 'Are you heading out to the Kimberley country again?'

'No. Going the other way. We're off down to Roper Bar,' said Jamie.

'Roper Bar! I've got a couple of boxes of supplies for the police station and the mission,' said Fred. 'Any chance you could take those with you? The Connellan Airways flight out there's not due till next week.'

'Happy to do that, Fred,' said Jamie. They all walked outside to the petrol bowser and Fred started filling the tank of the jeep.

'G'day, Sarah. Nice to see you again,' said Fred when he saw her sitting in the back of the jeep.

'G'day, Fred,' she replied, smiling shyly at him.

After a while, Fred exclaimed, 'Geez! This little jeep takes a lot of fuel.'

'Yeah. Good thing we don't need petrol ration books any more. Long-range tanks, Fred.'

'You need them out there,' he agreed.

As they went back inside the store, he said, 'There's more than a couple of boxes, I have to admit. If you could take the five most urgent, there should still be room for Sarah, but you don't have to. There's a mailbag too. I'll make your sandwiches now.'

'We'll take your boxes,' said Jacko. 'Sarah won't mind. How often does the aeroplane go out to Roper Bar, Fred?'

'Weekly. Sometimes fortnightly,' said Fred, cutting into a loaf of bread. 'Connellan flies a de Havilland Dragon Rapide. Twin biplane. Regular orders come in by radio from the Roper Bar police and the mission.'

'Do you get any orders from other groups down there?' asked Jamie.

'No, not usually. Only if there's a government survey crew there, or something like that,' replied Fred. 'Why do you ask?'

'No reason,' said Jamie. 'Are there still lots of military fellas around here, Fred?'

'Just a few, Jamie. Not as many as there were last year when you were here.'

'Makes sense. Now where are those boxes?'

The five boxes were of varying sizes. After carefully stowing them in the jeep, there was just enough room for Sarah to sit comfortably in the back.

'Would you like to sit in the front, Sar?' offered Jacko gallantly.

'You too bikpela, Jacko,' she said, laughing.

'Okay, Sar,' said Jacko, as they set off down the road. 'Just sing out if you're getting squeezed.'

This was greeted by a giggle from the back. Jamie said, 'About an hour and a half to Mataranka, Jacko.'

'Hope we've got room to fit in a case or two of beer, Cap.'

'Always room for that, Jacko.'

'Yeah, I reckon, Cap.'

The country changed from low rocky hills to grassy plains with several stands of eucalyptus and paperbark trees, mulga, and scrub persisting all the way until they sighted the green corrugated iron roof of the Mataranka Pub at the junction of the bitumen. A gravel road stretched out towards the Elsie Downs homestead to the east.

'We could have a cool one while we're here, Cap,' suggested Jacko.

'You'll be taking over the driving from here, Jacko,' warned Jamie.

'Just the one, eh Cap?'

'Yeah, that wouldn't hurt.'

'C'mon, sis. I'll get you a nice cold orange juice.'

'Aye yu, bikpela brother,' said Sarah, emerging from amongst the boxes. 'Good proot, Jacko.'

'Fruit, Sar. Fruit.'

'Proot. I said proot, Jacko.'

'Never mind, Sar. Let's go.'

The bar was busy, considering it was still morning. Jamie went up and ordered. 'A couple of cold middies of beer and one of orange juice, Harry.'

The barman looked at him in surprise. 'Do I know you, mate?'

'Yeah, we were here last year,' said Jamie. 'We were chasing a gang of criminals who'd dropped in here.'

'Ah, yeah. I remember you now. Those fellas were rough buggers. Did you catch 'em?' he asked.

195

'Yep. Put them away for keeps,' said Jamie. 'You've got a good crowd in here this morning.'

'The fellas on the cattle stations around here are up and about real early,' said Harry. 'They're hungry by about ten o'clock. Come in here for an early counter lunch with a beer chaser. Anything else I can do for you today?'

'Yeah. We'll take a couple of cases of beer, Melbourne Bitter, for the road,' said Jamie.

'Okey doke! What road are you taking?'

'Going down to Roper Bar,' Jamie replied.

'Dusty old road,' Harry observed. 'You might need a beer by the time you get there. I'll get them for you now.'

He placed two cases on the bar and Jamie paid for them and asked, 'Have you heard of any other groups, recently arrived, around Roper Bar? That is, other than the police, the local Aborigines, cattle stations, and the Roper River Mission?'

Harry scratched his chin, screwing up his eyes as he pondered the question. 'Other groups? No other groups from down that way buy anything from here, except for the ones you mentioned. Nothing I know of. There is, however, a rumour about a mob downriver from the Bar, but that's all it is. A rumour.'

When the beer cases were stowed in the jeep, they set off down the bitumen with Jacko in the driver's seat. After five miles, they turned east along the rough gravel road through Elsie Downs cattle country towards the Roper Valley.

The road led over plains with scattered bloodwoods, box eucalypts, and stringybark trees interspersed with lancewood and other acacias. The road was dry at this time of year. In spite of the bumpy and rutted surface, the jeep maintained a speed of around forty miles an hour. Jamie estimated they would take about three hours from the bitumen turnoff to Roper Bar unless they had a mishap such as a flat tyre or a breakdown.

Jacko put his hand on his head and said, 'Touch wood! We'll be okay, Cap. Though we could do with better shock absorbers.'

After hitting a pothole, Jamie turned around and asked, 'Are you all right back there, Sarah?'

'Aye yu! Plenty bumpy. Me and boxes. Orright!' she cried from the back.

The gravel road slowly descended through raw-red hills into the river valley where large isolated herds of cattle grazed, mainly in the shade of eucalypt trees and banyan groves. Occasionally, where the road ran beside the glittering river, they passed through majestic rocky brick-red gorges with pandanus growing along the riverbanks, then out onto open plains again. It was already early afternoon by the time they sighted a homestead in the distance. Beside the homestead they saw various sheds, silos, and cattle yards. A signpost indicated that they were on Roper Valley Cattle Station.

Pulling up beside the homestead, Jamie and Jacko alighted from the jeep as a tall man with a large wide-brimmed hat stepped onto the verandah and called, 'G'day! I saw your dust from miles away. Where are you headed?'

'We're going to Roper Bar to visit with Jake Bradwood, the policeman,' said Jamie. 'I'm Jamie Munro, this is Jack O'Brien, and hidden amongst the boxes in the back of the jeep is Jacko's sister, Sarah.'

The tall man smiled broadly and said, 'You fellas are just in time for lunch. My wife, Beryl, can throw a few more steaks on the fire, no problem. My name's Ray Turner, owner and manager of this cattle station. Come in and meet the wife.'

'We've got some sandwiches for lunch,' protested Jamie, but not strongly. The smell of grilling steak was alluring. 'We don't want to put you out.'

'Won't put us out, mate,' said Ray. 'Don't get too many visitors, and any friend of Jake's is a friend of mine. Come on in.'

He led them into a large kitchen where a woman in a floral dress, her hair done up in a bun, was cooking steaks on a grill in a large fireplace. As they walked, in she rubbed her hands on her dress and faced them.

'Beryl, these fellas are on the way to the Bar and they look a bit hungry,' said Ray in his booming voice. 'This is Jamie and Jacko. The little black girl is Jacko's sister. Half-sister, I suppose, eh, Jacko?'

'Yeah, Sarah and I have the same mother,' explained Jacko.

197

In the background they could hear a chorus of children's voices, 'Four times five is twenty, four times six is twenty-four, four times seven is twenty-eight …'

'That's the school out the back of the house,' said Ray. 'School's almost finished for the day. In a moment you can meet my two ankle-biters, Tod and Susan, as well as our governess, Lynette. We call her the governess, but she's really the schoolteacher, radio operator, and general factotum.'

'I'll just throw three more steaks on the grill,' said Beryl. 'You fellas relax.'

They sat down at a large wooden table in the middle of the kitchen and in a short while, two children, a boy and girl, rushed in screeching followed by three dogs.

'Get those bloody dogs outta here!' roared Ray.

The children screamed at the dogs, who fled. Then they stopped wide-eyed when they saw the new arrivals. They were followed by a pretty young girl with light-brown hair and freckles around her nose. The men stood, and Ray introduced her as Lynette the governess. She smiled back at them and asked where they were from.

'We came from Darwin this morning,' said Jamie. 'Just on the way to Roper Bar.'

When they were all around the table eating, Jamie asked, 'How big is this cattle station, Ray?'

'Aw, not that big by Territory standards,' replied Ray. 'It's about 3,800 square miles.'

'Must take you a bit of time to get around the whole area,' observed Jacko.

'Aw yeah. I've got some bloody good cattle hands though. The blackfellas on this station are good workers and they can ride anything with four legs. They can tell where the cattle are from miles away.'

'Are you the only white man on the place?' asked Jamie.

'Yep. The hands and their families have their own quarters out the back of the homestead,' explained Ray. 'As well as the salaries for the station hands, we look after their families and educate their children. Lynette does a great job as the schoolteacher.'

'Thanks, Ray,' Lynette smiled. 'Ray exaggerates everything.'

'We also have School of the Air for an hour in the afternoon,' said Ray. 'That's run by the Royal Flying Doctor Service. The kids love that.'

After lunch, Jamie thanked Ray and Beryl for their hospitality and Ray asked them for a favour. 'I've got a package of meat in the fridge for Jake Bradwood. I'd be grateful if you could take that with you, as long as there's still room for Sarah in your jeep.'

'Not a problem, Ray. We'll fit it in, even if Sarah has to sit on my lap,' said Jamie. This was greeted by a squeal of laughter from Sarah.

After travelling the first few miles, the road, which could only be described as a two-wheel track by now, ran mostly close to the river. It passed over dry black-soil floodplains with occasional wild red crags bearing scattered vegetation rising above the plains in abrupt, fantastic shapes. The track had been roughened by cattle hoof prints from the previous wet season. Apart from the large eucalypts on the plains there were stands of yellow cheesewoods, known locally as Leichhardt trees, acacias, banyans, and woolly butts, interspersed with native grasses, while pandanus and riparian trees marked the course of the main river.

'Not long to go now,' said Jamie. 'Are you still all right back there, Sarah?'

'Aye yu! Bloody orright, Jamie.'

CHAPTER 21

Fifty miles downstream from Roper Bar, three men sat in the shade of a banyan grove watching a billy of water coming to the boil on a wood fire.

'Tea's up!' barked the tall man with the soiled broad-brimmed hat. He jumped to his feet and lifted the billy from the fire, throwing in a handful of tea leaves.

The tall man was Vince Rutter, a tough-looking character with hard dark eyes and a few days' stubble around his mouth and cheeks. The other two mumbled as he poured hot tea into their tin pannikins.

'There! That should put a bit of hair on your chest,' Vince said, plonking himself down with his back up against a banyan tree. Slowly sipping his tea, he studied his companions through narrowed eyes. Ernie Smith was a dumpy fellow with a perpetual smile, a belly that hung over his belt, and his baldness hidden under a comb-over. Ernie was not much for manual labour, but he was good with figures and kept a close tally of their stock. He also handled their radio equipment.

The third man, Pat Healy, was a short skinny fellow with untidy long hair under a Texan cowboy hat which he hardly ever took off. Probably sleeps in it, thought Vince. He was a good worker, in spite of his small stature, and almost never uttered a sentence longer than about six words.

They had been hard at it for most of the day, separating half a ton of opium into bags from a ton of copra. They had stacked the bags in their shed of raw wood, corrugated iron and tarpaulin.

Suddenly Vince asked in a loud voice, 'Where'd you say that boat was this morning, Ernie?'

'It's already in the Arafura Sea southeast of Trangan Island,' Ernie replied. 'It's still motoring along at about eleven knots. Not bad!'

'So ya reckon another three days before it gets here, eh?'

'Yeah, Vince. Couldn't make it any earlier than that.'

'Bugger!' said Vince, aiming a spit at the ground in front of him. 'The truck's gonna arrive tomorrow or the next morning. We'll be sitting here twiddling our thumbs after loading what we've got now. How much more will we need to load when the bloody boat gets here, Ernie?'

'Well, as you know it's a 10-ton truck. We can fit almost three tons of opium under the false tray, leaving room for just over seven tons above the tray,' said Ernie, looking at his notebook.

'Yeah, yeah, yeah, I know that, Ernie,' said Vince belligerently. 'Not much for maths meself. How much more do we need from the boat to fill the truck?'

'Two point four tons of opium and just over five point eight tons of copra, Vince,' said Ernie.

'Gawd! We'll be working our arses off to get the truck away after the boat arrives,' exclaimed Vince. 'Anyway, as soon as you've finished your cup of tea, Pat, you'd better have another burst at winding the handle on the debil-debil to keep the natives away.'

'Yeah, boss,' said Pat, remaining where he was while he rolled a cigarette.

'Yeah, boss,' Vince repeated and sighed impatiently. What a mob of pissants I've got to work with, he thought. Thank God the money's bloody good.

The debil-debil he had referred to was a type of siren that emitted a fluctuating mournful whine when its handle was turned. It was designed to make the local Aborigines stay away, as they were inclined to interpret the distant howl of the siren as an evil spirit, a debil-debil.

The truck would be driving up from Borroloola on a track so rough and rutted that the 240 miles often took up to three days or more, particularly if there were stoppages owing to tyre punctures, common on this overland track. The truck would be carrying their regular supplies as well as a few 44-gallon drums of diesel fuel for the return journey through to Queensland via Borroloola. The route had been chosen so that the inhabitants of the settlements to the west, up the Roper River, would have no clue as to what was going on downstream from them. The truck carried a radio to transmit its estimated time of arrival.

Vince was nibbling on a stalk of kangaroo grass when the debil-debil siren started its dismal whine, causing myriad birds to fly away screeching into the distant bush. When the whining ended it was followed by the melancholy howling of a wild dingo, raising a laugh from Vince. Must be going stir-crazy, he thought.

They had selected this site south of the river for their camp four months before as there was a nearby spring for fresh water. The river at this location was tidal and its water salty. They had cleared a pathway through the thick vegetation on the banks of the river for the purpose of unloading boats. Over the period, tension had built up amongst the men because of the isolation. There had been a routine of unloading boats, separating the cargo, loading trucks, and in between, sitting around with nothing to do. It seemed endless and no one knew how much longer they would be staying. They were well paid, but Vince was starting to think they would all go mad if they didn't get a break. Somewhere. Anywhere, away from this crocodile-infested river. The crocodiles hadn't bothered them so far as they had set up their camp a few hundred yards from the riverbank, but they had sighted some giants at times and were alert to the danger.

Just a day or two at the Mataranka pub, thought Vince. That'd wash away the cobwebs a bit. Ain't gonna happen though. The bloody police would want to know what they were doing down there. And too far to go to Borroloola for a drink. Vince sighed again. I guess we're stuck here for a good while longer, he thought. With the flies, the crows, the snakes, the flying foxes, the dingos, and the crocs. Bugger!

* * * *

The first thing that came into sight as the jeep approached Roper Bar was a large white house raised up from the ground on pylons at least eight feet tall. It already stood on higher ground above the river and there were several small buildings scattered around. Jacko pulled up in front of the house and they looked down upon the river where a natural weir of smooth flat rock crossed the stream, the water higher on the upstream side as it flowed continuously over the weir.

'So that's the famous Bar,' said Jamie. A shout from the house made them jump. As they emerged from the vehicle, they saw a tall athletic young man with a thin moustache inspecting them from the top steps of the house. He was dressed in a khaki uniform.

'G'day!' yelled Jamie. 'Are you Sergeant Bradwood?'

'Yep. You must be the coves that Fitzy radioed us about,' he replied. 'C'mon up and I'll put the kettle on. We'll have a cup of tea.'

'We've got some boxes for you from Katherine and some beef from Ray Turner,' said Jamie.

'Ah! Fair dinkum? Hang on. I'll come down and give you blokes a hand,' said the policeman.

He ran down the steps and Jamie introduced himself and Jacko and, after unloading some boxes, Sarah who emerged from the jeep with a shy smile.

'So, you brought your own black tracker?' Bradwood said with a chuckle, looking at Sarah.

'She's me sister, Sergeant,' said Jacko warily. 'Bloody good tracker too.'

'Didn't mean any offence, Jacko. You can call me Jake. I'm really happy to see you, fair dinkum. You're all most welcome to stay here. I've got plenty of rooms. We'll get these boxes up into the house and have a chat over a cup of tea.'

'Sounds good to me, Jake,' said Jacko.

'Sounds good to me, Jake,' repeated Sarah.

A short time later they were seated around the kitchen table drinking tea while Jake chatted about the region around Roper Bar. Then he said, 'Can't thank you fellas enough for bringing all that stuff. It's not always easy to get our supplies here, particularly if the Connellan Airways plane breaks down. Often happens. So, can I ask what's happening? I'd be interested to hear what you fellas are going to be doing while you're here.'

'We've recently returned from China, Jake,' Jamie began. 'We were there to investigate an opium-smuggling operation with a base up the Yangtze River, west of Shanghai.'

'Geez! China! That must have been interesting,' said Jake.

'Yeah, interesting place. It's a bit unstable at the moment, with different groups vying for power in the aftermath of the Japanese occupation,' explained Jamie. 'Anyhow, I think the smuggling operation in China is finished now. Kaput! But we believe that some

203

of the opium has been coming into Australia regularly up till now, brought in by boats carrying the stuff up the Roper River.'

'The Roper River! Here? Why would they bring it here?' Jake exclaimed.

'To escape detection, Jake,' said Jamie. 'The opium is wrapped in bundles of copra from the Philippines. Once it's offloaded in Australia, it's probably split and trucked separately, south from the river to the east coast. The copra would be sold to pharmaceutical companies for coconut oil products and the opium would end up in the streets of the big cities.'

'Bloody long journey, that one,' observed Jake.

'Yeah, but there'd be big money in it,' said Jacko.

'That's for sure,' agreed Jamie.

'I thought you said the smugglers were finished,' said Jake.

'Only the supply end in China. We know there's still a boat on the way, full of the stuff,' said Jamie. 'It's probably due into the Roper River in about three days. The freighter is a sailing ketch with considerable engine power. We reckon it's been travelling at more than ten knots.'

'Fair dinkum? That's bloody swift for a sailboat, eh?' said Jake, shaking his head.

'Fair dinkum!' said Sarah, chuckling.

'Have you or any of your people heard anything about recent unusual activities down the river, Jake?' asked Jamie.

'Yes and no,' said Jake with a serious expression. 'There are rumours about something going on about forty miles downstream. We haven't seen anybody coming through here though. I sent some of my native police down there in the boat to have a look, but they reckon there are debil-debils down there and so they didn't go all the way.'

'Debil-debils?' exclaimed Jamie with astonishment.

'Yeah. Something spooked them. I'm not sure what,' said Jake. 'Anyway, as I said, we haven't had any strangers passing through here.'

'You're a long way above the river here, Jake,' said Jacko. 'Do you get many floods?'

Jake laughed bitterly, shaking his head. 'Floods! Yeah, we get floods. The old police station near the Bar was always flooded. They built this new station on high ground before the war, back in 1937, but even with these eight-foot-high pylons, we've had floodwaters inside the house on a couple of occasions. When the river comes down, she really comes down. Fair dinkum.'

'Fair dinkum,' said Sarah.

'Yeah, that's right,' Jake chuckled. 'You've got nothing to worry about at this time of year though. So, what's the plan of attack? When do we go to take these smugglers into custody?'

'Our plan is for Jacko, Sarah and me to go downriver first and have a look, Jake,' said Jamie. 'We want to find out where and how many there are. They are likely to be heavily armed. Fitzy will be arriving in a couple of days with some of his troops and by then, we'll have a lot more information.'

Jake nodded. 'Okey dokey. When do you plan to go?'

'Tomorrow morning early. Piccaninny light, as Jacko would say,' said Jamie.

'Well, in that case, we've got time to drink a couple of those beers you brought with you. This evening, you can join me for a fine dinner of wild roast brush turkey,' said Jake. 'How does that sound?'

'Sounds bloody good to me,' exclaimed Jacko.

'Sounds bloody good,' said Sarah with a beaming smile.

'If you've got some orange juice, Sarah would prefer that,' said Jacko.

'Fair dinkum,' she said.

* * * *

They left the police station in the morning after listening to the position of the opium boat on the police radio at seven o'clock. Jamie drove the jeep and it took them over three hours to travel forty miles downstream, keeping the winding river in sight as much as possible on their left. The course of the river was easily visible by the heavy growth along its banks, largely paperbark trees, river gums and pandanus. Myriad birds nesting near the river flew and whirled, disturbed by their approach, while a few hawks glided high above

205

them. On two occasions, troops of kangaroos leapt across the path in front of the vehicle.

Finally, Sarah tapped Jacko on the shoulder and pointed ahead where birds were flying in agitated circles over the trees.

'Yeah, thanks, Sar. I saw it too,' he said, then asked Jamie to stop. 'There's some activity ahead of us, Cap. If it's the baddies, we don't want to alert them. It's best if Sarah and I go ahead to see what's up. If you stay with the jeep, we'll be back in a jiff and tell you what's going on.'

'Okay, Jacko,' said Jamie, who couldn't see anything ahead except more trees. 'Do you want to take a gun?'

'Naw. We'll just take a quick peep without disturbing anyone, Cap,' said Jacko, helping Sarah out of the back of the vehicle.

'Okay. Take care, you two.'

They approached on foot and hid behind some bushes next to a large termite mound which looked like a gigantic monument in a cemetery. When the mournful wailing broke out in front of them, Sarah jumped into Jacko's arms and buried her head in his chest.

'There's your debil-debil, Sar,' Jacko whispered in Sarah's ear. Sarah looked up, nodded and smiled at him. A short skinny man in a large ten-gallon cowboy hat was winding the handle on an instrument with a metal trumpet-shaped horn emitting a loud fluctuating whine. Behind him they could see a dilapidated shed which looked like it had been haphazardly erected. A tall tough-looking man with a dirty hat was sitting with his back against a tree, fast asleep. How the hell can he sleep through that horrible din? thought Jacko.

'Debil-debil,' she muttered.

'Sounds like a siren, Sarah,' said Jacko, patting her back. 'I think that's white man debil-debil. Stick by me and you'll be okay. I guarantee.'

Now as they watched from their place of concealment, the thin man stopped turning the handle and the whining faded away into distant echoes.

'We'll slip down to the river and see what they've set up there, Sar,' whispered Jacko. She smiled and nodded and they both crept towards the riverbank where they observed the cleared passage on the river where a boat could moor. There was no one about and Jacko

206

stood studying the landing point before tapping Sarah on the arm and heading back towards the camp.

Skirting around the back of the camp, they found the tracks where large trucks had entered from the south. From the tyre tracks, Jacko reckoned they would have to be big trucks, maybe eight to ten tons. They'd have to be six-wheel drive too, he thought.

They could still see only two men. As they watched from the south side of the camp, the tall rough man woke up, stood and stretched. Ugly-looking brute, Jacko thought. The man yelled out to someone in the shed and a plump man with a nearly bald head and a protruding belly walked out into the sunlight and said something to him. So, at least three of them here, thought Jacko.

'We'll go back to the jeep, eh, Sar?' he whispered. 'Nothing much more to see here.'

She smiled and followed him silently back through the bush.

Back at the jeep, Jacko said, 'Three of them there, Cap. Could be more, but I don't think so. Their camp is about half a mile downstream from here.'

'No more. Just three pelas,' said Sarah, shaking her head. 'Just three.'

'Yeah, just three,' repeated Jacko. 'Their leader's an ugly-lookin' character. The others aren't much. They've got a gadget that makes a whining noise when they wind a handle.'

'Yeah, I heard that after you left,' said Jamie. 'What the hell was it?'

'They're trying to make the locals think there are debil-debils around there to keep them away, Cap,' said Jacko. 'Sarah nearly jumped out of her skin when it started up.'

'Ay! Bullshit,' cried Sarah. 'You full of it, bikpela brother.'

'Okay. Okay. Sorry, sis,' said Jacko. 'She's happy now, knowing what it is.'

'Aye yu! Happy,' she said, beaming.

'There's a rough track heading south from the camp,' continued Jacko. 'That's the way they truck it out. It looks like they're waiting for another truck to arrive. Probably arriving any day now. They're also waiting for the boat, I'd reckon.'

'Good work, you two,' said Jamie. 'No sense in moving on these fellas yet. We'll be able to confer with Fitzy tomorrow and together work out the best way to handle it. It'll probably be best to round the lot up when their boat gets in. At least we'll have some idea when that is. It should be in sight of Gove Peninsula by now. Less than two days out.'

They had been talking while standing beside the jeep. They were about to turn to get into the vehicle when Jacko suddenly yelled, 'Freeze! Jamie! Don't move! And don't look down!'

They all stood motionless for about thirty seconds before Jacko stepped up to Jamie and showed him a dark-brown snake, about six feet long, gliding across the ground ten yards away from them into some bushes. He pointed at the snake's trail where it had passed two inches from the heel of Jamie's boot.

'Him badpela snake,' said Sarah. 'Quick dead.'

'Yeah. That's a taipan, Cap. Most deadly snake in Australia,' said Jacko. 'When you didn't move, he ignored you. Mighta been different if you'd stepped on him.'

'Christ, Jacko! Thanks for the warning, mate,' said Jamie. 'I'll watch my step in future. Let's get out of here.'

By the time they had completed the tortuous drive along the winding river back to Roper Bar, they were all ready for a cool drink. At the kitchen table of the police station, Jake Bradwood listened intently as Jacko described in detail the situation at the smugglers' camp forty miles downstream from the Bar. He was amused to hear about the whining siren which had fed the superstitions of his native policemen. Jacko suggested that it would be better if Sarah explained it to them.

'They probably wouldn't believe a white man, but they'll believe her okay,' he said as Sarah nodded with a shy smile.

'Aye yu! No debil-debil,' she said.

'Okay. Good idea,' said Jake. 'Please come with me, Sarah, and I'll introduce you to my men.'

After Jake and Sarah had left, Jamie and Jacko plotted the opium boat's positions on a map of the Gulf of Carpentaria.

'Unless they have engine trouble or something like that, I reckon they'll be somewhere around Groote Eylandt when they radio in tomorrow morning,' said Jamie. 'That means they'll be well into the Roper River, probably already at the campsite, early the following morning.'

'Yeah. With Fitzy and his men arriving tomorrow, we'll be in good shape to welcome them, eh, Cap?' said Jacko.

'Yep. I reckon, Jacko.'

CHAPTER 22

Superintendent Russell Fitzgibbon arrived in the early afternoon of the following day with three of his men from the Darwin police.

'Sergeant Terry Walker's my right-hand man,' he said. 'These other two fine-lookin' fellows are the two "ARs", Constables Allan Read and Andy Rowley.'

After handshakes all round, Jacko described what he and Sarah had seen at the smugglers' camp. Fitzy suggested that Jake bring two of his native police, increasing the police presence to seven.

'No problems,' said Jake. 'Constables Billie and Tommy are my two best men. Both first-class trackers and straight-shooters.'

'Don't count us out,' said Jamie. 'You'll need Jacko to show you where the camp is. I'll come along too. Jacko has drawn up a rough plan of the campsite. It's a cleared area leading down to the river where a shallow-draft boat can moor.'

'The main shed is in a clearing a few hundred yards south of the river,' said Jacko, spreading out his sketched map on the kitchen table. 'They've cleared a pathway about forty yards wide through the scrub and trees from the clearing to the river.'

'What about the jeeps? How close can we drive those?' asked Fitzy.

'When we went there yesterday, we stopped about half a mile short of the camp and Sarah and I walked from there,' replied Jacko. 'I suggest we drive to the same spot tomorrow. They won't hear us from there. Sarah can stay and look after the vehicles.'

'Well, that seems cut and dried,' said Fitzy, closely studying the map. 'Pretty much a straightforward police roundup. We'll all be armed with rifles and handguns, so I expect there'll be little if any resistance. There'll be nine of us. We'll spread out when we get close. Allan and Billie close to the river. Then Andy and Jake further away. I'll take the centre, with Tommy and Terry to my right. Jacko and Jamie will be the closest to the sheds. When I give a loud whistle, we'll all rush into the clearing together guns at the ready. Then we'll handcuff the lot and put them in the truck if it's there. How does that sound?'

'Sounds all right to me,' agreed Jamie. 'We don't know how scattered they'll be but that should provide a wide enough net to round them all up. What do you want to do with the boat?'

'We'll leave it where it is at the time,' Fitzy said. 'Jake can send some of his boys down later to see if they can bring it up here to the Bar.'

Jake nodded. 'Not a problem, sir.'

Fitzy patted Jamie on the shoulder and said, 'You fellas have done a superb job. We now know exactly where and when. Show me again just where that opium freighter was this morning.'

'On the seven o'clock radio sched, the position given was here on the police map,' said Jamie, pointing to a map on the wall, 'about sixteen miles southwest of Groote Eylandt. They must have sailed through the strait between Bickerton Island and Groote.'

'Yeah. At the rate they're going, they'll certainly be well up the Roper by dawn tomorrow,' said Fitzy.

'We still don't know whether their truck has arrived yet,' warned Jamie. 'It's a fair bet that it could be there by now though.'

'Doesn't matter,' said Fitzy. 'If it hasn't arrived when we get there, we probably won't have long to wait after we've rounded up the men there. From what you say, they should have tons of opium there. Certainly enough to provide evidence for a conviction.'

'Yeah, that's for sure,' agreed Jamie. 'We can drive them back here and then on to Darwin in the back of their own truck.'

Fitzy turned to Jake and asked, 'How are things going here? Had any more trouble with tribal wars?'

'No, not really,' said Jake. 'There's the odd flare-up amongst the Myall tribes in Arnhem Land, but we usually manage to calm them down. One tribe steals a lubra from another tribe, or some fella fishes in another tribe's billabong. That sort of thing.'

'That's good,' said Fitzy. 'The tribes were pretty hostile to each other years ago. Hammer and tongs in those days.'

'Pretty calm now,' said Jake. 'I've got a written report for you when you leave. The mission schools are helping a lot. The pupils are from different tribes and they get on well together. They adapt really fast. My native police all send their kids to the Roper River Mission school the other side of the river. Most of the cattle stations have schools now too.'

'Well, that's good news,' said Fitzy. 'You'll be happy to know that we've brought a couple of cases of beer with us. So if you've got some coldies in the fridge already, open some of them now and replace them with our warm ones. I think we all deserve a drink.'

'No worries, boss,' said Jake, taking some cold beers from his refrigerator and handing them around. 'Hopefully, we'll be doing the same thing tomorrow night in celebration of a job well done.'

'I'll drink to that, my boy,' said Fitzy.

* * * *

The sun had just started to rise when the Brown Dolphin edged up to the loading point on the south bank of the Roper River. They had sailed up the river under motor and with bare masts through the night. A powerful spotlight on the bow provided ease of navigation along the winding river, which had heavy vegetation marking its banks. The hull of the ketch was equipped with a centreboard which had been raised when the yacht was not under sail. It significantly reduced the draft of the vessel.

'All secured!' cried Fred Walsh, the for'ard hand, having leapt ashore and tied the bow hawser to a stout river gum. The other crewman, Tom Stratton, followed suit with the stern hawser. The skipper, Colin Flinn, switched off the engine and looked to the shore where Vince Rutter was waving his hat at him.

Colin called out, 'I've got some extra passengers for you, Vince. Three of 'em came with me from Samar. They'll be able to help us unload this stuff. Weren't much good as sailors, though.'

'The more hands the merrier, Colin,' Vince called back. 'Why'd they come?'

'No more shipments, mate,' said Colin. 'Done and dusted. This is the last load.'

Vince scratched his head, slightly puzzled, as three men jumped ashore. He knew Luke Atkins, but he hadn't seen the other two before. The first one off the boat, a burly man with a large untidy beard, introduced himself in a strong Scottish accent as Hamish McIntyre.

'Och! It's guid to be on dry land, laddie,' he said. 'Though the land still seems to be rocking. This next gentleman is Nick Bradford and this...'

'I know Luke,' Vince interrupted. 'What's this about the last load?'

'We had word from China that there'd be no more supplies from there,' replied Luke. 'Dunno why, but Trevor Clark told us all to leave. So here we are.'

'Where do we go from here?' asked McIntyre. 'Where's the nearest town?'

'Aw, I reckon about three days away, mate,' replied Vince. 'Borroloola. It's not that big a town, neither. At least there's a pub there.'

'Three bloody days!' exclaimed McIntyre. 'Och! What sort of country is this?'

'It's called Australia, mate,' said Vince with a sardonic smile. 'If you don't want to come to Borroloola we can leave you here if you like.'

'No, no! I'll come with you for sure. I'm not going on that damned boat again,' said McIntyre, shaking his head as he walked away muttering, 'Three bloody days to a town. Hell's bells. Where do all these damned flies come from!'

'I'll go and get the boys to bring the truck up to the boat,' said Vince, walking back to the camp.

The truck drivers were waiting for him beside their 6x6 10-ton truck which had a high metal structure over the tray and doors at the back. One, Noel Corder, was a muscular stocky man with fair hair and a grizzled face. The other, Stan Crippin, was skinny, unshaven, and had thinning black hair.

'You can get your rig down to the boat now, Noel!' Vince called out to him. 'We'll start loading the truck right away. We've got some extra hands to help.'

'Okey doke, mate,' said Noel. 'The sooner we get loaded, the sooner we'll be on the road.'

'It looks like we'll all be coming with you, Noel,' said Vince.

213

'Wha... All of you?' exclaimed Noel.

'Yeah, mate. All of us except the boat crew,' replied Vince. 'There'll be six of us now.'

'We'll have to take a ton or two less of the copra,' said Noel, starting up the engine of the truck.

'No worries, Noel,' said Vince, who then went over to the shed and told Ernic Smith and Pat Healy to accompany him down to the boat to help.

They arrived as the truck was slowly backing up to the boat to get as close as possible, prompting Vince to yell out to the driver, 'That'll do, Noel! We've got to leave a bit of room to pull the copra stacks apart and separate the opium. First, we'll unload from the truck the drums of diesel for the boat.'

Noel and Stan jumped out of the cabin of the truck and opened the doors at the back.

'After unloading the drums, we'll lift the false bottom on the tray and then go to work,' said Noel. 'We've got plenty of hands for the job.'

Vince spoke to Colin Flinn, who had stepped ashore. 'There's already half a ton of opium that we loaded yesterday. We just need another two and a half tons for a full load in the concealed storage space under the tray.'

'What about the copra?' asked Colin. 'How much of that will you take?'

'Bugger the copra,' said Vince vehemently. 'We've got to travel in the truck ourselves. I'm not riding with any of that stuff. Can't stand the stink!'

'Fair enough,' said Colin. 'We've got a few hours' work ahead of us, fellas. Let's get to it.'

They had to unwrap the copra stacks and extract the bags of opium for loading in the truck. The copra was discarded to both sides of the clearing and soon grew into large heaps.

By mid-morning most of the work had been completed, but with the sweating men complaining of the heat, Vince called for a break. 'Time for smoko. Ernie! You and Pat fill up the billies from the spring and fetch some tea. The rest of us'll start a fire.'

Except for Colin Flinn who had jumped aboard his boat to organise hoses for refuelling the boat from the diesel drums, the men settled down in the shade, watching the billies on the fire which was well back from the river and ten yards in front of the truck. The bush around them was silent except for the incessant buzzing of flies and the twitters and squawks of birds along the river.

With their attention on the billies, which had just started to boil, they did not hear the rustling of some bushes in the surrounding scrubland where the police were hiding, spread out and awaiting a signal from the superintendent. The rustling was caused by Constable Andy Rowley who had caught the toe of his boot in the exposed root of a gum sapling and was trying to free it. Sergeant Walker, who was nearby, thumped him on the shoulder to keep quiet.

'Tea's up!' shouted Vince, throwing handfuls of tea into the boiling billies.

Immediately following this, Superintendent Fitzgibbon whistled loudly, stepped forward into the clearing, and yelled, 'Freeze!'

He, Jamie, Jacko and the other policemen rushed into the clearing, but Andy Rowley was still trying to free his boot. They were greeted by stunned silence and shocked looks from the ten men around the fire.

'My men have you all covered,' said Fitzgibbon in a steely voice. 'Drop any firearms on the ground and stay where you are. You're all under arrest. Consider yourselves prisoners of the Northern Territory police. Hold out your arms and my men will handcuff you. We'll shoot anyone who moves.'

While their eyes were on the men who were holding out their hands, they did not detect Colin Flinn who was crawling up to the bow of the Brown Dolphin carrying a Thompson machine-gun with a 30-round box magazine.

Hardly anyone had moved before the first burst of machine-gun fire. Constables Allan Read and Billie, who were closest to the vessel, took the brunt of the attack, falling in a shower of blood and gore. The second burst erupted while the stunned police group were in the act of throwing themselves to the ground. Sergeant Walker took a .45-calibre slug in his heart while Jake, Fitzy and Tommy were also hit. As he aimed his rifle at the assassin from his prone position,

215

Jacko thought he had been kicked in the head by a horse as a round from the third burst creased his skull. Fighting unconsciousness, he loosed off a round and then everything went black.

Except for the splash as Colin Flinn, caught by Jacko's rifle bullet, fell overboard into the river, sudden silence descended on the scene. Andy Rowley, who had just freed his boot, looked out from his hiding place and decided to stay where he was.

Vince was the first to move. Pulling his pistol from his belt he viewed the prone bodies, including some of his own men, and yelled, 'Everyone stay where you are, or I'll shoot!'

Noel Corder, also holding a pistol, walked around from behind the truck and exclaimed, 'Goddamn! Bloody hell!'

Fred Walsh, one of the crewmen, rose to his feet and said, 'I think Colin's bought it. What do we do now?'

'Find out how many of these bastards are still alive and tie them up!' shouted Vince. 'Be quick about it. Noel and I'll keep them covered.'

'There's plenty of rope on the boat,' said Tom Stratton. 'I'll go and get it.'

Holding his gun in front of him, Noel stepped up to where the bodies of Allan and Billie lay in grotesque blood-soaked heaps and started to walk back along the line of bodies, most in khaki police uniforms.

'These first three have had it,' he said. 'So has the fourth. The next fella is only wounded. Hey, Vince! He's wearing real flash insignia. Must be a police chief or something.'

'Yeah. He was the bastard who told us to freeze,' said Vince. 'He's not too badly wounded. A flesh wound in the shoulder is all I can see. Not bleeding too much. We'll take him with us. Fix him up and tie him up. He'll be useful as a hostage.'

'The next bloke's a blackfella,' said Noel, looking down at Tommy who lay unconscious at the side of the clearing. 'Badly wounded by the look of him. He's not going anywhere.'

'Yeah. Just leave him,' said Vince. 'What about the others?'

Noel had walked further away from the river and was pointing his pistol at Jamie who had just sat up with his arms in the air. He then looked down at Jacko, the side of his face covered in blood, and said, 'There's a live one and a dead one here, Vince.'

Vince walked over and looked at Jamie. 'Who are you, mate? You with the police?'

Jamie was stunned and couldn't bring himself to speak. He looked at Jacko with dread, unable to believe what had happened. Finally, he found his voice and croaked, 'Not police. Can I look at my friend here?'

'Just stay where you are, digger,' Vince said. Then, looking back towards the river, he shouted, 'Bring some rope here and tie this bloke up!'

'I think he's breathing,' persisted Jamie. 'He needs attention.'

'Shut up and stay where you are!' yelled Vince.

Noel walked over to where Jacko was lying and prodded him with his boot. 'I think he's still breathing, but he won't last long. He's been shot in the head.'

'Can I have a look at him?' pleaded Jamie.

'Who the hell are you?' asked Vince.

'My name is Munro. This man lying here is my friend. I think the bullet grazed the side of his head and knocked him out. I want to have a look. Please.'

Vince rolled his eyes, spat, and looked at him. 'Hell. Okay, you can have a quick look at your mate. Keep him covered, Noel.'

'Wha' the hell are you doing?' cried Hamish McIntyre angrily as he approached, pointing to Jamie. 'How come dinnae ye shoot thaim all?'

'Because, mate, we're gonna need hostages,' replied Vince sarcastically. 'Stands to reason. When this lot go missing, they'll come after us for sure. They might even send the bloody army after us. That police chief is not too badly wounded, so we'll take him and this bloke, Munro, with us. As for the rest, those who aren't dead will die anyway.'

'We should take my friend here as well,' protested Jamie. 'I just need some bandages to fix his wound.'

One of the Brown Dolphin's crewmen, Fred Walsh, stepped forward and said, 'We've got a first-aid kit in the boat.'

Vince looked at him, then at Hamish, who was still glaring at him, and said, 'Yeah, go and get the first-aid kit and give this fella what he wants. The rest of us can concentrate on finishing the loading of the truck and getting ready to leave.'

Andy Rowley, still hidden in the nearby bushes, observed all this with horror, too scared to move. Finally, when most of the criminals were talking loudly to one another and heading back to the truck and the boat, he shook his head and crept away towards where they had left the jeeps. Having covered over a hundred yards, he looked down and was ashamed to discover that he had urinated in his pants. However, the thought of getting back to Roper Bar and raising the alarm spurred him on to quicken his pace in spite of his discomfort.

In the meantime, Jamie was studying the wound in Jacko's head. He caught a glimpse of the skull where the skin had parted. The bleeding had stopped and it was obvious there were small hairline fractures, but the skull hadn't been penetrated by the bullet. After Fred returned with the first-aid kit as well as a damp towel, Jamie carefully washed the wound with antiseptic and was able to roughly close the skin by bandaging it. He then wound a long bandage tightly around Jacko's head. Dear God, he thought, he mustn't die. He mustn't! He wondered who would be the more devastated. Monique or himself. Or Sarah! Christ!

There was a sudden shout from Tom Stratton who had started refuelling the boat. He pointed downstream at a large saltwater crocodile which had just broken the surface of the river. 'Holy cow! That bloody monster's got Colin in its bloody great jaws.'

'He won't care,' laughed Noel Corder. 'He was already dead, Tom.'

'I don't know how we're gonna get this boat down the river without him,' mumbled Tom.

'Hamish or Nick can go with you,' said Luke Atkins, smiling. 'They're experienced sailors now.'

'Ye wull ne'er git me on that boat again!' yelled Hamish. 'Na way!'

'Me neither,' said Nick. 'I'm staying on land from now on.'

Vince laughed and said, 'Looks like you and Fred are on your own, Tom.'

An hour later, they were all aboard the truck with Noel, Stan and Vince up front. Ernie, Pat, Luke, Nick, Hamish and the three hostages, Fitzy, Jacko and Jamie, were all in the back. Fitzy, lying out on the tray with his shoulder bound up in bandages, moaned softly. Jacko hadn't moved since being lifted aboard. His head was cradled on Jamie's lap to protect his injuries against the expected bouncing along the rough road to Borroloola.

CHAPTER 23

Sarah sat up straight when she heard the distant bursts of machine-gun fire. She jumped out of the jeep she had been sitting in and noticed flocks of birds whirling above the trees in the direction of the shooting. She was certain the shots had come from the campsite which she and Jacko had reconnoitred the day before. After a brief hesitation, she swung her dilly bag over her shoulder and headed off downstream through the trees towards the distant location where the birds were still frantically flying around and shrieking. As she walked, the birds settled down in the silence.

She had a sense of apprehension as she was sure that Jacko, Jamie and the police had single-shot rifles and the shots she had heard hadn't come from a pistol. She was confident that on arrival at the scene, she could remain undetected until she ascertained what had happened, but she couldn't help worrying over whether Jacko and Jamie were all right. She could see five hawks gliding lazily in circles ahead of her. A sign of death.

She was within about 200 yards of the campsite when she heard twigs snapping and realised that someone was walking towards her. Melting into the nearby scrub, she stood immobile as the sound of footsteps drew closer. When the source of the footsteps appeared, she recognised one of the police constables from Darwin who had accompanied their friend Fitzy. She couldn't remember his name. He looked as though he had seen a ghost.

When the policeman was abreast of her position, Sarah stepped out of the scrub and touched his arm. He jumped as though hit by an electric shock and cried out.

'No, no, no!' he whimpered and looked as if he was about to run away.

'Me Sarah,' she said loudly. 'Meet you at Roper Bar.'

The young policeman looked closely at her and it dawned on him that the small black girl was Jacko's fabled sister who had been left behind to wait with the vehicles. Her exploits, as well as her brother's, had been much talked about in Darwin.

'I... I'm... I'm sorry,' he spluttered. 'Didn't recognise you at first. I'm Andy.'

'What happen? Shots?' she asked.

'All dead. All dead,' he said despairingly. 'Machine-gun on the boat.'

'All dead? Jacko too?'

'Yes. Yes, I think so,' Andy mumbled. 'I didn't wait to find out. They didn't see me. Otherwise I'm dead too.'

'Come with me, Andy,' she said firmly. 'We find out.'

'I can't. I can't go back. They kill us,' he cried.

'You policeman. You come. Not all dead. They need us,' she insisted.

Andy wilted under the unblinking disdainful glare of the large whites of Sarah's eyes, and finally nodding, he gestured for her to lead the way.

'Walk quiet. Walk on toes,' she said, leading him towards the campsite.

As they slowly approached, they could hear voices followed by the sound of a large vehicle starting up. She presumed it was the truck Jacko had talked about. As they came near to the clearing, they heard the truck driving away to the south.

Once the sound of the departing truck had diminished, Sarah peered carefully into the clearing. She could see a figure moving about and on closer inspection realised it was one of the native police from Roper Bar.

'Hiya, Tommy,' she said as she stepped into the clearing.

Tommy looked at her, laughed and said, 'I could hear you coming.'

'That Andy,' she said as the policeman from Darwin stepped gingerly up beside her. 'Him walk like elephant.'

She looked around at several blood-splattered bodies lying on the ground close to the fringe of the trees. Tommy was bending over and applying bandages to the prone figure of Jake Bradwood, the Roper Bar sergeant, who was moaning softly.

'Sergeant Jake, bad wound. Collarbone near neck,' Tommy explained. 'Two fellas from Darwin and Billie cop it. Dead. I pretend I'm dead. They think I'm dead.'

221

'Where Jacko and Jamie?' she asked sharply.

'They take 'em with truck,' replied Tommy. 'Also, Super Fitzy from Darwin. I think Jacko near dead. Others okay.'

'Near dead?' Sarah cried, almost choking on the words.

Tommy saw her concern and said softly, 'Jamie look after Jacko. I think maybe all right.'

'Maybe orright?' she mumbled.

'We have to get Sergeant Jake back to Roper Bar. He need treatment,' Tommy said urgently. 'Hospital and nurses at mission.'

'Where boat?'

'Boat gone.'

Meanwhile, Andy had been silently staring at the three bloody dead bodies in a daze, finding it hard to believe. When Sarah tugged his arm and told him he was needed to support Jake back to the jeeps, he nodded and helped Tommy lift the wounded man to his feet.

Supporting Jake on both sides, they staggered after Sarah who carefully picked out the easiest paths through the trees and scrub. Supporting Jake with great care, it took them nearly an hour to reach the jeeps. Gently putting Jake into the front seat of one of the jeeps, Andy started up the engine.

'I stay here. You go,' said Sarah.

'Are you going after criminals?' asked Tommy. 'I come with you.'

'No. Need you take care Jake,' she said firmly. 'Take to mission.'

'Okay, Missie Sarah,' said Tommy, sitting in the back seat of the jeep behind the hunched-over bedraggled figure of Jake and putting his hands on his shoulders to support him. 'Wish lots of luck.'

She waved as the jeep drove away back towards Roper Bar. After watching the dust cloud kicked up by the jeep vanish into the trees, she took off at a brisk trot back to the campsite with a determined look on her face.

* * * *

The road headed inland away from the coast and into the hills to avoid the mud flats of the Limmen Bight. It became rockier and rougher, often throwing the passengers in the back of the truck around. Jamie tried as best he could to keep Jacko's damaged head as stationary as possible. In the darkness of the enclosed truck, he could hear Fitzy's occasional groans overwhelmed by the loud swearing of the five smugglers. This is going to be a great trip, he thought grimly.

As the truck laboured along the rough track, the three in the front seat paid no attention to the spectacular scenery. The escarpments of ancient bedded sediments, bright red quartzites, and sandstones enveloping lighter beds of dolomite, were dotted with displays of sparse foliage. Erosion had carved the rocks into fantastic shapes, their colours changing between red and purple through the heat haze. A few termite heaps, some up to twenty feet high, stood like sentinels beside the track.

A half-full 44-gallon drum of diesel in the back of the truck permeated the space with fumes, making both Hamish and Nick feel as nauseated as they had been when they had suffered seasickness.

Jacko started to dream. He felt his body rising, higher and higher through the atmosphere, although jerked around by wicked gusts of wind. He passed through clouds and saw the sky above him, a deep azure. It grew darker as he ascended, and he felt himself tossed around by some outer force. He instinctively knew that the force was Wollonqua, the giant mythical water snake which had originally risen from deep down in the bowels of the earth and now spiralled around in the darkness of the skies. He smiled, knowing that his mother and his ancestors lived with the snake. Wollonqua, the father of all humanity, tried to swallow him but was unable to reach him. After several failed attempts to get to him, he saw the giant snake smile, a great big all-encompassing smile, and descend again. It was the reverse of his ascent, with the blue of the sky becoming lighter as he descended, while the jerky gusts of wind still threatened to toss him around. By the time he reached the earth, it was suddenly dark and still and quiet. He sensed a strong light come on, dispelling the darkness, and felt a strange calmness wash over him.

Jacko still had a smile on his lips when he slowly opened his eyes. He studied the light and realised he was in some sort of enclosed space with open doors. Looking up, he was aware that Jamie was with him and watching him carefully. He tried to sit up, but a searing pain shot through his head and he lay back.

'Glad to see that you're back with us again,' he heard Jamie say hoarsely. 'Just stay where you are, and I'll get some help to lift you out of the truck.'

The truck? He wondered what Jamie was talking about. Why did he have such a monstrous headache? Then it all came flooding back. The failed capture of the smugglers. The sudden burst of machine-gun fire. Blood and gore everywhere. The powerful kick to his head. He had managed to fire off a shot from his rifle before he passed out but he didn't know if he had hit anyone. Where are we now? he wondered. How bad is my head? Thank God Jamie's with me.

'I'm alive, Cap,' he muttered through chapped lips.

'Yes. You're alive.'

The two truck drivers, Noel Corder and Stan Crippin, had just opened the doors to the back of the truck and were looking in at their other men. Noel said, 'I hope you fellas are okay in there. We'll be stopping here for the night. We're just north of the Limmen River crossing. There's a great waterhole here where we'll camp. I suggest you all help our esteemed police chief out of the truck. Be careful. He might be valuable to us.'

There was movement and mumbling from the men in the back of the truck as they stood and stretched, blinking in the light.

'Yeah, we'll help him off the truck,' said Luke. 'C'mon Nick, Hamish, Ernie. Give us a hand here.'

As they were helping Fitzy down from the back of the truck, Vince appeared and called out, 'Is that other half-Aboriginal bloke dead yet?'

'No! He's very much alive,' Jamie called back.

'Well, if he can't walk by tomorrow morning, we'll leave 'im behind,' said Vince. 'No value in keeping him.'

'He's a senior officer in the Commonwealth Investigation Service,' protested Jamie. 'He'll be a valuable hostage for you.'

'Really? Commonwealth Investigation Service?' said Vince. He looked at Ernie and asked, 'Do you know anything about that, Ernie?'

'Yeah. It's a branch of Australian Intelligence,' said Ernie. 'I've read about it. Fairly big time.'

'Big time, eh?' said Vince, only half-convinced. He asked Jamie, 'Are you with the same big-time mob?'

224

'Yes, I'm with the CIS too,' agreed Jamie.

'Okay! Let's get the big-time half-caste outta the truck, fellas,' said Vince. 'Doesn't look like he's in any condition to go running off anywhere.'

With five men helping Jamie, Jacko was laid on the ground beside a shady ghost gum tree. Stan handed Jamie an old blanket which he put under Jacko's head.

'Thanks. I need to get some water into him,' Jamie told Stan.

'No worries, mate,' said Stan. 'I'll bring you some from the billabong. It's good water there.'

'Thanks, mate. I appreciate it,' said Jamie, adjusting the blanket under Jacko's head.

Jamie managed to pour some water into Jacko's mouth, and he opened his eyes and muttered, 'Thanks, Cap. Where was I hit?'

'You are going to have an ugly scar above your right eye,' explained Jamie. 'Monique might find you're not the handsome devil she married.'

Jacko smiled. 'I always was an ugly bastard, Cap.'

* * * *

Sarah kept up a brisk trot as she followed the track in the unfamiliar countryside around her. The spectacular escarpments, the hills and crevices, the ghost gums, acanthus bushes and paperbark trees were all as foreign to her as the Philippines and Malaya. Like the countryside around the Daly River and the Kimberleys, where she had previously worked with her half-brother, this was very different from her own tribal lands, the flat red plains around Tennant Creek. Here, she was all alone in a strange land.

She was nervous that she might encounter local tribes who could well be hostile to her, but there had been no sign of humanity so far. The only signs of life along the track were the birds that flew off at her approach, the mournful cries of crows, the scurry of startled kangaroos, and the occasional howl of a distant dingo. The thought that Jacko was in serious trouble kept her pressing on ahead with grim determination.

225

When she had earlier returned to the smugglers' campsite, she had looked around with great care. The tracks on the ground had told her that Jamie was uninjured. She was comforted by the realisation that he might be in a position to help Jacko. The tracks also told her that Fitzy was wounded but not too badly. She counted eight different tracks left by the bad men. Looking through the shed, she found some cans of food and two knives left behind which she put in her dilly bag. There was also some fishing gear, so she took that as well.

In the late afternoon, she stopped briefly near a small rock pool, splashed herself all over, drank water, and ate some food. She worried that if she stopped too long it would be harder to get going again, so she was soon back on the track, as determined as ever. She began to realise that if the truck continued to drive through the night, she would never catch them, although that was unlikely. They must rest sometime. She must keep going! Gritting her teeth and ignoring the heat, the sweat and the flies, she kept up the pace. *I must keep going.*

It was already getting dark when she heard the murmur of voices in the distance. Suddenly alert, she stopped, listening. For the past few hours she had been half-running in an unthinking trance and now, it was like waking from a dream. She moved more slowly, peering into the darkness. Climbing over a slight rise in the track, she looked down into a broad valley where she could see a campfire through the sparse trees. She shivered, relief flooding through her. *Jacko and Jamie must be here, and there must be some way to free them,* she thought. Moving steadily, she crept towards the campfire until she could make out several men sitting and standing close to a large billabong to her left. She also noted the truck parked beyond the fire. The men were talking and occasionally laughing, oblivious to her presence.

Scrutinising the scene, she recognised Jamie sitting next to a man lying on the ground. *That must be Jacko,* she thought with rising excitement. Another man, sitting with his back against a tree, she realised was Fitzy. He had a sling on one arm and looked exhausted. She surmised that the men had already eaten their dinner because they were drinking from bottles of beer while they chatted. Deciding there was nothing she could do until they settled down to sleep, she withdrew about 100 yards away and lay down. Until then, she hadn't realised how tired she was. Closing her eyes, she fell into a deep sleep.

When she woke about three hours later, she listened intently for any movement from the direction of the truck. There was no wind and the only sounds in the night were the strident chirping of crickets and the occasional scurry of small nocturnal animals.

She stood and made up her mind on what action to take. Setting off to the far side of the billabong until she was beside a giant ghost gum, she focused her eyes on the distant campsite. From where she stood, the waterhole was about 250 yards across, but owing to a bright starry sky with a half-moon shining on the water, she could easily distinguish the truck. After drinking some water and washing her face, she set off back towards the other side of the billabong, carefully surveying the scene when she was close to the truck. With her excellent night vision, she could see that no guard had been posted and all eleven men were asleep, a number of them snoring loudly. She took special note of where Jacko and Jamie were lying, surrounded by other sleeping bodies.

Creeping to the rear of the truck, she noted that the back axle had twin tyres on both sides. Once she was on the right-hand side of the truck, furthest away from the sleeping men, she took a sharp knife from her dilly bag and stuck it into the nearest tyre. She stayed perfectly still as the air hissed out of the tyre, listening for any movement from the men on the other side of the truck. She relaxed when the snoring continued uninterrupted, and then crept under the truck where she pierced the inside tyre with her knife. She silently scurried away as the right-hand rear of the truck slowly subsided, the air hissing from both tyres. When the rear of truck settled down, she waited another few minutes until she was satisfied that none of the men had woken up.

Walking back along the track about fifty yards to the north, she cupped her hands to her mouth and emitted a loud shrieking howl, which pulsated up and down and lasted a minute.

The men at the campsite woke up and Vince sprang to his feet. 'What the bloody hell was that!'

'Sounded a bit like that bloody wailing machine we had back at the river,' said Ernie. 'Bit different though.'

The men, some sitting, some standing, all peered into the darkness towards the direction of the sound.

Noel shook his head and said, 'Weird sort of dingo maybe.'

'Don't think so, mate,' said Vince. 'Someone's out there.'

The next moment the silence was broken again by the same howling sound, this time from the opposite southerly direction.

'What the hell!' yelled Vince.

Nick Bradford fired two shots from his pistol in the direction of the latest howl.

'Don't be an idiot, Nick,' said Hamish grimly. 'Just shooting at ghosts.'

Jamie, sitting up next to Jacko, whispered, 'What do reckon that is, Jacko?'

Jacko smiled and whispered back, 'She's here, Cap.'

Jamie blinked and whispered, 'Sarah?'

'Yep. She's out there somewhere, Cap. Could you help me sit up?'

'Are you sure? How's your head, Jacko?'

'There's a fella hammering away inside, Cap, but I'll be right if I sit up for a while.'

Another howl broke out, this time west of the truck, and three of the men ran past the truck into the bush, rifles poised to fire. They stopped and meandered around when they couldn't see anything. By the time Jamie had helped Jacko, groaning softly, to sit up with the tree at his back, the men had returned. Soon after, the silence was again broken by a succession of high-pitched shrieks to the north. By this time, the smugglers were in total confusion.

Vince walked over to where Jamie and Jacko were sitting and demanded, 'Do you bastards know what's going on?'

'There's some Myall blackfellas out there,' said Jacko hoarsely. 'They're a bloody hostile mob, those Myalls.'

'Myalls?' exclaimed Vince.

Although it was painful to do so, Jacko nodded and said, 'Yeah. Looks like they've got us surrounded.'

'Surrounded?' cried Vince. 'Do you think they're about to attack?'

'Don't know about that, mate. They're a bit unpredictable.'

A series of shrieks broke out to the south of the camp and Noel yelled, 'I'm not waiting for those blackfellas to attack! Let's get out of here.'

'Good idea,' agreed Vince, as most of the men packed up their swags and ran towards the truck.

Noel, holding a torch, went to open the back doors of the truck, which seemed to be leaning over. He looked down at the rear wheels in the torchlight and said, 'Oh shit!'

CHAPTER 24

It was after midnight when Noel had retrieved the jack, tyre irons and a vulcanising kit from under the front seat of the truck and carried them around to the wheels at the back, yelling, 'Get that spare wheel out of the back of the truck, Stan, and bring a couple of torches!'

'We've only got one spare tyre, Noel,' replied Stan, jumping up into the back of the truck.

'Yeah, I'll have to put a vulcanising patch on the tubes of the flat tyres,' said Noel. 'You other blokes can give us a hand.'

As they all filed around to the other side of the truck, Jacko slowly stood up and shook his head. He looked at Jamie and whispered, 'Are they all looking away, Cap?'

Jamie nodded. 'Yes, Jacko. They've all gone behind the truck.'

Suddenly there was a continuous series of loud shrieks, 'Owyoo! Owyoo!' as Sarah ran up and down in the dark through the bushes. The men all rushed back to the left-hand side of the truck and picked up their firearms.

Vince shouted, 'They're about to attack! Fire when you see them.'

Jamie looked back at Jacko, but he was gone.

As suddenly as it had started, the shrieking, which seemed to come from a widespread area, stopped. The men looked at one another and nervously kept their guns trained on the trees and bush on the other side of the truck.

Jamie smiled and sat down next to the wounded police chief who was still propped up against a tree with a look of consternation on his face. Fitzy was startled but relieved when Jamie whispered to him that it was probably Sarah making all the noise and Jacko, despite his wound, had gone to join her.

'Bloody hell, Jamie. I thought he was close to death!'

'I don't reckon a mere bullet wound could slow Jacko down, Fitzy.'

Soon after, they heard the hoot of an owl in the trees. This was followed by the screech of a cockatoo from a different direction. Jamie smiled again.

Vince walked over to Jamie, looked around, and demanded, 'Where's that mate of yours, Munro?'

'I think he's gone for a crap,' answered Jamie.

Vince was angry, 'Oh, shit!'

Jamie smiled. 'Precisely.'

'Smart-arse!' was the rejoinder. 'Anyway, the Myalls will probably get 'im.'

He then yelled out to Pat Healy, 'Cover these blokes, Pat! Shoot 'em in the legs if they try anything. We don't want anyone else vanishing into the dark.'

Jamie watched him as he went back to the truck and tried to get the men to fix the flat tyre. There was a lot of muttering, but nobody seemed keen to move to the other side of the truck. Noel finally yelled out to Stan and the two of them went back to work on the rear wheels. Noel had positioned the jack under the truck and was just about to start working on the jack handle when there was a loud scream. A rock, thrown out of the nearby bushes, hit him on the back of the neck.

'Bugger this!' he exclaimed as he and Stan ran back to join the rest on the camp side of the truck. Swearing loudly in Scottish, Hamish pointed his pistol at the trees and fired off six rounds.

'Waste of bloody time and ammo, Mac,' Vince told him. 'Better we wait until daylight to fix the bloody tyres. We can see what to shoot at then. Stir the fire up again and we'll take it in turns to stand guard. There's eight of us. Four can keep guard and the other four can sleep for two hours at a time.'

'Don't think we'll get much sleep, mate,' murmured Noel.

Two hours later, from the other side of the large billabong, Jacko and Sarah studied the distant campfire, its flame reflected on the surface of the water. She giggled when he showed her the ignition key to the truck.

Except for some dizziness which came and went, Jacko was feeling considerably better and he was happy to be reunited with his sister. Sarah had rewound the bandage on his head after dabbing the wound with oil from the leaves of a ghost gum tree. She had reapplied the dressing and smeared it with mud from the waterhole so that the white bandage would not be easily seen in the dark.

Jacko sat back and contemplated his diminutive half-sister. Having now spent months away from her own environment and amongst his friends, her English had greatly improved, although she still had trouble pronouncing the letter 'f'. She only reverted to her broad pidgin when excited or angry, which was not often. He marvelled at her strong determination which had enabled her to reach this location, a run through country unknown to her and involving many miles, some of which had been covered in the dark. She noticed him looking at her and smiled shyly back.

After talking softly together, they gathered a large quantity of dry branches and leaves, heaping them up into two separate piles about five feet high. The piles were ten yards apart and close to the edge of the billabong. Jacko then gathered some handfuls of wet clay to be used to stuff into the exhaust pipe of the truck. He took off his shirt and wrapped the mud in it.

'We'll have to rub sticks together to start a fire here, Sar,' said Jacko.

'Got matches with me,' she replied, pulling a box out of her dilly bag.

'Good girl! Much easier. Let's give these bad fellas something to think about.'

This was greeted with Sarah's soft but high-pitched giggle. 'Aye yu, brother. Something to think about.'

As soon as he lit them, the piles burst into orange flames, reaching up to satisfying heights.

'It's still a few hours until dawn. Let's go, Sar,' he said, trotting off to circle the north side of the waterhole towards the smugglers' camp.

'Yeah! Let's go!' she repeated, following close behind him.

'What the bloody hell!' Vince shouted, staring at the two fires burning fiercely half a mile away on the other side of the billabong. Orange reflections twinkled in two straight lines on the surface of the barely rippling water. All the men, unable to sleep, were immediately on their feet staring at the fires.

'Those blackfellas musta set up camp over there,' said Nick.

Pat Healy, who was nearly demented by itchy insect bites, looked at Hamish and said, 'What about creeping up there and blasting 'em to kingdom come? What do you say, Hamish?'

The Scotsman scratched his beard, 'Dunno, Pat. It's a damned long way over there.'

'Might be a trick,' said Vince. 'What ya reckon, Luke?'

The lanky Australian was intently staring at the fires. Finally he said, 'I think Vince might be right. Could be a trick, but we're all stuck here like a mob of nervous nellies. Wouldn't hurt for a few of us to have a look. See if we can shoot some of 'em. We'll have to be careful, but!'

'Leave me out of it,' said Noel. 'Stan and I have to watch the truck.'

'What about you, Nick?' asked Vince.

Nick, his face set in fractious discontent, exclaimed, 'No! No! It's your bloody Australian bush and they're your wild savages, cobber. It's all foreign to me. It's safer in the bloody gangland streets of Birmingham.'

'Ernie?' Vince asked.

The balding plump bookkeeper looked at him with disbelief, his bloodshot eyes blinking. 'I'm no gunman. Leave me out of it.'

'What a mob of heroes!' said Vince with a loud sigh. 'Looks like it's you, me and Pat, Luke. Rifles and pistols.'

'I'll come wi' ye,' said Hamish.

'Good for you, Mac,' said Vince. Turning to Nick he said, 'I hope guarding those prisoners ain't too dangerous for you, Nick.'

Nick turned his back, mumbling as the four men checked their firearms.

'Shotgun or rifle?' asked Pat.

'You can take your shotgun,' replied Vince. 'Rifles for the rest of us.'

Vince set off to skirt the waterhole along the south bank, with Luke, Pat and Hamish following.

The going was slow as the group stumbled over fallen logs and sometimes walked into mud puddles or mulga shrubs and had to backtrack. Pat, who seemed to be a magnet for all manner of bugs, constantly scratched and groaned, occasionally dropping his rifle.

As he picked his way through the darkness, Vince thought to himself, what the hell am I doing here? This simple journey has become a nightmare.

He often stopped and shushed his men who swore a lot and complained about scratching themselves on scrub bushes in the dark. Startled birds took to the air, shrieking, as the men progressed up the side of the billabong and every stumble seemed loud in the stillness of the night.

Those bastards up ahead must know we're coming, thought Vince. We sound like a herd of elephants. We're not going to be able to get too close.

He whispered to the others, 'Listen! We'll creep up until we're about eighty yards away from the nearest fire, with our rifles at the ready. If we keep up a rapid fire for a few minutes, we should be able to hit some of them. We'll start when I whistle. Fire low. Until then, for Christ's sake, keep as quiet as you can!'

The other three murmured agreement and crept towards the fires. They still tripped over roots and walked into bushes as they advanced, but they didn't detect any alarm or movement at the Aboriginal camp.

Half a mile to the east, the smugglers' camp was quiet. No sound of birds or wildlife. Noel and Stan were sitting in the front of the truck, dozing. Ernie and Nick were lying on the ground, vainly trying to get comfortable.

Jacko lay quietly in the scrub close to the rear of the truck. He only moved when the sound of rapid gunfire, accompanied by the shrieking of many birds taking to the air, suddenly broke the stillness around the billabong. Creeping up to the truck, he stuffed several handfuls of clay mud into the exhaust pipe and then retreated into the bushes.

Ernie and Nick stood and stared out towards the distant flickering fires. Noel and Stan soon joined them.

Jamie stood up next to the tree Fitzy was propped against and whispered something to him.

'D'ya reckon they shot 'em all?' asked Nick as the distant gunfire faded away.

'Woulda given them a bloody good fright, anyway,' said Noel.

'Gave me a bit of a bloody fright too,' said Ernie.

'M-m-might be s-s-safe to go f-f-for a l-leak now,' stammered Stan, scratching his beard and heading off to the other side of the truck. 'I'm b-b-busting!'

Jamie was standing unmoving next to the large gum tree, watching the activities in the flickering light of the campfire and wondering what to do. He decided it would be best to wait for a move or signal from Jacko. Fitzy was calmly watching the hustle and bustle of the men near the truck. His condition was much improved by the long rest, but he was resigned to staying where he was for now.

Jamie was startled when a hand came out of the dark and grasped his arm. Jacko whispered, 'Get Fitzy on his feet, Cap. Come around the other side of the tree when you hear a scream.'

With that, the hand was gone. Jamie bent down and whispered in Fitzy's ear. He then helped him to his feet so that they were both standing with their backs against the tree.

'What the hell are you doing!' Nick yelled in his coarse Midlands accent.

'Just needed to stretch, mate,' said Fitzy with a pained expression. 'I was getting cramp in my leg.'

'Well, stay where you are. Don't move,' said Nick, threatening them with his rifle. His facial tic became more rapid and gave him the appearance of winking. Then his attention was diverted by a blood-curdling scream from the bushes on the other side of the camp behind him. All three of the armed men nervously pointed their firearms in the direction of the scream echoing through the trees.

'What the bloody hell!' bellowed Noel. 'If you see any movement, shoot.'

'Don't see a bloody thing!' Nick shouted back.

He turned back around to say something to the prisoners but instead, stared open-mouthed at the tree with a stunned expression on his face.

'The bastards are gone!' he shouted. His face seemed to come alive, his nervous tic out of control.

'What? Where?' said Ernie unhelpfully.

In a rage, Nick blundered into the scrub behind the tree, firing his rifle from the hip as he disappeared from sight. Eventually the firing stopped, followed by silence. Noel and Ernie looked at each other. Ernie picked up a rifle and joined Noel, standing with their backs against the truck, both looking nervously around with their firearms at the ready.

Time and space scarcely existed for Jamie and Fitzy, who waited for about ten minutes hidden from the camp behind a large spikey bush. Eventually, Jacko appeared out of the darkness and gently led them through the trees. They crept to a point about 100 yards west of the truck. By this time, Jamie's eyes had become adjusted to the darkness and he was able to make out two sprawled figures bound by rope to the trunk of a large tree.

Puzzled, he looked at Jacko who whispered to him, 'These gentlemen, who were your previous captors, have come to pay us a visit, Cap. Don't worry, they both have gags in their mouths. Ugly lookin' brutes, aren't they? Only a mother could love 'em. Someone's coming...'

They all listened. Jamie couldn't hear anything except the slight breeze rustling the leaves overhead; however, in a short while he noticed something that looked like a disembodied set of smiling white teeth floating towards him, about chest height.

'Hello, Jemmy!'

'Sarah! Was that your scream we heard earlier?'

'Aye yu, Jemmy. Scream real good.'

Jacko whispered to her, 'Really good, Sar.'

'Scream really good,' she repeated with a giggle.

'You fellas are amazing!' exclaimed Fitzy.

'Aye yu. Amazing! Yeah.'

'After you've stopped patting yourself on the back, Sar, remember we've still got work to do,' said Jacko in a low voice. Turning to Jamie, he said, 'It's best if you and Fitzy stay here and look after our guests, Cap. Sarah and I'll see if we can't invite a few more to join them.'

'How's your head, Jacko?' asked Jamie.

'Getting better all the time,' said Jacko. 'A bit of action does wonders. We'll see you in a while, Cap.'

236

'Good luck, you two,' said Jamie quietly, as Jacko and Sarah vanished into the dark of the forest.

'My God!' Fitzy whispered to him. 'I don't know exactly how far we've come from the Roper River, but that little girl must have run the better part of fifteen miles to get here.'

Jamie nodded. 'Yeah, and she doesn't show any signs of exhaustion. I feel so useless. However, it's best to leave it to those two. They're in their element.'

'Might as well settle down here,' agreed Fitzy, grunting as he sat down on a fallen log. 'It's not going to be hard work to look after these two crims.'

* * * *

With their backs against the truck, Noel and Ernie were still nervously looking around and jumping at shadows when they heard the rustle of footsteps coming towards them from the direction of the billabong. Pointing his rifle that way, Noel was relieved to recognise Vince leading Hamish, Luke and Pat out of the scrub.

'Put that bloody rifle down before you shoot me, Noel,' said Vince gruffly. 'Where the hell are the prisoners and where's your mate Stan?'

'Dunno! He and Nick have vanished along with the prisoners, Vince,' he replied. 'Can't explain it. Must have been taken by them Myall savages. How'd you go? We heard the shooting.'

'Nothing, mate. Bloody nothing,' said Vince bitterly. 'We were shooting at thin air. If there were any blacks there they musta heard us coming. We were as quiet as a bloody herd of elephants.'

'I think it was a trick,' said Luke. 'To get us out of this camp for a spell.'

'Yeah, well, it seems to have worked,' said Vince, looking around despairingly, his gaze falling on the campfire which was reduced to glowing coals. 'It seems while you fellas were in charge, we've lost two men and all the prisoners. We'd better stack up that fire before anything else happens.'

Later, when they were all seated around the fire holding their firearms, they heard a plaintive cry from the trees, 'Help! Help me!'

'Who's that?' asked Hamish.

'Sounds a bit like Stan,' Noel muttered.

This was followed by a strangled plea for mercy and more cries for help.

'It's a bloody trick,' said Vince.

'We've got to do something,' said Noel.

Hamish shook his head. 'I'm not going out there.'

'Perhaps if we all go and stick together...' offered Luke.

More cries for help. Vince snorted and said, 'I still think it's a trick.'

Luke stood up and looked down at Vince. 'C'mon, mate. How smart do you think these Myall blackfellas are?'

'Smart enough to have us all cowering in the dark,' said Vince.

Luke laughed sardonically. 'Cowering is right, mate! Don't you think it's time we stopped being the victims? What ya reckon, Pat?'

Pat stood up, scratched his groin, and said, 'Yeah, doing something's better than just sitting here.'

More but softer cries from the scrub.

'Okay then,' said Vince as they all stood. 'We'll go and have a look but keep your guns ready and stick closely together.'

They checked their rifles and followed Vince when he headed off towards the plaintive cries. Sticking closely together proved difficult as they stumbled into mulga and other unknown but prickly bushes. Vince sighed with frustration at the swearing and loud noises as they moved forward. After progressing about fifty yards, Vince stopped and signalled to the others to keep quiet. Vain request! Once they were all together again, they could hear someone whimpering just ahead of them. Vince pushed ahead, the others following. Another twenty-five yards and silence surrounded them.

Vince whispered to them, 'It's a trick for sure. We'll go back. You can see our campfire through the trees. And stick together, for Christ's sake.'

'We can't leave Stan out there. He's in trouble,' objected Noel.

'You can stay here if you like, Noel,' countered Vince. 'I'm going back.'

'Yeah. Maybe you're right, Vince. I'm not staying out here on me own.'

After considerable muttering amongst themselves, they all headed back, following the flickering glow of their campfire with Vince again in the lead.

On the way back, the bushes seemed to be more numerous and thornier as they blundered into one after another, but after ten minutes they stumbled back into the clearing. Ernie, Noel and Hamish were much relieved when they returned. The fire was still blazing brightly and gave them a feeling of security.

Noel leant back against the truck and looked around. 'Where's Pat?' he asked.

They all quickly looked at each other, realising Pat was not with them.

Vince yelled, 'Pat! Pat!'

The others joined in shouting his name without response.

'Och! This is getting spooky,' said Hamish.

'Bloody oath!' agreed Vince. 'Whatever happens, we'd better stay put until daylight.'

'Yeah, you're right,' agreed Luke. 'Whoever's out there, I don't think it's a mob of tribal Aborigines.'

They all looked around nervously, clutching their rifles tightly. They were further spooked by the howl of a dingo, quite close. Huddled together between the truck and the fire, none of the remaining five attempted to sleep. Luke suggested that if anyone wanted a leak, to stay in sight. Their nervousness increased as the night went on.

When the sky finally began to lighten in the east, the five men were all still awake. Colourful birds flew around the billabong and a soft breeze blew in from the Gulf of Carpentaria. None of this provided any comfort for the men, whose faces were all set in expressions of anxiety and weariness. Flies had started buzzing around them, adding to their irritation.

Vince stood up, stretched, and said, 'I think we should get out of here. Let's fix those goddamn tyres. Noel and I'll work on that and you other three can stand guard. Shoot at anything that moves.'

'We can't just leave not knowing what happened to Nick, Pat, and Stan,' Luke protested.

'No? Well you can stay behind if you like,' said Vince. 'Come on Noel, let's get to it. You get your vulcanising kit and wheel spanner and I'll bring the tyre levers and the jack.'

'No worries, Vince.'

CHAPTER 25

Hidden in the scrub amongst the trees, Jacko, Sarah and Jamie patiently watched the men jacking up the rear of the truck and getting ready to fix the flat tyres. While two of the men worked on the wheels, the other three stood close to them, nervously pointing their rifles at the trees.

The two men lifted the two right-hand rear wheels off the back axle and laid them flat on the ground. They had just started to separate the tyre from one of the wheels with the tyre irons when Jacko and Sarah noticed a large grey brolga stepping its way through the trees towards the billabong. The movement was spotted by the armed men who opened fire in a panic. The large grey crane took to the air, gained height, and glided with its seven-foot wingspan to the other side of the waterhole.

Vince stood up and swore loudly at them. Then he and Noel continued working on the wheels. It was about an hour and a half before they had vulcanised the holes in the inner tubes and replaced the tyres in the truck wheels. The other three men helped them lift the wheels onto the axle and after the truck was back with all wheels on the ground, the men started loading their gear in the back of the truck.

Jacko smiled when he heard Vince say, 'Noel, get this heap started.'

'Someone nicked the bloody ignition key! But luckily, I've got a spare,' said Noel, climbing into the cabin of the truck.

There was a loud revving as the driver pressed the ignition, causing a variety of birds to rise screeching into the air. Beyond that, nothing happened.

'What the bloody hell's wrong?' shouted Vince.

The revving started again and then stopped. Noel jumped out of the driver's cabin and yelled, 'Won't start! I'll have a look under the bonnet.'

Noel fiddled around under the bonnet and then asked Vince to get into the driver's seat and start the engine.

The revving started again with Noel fiddling with engine parts under the bonnet. He finally yelled out to Vince to stop before the battery ran out. Jacko winked at the other two who were watching intently. They saw the men milling around until they were all looking at the engine. Noel shook his head and said he didn't know what was wrong, that he'd have to work through it and everyone should leave him to it.

Some of them sat down wearily until Vince shouted at them to stay alert for any attackers. While Noel worked on the engine, the others all stared into the trees with their guns at the ready. As they grew more tired and nervous, they fired occasional shots at rustling leaves and targets of imagination. Finally, Noel left the engine, telling the others he would get back to it after he had eaten some breakfast.

Jacko, Sarah and Jamie silently withdrew to where three figures sat bound together 200 yards west of the truck. Fitzy, sitting with his back against a tree, waved his hand with relief at their return.

'Hope you're okay now, Fitzy. You look a lot more comfortable than these other fellas,' Jacko said. 'Don't think it'll be much longer now.'

'Do you think they'll be able to get that truck going, Jacko?' asked Jamie.

'I don't reckon, Cap. Not with that blocked exhaust pipe.'

'We might as well get going on Plan B before they run the battery down, eh?' suggested Jamie.

'Yeah, Cap. You take one of the rifles to the north side. Make sure they can't see you. If they fire at you when you tell them to surrender, I suggest you wing one of them with your rifle. Preferably that Vince fella. He's the leader,' said Jacko. 'I'll be on the south side. I'll fire a volley over their heads after you yell. Sarah will be this side of the truck making her noises. Sorry! Looks like I'm the one giving orders to you, Cap.'

'Don't worry, Jacko. You're in your element here,' said Jamie. 'Happy to follow your instructions.'

'Yeah, well it's a pretty simple plan, Cap.'

'Yeah, simple, Jacko. I think the baddies are pretty exhausted now and should be ready to give up,' agreed Jamie. 'It might take me a little while to get set.'

242

'No worries, Cap. We've got plenty of time.'

It took time but finally Jamie had worked his way to a position north of the truck where he was concealed by thick scrub with a good view of the men milling around their campfire. Most of them were eating on their feet. Two of them were arguing. All were carrying rifles under their arms.

Jamie settled down with his rifle aimed at the rangy figure of Vince, who was shouting something unintelligible at one of the other men.

Taking a deep breath, he yelled, 'Drop your rifles! You're surrounded!'

The men all froze, baffled, squinting in his direction. Suddenly, Jacko fired a loud volley of shots over their heads from the opposite direction. This was accompanied by maniacal screams from the bushes on the other side of the truck. Four of the men instantly dropped their rifles and put their hands in the air. Vince, on the other hand, whipped around and fired three shots in the direction of the latest shots, shouting at the others. Jamie carefully aimed at Vince's right arm and squeezed off a shot. The bullet caused Vince to spin around and fall to the ground, his rifle landing well out of reach.

The Scotsman, Hamish McIntyre, screamed, 'Don't shoot! Don't shoot! We surrender.'

He and the other three, with their hands in the air, stayed where they were. Their eyes bulged with disbelief when Jamie strode into their camp to cover them and methodically threw all their firearms into a heap near the back of the truck. They were further astonished when Jacko appeared amongst them and tied their hands tightly behind their backs while Jamie aimed his rifle at them. Vince lay groaning on the ground. Nobody spoke for a while until Ernie asked what had happened to the tribe of Myall blacks.

There was an audible gasp of astonishment when they saw a diminutive black girl appear at the edge of their camp. She stood like a statue staring at them with a slight smile on her lips.

Luke shook his head in disbelief and asked, 'Is that all? Just the three of you?'

Jacko laughed, 'You don't see anyone else, do you?'

'I knew it was a trick. Where are Nick, Pat and Stan?' asked Luke. 'Are they dead?'

'If you all stay where you are, I'll bring them here,' said Jacko. 'After that we can get underway.'

'The bloody truck won't start,' said Noel. 'Have you got another set of wheels?'

Jacko smiled at him and vanished into the trees. In a short while he reappeared with Fitzy, his arm still in a sling, and three bedraggled figures, the missing smugglers. There was little joy amongst the reunited criminals as they eyed one another and looked enquiringly at their captors.

Jamie asked where the first-aid kit was. Noel said it was under the front seat of the truck, and Jamie removed his bonds and told him to take care of Vince.

'It shouldn't be too much of a wound,' Jamie said. 'I only nicked him. A bit of antiseptic and a dressing, he'll be right as rain.'

When Noel went to collect the first-aid kit from the truck, Jacko asked him for a screwdriver which Noel extracted from his toolbox. With screwdriver in hand, Jacko went to work on the hardened clay plugging up the truck's exhaust pipe. It took several minutes but he was finally able to push the screwdriver through the clay and pull most of it out.

By the time he had finished, Noel had applied a dressing to Vince's arm and propped him up against the rear wheel of the truck. Vince stared at his captors with pure hatred in his eyes while the other smugglers stood around dispiritedly.

Jamie broke the silence. 'You fellas have already eaten, but we're hungry. We'll have a bite of food from your stores and then we'll be off.'

'Are you going to keep us tied up when we go?' asked Hamish.

Jamie laughed, 'You want to come with us? We thought you'd want us to leave you here.'

'No! No!' cried Ernie, his round glabrous face already sweating in the morning sun.

Jacko grinned and said, 'Don't worry, mate. We won't leave you here.'

Jamie turned his attention to Noel. 'How's the fuel tank, Noel?'

'I've already filled it from the petrol drum in the back,' he replied.

'Okay. We'll be off in about twenty minutes,' said Jamie. 'We'll remove your bonds and lock you in the back of the truck before we go.'

'Are we going through to Borroloola?' asked Luke.

Fitzy looked at him, smiling. 'Not bloody likely, mate. We'll have you in the Roper Bar police lockup by late this afternoon.'

Vince shook his head. 'Bloody hell! You bastards!'

'Steady on, mate. There's a lady present,' warned Jacko.

Later, as the smugglers were all climbing into the back of the truck, Jacko provoked more hostile murmurs by thanking them for fixing the flat tyres.

Heading back north towards the Roper River, they negotiated the pot-holed gravel track, with the morning sun shining through a light mist casting varying colours on the great iron-stained sandstone and quartzite escarpments to their west.

Jacko, Sarah and Fitzy were squeezed into the front seat of the truck beside Jamie who was driving. Muffled curses above the noise of the engine came from the men in the back every time the truck bounced over a rough patch.

After a while, Jamie found that he had no one to talk to, his three front-seat passengers having all fallen into a deep sleep. He shrugged and focused on the track, humming to himself, his concentration unbroken by the occasional rock wallaby, kangaroo, dingo, goanna, and other wildlife darting across the track in front of the slow-moving truck. Neither did the occasional loud swearing from the back of the truck disturb him.

After several hours, he felt the track slowly descending into the Roper River valley and just before reaching the old smugglers' camp on the river, he stopped the truck. With his eyes growing heavy, he woke up his passengers and suggested a brief spell and a change of driver. Fitzy greeted this with enthusiasm and said he was busting to relieve himself. Jamie told Sarah that according to the mileage on the truck, she had run over fifteen miles. Sarah smiled shyly. They got out of the truck, walked around a bit, then decided to let the eight prisoners out of the truck briefly to stretch their legs.

Jacko opened the back door of the truck while the others covered the smugglers with their rifles. The eight men emerged, squinting in the bright sunlight and mumbling complaints which were totally ignored. A couple of the men helped the wounded Vince out of the truck. The rough track had done nothing to shake the bitterness from his face. He glowered with undisguised hatred at Jacko but kept his silence.

'Where are we?' demanded Hamish.

'On the way, mate,' replied Jacko.

'I hate your damned Australian bush,' Hamish retorted.

'I'm not too keen on you either, mate,' was Jacko's response.

Fifteen minutes later, they were back on the track with Jacko driving. A short time later, the truck entered the clearing where the smugglers had set up their original camp. Looking around, they realised that there were no dead bodies around and the area had been partially cleared. The large heaps of copra were still near the riverbank. Nodding at Jamie, who had been dozing but had woken when they stopped, Jacko drove away from the clearing towards Roper Bar along the southern side of the river.

'Should be there by early afternoon,' he observed.

'Yeah, a bath and a feed would be good, eh?' exclaimed Jamie.

'The bath especially, Cap,' said Jacko, laughing. 'We probably all smell like an Afghan camel driver's armpit.'

Led by Jamie, they all broke into lusty song, belting out the verses of 'Click go the Shears', 'Waltzing Matilda', 'The Road to Gundagai', and 'Don't Leave your Waterbag Nearly Half Empty', with varying efforts of staying in tune. Sarah's shrill treble added an extra descant to the fractured melody. The jollity was not appreciated by some of the men in the back of the truck who yelled out curses, making the singers increase the volume of their discordant chorus.

They were still singing when they came in sight of the Roper Bar police station perched on top of its hill. As the truck drew closer they could see Sergeant Jake Bradwood standing on the landing above the steps, his arm in a sling and his neck and shoulder swathed in bandages, watching them in sheer astonishment.

'My God! I'm glad to see you fellas,' he shouted down to them as they pulled up. 'How did you get away?'

246

'Long story, Jake,' said Jamie as he climbed up the steps to the police station. 'We were saved by our guardian angel. We'll tell you all about it when we've had a bath and something to eat. A cold beer if you've got one. There are eight desperados in the back of the truck. Do you think your fellas could put them into your lockup?'

'Eight? Bloody hell! The lockup's only designed to hold five, maximum. But no problem, Jamie. We'll squeeze 'em in. It's as good as done.'

'Did you take care of the men who were killed at the smugglers' camp?' asked Jamie.

'My boys brought their bodies back here,' said Jake. 'They were buried this morning with full honours in the church graveyard at the Roper River Mission.'

'That's great, Jake. Thanks for that,' said Fitzy.

'Least we could do, sir.'

Half an hour later, washed and scrubbed, they joined Jake Bradwood around the kitchen table. Also at the table was Constable Andy Rowley, the Darwin policeman who had stayed in the bushes, his foot caught in a tree root, when the machine-gun from the boat had opened fire. Jake explained that he had asked Andy to stay for a few days while Jake recovered from his wounds. They were all eating a mixture of sausages, beans and local steak when Jake got up and asked if they would like a cold beer.

'Aw, mate!' exclaimed Jacko, 'that'd be better than a poke in the eye with a sharp stick!'

'Yeah. I suppose it would,' said Jake, putting a couple of large bottles of cold beer and four glasses on the table with a glass of orange juice for Sarah.

Jake suggested that he take Jacko over the river where one of the nurses at the Roper River Mission could have a look at his wound. Jacko told him he was sure a cold beer would do the trick.

'Half the bloody police force in the Territory is waiting for you in Borroloola,' said Jake as he sat down. 'When the smugglers left in the truck, your locked-up friends thought Tommy and I were both dead, and they didn't see Andy Rowley. As soon as we got back here, before I went to the hospital at the mission, I got on the radio and told the police in Darwin, Tennant and Alice Springs that the truck was on its way to Borroloola. I think they're gonna be disappointed when I radio them and tell them all to go home. So, tell me about your amazing escape.'

'Amazing it was,' said Jamie. 'It all started when this little girl here decided to run after us. She caught us up after running fifteen miles mainly in the dark.'

'A regular marathon runner!' exclaimed Jacko.

Sarah giggled and repeated, 'Aye yu! Marathon runner.'

As Jamie continued recounting the details of their escape and final capture of the smugglers, Jake kept shaking his head and mumbling, 'My God. Unbelievable!'

He laughed out loud when Jamie told him the parts about Sarah convincing them they were surrounded by Myall tribal natives, about Jacko stuffing mud into the exhaust pipe, and how they had left them alone while they fixed the truck tyres.

When Jamie finished, Jake said, 'That's the most amazing story I've ever heard. I'd have never thought it possible. When do you plan to move on?'

'We all need a good sleep,' said Jamie. 'If you can put us up for the night, we'll set off early in the morning.'

'You're most welcome. I'll get Andy here to deliver some palliasses to the lockup so our guests can spread them out on the floor of the gaol. We've got plenty of beef here to feed them on, but the way I feel about them, it's an awful waste of good beef.'

'I could sleep on a clothesline tonight,' said Jacko.

'No worries, Jacko. We've got plenty of beds for you fellas tonight. How about another beer?'

'You're speaking my language now, mate,' said Jacko with a happy smile.

* * * *

Vince Rutter sat in a corner of the lockup, sweating and inwardly cursing with frustration. Even inside the lockup, flies were buzzing around his head. How the hell could this have happened? He couldn't believe that he had been tricked by that tiny black girl. Eight armed men! It wasn't possible. They were now all cramped into this small barred lockup on the Roper River like rats in a trap.

'We've gotta break out of here!' he said to no one in particular.

'Those bars look a bit impossible, mate,' said Luke with a wry smile.

'Yeah! Yeah! I mean they're not going to keep us in here forever,' said Vince bitterly. 'When they next let us out of here, we'll make a break for it.'

'Where would we go?' asked Hamish.

'Outta here, mate,' replied Vince. 'Maybe we can kill a few of them when we run for it.'

'It's all bloody scrub out there, Vince,' said Luke. 'There's nowhere to go.'

'Well you can stay behind,' said Vince. 'What about the rest of you?'

There was an awkward silence as the others stared at him, not sure what to say. Pat Healy started feverishly scratching himself while others mumbled and shook their heads. Vince glared at them. Bloody mob of heroes!

'Are you scared of that little black girl?' he said sarcastically.

'We ain't got any guns, Vince,' said Noel.

'Doesn't matter. Apart from the ones who captured us, there's only one or two cops here and a handful of blackfellas. If we stick together...'

'I don't know, mate,' said Luke.

'Well, damn you and damn them. I'm gonna try to make a break for it,' exclaimed Vince.

* * * *

It was early the following morning when Jamie backed the truck up to the lockup to load their prisoners. He told them they would be driving straight to Darwin and to be prepared for a long day. Covered by Jake and Tommy as well as Jamie and Jacko, the smugglers climbed into the back of the truck. Vince was lingering back, complaining about his arm. As Jamie stepped forward to look at his wound, he pushed him and Tommy aside and sprinted away, heading upriver.

Jacko raised his rifle but Jake put his hand on his arm and said, 'Let him go, Jacko. There's nowhere for him to go.'

'Yeah, you're right, Jake. Anyway, he's going in our direction.'

'That's right,' Jake laughed. 'Tommy can follow his tracks and you'll follow him in the truck.'

Sarah put up her hand and cried out, 'Me too go after him.'

Jacko grinned and nodded. Soon, Tommy and Sarah were distant figures through the bush, the truck following them with Jamie at the wheel.

'That sister of yours likes to be involved, Jacko,' observed Fitzy.

'Yeah, she sure does. Never gets tired, my Sarah.'

They drove in companionable silence for about five miles upriver until they came across Sarah and Tommy standing over Vince, who was propped up against a tree looking sorry for himself.

Jacko leant out of the truck window and shouted, 'Anybody want a lift?'

After helping an exhausted Vince into the back of the truck, Jamie asked Tommy if he wanted a lift back to the police station.

Tommy shook his head and replied, 'No boss. Easy walk for me. Bye all.'

Sarah muttered, 'Tommy not bad tracker.'

'That's a huge compliment coming from you, Sar,' said a laughing Jacko. 'All aboard now for Darwin.'

The truck headed west along the rough gravel track and the conversation in the front turned to waiting wives.

CHAPTER 26

The truck passed through cattle country, Roper River Downs, Hodgson Downs, and Elsie Downs, finally reaching the bitumen at Mataranka by late morning. They had changed drivers a number of times during the morning. There was an attempt to give Sarah a turn; however, when she stretched to reach the pedals she couldn't see over the dashboard of the truck.

After a brief stop for lunch at Mataranka, including for the prisoners, they headed northwest up the bitumen.

With growing anticipation at seeing their wives again, the men found the driving seemingly never-ending as they passed through Katherine, Pine Creek and Adelaide River, hardly noticing the townships they passed through, mesmerised by the straight, narrow black road ahead of them. After Adelaide River, the road turned due north for the last stretch to Darwin, and their anticipation grew with every mile.

The sun was already low in the sky by the time the truck reached the outskirts of Darwin. Jacko was behind the wheel when they pulled up outside the Fanny Bay Gaol. Fitzy spoke to the guard at the gate and soon, five armed guards were ready to escort the smugglers to their new quarters. Following a torrent of muttering and swearing, they were finally rid of their passengers and able to drive into the city centre. Jake had sent messages to Monique and Carna that morning through VID, Darwin radio, so they would at least know their husbands were alive.

They decided to drop Jacko and Sarah off first at the Hotel Darwin with the thought that the wives might be there together expecting their arrival. This turned out to be correct. They pulled up outside the hotel to see on the verandah Mary Fitzgibbon with Monique and Carna standing beside two constables and their CSI assistant, Sparky Speck, waving enthusiastically to them.

The four in the front seat descended from the truck to be greeted by what appeared to be a flying white dress as Carna hurdled the garden bed in front of the verandah and threw herself into Jamie's arms, and then hugged him and Sarah together. Jacko moved swiftly in the opposite direction, hurdling the garden bed onto the verandah to gather a laughing Monique into his arms. Mary and Fitzy, his arm still in a sling, stood looking at each other for a moment bemused, until Fitzy shook his head and walked sedately to the front door of the hotel. He shortly appeared on the verandah, nodded to the two policemen, and then hugged his wife using his one good arm.

There was silence for a while as the constables looked on, then Monique broke it when she stood back, staring at Jacko's rough bandage, and demanded, 'What happened to you, mon chèri?'

'Aw, just a little brush with a bullet. It sort of bounced off my skull,' he replied.

'Merde! Bounced off your skull?'

'Yeah. I'm afraid I'll be even uglier now than I was before,' he said with a grin.

'Not ugly, but we must go immediately to the hospital to look at that,' she fussed.

'No, she'll be right, my love.'

'Non, non. You are stubborn as ... as ... le taureau!'

'What's a taureau?'

'A bull.'

'Ah, yes. I'm a bull. That's me. Sarah's always telling me I'm full of it.'

'Sarah must be right. But you must come to Darwin Hospital with me.'

'Okay. But I've just got to have a cold beer first,' Jacko laughed.

Jamie's voice came out of the darkness from the road. 'Did someone just mention a cold beer?'

'I'll be in that,' agreed Fitzy, who turned to the two constables waiting beside him and said, 'Take that truck to the garage at the police station and lock it in. There's a few tons of opium in the back.'

The two officers left and the others all sat down at a table on the verandah while Monique went in search of a waiter to organise drinks. Sparky told them that a sailing ketch had run aground near the mouth of the Roper River and the crew of two had been taken into custody by the coastguards who had been looking for them in the Gulf of Carpentaria.

252

'Bravo!' exclaimed Jamie.

Carna and Mary insisted the men explain in detail everything that had happened over the past week. They had heard the radio reports of the deaths of the policemen in the Roper River country and had been terrified that their own husbands were amongst them.

'You've gotta realise, we're indestructible,' Jacko chuckled. 'Bullets stop and go around Jamie.'

'Yeah, and they just bounce off Jacko,' retorted Jamie.

'Speak for yourselves,' said Fitzy morosely. 'Bullets seem to go through me. Unfortunately, several of our police officers were not so lucky. The fact of the matter is that we'd probably all be dead now if it wasn't for Sarah.'

Sarah was looking embarrassed to be the subject of conversation and Carna gave her shoulders a squeeze. 'We are waiting to hear the whole story,' she said.

Over a couple of drinks and snacks, the whole story of the Roper River incident was related, somewhat embellished by Fitzy but excluding the gorier details of the shoot-out.

Carna shook her head and said, 'So this little girl ran fifteen miles to save you?'

'Yeah, we're thinking of entering her in the marathon at the 1948 Olympics in London,' said Jacko with a cheeky grin.

'Aye yu! You crazy man, bikpela brother,' Sarah giggled.

'Before you go completely foufou, I'm taking you to the hospital now,' said Monique firmly. 'The emergency section is open all night. It's just at the other end of Mitchell Street, so it's not far. You can drive.'

Driving northwest along Mitchell Street, Jacko glanced at Monique and said, 'You seem to know a lot about the hospital. Was something wrong with you?'

With a secretive smile, she replied, 'Non. Nothing wrong, Jacko. Everything's right. C'est bon!'

'So, what's so good?'

She smiled and patted her stomach.

On their return an hour later and with the top of Jacko's head swathed in new bandages, they found that the Munros and

Fitzgibbons had already departed. Sparky and Sarah were still sitting on the verandah talking quietly to each other.

'We'll go and say hello to those two,' suggested Jacko. 'Tell them our good news.'

'Non, non. We won't,' said Monique firmly. 'We'll go very silently up to our room and go to bed, Jacko. Leave them alone.'

'Alone?'

'Oui, on their own.'

'You reckon they're...?'

Monique's green eyes flashed in the dim light from the hotel. 'Shhh!'

By the same author

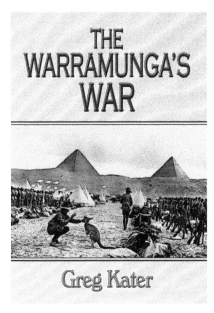

Reviews for
The Warramunga's War

Rosemary Wright. Official Review, Online Book Club

Review Rating: 4 out of 4-Stars
The Warramunga's War is the first novel in a trilogy. It's a historical fiction about war and espionage. Being suspenseful and absorbing, the tale is well written, easy to read and full of fascinating historical details. The characters are unique, exciting and well developed, particularly the focal characters. The book is balanced consisting of enthralling conversations, action and narration. Undoubtedly, it will be a feast for fans of historical fiction blended with mystery and romance. Rosemary Wright. Official Review, Online Book Club, 23 March 2018

Review by Ruffina Oserio, Readers' Favorite

Review Rating: 5-Stars
The Warramunga's War by Greg Kater is a gripping tale of war that features political intrigue, espionage at its best, and a friendship that develops in unusual circumstances. In a story set against the backdrop

255

of WWII, we encounter two compelling characters: Jamie Munro, a young Australian officer, and the half-Warramunga aboriginal, Jack O'Brien.

The narrative has both emotional and psychological depth, and it will be easy for readers to feel connected with the characters. One gets the impression that Greg Kater must have put a lot of research into this novel, because of its resounding realism and relevant historical details. *The Warramunga's War* is an utterly enjoyable read.   Readers Favorite

Review by Darryl Greer for Readers' Favorite
Review Rating: 5-Stars
The Warramunga's War is a war story with a difference, a crime novel with a difference, an historical novel with a difference, an adventure story with a difference and I can't wait for the movie.

Review by Amazon Reviewer
Review Rating: 5-Stars
A captivating, gritty, historical fiction novel The Warramungas War is well written, detailed, and hard to put down. The characters were very well-developed and relatable, as is some of the betrayal they face throughout the novel. I enjoyed this novel and would recommend it to historical fiction fans.

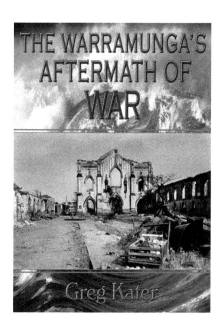

Reviews for
*The Warramunga's Aftermath
of War*

Review by Online Review Cub Reviewer, Timd
Review Rating: 4 out of 4-Stars
The Warramunga's Aftermath of War, by Greg Kater is the second book in the trilogy by the author and follows the exploits of Jamie Munro and his friend and wartime comrade, the half-aboriginal or Warramunga, Jack O' Brien, in the Philippines and further on in the rugged Australian outback as they hunt for members of a ruthless paedophile gang.

Throughout the book, and writing in a fast-paced yet compelling style the author captures the lost atmosphere of a past era. The story is fast-paced, packed with interesting details, yet engaging and entertaining.

Review by Romuald Dzemo for Reader's Favorite
Review Rating: 5-Stars
The Warramunga's Aftermath of War by Greg Kater is a meld of political thriller, mystery, and historical narrative, a tale with a strong historical setting. It covers a variety of themes and that make the narrative relevant — human trafficking, war, and adventure. The

257

novel is engaging and filled with unexpected surprises and an unpredictability in plot that keeps readers turning the pages. It's an exciting read, indeed!

Review by Kathie Denver for The International Review of Books
Review Rating: 5-Stars
Greg Kater's second book in the Warramunga series does not disappoint. For those seeking a realistic 1940s Action- Adventure novel, this is it. The story reads like a period movie filled with thrills and characters the reader will want to know. Kater manages to capture the setting of and culture of the Philippines in an exceptional way. Very well written to the point that one would think Kater was a first-hand witness to the events. Characters and settings are extremely well done.

Review by Ella James for Artisan Book Reviews
The Warramunga's Aftermath of War is the second book in a trilogy. Book one introduces the reader to Jamie and Jacko, and this second book follows them on an adventure in the Philippines and the Australian Outback that is truly captivating. All of the characters are believable, the dialogue is spot on, including the clever use of Aboriginal language in one of the characters, and this is definitely one of the books that is written with a visual experience, and would certainly be ideal to be portrayed as a movie. This reader certainly can't wait for Book Three.

Reviews for
Skills of the Warramunga

Cecila L, Official Review, Online Book Club
Review Rating: 4 out of 4-Stars
Skills of the Warramunga is the third book in the Warramunga Trilogy by author Greg Kater. Set in 1946 Malaya, the plot of this intriguing historical fiction includes kidnapping, theft, and murder. The plot is supported by a diverse cast of well-developed characters. I particularly enjoyed the way the author brought his characters to life through the use of their native dialects. I would recommend it to readers who enjoy historical fiction and action adventures. However, the book would appeal to a broader audience as well.

Review by Ruffina Oserio for Readers' Favorite
Review Rating: 5-Stars
Skills of the Warramunga by Greg Kater is a gritty tale of espionage, a rescue mission with untold challenges, featuring likeable characters. The story is emotionally rich, with twists no one could predict and tight spots that will have readers on the edge of their seats. The prose

is gorgeous and I enjoyed the author's ability to paint vivid images of the landscape and create a direct link between the environment and the characters. It is a 'hard to put down' thriller.

Review by K. C. Finn for Reader's Favorite
Review Rating: 5-Stars
Skills of the Warramunga is another fantastic work of mysterious historical fiction by author Greg Kater, and the third book in the series following Jamie Munro and 'the Warramunga', Jacko O'Brien. Reading the three books of the Warramunga series in such a short space of time has been a fantastic experience. I hope there will be more in the future as this intriguing setting on the other side of the world has really opened up post-war history for me in a brand new way. *Skills of the Warramunga* is a novel not to be missed.

Review by Kathie Denver for The International Review of Books
Review Rating: 5-Stars
Skills of the Warramunga by Greg Kater is the third book in the Warramunga series although it is more than fine as a stand-alone novel. Kater fully develops the good guys' characters in a smooth and even way for readers who have not read the other books in the series. The bad guys remain mysterious with just enough information to produce a villainous shadow. The post-war era, Kuala Lumpur, and the jungle are captured brilliantly. The historical fiction presented will not disappoint the historian, and the flow of the novel will not disappoint the adventure reader. Extremely well done.